The Spindle Tree

A Story of Lost Childhood and Redemption in the Irish Midlands

Danny Dunne

ORLA KELLY PUBLISHING

978-1-912328-13-0

Dedication

Who is this book for?

There are so many I dedicate it to. Here are but a few:

Betty, Gerard, Greg, Rita and Kathleen – who must put up with me every day.

My siblings, extended family and relations, at home and abroad, as well as the people of Westmeath – the place of my birth, who have inspired me all my life.

But this book is specially for a lady, who was the greatest story teller of them all, my mother Kathleen, who touched our hearts for more than ninety-two years.

About the Author

Danny Dunne is a historian and retired School Principal from Mullingar, Co. Westmeath. He has ten books to his credit including, The Little Silver Bell (1995), a book of poetry Along the Gravel Road (1996) and compiling and editing eight books documenting the local history of communities in the Mullingar area. He is married to Betty and they have three adult children.

SPINDLE-WOOD, spindle-wood, will you lend me, pray,
A little flaming lantern to guide me on my way?
The fairies all have vanished from the meadow and the glen,
And I would fain go seeking till I find them once again.
Lend me now a lantern that I may bear a light
To find the hidden pathway in the darkness of the night....

from

Alms in Autumn, by Rose Fyleman

Contents

Dedication   iii

About The Author   iv

Part One: The Travelling Show

    Chapter 1: August 1962   1

    Chapter 2: The Harvest   17

    Chapter 3: Meg   27

    Chapter 4: A Night of Melodrama   35

    Chapter 5: The Dance   44

    Chapter 6: The Flicks   51

    Chapter 7: The Promise   60

    Chapter 8: Confrontation   69

    Chapter 9: Departure   77

    Chapter 10: The Sally Army   83

    Chapter 11: The Long Night   94

    Chapter 12: Packy's idea   106

Part 2: The Mausoleum

    Chapter 13: Night Journey   115

    Chapter 14: An Angel returns   124

    Chapter 15: Meg's Story   135

    Chapter 16: The drama begins   141

    Chapter 17: Mad Mary Strikes   150

    Chapter 18: Birth   157

Contents Cont.

Chapter 19: Fr Doyle's Concerns   161

Chapter 20: Sunday Mass   166

Chapter 21: Seán   171

Chapter 22: Mr Thomas   176

Chapter 23: Merry Christmas Sergeant Greene   182

Chapter 24: Eileen   186

Chapter 25: Christmas 1962   189

Chapter 26: 'The Wren! The Wren!'   199

Chapter 27: Walking Back to Happiness   207

Part Three: Snow

Chapter 28: The Fender   215

Chapter 29: Cars and Trains   231

Chapter 30: The Snowstorm   247

Chapter 31: Happy New Year   252

Chapter 32: Snowball Fight   255

Chapter 33: The Telephone Call   258

Chapter 34: A Letter from Glasgow   265

Chapter 35: The New Master   274

Part Four: Convalescence

Chapter 36: John's Return   289

Chapter 37: Let her rest in peace   299

Chapter 38: Sarah the thief   304

Contents Cont.

Chapter 39: Meg's departure   315

Chapter 40: In the doldrums   322

Chapter 41: Joe's Shiner   326

Chapter 42: The Decision   330

Chapter 43: All's well in love and war   338

Chapter 44: Thinking of nice things   343

Chapter 45: Easter 1963   347

Chapter 46: The Sweetheart I once knew   356

Part Five: The Lake

Chapter 47: Measles and Nursemaids   371

Chapter 48: The Fishing Trip   378

Chapter 49: A Great Big House of Cards   385

Chapter 50: Departures   396

Chapter 51: Moving on   404

Part Six: The Return

Chapter 52: 'I will care for you for the rest of my life.'   411

Chapter 53: The Return   422

Chapter 54: The Funeral   430

Chapter 55: Pat's Story   436

Chapter 56: Requiescat in Pace   459

Epilogue   463

Part One

The Travelling Show

Chapter 1

August 1962

I suppose 1962 was the last summer of childhood for me. I was fifteen that year, but I was very much a child still. My days were spent running through the fields where we threw off our shoes, skipping through the long grass, and feeling the cuckoo spit wetting our legs and stepping on the occasional thistle. Our quest on days like this in August, saw us slow down to gather mushrooms hidden in the long stringy pasture, visible only when they emerged as mature platters, to be taken home and tossed on the pan to be eaten with new potatoes and cabbage. We explored the hedgerow to find the first August blackberries, returning home with the tell-tale purple lips from gorging on such rich natural bounty. We were brave enough also to find a fresh cowpat on the grass, and dared each other to step on it, and feel it ooze through the toes, bringing shrieks of laughter to attempt such a daring thing. It was something we wouldn't dream to tell our mother. Then before we went home, we ended our adventure at the little stream to wash the offending cowpat away, in the cold spring water.

It was a day like this in August that we ran to the top of the hill near our house, to watch for the Galway bus, which was scheduled to leave town at four o'clock, on its journey across the Shannon into the west. This was the day Dad came home for a few weeks to save the harvest, and then would have to return to England to work on the buildings. He had been home at Easter that year, and the Christmas visits were always welcome as well.

But for some reason this time, Mam made no preparations for his return. The house would usually be scrubbed from top to bottom, and apple tarts made and cooked for the evening tea. But Mam hadn't been well, and she had gone to the doctor on many occasions. She wouldn't tell me what was wrong but when I questioned her about it, she warned me not to tell Dad.

I had been doing most of the house work and she spent a lot of time lying on the bed. She called me her little angel of the morning, as each day when I got up, I brought her a cup of tea. Sometimes she finished it, but other times I watched her hand shake, as she brought the cup to her lips.

1

She would rise at about eleven o'clock and begin the daily tasks, moving very slowly. I spent a lot of the summer days with her, and worried so much about her, I cried myself to sleep at night. I knew what was wrong with her. Her lack of energy and her breathing, it was a heart problem she had, and she had to take things easy. She used to talk about how frail her own mother was, and how she died young in her sleep, leaving her, their only child to be cared for by her father. I was determined *she* would not die young. I would look after her every need. I left school at thirteen and I spent my time at home, helping her around the house. I didn't tell the boys what was wrong with her, but I knew that Tom and Joe were aware that things were not right with Mam's health. Packy, on the other hand, was told that Mam was tired a lot, because she worked very hard.

'That's why you left school Sarah, isn't that right?' he asked.

'That's right little man, and I always want to look after you.'

'I'm not a little man, stop saying that. I'm big, now that I am eight, and I can do joined writing at school.'

'It's beautiful writing, so it is,' I said, 'and so are those lovely drawings you do.'

'I am going to be an artist someday, Sarah. Do you know that?'

'Will you draw my picture for me?'

'When Dad comes home, and the hay is in the haggard, I will draw your picture at the cock of hay.'

'That would be lovely,' I said.

'But I will have to get you to make some of the black chalk for me, you know, with the twigs and the tin can. I have some thin willow sticks drying out in the shed.'

'We'll do that so,' I said.

I was a little mother to Packy. I was seven years older than him, but I always bent down to his level when he needed me, to solve some little problem. The older boys had no time for him as Packy was never able to keep up with them. He was useful when they needed a goalie in the garden to play football, or to push them in the go-cart made from the remains of the old pram. Packy resented this as he was still the little brother who could not keep up with them.

So, on this breezy August day we were sitting on the top of the hill, waiting for the bus. Great white clouds raced across the sky, playing with the sunlight, and throwing dappled shades on the fields below. A field of barley shimmered in the dancing breeze, causing ripple effects across the shining seed heads. It was an afternoon of happiness, and we waited in anticipation for the drone of that big heavy bus.

At ten past four there was no sign of it and we were about to give up, when we heard it rev going around a corner, a half mile nearer to the village. It was then that the race began, and the two older boys took off like the wind. I stopped in my tracks and waited for Packy. I took his hand and ran at his pace to meet the bus at the bottom of the hill. My father would get off at the crossroads where the boreen led to the bog, and our place was further on across the hill.

The two older boys got to the bottom first, and jumped the stone wall, just as the bus slowed down at the turning. By the time I got Packy across the stone wall, Dad was dismounting from the bus, carrying his battered old suitcase, and a shoulder bag, which I knew had the usual surprise gifts for us all.

Joe and Tom were busy running rings round him, arguing who was going to carry the suitcase, as Packy ran into his arms and embraced him.

'Well, look at you lot! You're not a little man anymore, you are getting bigger by the day!'

'Well, I eat my porridge every day, and all my spuds, and all my cabbage. I go to bed on time at night, not like these fellas. Mam says they are always gallivanting around the countryside.'

'How are the cocks of hay, Joe?' he asked.

'They were done three weeks ago. They are dry as a bone.'

'Pat Reardon gave us a hand to make them,' said Tom.

'What would we do only for Pat,' he said.

'He wouldn't take any money from Mam,' said Tom, 'and he brought some spuds and cabbage from the garden.'

'I'll give him a few bob for his work alright, when we bring them in.'

I stood some distance away, waiting, and when all the excitement with the boys slowed down somewhat I saw him lower Packy to the ground, and he came to me. The boys decided to bring the suitcase, carrying it shoulder high, but I knew that my father would take it from them, once we began the journey of the quarter of a mile up the boreen. Packy ran to keep up with them.

I threw my arms around him, and I began to weep into his tweed coat.

'What is it, alana?' he asked, stroking my hair and holding me close to him.

'I'm so glad you are home. I had no way to contact you.'

'Tell me, what's the matter, love?'

'Mam isn't well, Dad. I know there's something terribly wrong with her. You can't go back, not this time, wait till you see her. I think it's her heart. She is lying a lot on the bed, and sometimes I hear her crying in the night. She won't tell me what's wrong, and I help her do all the work.'

'Well, you're the best daughter any man could have, and don't be upsetting yourself about it. I'll look after her from now on.'

'Will you be going back to England?'

'I won't go back if your Mam is not well. I will have to stay here, won't I?'

He threw his arm around me, and we walked together to the boreen. For the first time in my life, I thought my father had grown smaller, but in fact it was me. Myself – I was growing up. As we walked, my feet hurt so I knew that I'd have to get some new shoes for the winter, as the ones I was wearing were getting tight on me, and the toes were beginning to wear thin. This would involve a trip for us all, someday before school started again, to buy shoes, and clothes with the money sent home from England.

Packy came running back and started teasing my father looking to know what he brought us from England.

'You will have to wait now till I get home,' he said, 'I think a man deserves a cup of tae, and something to eat, after a long train journey, and then the boat crossing, and not to mention that rickety auld bus.'

There was precious little said, but there was a spring in my father's step, as we made the short journey to our farmhouse at the edge of the bog.

My mother was lying on the bed and when she heard us coming she brought herself slowly into the kitchen. She sat herself down on the armchair beside the range. She had spent the morning with some black lead, polishing the great metal fender which skirted the range. She always said that the house looked dirty if that fender wasn't clean. The place was quite tidy, and she had the great big metal kettle on the boil, to make the tea when my father came home.

For the first time in many months, I saw her smile when we all dashed in the door, followed by my father. He stood in the doorway looking at her, and she sat still in her chair looking at him. I knew by that look, that there was still a great bond between them, and that the distance of months, and years of necessary separation, didn't break that link in any way.

'Are you coming in the rest of the way John Cregan, or are you going to high tail it back to England again?'

'I'm looking to see if you are alright, girl. Sarah tells me that you haven't been well.'

'Don't mind that little scut. I'm fine, just overworked, and tired lately. She worries too much about her Mam anyway. Will you come along now girl, and set the table, and make ready for the tea. Boys, you get off and start the jobs, and the milking?'

'But Mammy it's early, and Dad hasn't given us our presents yet,' protested Tom.

'Get along with ye now, or you'll find the track of my hand on your backside.'

The boys went quickly out the door to tend to the evening chores. I began getting the tea ready, and my parents went to the room to have a private chat. I knew that my father would quiz my mother up and down about her illness, and what they were going to do about it. I delayed the tea a little, as I knew they wanted some private time together, but that came to an end when the boys arrived back with a bucket of milk, which had to be strained into a milk crock on the table, at the front window.

My parents heard the commotion, and they returned to the kitchen to sit down for the tea.

My father was hungry alright and settled into a meal fit for a king. I had prepared him fried bacon with new potatoes, and cabbage, while we settled for brown bread, and blackcurrant jam with apple tart.

I had made it earlier that morning, while Mam slept in late.

She was very quiet at the table, but I knew she was happy to see him home, and I felt somewhat relieved, that he was back among us again.

When the tea was over, he reached into the shoulder bag he was carrying and began taking out presents for us all.

First up, was Packy, who tore open the brown paper parcel, to find a box of tempera paints, with brushes, pencils, and a small pad to draw on.

He was so excited, it felt like Christmas all over again, and he danced for joy on the cement floor. He threw his arms around Dad's neck, and disappeared into the room, to explore his new gift further.

'Don't let me see any paint stains on the bed, or you'll be in trouble,' Mam shouted after him.

'I won't!' he answered.

The next parcel, he gave to Joe, who opened it to find a model airplane with glue, and paint to piece it together.

'Oh thanks, Dad!' he exclaimed. 'I love this. My friends in school get them sometimes, and I never got one before.'

'It's a spitfire,' said my father, 'Now, I want plenty of help on the farm with the hay, and the harvest.'

'Of course, Dad, you know I always do.'

'I don't doubt it one bit, lad.'

'I always help too,' said Tom, thinking that he was left out in the whole conversation. Reaching into the bag he said, 'That's why I have another here for you. You know how you like puzzles, and things like that…'

It was a larger parcel, and Tom opened to reveal a thousand-piece jigsaw, showing a picture of an English village pub, and flowers growing everywhere.

'That will keep you quiet for a while, Tom,' said Mam.

'I am going to put this by for the winter. It will be great, when the long nights come. Thanks Dad, I really like it.'

Reaching in again, he produced another brown parcel. Smiling at me, he said, 'A pretty young face needs to be seen young lady, so I got you this.'

I opened it, to find a hand mirror, a hairbrush, a comb, and some hair slides in various colours. They would look lovely on my dressing table, and I knew that I would spend a lot of time doing my hair and changing my hair style.

I gave him a big hug, and at the same time, he took another parcel out of the bag for Mam. She opened it, to reveal a long-sleeved dress, with frilled cuffs and decorated with small flowers, resembling primroses on a blue background.

'This is too extravagant,' she said, 'We could have done better with the money.'

'When did you last get a new dress?' he said.

'I don't know. What will everyone think, when they see this?'

'They'll say, there goes the belle of the ball. Can't you wear it to the harvest dance in the village later?'

'I'm not going on my own,' she said.

'I'll be with you. I'm not going back until you are better, and you know that.'

'What will we do for money? How will we get through the winter?'

'We will manage. I have plenty put by. I was thinking of coming home for good, in a year or two anyway. Things are getting better here.'

'We will never make a go of it on a small farm, you know that.'

'I will get a job here. I can try anyway.'

So, the conversation continued into the evening, where they talked about their dreams and plans. I listened quietly to all this and hoped that their vision for the future would come true.

I could see us all going to mass together on Sunday, or travelling to the town in our own car, or going to a hurling match on a Sunday afternoon.

Dad would be with us, and we could be a complete family again. I went to bed that night thinking now that I was fifteen, I could get a job, and bring some money into the house as well. On my sixteenth birthday, I could go to my first dance, and buy a record player. We could play records at home, and listen to music all night long. I could buy one of them new transistor radios and bring it with me everywhere. The greatest dream of all, would be to buy a television, and watch all those great shows. These were only dreams. I went to sleep that night, thinking that the future was going to be great, and that our lives were going to change, but this was not going to happen. Fate had a more challenging and sinister fate in store for us all. The future mapped out for us, could never happen any family in our wildest dreams. The outcome of these events would haunt us for years to come, and returning for our father's funeral, would awaken this nightmare once again.

Two days later, the hay harvest began, and Dad sent me to the village to find Pat Reardon. Pat helped always at home, at times when work needed to be done. His needs were simple, the only pay requested was a good dinner, and an evening tea, but Dad paid him with money as well, as Pat was very reliable, and dependable, when the message was sent to him. Dad and Pat were very good friends, having gone to school together. He always protected him in the school yard during those childhood years, as this simple soul was picked upon, and laughed at, because of his speech impediment. When he was nine years old, his mother died, and his father was unable to care for him. He spent the next six years in an orphanage. It was a part of his life, he never wanted to talk about. His treatment there, influenced him psychologically. He returned home when he was fifteen years old to stay with his father. Pat could talk normally to anyone, but when he got excited or confused, he began to stammer and lose control of his body, shaking and jerking, till he began to scream with confusion. To stop him, one had to take his hand, and start reassuring him that everything was alright.

On a few occasions during their childhood, Dad challenged the culprits who dared to tease Pat, resulting in a fight at the crossroads, where he received many a bloody nose, and a black eye, until one weekend, my grandfather took him to a big burly sergeant in town, who trained all the young lads to fight in the ring, and take on challengers at another club. He spent a season training with them, and the inevitable happened, one afternoon when he took two challengers on at the crossroads. They had upset Pat that afternoon, causing him to run away from home, and Dad settled the score once and for all that day. He was only nine years old at the time.

He went home with not as much as a scar on him, and telling his mother all about it, headed off to find Pat, and to bring him home.

Pat had a secret hiding place. One day when he was exploring with my father, he decided to share his hiding place with him. Their adventure led them into the old cemetery, which was still in use at the time. The remains of the medieval church stood abandoned in the middle of the cemetery, overgrown with ivy, and sealed off from the world. Its stone roof was still intact, and the entrance was covered with hanging ivy.

Close by, was the mausoleum, belonging to the Wilson family. Pat had a key to get in, and it was here among the old wood, and lead coffins that he hid to get away from it all. They made an agreement that this spot would always be their secret place, and Pat found it a haven to go to, when he couldn't cope with the world around him. This was the place Dad went to, when he needed to take Pat home again to his mother. When she died, Dad missed him very much, and was so glad when Pat returned once more. Pat never forgot my Dad's kindness, and this paid off for us always, when he was needed in later years to help on the farm. All that had to be done, was to ask him, and he was there bright and early in the morning to begin the day's chores. Pat continued for many years hiding away in the old mausoleum when trouble came his way. He was the victim of jeers and taunting, by certain people in the village, who did it for fun, to see him stammer, and work himself into a frenzy just for a laugh. Whenever Dad heard about it, he went and brought Pat home.

When a new parish priest came to the village, Fr Doyle took Pat under his wing, and gave him some little responsibilities, collecting money in parish dues, as well as selling raffle tickets as part of the fundraising for the new hall. He spoke one Sunday morning that he'd denounce any person off the altar, who was cruel and unkind to Pat. He threatened also, to report them to the Gardaí. There was an immediate reduction in the taunting and jeering, but Pat was still nervous, and went about still peeking around corners, or looking in windows, before he entered a shop, or a house, to make sure that those inside were not a threat to him. He was often referred to as a peeping Tom or a hide-in-the-corner. But Fr Doyle kept a close eye on him always.

I made the journey to the village at noon the next day to find him.

I didn't expect to see him at his little cottage at the edge of the village, but the door was unlocked. I knew he had gone to the shop for a loaf of bread or other messages, so I followed my nose to see if I could locate him.

He wasn't at the post office, because it was closed for lunch. I found him paying for his few messages at the grocery shop. He was putting them into a sackcloth shopping bag and was just leaving when he saw me.

'Ah Sarah!' he exclaimed. Pat's speech was slurred, and he spoke through his nose in a slow manner, sounding as if he was bordering on being drunk.

'Dad needs you Pat to bring in the hay tomorrow,' I said.

'Ah, he's home, then is he?' he asked.

'He arrived last night, and he wants to get cracking on it in the morning.'

'I will be there,' he replied. 'Now I want you to bring home some chocolate for everyone.' He shoved the bag into my hand and dashed back into the shop. He arrived out a few minutes later with a paper bag containing bars of Cadbury's Dairy milk, peeping out of the top.

'They're for the boys as well,' he said, with a smile on his face, and sounding as if his whole voice was coming through his nose.

'Can I walk with you to the house, Pat?' I asked.

'Of course, you can girl. I didn't make any morning tea yet, and I had to get a loaf of bread.'

I wheeled the bike, and he hung the sackcloth bag on the handlebars. It was lucky I went with him that morning, as this was the day Pat was to declare that he would watch over me for the rest of his life. It was one of those days when there was a lot of men in the village collecting dole, and then heading off to the pub to spend some of it on drink, not thinking that there were mouths to be fed at home. Pat never frequented the pubs, but stayed away, as he would often be the subject of many jibes and jokes. He avoided confrontation as best he could, and went to the shops only when necessary, but enjoyed moving quietly through the countryside, exploring the fields, and listening to conversations through ditches and hedges. For most people, he was regarded as a harmless soul. To others, he was a nosey parker, listening to things that were none of his business.

We had no fear of him, and in fact, during those days he helped on the farm, when my father was away, I felt happier, and more secure that he was there, as he was well able to handle a horse, or a plough and he could even drive a tractor.

Something happened on this particular morning, which would seal forever his devotion to me.

We were walking slowly down the street, when two men emerged from the pub half drunk. I didn't know who they were at the time, but obviously, my father would have known them from his younger days. They were about to climb on to the David Brown tractor parked on the street, when they saw Pat with me. They stopped in their tracks and sidled up to Pat.

'Why if it isn't the bould Pat Reardon?' Then Pat got a slap on the back.

'How's it going, me ould segosha?'

'Haven't s-s-see seen you in a long time!'

'That-that-that-that's right,' they mocked.

'Ya know. he'd nearly talk to ya, wouldn't he?'

I intervened at this stage and stepped in front of them. 'Would you please leave this man alone,' I said, 'He has done no harm to you, or anyone.

Why don't you mind your own business?'

'Who's she?' asked the man who owned the tractor.

'The young Cregan one from in near the bog. You know the auld man couldn't run that swampy farm and had to head off to England. Not like us, Jim, we know how to make a living off the land.'

Pat began to shake as I knew he was angry at what he was listening to. 'L-l-leave the l-l-little g-g-girl alone.'

'Are ye going to take me on, Pat. Remember the way you used to win when you were a little fella?' said Jim, 'You'd take to your scrapers, and run away. Why don't ye do it now, ye demented scrappy little cur.'

I turned and faced him. I could take no more. 'How dare you!' I shouted at him, and with that, I drew a punch hitting him in the nose.

Jim stumbled back, and his partner gave me a push so that I fell over the bike, and the bag of shopping. He drew out a hazel stick, and was ready to hit me with it, when a soft voice spoke from behind them.

'Are you in the business of beating little girls with hazel sticks like that every day now? Are you, Mr Flynn?'

Startled, Flynn turned around, and came face to face with the parish priest.

Fr Doyle was a softly spoken man, and moved quietly through the parish, carrying out his duties. His soft voice demanded that people listen at mass with an alert, and keen ear, to hear his gospel message on Sundays. Revered as a saintly and holy man, he had a wry, and gentle humour, which endeared him to people of every age.

'Oh, hello Father,' said Flynn, lifting his cap to greet the priest.

'Are you alright, Sarah?' he asked gently.

'I'm fine, Father. Thank you,' I replied.

'Are you alright, Pat?' he asked. Pat was shaking, and he could not answer.

'I see gentlemen, that Pat may need some medical attention. I wonder what brought on this attack of nerves on the poor man.'

'He is being bullied by these two, Father,' I intervened, 'I'm just sick of this sort of carrying on. Pat is my friend, and they do this to him all the time.'

I began to cry, and I put my arms around Pat to try and reassure him that everything was going to be alright again.

'I wonder do you want to get the sergeant, and press charges against these fellas, Pat?' said the priest.

'I'll go for him if you like, Father,' I said.

'You shut up now, you impudent little strap,' said Jim.

'Now hang on there, my good man,' said Father Doyle. 'Let me see if I have this right… Here on this little village street, on an ordinary autumn day, Pat Reardon has been shopping. He is talking to his neighbour and friend, Sarah Cregan. So, I don't see why their little innocent conversation should be violated by a pair of drunken thugs.'

'We were only having a bit of fun, Father,' muttered Flynn.

'At everyone else's expense. I see!' the usually quiet Fr Doyle roared at him with anger. Flynn was startled by the priest's outburst, resulting in him dropping his cap to the ground, and he stooped down quickly to pick it up, shoving it into the pocket of his dirty grey raincoat.

'I think Pat Reardon deserves an apology for this sort of carrying on, and so does this little girl. You ought to be ashamed of yourselves. What would your wives think of this carry on? I see you have been in to collect your dole. Why isn't that money brought home to your families, instead of being spent in the pub.'

'Apology my foot,' said Jim, 'I ought to have that little strap up for assault. If one of my kids did that to me, I'd have the strap of my belt to them.'

'If you are not careful, someday the tide will turn my good man, and they will all gang up on you.'

'It's alright, Father,' said Pat, who had recovered from his spasms. 'I don't need any apology.'

'Ever forgiving as always, Pat,' said Fr Doyle. 'You know there will be a place in heaven for you someday, my good man, and it will be well earned.'

He turned to the two men, and rather calmly said, 'Get yourselves up on that tractor, and out of this village. Get home to your wives and families and be good dutiful fathers and husbands.'

'We're sorry, Father,' said Flynn.

'Get yourselves gone now before I put a curse on you both.'

Within less than a minute, the tractor had left the village, and as fast as such a vehicle can go, it sped out into the country, leaving the three of us standing on the street.

At this point in time, a group of people began to gather. I was ready not to say a word to anyone about the incident, but I knew the story would reach home, and I feared that Dad would go after the two of them, to give them a good hiding, but then another thought struck me, that if he did, he wouldn't be making things easier for Pat.

'Will you both be able to manage now?' asked Fr Doyle.

'We are fine, Father,' I said, 'I just want to get Pat home, and make him a bit of breakfast. Dad wants him to help bring in the hay tomorrow.'

'He's home again, is he?'

'Yes Father, but I don't think he'll go back for a long time. Well, not until Mam is well again.'

'Tell her I send my blessing, I'll call to see her soon.'

'I will Father and thank you again for your help.'

He doffed his hat at us and made his way to the shop to buy his morning tobacco, greeting all and sundry with a smile, and a good morning, as he went along.

I put my hand on Pat's arm, and said calmly to him, 'Come on Pat, and I'll take you home.'

He picked up the bicycle for me, and I put his shopping bag back on the handlebars.

We made our way swiftly to the little cottage at the edge of the village. There was smoke rising from the chimney, as Pat had the range lit from early morning, to have the kettle boiling, when he got back from the shops.

It was a little place with a kitchen, and two small bedrooms. It had a thatched roof originally, but some years earlier, a few local people covered the thatch with corrugated iron. The thatch was still beneath the iron, and it left the cottage a tad cosier in the winter.

Pat had no electricity in his little house, and he still had to light an oil lamp at night. This stood in the middle of the table. It had a blue glass base on a gold coloured stand, and a tall globe to control the flame, so that it could be adjusted, and made brighter, and present a reasonable light on a dark night.

The big steel metal kettle was boiling, and I made a pot of tea, putting the tea leaves into the heated brown Delph teapot, filling it with boiling water, and placing it on the table.

Pat had bought a batch loaf of bread, a packet of Galtee cheese, and a pound of Westmeath Butter. He made me sit down to eat a big doorstep of a cheese sandwich, and I must say I was hungry. When he poured the tea, he put plenty of milk and sugar in it, and he sat down at the table, saying nothing, and began eating his sandwich quickly. After three or four bites, he stopped, and looked across the table at me smiling.

'You know what, Sarah, there's something I'm going to tell you.'

'What is it, Pat?' I asked.

Then he shied away from me and held his head down. He wanted to tell me something. He began to stammer. I knew that whatever he was going to say was difficult for him, and it was his nerves acting on him again.

'It's alright, Pat, if you cannot tell me, you can tell me another time. It's alright.'

Then he composed himself a little and stopped shaking. 'I h-h-have b-b-been trying to tell you for a long time.'

'Well, if you are going to marry me, Pat Reardon, you can forget about it. I'm never getting married.'

Then he began laughing out loud, and I knew that this was not his intention.

'I could never marry you, Sarah Cregan. You have always been my little girl.'

'I know that, Pat, but what are you trying to tell me?'

'As long as I live, Sarah Cregan, I will always protect you. Someday, I hope I can pay you back for your kindness.'

'You are my friend Pat. You are my Dad's friend, and Mam's friend, and Packy, and Joe, and Tom. You are always welcome at our house.'

'Your family have always treated me very well, when other people were cruel and unkind to me. I can trust you all with my life. I will always look out for you Sarah, please God, and Saint Joseph, and Holy Mary of the Holy Family Amen.'

'Now Pat Reardon, will you eat up your sandwich, because I know you are hungry and stop all that silly talk.'

'I'll say it again, little girl. I will always look out for you, and your family, as long as there's a breath in my body.'

Then he stopped talking and began eating again. He made another sandwich, and wanted me to have more, but I was finding it hard to finish the one I had. When I left him, he was tidying up the kitchen, and sweeping the floor, and I wondered to myself what would ever happen to him, Pat needed protection from the world that was cruel, and uncaring at times.

Chapter 2

The Harvest

The harvest began when the hay was brought into the haggard. Dad had borrowed Walsh's David Brown Tractor and buck rake to take the cocks in, so that the ricks could be made. Pat arrived at seven o'clock the next morning, and the first thing we made him do, was sit and have some breakfast. Dad had heard what had happened the day before. I told them when I got home before any of the neighbours or villagers could do so.

His only comment was, 'Aye! No one is going to walk on you, girl. You know what, that's your mother coming out in you now.'

Mam hit him a crack with the tea towel, and he nearly choked laughing.

She had come back to herself a little, and he was glad to see her cheering up. She was still weak and tired, but she sat at the table ironing the clothes, which had been taken in off the line the evening before.

Packy wanted to keep his promise to draw my picture when the hay was being brought in. While Mam did the ironing, we decided to make willow charcoal sticks. I had read in a book how to do it. It was not possible to buy charcoal in the town, so we decided to try the experiment ourselves. The theory was that if you burned the sticks in the open fire, they would reduce to ashes because of the presence of oxygen. We had put some willow canes by in the shed the evening before, to save time gathering them the next day. There was always a heap of twigs in the shed, which were collected regularly, and were used on winter mornings to help light the range, if it ever went out during the night.

The process involved getting an open pea tin with the lid still attached, so that it could be closed in on itself again. The space where the tin was cut open provided a little room for gases to leave the wood, but oxygen could not get in.

It was then packed with small canes of willow and the lid closed again. It was placed in the fire and left to burn or roast, turning the little willow canes into carbon.

We left them in the fire for about an hour and lifted the tin out with the tongs, leaving it to cool outside the door. It was important not to open the tin immediately, as the presence of oxygen could cause the sticks to burst into flames.

When it was cold, we tossed the charcoal sticks out on to the ground, and Packy cheered with delight at the result. Some of the sticks had broken, but that didn't matter. Straight away he found some large pieces of brown paper and began drawing the hedge and the gate leading on to the road. He could draw the angle of the half open gate with the long shadow of the evening sun. I left him quietly and went back into the kitchen to begin churning the butter, as it would be a job less to do the next day.

'He has a great gift for that,' said Mam. 'It makes him happy. He wants to draw my picture tomorrow in the haggard. He's been talking about it for a long time, so I hope I have time for him to do it…'

'Why don't you head off, alana, as soon as the dinner is over. You will have a few hours before the tea begins.'

This is exactly what I did.

The busy day began after breakfast when the tractor revved at the gate and away Dad went with Pat driving to the hay field. The boys had gone on ahead to open the gates, and their job that morning was to watch when the buck rake lifted the cock of hay, to see if there were any field mice hiding underneath, and to chase them into the after grass. There were also mushrooms there, having found space to grow when the grass was shorter. These, they gathered as well, putting them into a sweet can they brought with them. They remained in the field, while the hay was brought home, and watched to keep the cow from coming into the after grass, as the tractor had to pass through the lower field to the road.

I began by digging some new potatoes, and cutting a few heads of cabbage in the garden, and preparing them for the dinner. The potatoes were clean, and fresh, and delicious to eat still in their jackets.

The heads of cabbage were white, and when cleaned, the few invading slugs were removed. They were peeled open leaf by leaf and washed in a basin of spring water at the table. The secret in cooking the cabbage was to boil the water, salt it and add a little bread soda. I began feeding in the cabbage leaves, leaf by leaf, and watched each one as they turned a bright green and sagged limply into the boiling water. After ten minutes, the whole bucket of cabbage had reduced to fill the large pot, and it was put to one side, to be boiled alongside the potatoes, so that they were ready together.

I had a big side of bacon boiling from early morning, and the sweet smell of the meat wafted out into the blustery August air, giving the impression to all and sundry that the kitchen was a busy place to be.

Dinner was ready at half past one, and all those men in my life, sat down to a hearty meal of bacon, cabbage, and new potatoes.

The smell of that country cooking stays with me still again, as it was a very happy time in our lives, and the last time that such happiness was experienced in our home.

Pat Reardon said very little but was more interested in eating a hearty dinner. This was something he didn't get every day, and he enjoyed such a meal when it was offered to him, when he also helped on other farms in the parish.

When dinner was over Packy stayed back and helped me to wash the dishes. Mam went and lay down on the bed. She didn't finish her dinner, and she was very quiet too. This did not go unnoticed by Dad, and it was *he*, who suggested she take a lie down.

Meanwhile, Packy took me out into the garden. I sat down in the sun under a small cock of hay and he began drawing. He wouldn't let me see it until it was finished. He used the pad of artists paper that Dad had brought from England, and he looked just like a professional artist at work.

He said very little, and once or twice, he had to get a fresh piece of charcoal, as the piece in his hand had crumbled. Occasionally, I saw him rubbing the charcoal in, for shadow or effect. I knew Packy had artistic talent that none of the rest of us had, and that there was a likelihood that he would never get to develop it further.

When he was finished, he turned it around, and I sat open-mouthed, not knowing what to say. Then Packy chirped up, 'Go on say it! You hate it, don't you?'

19

'No, I don't! I think it's just wonderful. It's fabulous. Don't let anything happen to that. You could get Dad to make a frame for it and hang it in the kitchen.'

'I think you are just saying it to please me, Sarah.'

'If I didn't like that picture, Master Packy Cregan, I would have said so. It is beautiful, and I never saw anyone draw like that before. I want that picture, it's gorgeous.'

'Well I don't like it, I might crumple it and throw it away.'

'Give it to me Packy.'

'I don't know.'

'Please!'

'Well don't be showing it to everyone.'

'I promise, I won't! Can I show it to Pat? He likes things like that.'

'You promised you wouldn't.'

'Alright then!'

He tore the picture out of the pad, and I brought it to the shed, to find some clear varnish. I wanted to seal the picture, to prevent the charcoal from wearing off. He captured my image very well, and he even had a smile on my face, and did the representation of the background hay, in a very realistic way. I lay the page flat down on the bench and began to cover it slowly and lightly with a coat of clear varnish from a tin on the shelf. I left it there to dry, and went back to the kitchen, to begin preparations for the tea. The varnish would take a few hours to dry, and then I would take it in, and hang it on the wall in my room.

At tea that evening, Dad told my mother that he saw some lorries and vans heading for the village.

'That's not unusual now in this day and age, is it?' said my mother.

'Darcy is written on the side of some of the lorries.'

My mother brightened up, and said, 'Oh they are back again, that means we will have some theatre for a week in the village.'

'Would you like to go?' asked Dad.

'Of course, I would! We'll be able to see Meg again.'

The coming of the Darcy's to the village used to be an annual event, but in recent years their visits were not as frequent. They were a travelling theatre group, and it was two years since their last visit.

Meg and my mother made friends many years previously, and they had been corresponding with each other for a long time.

When Mam worked in a women's clothes shop in the town, Meg Darcy walked in one day to buy a coat.

So, began a friendship, which deepened as the years went on, and Mam asked Meg to be her bridesmaid at her wedding in 1944, when the show returned for the summer season.

'Do you want to call up to see her?' asked Dad.

'No, I'll wait. I'm sure she'll be here, when they have settled in. I don't feel up to going to the site to listen to that Darcy.'

'You never have a good word for that man,' said Dad.

'I don't know what she ever saw in him. I suppose it was a marriage of convenience for two people who just wanted an acting career. She could have graced the stages in London, or New York, or anywhere in the world, but she spent her time, traipsing around Ireland in a cold draughty caravan performing plays and making them up as they went along.'

'But he never did, or said anything to deserve your criticism, and contempt.'

'It is true, you know, that he had his sister Eileen committed to a care home, when she got a stroke. Eileen could only talk in slurred or broken speech, and she was surplus to requirement in the travelling theatre. She was an expense, and he had her committed. Meg has been pleading with him ever since, to take her out. She is in relatively good health, except for her speech.'

'I know that!' said Dad, 'but at least she could help out somewhat, backstage or something.'

'Darcy is not a nice man, and this I know.'

When Pat Reardon had the last cock of hay in the haggard, he parked the tractor in the yard, and came in for tea.

Again, there was cold bacon, and hard-boiled eggs with plenty of brown bread and home-made butter.

Pat was hungry, and he ate quickly. Mam had to tell him to slow down, or he'd get indigestion.

'I'm sorry, Mrs Cregan, but I am really hungry.'

'There's no hurry on you now, you did a good day's work, and it is time to relax.'

'Do you mind Mrs, if I have a smoke?'

'Go ahead, you might as well light up.'

Pat began to prepare his pipe for his evening smoke. He placed everything on the table in front of him, taking each item out of his pocket, a pen knife, a plug of Benbow tobacco, his pipe and a great big iron key.

It looked like a key to a great prison door, and it was heavy.

No one passed any comment on *this* key but watched as Pat emptied some of the ash from his last smoke, on to the side of the range. He kept the remainder in the pipe. He cut a few pieces of tobacco from the plug and began rubbing it in his palms to break it up. He then added the remainder of the ash with it, and he filled the pipe to the top. Lighting a match, he sucked the smoke into his lungs, as the air went down the pipe, like a wind tunnel. Happy that it was lit, he placed a lid on top, and sat back smoking his pipe contentedly. But the key still held a great fascination for us all, and it was Joe who decided to ask the question.

'Pat, what does that key belong to?'

Quickly, Pat's contented pose froze, and he put the pipe down on the table, and seizing the key, he put it back in his coat pocket. His personality changed, and he tried to speak.

'Th-th-that's a secret. I c-c-can't say.'

'It's alright, Pat,' said Dad, 'don't start upsetting yourself. You should be proud of that key. I know what it is for, and I'm sure the children here would love to hear all about where it came from.'

'Well, I-I-I'm not supposed to have it really.'

'Were you in jail?' asked Packy.

'Did you steal it from somewhere?' asked Tom.

'Don't be asking too many questions,' said Mam. 'That's Pat's privilege to tell you or not.'

He reached into his pocket, and took out the big heavy key again, which was now beginning to show signs of rusting. He placed it on the table once more.

He resumed smoking his pipe. When he composed himself, and when he had relaxed, he spoke, 'It's my secret place.'

'You mean you have a hideout?' interrupted Joe.

'Cor!!' said Tom.

'You read too many comics,' laughed Mam, and gave us all the eye, to stay quiet.

Pat cradled the key in his hand, then clinging to it tightly, said, 'If I tell you this childer, you can't tell anyone… Is that a promise?'

We all nodded and promised to keep it a secret. We sat wide-eyed in wonder as Pat began his tale, speaking in his slow drawl voice…

'Before I was born, in fact, before my father ever got married, he was on the run. It was back in 1921, when the War of Independence was on. He was one of the rebels, the old IRA, and together with his comrades they were wanted by the Black and Tans, following an ambush up at Broken Hill. They surprised the Tan Lorry full of soldiers, and two of them were shot. In that same ambush, my father's brother was killed too. The Tans knew that a man was killed, and that being a Catholic, they'd want him buried by a priest in a proper ceremony. Poor Fr Maloney was watched like a hawk, day and night, to see if anyone would approach him to hold a funeral. My father decided to wait it out. and to hide the body until such a time, even if it took years, to have his brother buried on holy ground.

23

For the first few days, he placed it in a rick of turf down in the bog. He was afraid that nature, and the elements would begin eating away at it, so he decided to do something which would either save or destroy him.

He knew that Wilson Hall was a safe house, and that her Ladyship Rose Wilson was a sympathiser with the cause.

For that reason, some of the rebels often hid in her sheds and barns. When it got to a point where she too might be discovered they moved away. It was a very wise move, as in time her ladyship came up with a plan which would save many of their lives at that time.

My father went to see her by night and Jones her Butler let him in. Jones had worked for many years at the big house, and her ladyship trusted him with her life. Jones hid him in the wine cellar, and after breakfast next morning, her ladyship met with my father in the drawing room.

He didn't have to tell her what was wrong, and her first suggestion to him, was that she would have him smuggled out of the country.

My Father wasn't having this, as he wanted to take care of his brother's body and see it safe somewhere. He was staying to fight, even if it meant he would lose his life in the process.

She then asked him if he was afraid of the dead, and my father laughed, knowing that he had often heard his mother say, never to be afraid of the dead, those who were living were more dangerous.

She went to her desk bureau which was in the bay window, looking out on to the front lawn, and the great chestnut trees. She had a large piece of sack cloth with something wrapped in it. She produced a great big key from inside. The key was well oiled, and the sack cloth was for protecting the inside drawer in her desk bureau.

You know where all the Wilsons are laid to rest, in the old graveyard in the family vault. Everyone knew it, and no one ever touched it, with its great big gothic iron door. The big lead coffins were placed there over the years, when deceased members of the Wilson family were laid to rest. The door was difficult to see in the cemetery, as the front of it was draped by the hanging branches of a spindle tree. When it was opened, the branches swept aside, and the dark chamber opened to the world.

Her Ladyship was the end of her line, and we all knew that she would be the last Wilson to be laid to rest there.

She told my father that night, that if they placed his brother's body in there, it could remain inside until it was safe again to have a proper funeral.

My Father promised to have the key returned within a few days, and she wished him the best of luck in his venture.

That night, he and his comrades placed a simple wooden coffin inside the vault and locked the door. Her ladyship didn't call it the vault, but the mausoleum. It's a great big word to use for a burial place. On their way home through the darkness, he had to take to the fields, as he was nearly discovered by a Black and Tan division, out on manoeuvres. Some of them gave chase, and he retraced his steps back to the cemetery, and locked himself inside the mausoleum. He could hear them talking a few yards from the door. Eventually, they went away, and he remained in the chamber for the night. He lay down on the floor and slept peacefully as he was exhausted from all those nights of hiding out in the fields.

After that incident, my father had a thought, that the mausoleum would make a great hiding place for some of his comrades. He knew he had to return the key to her ladyship, so he decided to have a copy made.

He went to the local blacksmith who had no problem in duplicating the key, and he returned the original key to her ladyship. She jokingly said to him, that when the good times returned, he would be able to tell his children, that he slept between the old major and his lovely wife.'

We all began to laugh when he said this, and he took his pipe and tapped the ashes on to the side of the range, keeping half of it for the next smoke.

We all held the key in our hands, and there were still traces of oil on it, which was keeping it in good condition.

'Did your father ever give her ladyship back the copy key?' asked Joe.

'That's the copy key. Her ladyship never knew he had it.'

'Is this your secret place Pat?' I asked.

'That's it, and it is still my secret place, and I don't want anyone else to know. Her ladyship died in 1932, and she was the last person to be buried there.'

'What happened the original key?' asked Tom.

'No one knows. There was an auction at the house, and all the furniture was sold. The key was probably given to the P-P-Protestant Minister, and it's in the Glebe somewhere. It hasn't been opened for a burial since 1932.'

'Well that's not exactly true now Pat, is it?'

Pat smirked when my father said this.

'I have often hidden there, when things didn't go well for me, when I was a young lad. I used to steal the key from the m-m-mantlepiece in the kitchen, and one of the times I was m-m-missing, my father found out, when he saw the key was gone. I thought he would flake the living daylights out of me, but he only took me in his arms and hugged me tight, thinking of the days when he found refuge there himself. Then I told your f-f-father what I had done, and we used to go there ourselves to play.'

'You shouldn't have been playing in a sacred place like that,' I said.

'Maybe those good dead people gave us welcome in their last resting place. It was our secret hideout, behind the spindle tree.'

'Sounds like a great adventure,' said Tom, 'Maybe we should go there some day.'

'Maybe it's time to let the dead rest,' said my mother, 'They were cruel days and it is time to let the departed be and move on.'

'When were you there last?' I asked.

'I h-h-haven't been there for many years, but it's still my secret place. W-W-Well that's not exactly true. I go there every year and I oil the l-l-lock. It is easy to unlock, but then you have to lift the b-b-big latch to open the d-d-door. I oiled the lock the other day and I forgot to put the key back in the big box I have at home.'

'It's *our* secret now,' said Packy, looking up into his face, 'and no one else is going to know, Pat. It's all like a great big adventure.'

'A great big adventure indeed, gosoon.'

Chapter 3

Meg

Meg arrived the next day. Darcy left her off at the gate, in his black Ford Anglia car. He was never welcome in our house, and Meg knew this. He was heading for a pub in town, and she didn't know when he'd get back.

We all stood in a line in the kitchen, as she surveyed us like a sergeant major, looking at us with a very angry and cross expression. In later years, it reminded me of the scene in the film *The Sound of Music,* where Maria meets the children for the first time, and their father frog marches them down the stairs like an army battalion, and they stand in line for inspection.

We knew her bark was bigger than her bite. We stood, pretending to be frightened, looking ahead, as if we were soldiers. Mam sat one side of the fire smiling, as the military drama unfolded.

'Chins up,' she shouted.

We obliged.

'Hands by your sides.'

Again, we obeyed.

'Let me see, these shoes are not shining.' She looked Joe straight in the eyes invading his space.

'Why are your shoes not shining, soldier?'

'They are Wellingtons, sir,' shouted Joe.

'Don't you tell me what I know already,' she bellowed, 'It's three days peeling potatoes for you in the slammer, soldier.'

'Yes sir,' shouted Joe.

'Why are you wearing braces at your age?' she roared.

'Because my trousers would fall down,' shouted Joe.

'Because my trousers would fall down, sir,' she roared back.

I began to titter and snigger.

27

'None of that from you now young lady,' she bellowed at me.

'Sorry!' I said.

'Sorry, sir,' she roared.

Then Tom saluted her with an American salute.

'Who told you to do that, soldier?'

'I thought I was supposed to,' said Tom.

'I thought I was supposed to, sir,' she shouted.

'I thought I was supposed to, sir,' he bellowed back, trying to prevent himself from laughing, wiping his nose with his sleeve, to stem the merriment.

'I gather there is an element of mutiny here,' she hummed to herself as she paced up and down by us. 'What am I to do about it? Let me see?' Then she saw Packy, who was beginning to get a bit tired of the game.

'Why are you looking so down and out, soldier?' She reached down peering into his eyes.

Packy had enough. He sat down on a chair and said, 'I think I have enough of this, Meg. I am dying to see if you have brought me some sweets or not.'

'Packy, have some manners,' said Mam.

'I think it's a good idea, soldier,' she said. 'Come on and give your Aunty Meg a big hug.'

Packy ran to her and hugged her tight.

'Why have you not come to see me in a long time?' demanded Packy.

'I have been a busy person trying to make a few bob so I could come visit you all and bring you some Galway rock.'

We cheered as she reached into her bag and started handing out long sticks of pink rock.

'You spoil them rotten, Meg,' said Mam.

'You know they are my kids also. I haven't chick nor child, and whether you like it or not Mary, I'll spoil them if I want to.'

'Let it be on your head then,' said Mam.

'Don't be such a grumpy biddy, Mary Cregan. I'd murder a great mug of your home brew tea.'

I pulled the kettle on to the left ring of the range and began setting the table. The boys disappeared with their sticks of rock into the room. Meg sat on the chair opposite the fire, and she kicked off her shoes. She sat back in the armchair, and put her two feet up on the fender, and stretched herself.

'I'm wrecked tired, Mary, had a long day rehearsing for the Saturday show. Are you going to come?'

'Please God if I can, pet. I haven't been so good lately.'

'Stop saying that, you are probably imagining it.'

'I don't imagine things, and you know right well I don't. Only for my own little girl here, I'd be lost, she's a little gem you know. She helps me out so much. I don't have to tell her to do it.'

'She is a blessing, and someday she'll find a handsome young man, and he'll fall madly in love with her.'

'Stop that!' I chirped, 'I'm not ever getting married, I'm staying here with my Mam, and I'm going to look after her.'

'Not alone that,' said Mam, 'she is very good to her brothers too. Packy depends on her so much. He turns to her whenever anything goes wrong, and she always seems to calm his fears. He's a nervous little craythur at the best of times.'

'You are blessed with your children, Mary. You are a very lucky person indeed. I never had a little boy or girl. Darcy says we are better off without them. They'd be just an extra burden, and expense and it could jeopardise the show, and the theatre. Sometimes I often wonder why I stick with him. You have a very good man you know. Even though he must go away to work, he comes back to you, and brings home the much-needed money.'

'I fear for them though, if anything ever happened to me, what would happen to them? I don't know if John would ever cope on his own...'

'Will you stop that?' interrupted Meg, 'Why are you saying things like this?'

My mother began to cry. Meg sat over beside her and cradled her in her arms.

'I know things are not right with me and I fear for my little children. I don't want them to be taken away from their home.'

'They won't be taken away, stop saying the likes of that. Have you been to see the doctor?'

'I have. My heart is weak, and I don't have a lot of strength left in me.'

'Well do what you are doing, and rest more. Stop worrying. Sarah will look after you. I know that she is a little treasure, and she will do her utmost. Please God, some day she herself will make a brilliant nurse. I can see it in her, you know. And I'm not joking young lady, when I say you will marry a handsome man someday. You may not think that way now, but you deserve a lucky break. All of you do. If I can be of any help, I will.'

'You are a very good person, Meg, you know that,' said Mam.

'Well to cheer you all up, I want to see you at the show on Saturday night. We are doing East Lynne. It's one of those stories that will have you all in tears. The only problem is I need someone to play the part of Little William. I'm working on it, and I will tell you about it later. Then next week, I must go to Dublin for a few days and I am bringing *you* with me, young lady. Darcy has to come back here again, but we will stay overnight, and return on the train the following day. Would you like that?'

I began to dance around the kitchen with excitement, and then she continued, 'I will take you to the flicks as well.'

'The Flicks – what's that?' I asked.

'We'll go and see a film in the evening and stay at my place for the night. We will call to Mrs McArdle's diner and have evening tea with sausages. They are to die for.'

'Why would they kill you?' I asked.

'What do you mean, love?'

'The sausages. You said you would die if you ate them.'

She laughed a little and she explained that it meant that they were so nice, you would die just to get to eat them.

'What I want you to do is look on the Independent and see is there any film advertised you might like to see. If it is still showing, we will both go there.'

'Oh, thank you so much, Meg. This is really great.'

'You are so good to them all, Meg,' sighed Mam. 'I'm not able to give them those extra things in life. You make it all look so easy. I haven't the energy to even make them laugh anymore.'

'Mary Cregan, you are here for them day and night. They are so happy, well fed, and getting an education. What more do they want? They just want you to get better. You worry far too much about them.'

'What's going to become of them, if anything happens to me?'

'We take things one step at a time. You stop worrying. You have a very good man. If Darcy were half the man John Cregan is, I'd be a very happy person indeed.'

'I know that, but he still needs to go away and earn money. He wants to make this a better place for us all someday, more land and means to make a living from farming.'

'As I have said already take it one step at a time, and after the show on Sunday evening I am coming over here, and John Cregan, yourself, and I will head off to the harvest dance.'

'You can wear the dress Dad bought you,' I said.

'There you are now, you'll be the belle of the ball. And we'll dance ourselves into the night.'

Mam laughed through her tears, and Meg embraced her in a big hug.

Then just as abruptly, Meg changed the subject.

'Now let me get back to the question of the little star of my show.'

Mam and I were both mesmerised again, wondering what she meant.

'What do you mean?' asked Mam.

'On Sunday next, we are putting East Lynne on stage.'

'What's that all about?' I asked.

'Basically, it's about a lady, Elizabeth Carlisle, who runs away from her husband and family and elopes with another man. In time, he abandons her. She returns in disguise as governess to her husband and his new wife. Later she hears that her son is dying from consumption, and she tries to see him.'

'What's consumption?' I asked.

'It's another name for TB.'

'What happens in the rest of the story?'

'Little William dies, and she is with him. He asks her a lot of questions about dying, and about his mother he believes is dead. After his death, she falls ill, and she too dies.'

'That's so sad!' I said.

'It's called melodrama. The Victorians loved it, the sadder the better.'

'Have you it all prepared?' asked Mam.

'We have, but there is a problem.'

'I never saw you before, Meg Darcy not being able to solve a problem,' chuckled Mam.

'That's where you come in, Mary Cregan.'

'Me! What can I do?'

'I want to borrow your eight-year-old son.'

'So, you don't have Little William!' I said.

'You've hit the nail on the head, child. The young fellow who was playing with us all the summer, has gone off to England with his parents, and I need a little urchin badly.'

'I don't know what John Cregan will say about this,' said Mam.

'Leave him to me,' said Meg.

The upshot of it all was that Meg needed Packy to play the part of Little William for four productions, the main one being on Sunday night in the village, followed by three more shows around the midland towns over the next three weekends. She was taking Packy with her on her travels and made every promise to take great care of him. She took him off to the village the next morning and spent the day rehearsing in the large tent parked on the GAA field. It was surrounded by many caravans and trailers used as dressing rooms and accommodation during their tour. She brought him to her caravan which was decked out with costumes, wigs, shoes, and all sorts of theatrical makeup. I spent the day with her tutoring Packy, who rose to the situation with great gusto. He was a natural at the acting, and she was thrilled to find that he could bring on real tears at the drop of a hat. But when she showed him the costume he had to wear, he wasn't too pleased. He had to lie on a bed as if he was dying, wearing a white nightshirt down to his ankles.

'I'm not wearing a girl's night dress,' he protested.

'It's a costume,' said Meg, 'you have to enter into the period.'

'I don't know what you mean.'

'Well the story happened one hundred years ago, and all little boys wore nightshirts. Even the men wore them.'

'Can I not wear pyjamas?'

'No Packy, you will wear a nightshirt.'

'I'll feel like a right sissy,' he grumbled.

'You will have to wear makeup as well.'

'What?'

'Theatrical makeup. It is to make you look ill. You are dying in the story, and it has to look so real.'

'They will all be laughing at me.'

'An actor rises above all that, you will have the power from your performance to bring everyone to tears. It's not real. You will be the envy of the village.'

'Packy! Mam said you are to behave yourself,' I said.

'Of course, he will,' said Meg, 'He will be my little boy, and I will be his Momma!'

'Oh, alright then, but no laughing Sarah.'

I crossed my heart, and expressed a hope to die, if I laughed at him, and I had to make a promise that Joe and Tom would not laugh either. On Saturday afternoon, there was a dress rehearsal for the Sunday night performance, and it looked fabulous. Packy played his part so well, it looked real. I felt like crying when I saw it, but I had to promise not to say a word about it, or I'd give the game away.

Chapter 4

A Night of Melodrama

On Sunday night, we all dressed up in our best clothes, and made our way to the village. Jim Walsh collected myself, Mam, and the boys to take us to the show. He had a farm not far from the village, and he was one of those people who was kind to us, when Dad was away. His wife Ellen was always sending up apple tarts or little bags of scones. Mam thought that she was treating us as a charity case, but she said nothing, as she felt that you always had a neighbour when you were in need. They had one son Seán. He was their one and only child. He was away in boarding school and he was home only during holiday time. He was about two years older than me, and he was going into his Leaving Cert class in the coming year. I fancied him a lot, but he didn't seem to have any interest in me.

Dad went on the bike to the village earlier in the evening for a few pints in the pub. He wanted to treat Pat for being so helpful in saving the hay and bringing it into the haggard for the winter.

The village was thronged with people, so Jim Walsh dropped us off at the church. The first person we saw was Father Doyle who doffed his hat as he passed by.

'You've nothing to worry about there, Mrs Cregan, no one will step on that young lady's corns.'

'She's a Molloy, just like her mother,' she said, 'the Cregan's are too soft-hearted.'

'I'm not soft-hearted,' protested Joe.

'I'm only coddin' pet,' said Mam.

'You boys are on for serving next Sunday, you know that,' he said.

'We do father,' replied Tom.

He doffed his hat again and headed for the football field ahead of us.

We hadn't seen Packy for two days. Meg took him back to her caravan to teach him his lines and to rehearse the show with the rest of the cast. The script was compiled during the winter and based loosely on the story. Darcy was the scriptwriter and it was his job to render down a four-hundred-page book into a play lasting two hours. It was a complete show, interspersed with singing and dancing. The musicians comprised of a piano player, drummer, violinist, trumpeter, flautist, and oboist. They were part of the show for the summer and played in bands and groups in the city during the winter months.

The tent was a tough green canvas type material, sewn together in sections with a thick cord-like rope and suspended on large poles, which went right to the top, just like a circus tent. It looked elegant decked out with coloured bunting and lit with bright electric lights, fed from a generator outside. You could hear the drone of the machine, but it was drowned out by the throng of people talking, and later by the music, singing, and dancing.

There was a girl going around the tent selling little tubs of ice cream, as well as bars of chocolate. When Dad and Pat arrived, Pat in his usual generous way bought ice cream for us all. He wanted to buy one for Packy too, but Mam told him it would melt, and it would be no good to eat. She warned the boys not to say anything to Packy in case he got jealous of their good fortune on the night. There was a man selling tickets for a raffle too, and at the end of the night, Mam won the prize which was a large Delph jug with blue stripes. She was delighted with it, as she had a matching sugar bowl on the dresser in the kitchen.

The tent was packed to capacity and it was opening on that Sunday night for four shows. Word got around that East Lynne was the production this season, and it had been a popular favourite down the years.

As was part of the production, ad-libbing was allowed, and they were so good at the acting, that no one would know the difference, even if occasionally, words had deviated somewhat from the chosen script.

We waited in anticipation for the show to start, and soon the curtain opened, and the Master of Ceremonies, dressed in a black suit with tails, bow tie, white shirt, bowler hat, white scarf, gloves, and a walking cane, welcomed all and sundry to this season's production. He spoke in a very grand English accent, but there were hints of a Dublin one, interspersed through his speech.

'Ladies and gentlemen, boys and girls, I come before you to stand behind you, to tell you something I know nothing about.'

There were a few gentle laughs from the audience, when he finished the sentence.

'I'm glad to know that someone out there is awake. I think I hear snoring out there.' He held his ear to the crowd to see would there be a reaction, when Tom, who didn't take too kindly to be told he was asleep shouted back,

'Ah heck! I'm awake anyway.'

The tent erupted with laughter, and Mam gave him a clip on the ear to behave himself. The man pretended to look down into the audience, shielding his eyes from the light, pretending to see Tom in the crowd.

'You know, young man, you worked magic. The whole audience has wakened up, and you are responsible.' With that, the audience broke into applause.

'That's fantastic, my dear people, now to get the show on the road. Tonight's production is East Lynne. We staged this play about ten years ago, and by popular demand, we have decided to reprise this production once more. We have a fine range of artistes, who will perform song, dance, sketches and many more surprises. Just to let you know that our production was hampered this week, with the departure of a young man to England, with his family. We lost Little William in the production, but tonight we welcome a young local thespian, Patrick Cregan, from this here part of the country. He is a very talented young man, and give him every encouragement, during his performance. So, without any ado, let's welcome the dancing girls and the singers as they go walking back to happiness...'

The audience applauded, and the girls arrived on stage in black outfits that looked like swim suits, with black jackets and tails, top hats and canes. Two ladies lifted the rafters, as Helen Shapiro's song, raised the canvas in the gentle breeze. They wore black patent high heels, and skin coloured tights with a line down the back.

'They have no shame,' said Mam, 'Brazen hussies.'

'They look l-l-lovely,' said Pat.

'You have a bit of manners, Pat Reardon. You should be down on your knees praying.'

I could see Dad chuckling, laughing to himself, and she gave him a gentle thump in the arm also.

'Stop encouraging him, you.'

I could see Joe and Tom, staring at the dancers and the singers, wide-eyed with wonder, as they began to immerse themselves in the entertainment. I looked behind me, to find that the Walsh family had joined us. Their son Seán, smiled at me. I turned around as he did so, I got such a fright, I don't think he ever looked at me before.

The show rolled on, and Packy appeared for a few brief scenes, and bellowed his lines to the audience so that he could be heard. He was wearing a little sailor suit, with knee breeches, white stockings, and a little sailor hat. Tom and Joe began to giggle, and I warned them to stop, just in case they'd distract Packy. I was looking forward to the climax of the story, when Little William was dying of consumption.

He lay in the bed, sitting almost upright, propped up with pillows. He was positioned on the stage, so that he was facing the audience at an angle, as the other actors in the story entered, and exited the stage behind the bed. His bed may have been against a wall, but it drew the audience into the story.

Packy's final scene was very sad, and filled with emotion, as I could hear the odd sob coming from people behind me, as well as some sniffles, and nose blowing. Meg played the part of Isabel, and Darcy was her ex-husband. He knelt by the bed, displaying the melodramatic pose of a father, on the verge of great loss. Meg stood behind him, the servant governess, her place being there to tend to the children, staying quietly in the background, as was her role in the society of the time. Then Darcy left the stage, and Meg knelt at his bed. The world knew her as Lady Vine, their governess. He was pretending to be wheezing, and his breath was laboured in the lasts moments of life.

'It won't be very long to wait now will it, Madame Vine?'

'For what, darling?'

'Before they all come. Papa and Mamma, and Lucy, and all of them.'

'Do you not care that I should come to you as well, William?'

Yes, I hope you will. I wonder will we know everyone in heaven? Or will it be only our own relations?'

Oh, child! I think there will be no relations, as you call it, up there. We can trust all that to God, however it may be.'

'There will be a beautiful city with lovely pearly gates and precious stones. There will be streets made of gold; and a river with clear water, and the trees with fruit, and leaves that can cure all sickness. There will be lovely flowers, and there will be harps, and music, and singing. I wonder what else there will be?'

'We may see all that we desire, and want to see William, but we cannot judge that here.'

'Madame Vine, do you think Mamma will be there?' he presently asked. 'I mean Mamma that was.'

'Ay, before too long.'

'But how will I know her? You see, I have nearly forgotten what she was like.'

Meg began to pretend to weep. Her little boy was not aware that his real mother was there. She was so broken-hearted that she would try to hint that she was there in reality, but her little boy couldn't see her.

'It is dark, Lady Vine. I cannot see you.'

'I'm here, my dear boy. I always will be.'

'I want Papa and the rest of my family. I want them. I cannot see. Can you open the blinds to let the light in?'

'There is light, my dear boy.'

Darcy and the rest of the family return. Meg takes her place behind them.

'Papa, I cannot see you.'

Darcy takes his hand. 'I'm with you, my little boy. Can you not see me?'

'It is you, but now there is a great light. I can see Mama. She is coming to me. I can see her. It is really her. She is coming to me.'

He sits up in the bed for about ten seconds and then falls slowly back on to the pillow. Meg collapses behind him, broken-hearted. This would later lead to the final scene where she dies too.

The actors held their pose on the stage, some dabbing handkerchiefs to their eyes, and sobbing. Darcy gently lifts the sheet up and covers Packy's head. Then the curtain closes.

The next song was an evocation of sadness also, as the show's tenor came onstage, and accompanied by some quiet music sang The Old Bog Road. The stage was set for the final scene and the conclusion of the story.

When the final scene was over, the curtain closed, and to bring the audience back on a happier note, the tenor, accompanied by the dancing girls standing in the background, lifted the canvas again, with the song, *Goodbye*, from *The White Horse Inn*. This gave the actors time to prepare for the final curtain, and the last sing song.

When the curtain call came, all the actors and dancers emerged on stage, as the audience clapped them on. At the end, Darcy and Meg emerged with Packy, dressed again in his little sailor suit, each taking him by the hand. Together with the two, he bowed like a gentleman, and stood smiling at the audience. Cheers and wolf whistles went up, and a call for more, rang out through the tent. The band struck up and the show concluded with *It's A Long Way To Tipperary* and *Pack Up Your Troubles*.

I turned and looked at Mam, and I could see pride written all over her face. She was so happy that night, and I was glad to see her smiling. She was holding Dad's hand, and every so often, she considered his face. They loved their children, and a moment like this, was something to remember forever.

As the people began to leave, a man dressed like a soldier, tapped Dad on the shoulder.

'Mr Cregan, Mr Darcy wants to see your family backstage.'

I had never been backstage in a theatre, and indeed never at the back of a theatre tent. It was just a continuation of the big tent and divided by black curtains each side. There were lights and mirrors, and seats behind the stage, where the performers dressed, the men's area divided from the ladies' area, by another black curtain.

Packy came running to us and Dad picked him up in his arms.

'Was I good, Dad?' he asked. He was full of excitement and was saying so much in one mouthful.

'You were famous, Packy,' said Dad.

'My little boy,' said Mam.

'Did I do a good job?' asked Meg coming to meet us, her face covered in cold cream. She was wiping the makeup off with it, using wads of tissue paper.

'How can you do it?' asked Dad.

'I did nothing, he's a natural, aren't you Packy?'

'Yeah, I'm a … What is it Meg?'

'Natural!'

'That's right. But I don't like that white nightdress.'

'It's a stage costume,' I said.

Then Darcy emerged from the men's dressing area, and he stood there aloof and debonair, as if he were Errol Flynn, or some great romantic Hollywood actor. He cast his eyes down at us, and then suddenly his focus fell on me.

'Is this a vision I see?' he said.

'Stop that Darcy,' said Meg, 'Don't mind him, he has had a few shots of whiskey when he got off the stage.'

'A maiden of extreme beauty to behold.' He took my hand and kissed it.

'Doubt thou the stars are fire, Doubt the sun doth move, Doubt truth to be a liar but never doubt thy love.'

He kissed my hand once again. I could feel Dad getting a little uneasy with the words he was saying.

'She's just a little girl, Darcy,' he said. 'She doesn't need to hear strange words like this.'

Meg grabbed him and pushed him away.

'Go away, Darcy, and drink a few cups of coffee. Go away now!'

She pushed him again, and he went away slowly, not saying anything, as if he were a dog, with his tail between his legs.

'I'm sorry John, I'm not going to let him spoil the night for you. The dance will have commenced by now and let's not delay. He won't be with us, and I'm glad. It's what I'm compelled to put up with. He has a penchant for young girls, and I must always watch him.'

'It's alright!' he said. 'She's my little girl, and I won't let anyone harm her.'

'Come on then, let's go,' said Mam. She looked radiant in the bright lights of the dressing area. She had done her face up earlier in the day, and Meg touched it up again for her, with something from her great big carpet bag. She made her look in the mirror, and as she smiled, she looked like Maureen O'Hara or Vivien Leigh.

'You have never lost it, Mary Cregan,' said Meg. She turned to Dad and laughingly said, 'You behave yourself tonight, John Cregan.' Dad gave a gentle laugh, and his usual sigh, 'aye!' She pushed us all out the door, and we watched as Mam, Dad, Meg, and Pat, got into her car, and drove the short distance to the dance. Jim Walsh brought us home in *his* car. We sat crouched into the back, and I was sitting beside Seán. Packy sat in the front on Ellen's knee.

'That was a great show,' said Seán.

'Yes, it was,' said I.

'Are you going to be an actor someday Packy?' asked Ellen.

'No, I'm going to be an artist,' said Packy.

'Well, you are a very talented young man.'

Seán kept staring at me, as we headed up the bog road to our house. He had a little notebook in his pocket and he wrote something on it. He handed it to me and I looked at it. It was short and sweet, it read, *will you write to me?* I looked at him, rather shocked and said 'Yes!' in a whisper. When I got home, I put the boys to bed. Packy fell asleep straight away. He had three other shows to do this week, and he had a fortnight on the road before he returned to school in September. By then, the troupe will have chosen a different play to perform. When they were all asleep, I looked at the note again, and Seán had written his school address on the back. He added another note also.

When writing, sign your name as Martin. The Priest sometimes opens the letters and they would not approve of a girl writing to me.

When I went to bed, I put it under my pillow, and I fell asleep smiling. I couldn't believe that an older boy could fancy me.

Chapter 5

The Dance

What happened at the dance that night was relayed to me in dribs and drabs by Mam and Meg the next day. Pat had the task of selling raffle tickets for Fr Doyle, and he joined them for tea towards the end of the night. It was the first dance Fr Doyle had in the new hall since the builders left two weeks previously. He was waiting until St Stephen's night to open the hall officially, with a gala dance for the whole parish. But tonight, Mam and Dad were together as if they had met for the first time. It was quite a while since they had been out, and they were all set to enjoy it. Little did they know that it would be the last dance they would have together. She looked radiant, having had her makeup put on by Meg in the tent. She was wearing the new dress Dad had bought her. He looked spruce and dapper in his grey suit, white starched shirt, and blue tie.

She spent a while dancing with Dad to the music, but after three or four dances, she asked to sit down. She wasn't feeling well, but she didn't want to tell him that. He sat with her in the room upstairs, where they served sandwiches and tea. When they sat down they were joined by Sergeant Mike Greene, and his wife Kathleen. He came to the village one year previously and they lived upstairs in the barracks. Their three boys were going to the national school, and one of them was in Packy's class. At this point in time, he knew most of the people in his district, but he had never met Dad or Mam before, with Mam unwell most of the time, and Dad being away in England. The sandwiches were brought to them on plates, and they settled into a light snack, and some tea. Mam didn't have an appetite to eat, but she sipped away at the tea, and she kept a chair for Meg to join them.

'A great show tonight, wasn't it Mrs Cregan?' said Kathleen. 'Your little boy is so talented.'

'He's my acting pupil,' said Meg.

'How long have you been teaching him the acting?'

'Just three days!'

'Janey Mac, you did a great job on him. It's as if he was used to acting, just like Mickey Rooney or Jackie Cooper.'

'You must like the movies,' said Mam.

'I do! Mike used to take me a lot before we were married, but now with the three boys, we get very little time for that. It's not easy bringing up a family, what with Mike being away on duty so much, and he is being called out at such unearthly hours, heaven knows, it can be taxing sometimes, when you are married to a Garda Sergeant. The government should pay us wives an allowance for being married to them. It's hard to live with them, and it's hard to live without them, isn't that right Mike?'

'Perhaps you'd like another sandwich Kathleen,' said the sergeant, trying to change the subject, and to halt her present train of thought.

'I'm sure you are very busy sergeant, having a big area of countryside to cover,' said Meg.

'It has its moments,' he said, 'but it has its trials too.'

'He's talking about what happened at the end of July,' said Kathleen.

'Listen, love,' he said, 'these good people don't want to hear that story.'

'But they *do*, Mike. It's a tragedy. He's really upset about what happened to the Larkin children.'

The Larkins lived halfway between the village and the town in a little cottage. Their mother died last year giving birth to her fourth child. The baby died a few days later. Danny Larkin, the father was left to care for the three children, two girls, and a boy.

'It's such a sad story, really,' said Kathleen.

'I hope I never have to do again, what I had to do then,' he said.

'What happened?' asked Dad.

'A neighbour of the children called to the station, wondering if they were alright. They hadn't been to school for over a week, and no one had seen them. That same day, young Dan was seen running away from a shop in the village, with a loaf of bread he had stolen. I went to the house and discovered that they had been alone for nearly two weeks. The girls, aged six and seven were filthy dirty, and very hungry. Dan was spending his time sneaking into the shops stealing bread, butter or anything he could lay a hand on to feed them.'

'Where was their father?' asked Meg.

'Gone!' said Kathleen.

'Where he is I do not know, but there is a search out for him. He has left the children and hightailed it to England.'

'The poor little mites,' said Mam.

'We took them away to the barracks, and had them cleaned up, washed, fresh clothes and food. The girls never stopped crying, and after we got to calm them down, I knew that they'd be sent away to the orphanage.'

'Mike has a big soft heart when it comes to children,' said Kathleen.

'If only we could have held on to them, but that wasn't to be. It's what I had to do, to spirit them away, to be picked up for the orphanage.'

'What do you mean?' asked Dad.

'They wouldn't leave the bedroom, and the young lad, Dan kept saying that he was going to care for his sisters.'

'What age is the lad?' asked Meg.

'He's ten!' said Kathleen.

'A great plucky little lad he is. I know he'd care for them, if he was let stay with them.'

'They were separated then,' said Dad.

'Yeah! I had to lie to those three little children. To get them into the squad car, I had to tell them, because they were so good, they were going to the seaside for the day.'

'That's not true of course,' said Mam.

'I wish it were,' said the sergeant. 'The poor little mites deserved a day at the seaside, or even a nice little holiday. They were so unfortunate.'

The sergeant reached into his pocket and took out a handkerchief. He was all choked up and couldn't continue. For a man who encountered all he did in his career, he could not face the breaking up of a family whose life was fraught with such tragedy. Kathleen continued with the story.

'When he told them they were going to the seaside, they went to the car with him. Himself and the young guard took them outside of town. They didn't want a scene in the village, having to forcibly put them in the car.'

'It was like leading little lambs to the slaughter,' said the sergeant. 'They didn't know what was going to happen.' He began wiping his eyes as he spoke, and Meg ordered one of the tea girls to pour him out another cup of tea.

'Listen, man, drink this,' she said. 'It's not your fault.'

'There were two hackney cars waiting for them out at the lay-by. When they pulled in, little Dan knew what was happening. Opening the door, he dragged his two sisters out of the car, and roared at them to run for it. We ran after them, and caught them, and carried them screaming to the cars. Two nuns took the girls away to the orphanage, and two men shoved Dan forcefully into the back of the car. They were taking him to Dublin. One of them gave him a good slap, and he continued screaming. I shouted at them to leave him alone, but they just ignored me, and drove off.'

Mam was in tears when she heard all this, and Dad put his arm around her, telling her not to upset herself.

'Poor little things,' said Meg.

'I rang that evening to find out how they were faring out. I got a very curt reply in both places. They were settling in.'

'What will happen to them?' asked Dad.

'I just don't know. They are gone, and we will probably never see them again. When they grow up, they usually go off to England. Even if the father came back, they will not be given back to him. He'll probably go to jail, for neglecting them.'

'I will try and keep in contact with them,' said Kathleen.

'They won't let anyone see them. I know that from experience.'

'It is really a very cruel world for some families,' continued Kathleen.

Mam had gone very quiet. Her enjoyment of the dance had soon waned, and she wished to go home.

'It's not over yet,' said Dad.

'I have had enough of that,' said Mam. 'This was something I didn't want to hear tonight.'

Meg left them home and said she would call around four o'clock the next day to take Packy back to her caravan for Monday night's performance. We were in bed asleep when they returned, and we heard nothing about the dance till the next day.

When Mam and Dad arrived down the next morning, Joe and Tom had the three cows milked, and Packy was still fast asleep.

Mam was very quiet and said very little all morning. Dad went out to the fields after breakfast to check fences, and to repair any gaps that might get bigger as the winter approached. He was all set to sell off the dry stock, before the winter, and to buy some calves in the new year to fatten them up. Molly and Daisy the two older cows were being considered for selling off too, as they were getting old for bearing calves, and giving milk. This was one of the reasons Dad was still anxious to return to England once more, to work for a few more months. He wanted to apply for a grant the following year, to build an extension to the house to include a bathroom and toilet. Now that they had electricity, water could be pumped from a well, to provide running water in the house, for toilet, bath, and sinks. They were plans he was making with Mam, and they were aiming to provide a much better life for us, and to have more home comforts, not to be depending on an old unsanitary privy at the back of the house. But Mam was reluctant to speak about her health situation, as she didn't want to upset his plans.

She did nothing all morning but sat by the range looking out the door. She said very little to *me*, and I knew that something was bothering her. As it happened, Meg called early, just before noon, wondering if she wanted to go to town. Mam declined the offer. She just sat there staring vacantly into space.

Meg was one of these people who could read situations as they happened.

'Mary Cregan, out with it?' she said.

'I'm fine, pet,' said Mam, smiling and reaching her hand over on hers.

'Well, I'm not leaving until I hear what this is all about.'

'Packy is still in bed, he might hear,' said Mam.

I peeped into the room. He was out for the count, so I closed the door tight, so that he couldn't hear anything.

'Do you want me to leave?' I asked.

'No love! I keep no secrets from *you*,' said Mam. I sat down beside Meg, and we waited for her to speak.

'From what I heard last night,' said Mam, 'What will happen my children if anything happens to me?'

'What do you mean? Will nothing happen to you? We've been at this point before, recently, and I don't want to go through it all again,' said Meg rather abruptly.

'I have a bad heart. I know I won't live long. My mother died young, with the same thing. It happens in our family.'

'Get that thought out of your head,' said Meg.

'Please stop, Meg. Stop telling me that. I know it! There is nothing I can do about it. It could happen tomorrow. It could happen next year, it could happen in ten years' time. I know it will happen. I have no energy. I cannot do the things I used to do. Poor Sarah couldn't go on to secondary school, as I needed her here. She's such a great girl. She does all the work for me. I don't tell John all this. He has all these dreams of extending the house, buying more land and building up a bigger herd. I don't want to stop that. He wants to go back to England and I don't want to stop him.'

'Why are you saying all this, Mary?' asked Meg, 'Why don't you tell him? He deserves to be told. If he knew you were so concerned about your health, all these ambitions could be put on hold.'

'It's not that Meg. If anything happens to me, will he be able to cope with rearing my children? Look what Danny Larkin did to his family.'

'What's all that about?' I asked.

'I'll tell you later Sarah,' said Mam.

'John Cregan is not Dan Larkin. John Cregan is a good upright man, who'd die, rather than abandon his family.'

'I'm afraid,' said Mam, 'I am so afraid for the future.' She had filled up to cry when the bedroom door opened, and Packy emerged, all dressed and ready to meet the day.

'How's my little film star?' asked Meg, defusing the situation.

'I'm not a film star,' said Packy.

'Well, you brought the house down last night young man.'

'Did the tent fall?' he asked.

'No pet, it's a way of saying that the audience loved you very much.'

'Were you crying, Mam? Are you alright?'

'No Packy, we were talking about the sad play last night, and how you acted so well, to make it look you were really dying, and going to heaven.'

'Oh! Is that it? Anyway, I'm hungry.'

'I'll get you some breakfast,' I said.

As I got up to get Packy some breakfast, Meg touched my arm and said, 'By the way young lady, I have something to say to you.'

'Did I do something wrong?' I asked.

'No! As promised, I want you to come to Dublin with me for a few nights. Well, that is if it is alright with your Mam and Dad.'

'I would love to go,' I answered, rather excitedly, 'Please Mam, can I go?'

'Of course, you can go. You need a break child. You have been working so hard.'

'Well, I want to take you shopping,' said Meg, 'I will be around on Thursday and Friday night. The show will move on, and I'll have to be back on Saturday to bring a young actor to the next town.'

I was all excited about going away. I was never in Dublin before, and the thoughts of going there intrigued me.

Chapter 6

The Flicks

I was so excited when Meg called on Thursday to bring me to Dublin. I was worried leaving Mam to cope with all the housework, but Joe and Tom promised to do as much as they could to help. It was a bright blustery August day, and Meg drove carefully on the road. When she got to the town, she didn't delay, and we were soon on the road to Dublin. Kinnegad was left behind quickly, and the road led us through Meath and Kildare, crossing the River Boyne at Clonard, and heading to Enfield and Kilcock. At Maynooth, we stopped for a cup of tea and a bun, and before long, the city suburbs approached, and the traffic was quite heavy. I had no idea where she was going, but she told me that their house was in Ranelagh. When we arrived there, it was a neat little street with pavements, lights, and brick on the front of the houses. Each house was a semi-detached, with a front garden and garage. It was a three-bedroomed house, and she showed me to my room upstairs. I had never slept upstairs before. It was a high double bed with a patchwork quilt. I sat on the bed and looked at the brown shiny wardrobe and dressing table with large mirror. When I left my bag down on the bed, she knocked on the door and sat down beside me.

'I want you to be careful Sarah at night. I don't trust Darcy anymore. You remember him quoting the lines from Shakespeare at the play, kissing your hand?'

'I do. Dad didn't like what he did. I thought he was being kind.'

'No Sarah! Darcy loves young girls. Now he loves them in a way that is not safe. He could do something nasty to you. You are quite safe when I'm around, because I have him under my thumb. Something has happened, and I want him to do something for me. I will tell you about it again. It concerns my best friend, his sister Eileen. If he doesn't do what I ask him, I have promised to quit the acting troupe, and to leave him for good.'

'Will I be alright?'

'I wouldn't take you here if it wasn't safe. I want you to take this key. It is the key to this bedroom, and at night, lock the door when you go to bed.

Only answer the door if I knock on it. I will speak if I must knock. He may not be here, but just in case he does, be on the alert. You will be with me all the time, so don't worry. We will go shopping tomorrow, and we will go to the theatre tomorrow night. Meanwhile, I want you to search through the newspaper and see if there is any nice film you would like to see.'

'That's great!' I chirped.

'Have you ever been to the cinema?'

'I haven't! I would love to go.'

'Well come on then and we'll have a look. When the film is over we'll go for fish and chips.'

'Meg, why are you so kind to me and my family?' I asked.

'I don't have chick or child, pet. I'll be kind if I want to. Do you not want me to spoil you all?'

'Of course!' I said, 'but how can I ever repay you for all this?'

'I just want you to do one thing,' she said.

'What's that?'

'Just be yourself. That's all I want. I have never had children. I have always wished for a child. I have never been blessed with one. I love coming to visit your family, as you make me feel at home, and I love being with you.'

'Thank you, Meg,' I said. She reached over and took my hand in hers. Her hands felt cold, and she sat smiling into my face.

'Will you come on now and let's see what flick we would like to see.'

The evening paper had been delivered. She rang the local shop, and a young delivery boy placed it through the letterbox. We sat in the dining room and searched through the pages for details about films on show in the city. She wanted to choose something suitable for me, and one that we would both enjoy. I had no idea which one to choose, and I didn't even know where the cinemas were.

'I don't think *Dr No* is suitable?' she said.

'What's *Dr No* about?' I asked.

'It's a spy film, James Bond. It's for older people. You will probably watch it someday.'

I looked at the listings up and down, and one caught my eye. I folded the broadsheet paper in half and handed it to her.

'*Whistle down the wind*,' she read.

'Yes!' I replied.

'You would like to see that one?'

'I would!'

'Well, Whistle down the wind it is then.'

We didn't take the car to the city centre. Instead, we went on the bus. It was a great big double decker, and I wanted to sit on the top. It was a bright sunny evening, and the light cast shadows on the red brick buildings. It was such a different place from our little rural world at the edge of the bog. I was sitting beside this elegant lady dressed in her fur coat and hat. She wore dark gloves. and carried a beautiful soft leather handbag. She had spent some time on her makeup also, and I felt as if I was in the presence of a movie star. I still could not believe that she came, and spent time in our house every year, sharing my room with her. She was still elegant when she was with us, yet she had no airs and graces about her, and my father and mother could converse with her as equals. It was her friendship with Mam, that sealed this great bond, and whenever she came to stay, I could see that her presence had a positive effect on my mother, and she laughed and smiled, and forgot about her failing health.

The city was thronged with people, coming and going, whether from work or shopping, each one was hell bent on their respective journeys. We got off the bus on Stephen's Green, and she took me to see the ducks who were always looking for morsels to eat, from people taking a walk, in that beautiful city space. It was a place I had never encountered. There was something of interest at every corner we turned, from shrubs to flowers, and little monuments to people who were of great importance to our country.

Little children played, while mothers sat minding prams and there were a few gentlemen looking smart in their top coats and trilby hats sitting reading their papers on park benches. One man was smoking his pipe, and I could get the whiff of Bendigo tobacco. It was no mistake about it. It was one of Dad's and Pat's favourite blends. I was a world away from the bog road, and I could only imagine if Packy were here, how he'd stand, and stare at the site of this lovely place.

On Grafton Street, the shops were so elegant with beautiful mannequins in the windows, wearing the latest in fashions, both ladies, and gents, as well as children. We went for tea in one of the cafés, and the aroma of fine coffee was something to remember. It was my treat, and I was allowed choose all I wanted. I settled for a bowl of ice cream. I had coffee too. It was the first time I had real coffee. The only coffee Mam had in the house was a dark liquid in a bottle, and it was made from chicory, and it was used mostly to flavour cakes. But sometimes I had a drink of it before going to bed at night, a spoonful dissolved in boiling water with sugar and milk. It was one of those treats that went hand in hand with cocoa, on winter nights. But this real coffee was just divine.

Meg knew that I was taking all of this in, and I could see the joy on her face at seeing me experience all of this for the first time. It was a great joy to her, and yet it was sad, as she wasn't sharing this with her own daughter. I suppose, I was the next best thing, and I was so happy to be there.

'You alright, pet?' she asked.

'It's just magic!' I replied.

'Well take it easy eating. We have plenty of time yet.'

Leaving the café behind, we went to College Green, past Trinity College and the Bank of Ireland. They were great elegant ornate buildings. The only other building any way like them at home was the county hall and the courthouse. They were the same colour, that grey weathered stone, standing the test of time.

I never saw anything as tall as Nelson's Pillar. The poor lonely soldier perched on top of his column, a landmark in the city centre, straddling the General Post Office and Clery's. It was this great colossus in the city centre, and always a meeting point for visitors. I didn't realise then, that less than four years later, Nelson said farewell to the city, when the IRA placed a bomb at the base and the column was no more.

The film was at eight o'clock, and we were early. The cinema was plush, with its velvet curtains and comfortable seats. I sat waiting in anticipation with some bars of chocolate and a bottle of Taylor Keith orange, with a paper straw sticking out of the top. Meg smiled at me and said, 'I hope you enjoy the film.'

The cinema was filling with people, but by the time the curtains opened, there were still seats empty. I didn't realise, that this was probably the second or third showing in the day, and that performance would continue until the next film came to town.

Whistle down the wind was a lovely story, based on a book by Mary Hayley Mills. She was the wife of actor John Mills and it starred Hayley Mills, Alan Bates and Bernard Lee. Three children are told by a lady collecting money for the Salvation Army, that Jesus would take care of them. Later they discover a man hiding in a hay barn on their farm. He is on the run from the law for murder, and when they asked him who he was, he answers with a swear, '*Jesus Christ!*' As a result, they think their visitor is Jesus, and the children keep it a secret. They bring him food and take care of him. But the inevitable happens, the law catches up, and the man is caught. It is a coming of age movie, where the heroine Hayley Mills is really in love with the fugitive. In fact, it is the little boy, who brings her back to reality, towards the end of the film, by saying 'It's not Jesus, it's just a fella!' He could see through the whole thing, when the so-called Jesus was unable to bring one of the kittens they had rescued back to life, when it died. It was a lovely story. I saw it again on ITV years later, and it conjured up memories of a beautiful time I spent in Dublin with Meg.

Next evening, we went to a show at the Gaiety Theatre, and the place had all the ambiance displayed in the cinema. When we had finished, the last buses had gone, and Meg ordered a taxi to take us home. The driver travelled down Abbey Street, and as we passed the site of the old Abbey Theatre, she showed me the building belonging to the Salvation Army.

'Is that the same as the Sally Army?' I asked.

'It is. The Sally Army in the film was a slang expression in that part of England where the story was set. We have it here in Ireland also,' she said, 'They do very good work, especially for people who are down on their luck. They try to help people, pick themselves up, rather than giving them handouts.'

'Do they sing like the people in the film?'

'I think so, and they have also helped find people who have been lost or missing.'

'They are great, the way they help people out,' I said.

'There are great people everywhere you go, even at home where you live.'

I thought of Ellen Walsh, and her kindness, Fr Doyle, and his dedication to the people, and of course Pat Reardon. I couldn't leave him out of the equation.

'No one ever knows when we need help. We should never be afraid to ask, if it is needed, young lady.' Those words have often gone through my head, and I didn't know then, that I too, would need some help before too long. For the moment, I was taking all the city in, the people, the lights, the traffic and a world that was so far removed from my quiet simple country life in the Midlands.

When we got back to the house that night, there was light in the front parlour window. Meg threw her eyes up to the sky and said, 'He's back!'

When we got in, we went straight to the kitchen, and I sat down at the table while Meg put on the electric kettle to make some cocoa. Darcy peeped in through the door and said, 'When I got home you were not here. Where were you?'

'We were at the theatre. We went to the Gaiety. It was Sarah's treat.'

'I see. How are you, my beautiful little princess?'

'Fine, thank you.'

He came in the door, and closing it behind him, began speaking some acting words again. I think it might have been Shakespeare.

'Doubt thou the stars are fire;

Doubt that the sun doth move;

Doubt truth to be a liar;

But never doubt I love.'

'Darcy, I think you should leave,' said Meg.

He went to speak again and bowed. He staggered as he did so.

'You have been drinking. Now get out, this little girl doesn't need to see you like this.' She shoved him out the door and closed it tight. He stayed out in the hall acting out some of his speeches again.

'Hear my soul speak: The very instant that I saw you, did my heart fly to your service.'

'Go away Darcy, I mean it,' she shouted.

After a minute or so, we could hear him going up the stairs to his bedroom. Meg and Darcy had separate rooms, and I had the guest bedroom. When she heard him go, she gave a sigh of relief and began to make the cocoa. When she sat down at the table with me, I knew she was a little bit upset with Darcy's behaviour.

'When he speaks like that Sarah, he's fantasising over young women. Please give him a wide berth. His behaviour will land him in jail someday. I'm usually there to pick him up, but be it long, or be it short, he'll have it coming to him.' She took a sip from her cocoa, and when she left it down she said,

'Make sure you lock that door tonight, and if he comes knocking don't let him in. He has been drinking, so I'd say he'll be out for the count.'

Meg was tired and when she went to bed, I knew she fell into a deep sleep. I locked the door and got ready for bed. I lay facing the window, as there was a beam of light showing from the street light outside. The only beam of light I had experienced coming through the window at night at home, was during the phase of a full moon, and the sky would have to be clear for that. I lay awake thinking of all I had seen and done for the past two days, and tried to remember the smells, and the tastes I had experienced. I drifted into sleep and I was dreaming of pleasant days in the future, when I could come to the city myself, and take my time going through the shops, and visiting places of interest.

At some point, late into the night, I was awakened by a noise. I thought it was a gentle knock on the door. I woke up and listened. There it was again a gentle knock on the door.

'Who's that?' I said.

'Sarah, it's me!' It was Darcy, speaking in a whisper.

'What do you want?'

'Can you open the door? I want to talk to you.'

'No! Go away.'

'Please Sarah, you are a nice girl. I just want to talk.'

'If you don't go away, I'll call Meg.'

'Don't wake her up. She's fast asleep. She is very tired, and she will be cross if you wake her.'

'I don't like you, just go away. I don't like the way you go on.'

'There's no need to be afraid. I thought you might like to join the show too.'

'No, I don't want to! Go away!' He kept turning the door handle, and I could see it rattling in the half light. I began to tremble with fear.

'Sarah! Please!'

I gave a muffled shout. 'Meg!' I tried to scream, but my fear made it more of a whisper than a scream.

'Alright, Sarah! I'm sorry if I frightened you. I'm going back to bed now. Maybe we will have a chat again sometime. Goodnight!'

Then there was silence. The rattling of the doorknob stopped, and I could hear his bedroom door close. The place was silent once again. As a result, I could not sleep, and I lay awake for ages thinking he might come back. When sleep finally came, it took me over. I woke with a start, when I heard a knock on the door again. It was broad daylight.

Then I heard Meg's voice, 'Wake up you lazy thing, are you going to stay in bed all day?'

'Alright!' I answered, 'I'll be down soon.'

When I got down, she made an announcement.

'I have to take you back by train to the village. Darcy left early this morning and took the car. Heaven only knows where he's gone. Had you a good night's sleep?'

I told her I slept like a log. I didn't tell her about Darcy knocking on the door. I didn't want to spoil what had been a few nice days for her. I helped her prepare breakfast, tidy up, pack our things and make our way to the station, to get the afternoon bus going to Galway.

Chapter 7

The Promise

I was in a dream world for days after. It was the nicest thing that had ever happened to me. It was the first time I was ever away from home on my own. Mam knew by me that I had really enjoyed my few days away and declared that she did not know how she was ever going to pay Meg for her kindness. There were times Mam had to call me back from my daydream world, and to continue with whatever job I was doing in the kitchen. Meg took me home in a hackney car from the station. Packy went with her in the same car to the next town for other engagements; the show had been extended by a further four nights. It was to be the last of that production, and Packy would finish the following Wednesday, just in time to go back to school. The theatre was to continue travelling until the middle of October when the show wound down for the season. Meg told Mam on the quiet also, that she wasn't sure if it would travel again, as it was difficult to draw audiences now, with newer attractions like dance halls and cinemas. A decision would be made in the new year in that regard.

Mam knew as well, that soon Dad would be thinking of returning to England. She began showing a braver face about her, when he was around, undertaking more jobs in the kitchen, such as baking bread, ironing and preparing meals. Whenever he left the kitchen, she handed the work over to me, warning me not to say anything. She was now hoping again he'd return to England to make more money, to carry out the proposed renovations to the house, and to acquire more stock. He spoke to Pat on a few occasions, that he'd begin by renting some land on the eleven-month scheme. He'd stock the land with dry stock and sell them each year. In that way, he could put money aside to purchase more land, and to increase his holding. Just in case he might have to remain longer in England, he got rid of the two old cows, and the younger one, now in calf would keep the house supplied with milk. He wasn't selling Tossie the donkey, as he was on the farm for so long. He had earned his retirement, even though he was yoked to the cart to draw turf from the high bank each summer, to the side of the road for transporting home. Where the tractor couldn't go, Tossie could and he was still valued on the farm. Mam had nothing to worry about regarding life on the farm. There was money in the house for our everyday needs, and there were the savings in the bank as well.

But it wasn't the farm and the work needed to keep it going that worried her, it was how she was feeling herself. During those few days Packy was away, Mam went to town with Ellen Walsh with the intention of buying new boots for the boys going back to school. This she did, knowing their sizes, and buying them straight off the shelf. I was left at home to mind the house and prepare meals. She didn't tell anyone that she had also visited Dr Sullivan at his dispensary. She didn't even tell Ellen Walsh what she had done. She arranged to meet her at the hotel where they'd share a cup of tea before coming home. When she returned, she told us that she wanted to lie down. I went to her, and she told me to leave her alone, she was alright. She warned me not to tell Dad she was resting. If he came home, she was tidying the room. I knew that Mam was acting strangely as well as not feeling well. Her mental state was not right too, as there were times when she was talking to herself, and on occasion, she started shouting for no reason. This never happened when Dad was around. It was only years later that I realised that Mam's health preyed on her mind, and her concerns for the future of her family affected her sanity. She was aware that I knew there was something wrong, and she kept warning me not to tell Dad. But I knew I had to tell him about it, and I didn't know when I was going to do it. It was Meg who came to me when she returned with Packy the following Thursday.

Mam asked me to take the boys down the fields to gather some blackberries for jam making. I knew she wanted to talk to Meg on her own. But what she told her that day, left her in a quandary. Meg came to me the next day, before she left for the last time that season, with some news I didn't want to hear. She brought me to town for as she called it, afternoon tea. It was something she had done with me for the past few years, as a little treat together, and this was the last time she'd see us until next year. While we sat together in the hotel, Meg told me what had happened.

'Sarah, you know your mother is not a well woman.'

'I've known that for a long time,' I said, 'There were times I could not sleep at night, and when Dad came home I told him. She keeps telling him she's alright.'

'I'm aware of that,' she said, 'and she's encouraging him to return to England to make more money for these pipe dreams she has. He should stay here with you and maybe get a job here. Why does she want him to go?'

'Dad has always been in England since they got married. Mam never wanted to go, and it is hard on him.'

'She was at the doctor the other day. She has some form of an inherited heart condition. He wants her to go into hospital, and she will not do it.'

'Why?' I asked.

'Ever since the night of the dance, things have been preying on her mind.'

'Like what?'

'When the sergeant told her, what happened to the Larkin children, she is afraid that something like that will happen to her children too.'

'I can take care of them….'

'Sarah, she told me she was going to die. I'm sorry, pet, to be so blunt about it, but she is obsessed with dying.'

'Is that what you wanted to tell me?'

'No! She asked me to care for you when she dies. She has tried to make me promise, that the boys would not be taken away to an orphanage.'

'But she is not going to die,' I said, sobbing quietly as I spoke.

'I hope not, but I could not take care of you, not the way she wants me to. I have promised to keep you all together. Your welfare lies at your father's feet. He needs to take responsibility for you all. He should not return to England, and leave you like this. You will have to talk to him. I really cannot take care of you all, the authorities would not let me. They might not let you care for the boys either, even when you are over sixteen, and able to work. If your father is not here, they will take your brothers away. Your father is a good man, but how will they perceive that? They could say that he abandoned his family like the Larkin man, and you would be left high and dry here. It's a terrible situation Sarah, and desperate situations can result in desperate measures.'

'I'm afraid, Meg. I really am.'

'You will have to get your father to stay at home then. Whatever it takes, it's up to *you* Sarah. Your mother is going to convince him otherwise.'

She hugged me tight and tried to reassure me that all would be well. I was silent all the way home, and Mam sat by the fire with smiles on her face, full of happiness and cheer. Dad was having his tea, and he hadn't a thing to worry about, as Mam was putting up a brave face to the world. She was up and busy sweeping the floor, tidying the kitchen. As usual, Dad went out to the sheds after the tea, and she sat down immediately when he left.

'You cannot hide it from him, Mary,' said Meg.

'Remember your promise, Meg,' she said. But Meg hadn't really made a true promise to her. I could see *why*, she was a friend and not family. She could support us as best she could, but she was on the outside. It wasn't fair of Mam to impose this request on her. She had enough problems of her own to deal with, without taking a whole family on.

Before she left, Packy clung to her, and thanked her for the great time he had on stage over the past few weeks. He promised to do his best in everything for her, and to work hard at school. Tom and Joe shook hands with her, but she grabbed each of them and planted a big kiss on their faces. They protested by giving little yelps as she did so, and Joe kept wiping his face with his sleeve.

'When are you coming back?' asked Packy.

'I don't know' she said, 'We may be acting in Manchester for the winter. I don't like making promises to little children, and then not carrying them out.'

'Will it be next year then?' asked Joe.

'Maybe! But then, you'd never know, I could come this way to see you if I'm not acting.'

'I hope it will be soon,' said Tom, 'We love it when you come.'

'Stop saying things like that, Mr Charmer,' she said to Tom, 'You'll have me hugging and kissing you again.'

'No way!' said Tom, stepping back from her. She had said goodbyes to Mam and Dad, and I saw her to the car. She was wearing her fur coat and gloves and looked the elegant self when she was in the city. Darcy had called to collect her, and he doffed his hat at me out the window. I ignored him and hugged her as she left.

'It's up to *you* now, Sarah, to hold on to your Dad.'

'I'll do my best,' I said.

The autumn season arrived with a bang. The weather was changeable at times, some fine days, but rain and wind were never far away. Dad was glad to have the turf in the shed, and the hay secure for the winter. He said that there was a likelihood that there'd be a plentiful supply of hay during the winter, as there were only two candidates for it, the one remaining cow, and Tossie the donkey. He said it wouldn't go to waste as someone in the neighbourhood might be short come April, and one never knew what the winter might bring. He was a happy man, having all the work done, fences and mearings secured, and as he said himself, he owed nothing to no one.

But reality showed a different picture. Dad was so absorbed in this work; he didn't see that Mam was keeping up this great barrier of pretence. She was obsessed with trying to keep both her physical, and mental state a secret from him. She knew I was aware of the situation, and she kept warning me not to say anything. Mam was perfectly healthy when Dad was in the house, but during September he went working on other farms, to help bring in the harvest, and secure the hay for the winter. He was gone each day from after eight o'clock, till about half past six each evening. She sat by the fire most of the day and when she heard Sputnik the dog barking, heralding his return, she was up, putting on the kettle for the tea, and cutting up a cake of brown bread, arranging the slices on a plate. She laughed and smiled at him, as he sat filling his pipe by the fire. I remained silent, as Mam had changed. She was liable to start shouting and screaming at me when Dad was gone from the house. I was afraid she'd get a heart attack in the process. I did not know how I was going to tell Dad. I decided to wait, and try to find a time, and place to get him on his own. It was difficult, as Mam was always in my presence, and I wasn't out in the evening milking the cow or feeding Tossie. The boys did that work. I was attached to the house all the time. The only time I could get away, was when I cycled to the village once or twice a week for some messages, such as tea, sugar, matches, flour or any produce we could not provide at home.

At the end of September, Dad accompanied Pat Reardon one day to Walsh's to stack the ricks of hay in the new hay shed they had just built. I decided to call to Walsh's before I went to the village.

Ellen was busy getting dinner ready for the work men, and she had a young girl I knew at school called Nan, helping her. Nan was good at cooking too, and it was some of her baking, in the form of apple tarts or barmbracks, that made their way to our house now and then.

'How can I help you, alana?' she asked.

'I just want to talk to Dad for a few minutes. It's important.'

'Come in and sit down by the Aga cooker, it's quite cold outside today. Will I make you a cup of tea?'

'No, thank you. I'm in a hurry. Mam isn't the best today.'

'Poor thing, she is suffering a lot lately. What's really wrong with her?'

'I don't really know,' I said, and changed the subject, 'Is there any word from Seán lately?'

'We went to see him on Sunday. He's doing fine, studying very hard.'

'That's interesting,' she said. 'He was asking for you as well. He wondered whether you were going to write to him.'

'I will soon,' I said.

'What's all this about then? What's that boy of mine getting up to?'

'He just wants to be my friend.'

'Well he has lots of decisions to make this year, and I hope he makes the right ones.' I didn't know exactly what she was on about. Seán would have to do his Leaving Cert before he made any decisions about his future.

Meanwhile, Nan arrived back with Dad. He knocked on the door and she invited him in. He looked at me wondering what I wanted him for.

'Is everything alright at home, Sarah?'

'I think Mary is a bit unwell today,' said Ellen.

'Does she need a doctor?' he asked.

'Dad no! I need to talk to you.'

'Well go on Sarah, go ahead.'

'I'll talk to you outside,' I answered.

'I'll tell you what, Sarah, take your Dad down to the parlour and no one will disturb you there.'

'I can't go there,' said Dad, 'my boots are too mucky?'

'Go down to the parlour,' she said, 'it's clean dirt. It wouldn't be the first time there were mucky boots in our parlour.' She directed us into the room, and shut us in. We sat on two dining room chairs which were placed at a round mahogany table, which smelled of wax polish. It was a pleasant room, and I would love to have had one in our house. Maybe someday, I thought.

'What brings you here Sarah?' asked Dad.

'Remember when you came home, I told you, when you got off the bus that Mam was not well.'

'I know that, love, but she tells me she's alright. I see a vast improvement in her.'

'No Dad, she's not. She's anything but fine.'

'What is really the matter with her, Sarah?'

'She has a weak heart. She went to the doctor the day she was in town with Mrs Walsh. She didn't even tell *her,* she was at the doctor. She told no one except Meg.'

'Why did she tell *her*? What's the matter with her? Why didn't she tell me?'

'She spends most of the day sitting in the chair or sleeping on the bed. When you come home, she pretends she was busy all day. I have been doing all the work, the cooking, the ironing, baking, and cleaning. Her mind is not right too. There are times she starts shouting at me, if I tell her I was going to tell you about her health.'

'That's not like her. I never heard her shouting at anyone ever. Will I get Fr Doyle to talk to her or Dr Sullivan?'

'Don't get the doctor whatever you do, he wants her to go into hospital for tests, but she's afraid of a number of things.'

'What's she worried about?'

'When the sergeant told her about the Larkin children, she is terrified that if anything happened to her, the boys would be taken away if you were away in England.'

'Then I won't go back to England, you know, love, that I'd never abandon you like Dan Larkin.'

'I know that, Dad, but there's something else, another part of her wants you to return to England. She wants a new bathroom and running water. She wants you to buy more land or increase your stock and rent land.'

'All of that will have to wait then,' he said.

'You will have to talk to her. She also tried to make Meg promise to take care of us. She told her she was going to die. Meg told her that you'd have to take responsibility for us.'

'You know I will take care of you no matter what happens.'

'If she has a weak heart, why is it affecting her mind? Dad, I'm afraid.'

'Listen, love, I'll talk to her. Will you take care of the boys and make sure they are fed and dressed for school? I will talk to her.'

'Dad, don't go home, and start giving out to her. She'll know I was talking to you. In fact, she'll wonder now what took me so long.'

'You go on to the shop. I won't go working tomorrow, I'll go down to Pat's place for a while in the morning, and I'll be back around midday. Shut the dog in the shed or tie him up down the field for a while so that she won't hear him barking. Sarah, you're a great daughter, you know that.'

'Dad, I have to go,' I answered. He gave me a big bear hug as he always did, and we thanked Ellen for the use of the parlour. I left him at the farm gate and cycled on to the village to buy the messages.

Chapter 8

Confrontation

He left the next morning and winked at me as he went out the door. Mam was up early, pretending to be busy getting the boys ready for school. She sat at the table giving orders and telling me to make sure their lunches were ready, making sure that Tom had the threepence to buy a new copy. They all got a penny each to buy a bar at the shop in the village on the way home. Dad had milked the cow and was finishing off his breakfast when they left. She didn't say anything to him but got up from the table and began to sweep the floor.

'You're doing that early,' he said. 'I never saw you sweep the floor so early in the morning.'

'Wouldn't you think you'd mind your own business John Cregan. Eat your breakfast and get off to work with yourself?'

She never spoke to him like that before, and he could read from her tone of voice that there was a change in her personality.

'I was only coddin' you,' he said.

'Well keep it to yourself and be off to work. In fact, it's time you went back to England.'

Dad got up from the table and left, winking at me as he went out.

I continued to busy myself with the morning chores. When I turned around, Mam had gone to her bedroom. I left it for about half an hour, and then peeped in the door. She was lying on the bed all covered up, facing the wall.

I left her so and didn't wake her. I was tired of this game she was playing.

Mam never mentioned her own mother very much. She said she was cared for by a maiden aunt in Tullamore and went to school from there. Her conversation was always about her Aunt Mary. She was named after her, but she said very little about her mother.

Dad returned at midday and whispered softly when he came into the kitchen.

'Where is she?'

'In bed,' I answered.

He went slowly to the room, opened the door quietly, and sat down on the bed. He placed his hand on her shoulder, and she turned with a start.

'What are you doing here?' she exclaimed.

'I was going to ask you the same question,' said Dad.

'I'm resting, so there!'

'Mary, what ails you?'

'There's nothing wrong with me John Cregan. Now get back to work.'

'Mary, I know there's something wrong. You were at the doctor and you didn't tell me.'

'It was Meg, wasn't it? I made her promise not to tell you.'

'She didn't tell me. She told Sarah.'

'Sarah! She shouldn't tell a young child like that.'

'Mary, you will have to tell me what's wrong. I'm your husband and you should have no secrets from *me*.'

I stood at the door, my eyes tearing up, keeping quiet and waiting for Dad in his own gentle way to bring Mam around to his way of thinking.

'You know we have the best daughter anyone could ever have, and three great boys. Why should you build a big wall from us all? We want to be there for you, and to help you get better.'

She sat up on the bed, and she began to shake, and breathe heavily as if she were in a panic attack. Dad put his arm around her, and speaking calmly, she began to relax after a few minutes.

'There,' he said, 'there's no need to be afraid. I'm here.'

'John, I'm going to die!' she whispered.

'Who said you were going to die? Was it the doctor?'

'No, John. He told me I had a weak heart.'

'And you are letting it prey on your mind. It's making you worse. There are loads of people who have a weak heart, and if they take care of themselves, what's to stop them living for years?'

'I don't know what to do? If anything happens our children, will you be there to care for them?'

'I will never abandon you, or my children.'

'Look what happened the Larkins?'

'So, this is what it is all about. Dan Larkin was a mean selfish man. He ran away from his responsibilities. He will never have luck for it.'

'What if it *does* happen? You need to go back to England to work. If anything happens while you are away, what will Sarah and the boys do?'

'Then I won't go back. I'll stay and get work here.'

'Yeah, working for farmers and getting a menial wage. We won't be able to build that new bathroom and get in running water.' She began to sob and weep uncontrollably. He sat calmly saying little, but all he could say was 'Aye!' Then 'Shush! It will be alright. Don't be upsetting yourself, acushla.' They sat like that for about ten minutes, and when she calmed down, she got out of the bed and sat by the range in the kitchen drinking a mug of warm, sweet milky tea to calm her nerves. She was shaking as she held the mug, and I took it from her, leaving it on the range beside her.

'You know John, we have a fine daughter. She's a great girl.'

'We'll go out and shout it from the highest treetops,' said Dad.

'Stop Dad!' I said. 'You are embarrassing me.'

'You're a treasure, girl and don't deny it.' A calm came over the kitchen and Dad stayed for the rest of the day. He spent his time in and out of the house, cutting sticks for lighting the fire, taking in turf and filling the corner box for the range, and seeing things like loose window catches needing screws, it was a clean and repair job for the afternoon.

I left them for a while and went to my room. I decided it was time to write to Seán. It was the first time I had ever written a letter to anyone, especially a boy. I didn't want Mam and Dad to know what I was doing. I'd write the letter and hide it under my mattress and post it the next day I went to the village. I decided to follow his guidelines.

Dear Seán,

I'm sorry I didn't write earlier. I was talking to your mother the other day and she told me how you were, and that I should write to you, so here it is.

I never wrote a letter before, so I hope I am doing a good job. Everything is quiet around here. Dad is still at home. Mam is not well now. She wants Dad to go back to England and earn more money as there are a lot of jobs needing to be done on the house. Dad said he will not go back until Mam's health is improved. I hope he stays, as I miss him a lot while he's away, and so do my younger brothers, especially Packy. He is only eight years old.

I'm looking forward to hearing from you, and it is still a long way till Christmas till I see you. I hope your studies are going very well. Your mother said you have a lot of decisions to make this year, as the Leaving Cert is next summer.

All the best for now,

Your friend,

Martin.

I read the letter again, and I hoped he could read my writing. I put it in an envelope, wrote the address on it, and left it under my mattress. I posted it two days later when I went to the village.

About two o'clock I began to get the dinner ready. Dad was sitting on the other side of the range, and Mam had dozed off to sleep in the chair. He sat staring into space and I knew that he didn't know what to think or do regarding Mam. I left him to his thoughts and did my work, boiling potatoes, cabbage and heating up a side of bacon I had boiled that morning. Dad loved his cabbage and bacon. I prepared some parsley sauce as well, it was one of his favourites. The house was quiet until around half past three, when reality kicked in and there was plenty of noise in the kitchen. The boys had returned from school. Mam woke up and she was much more cheerful in herself. I didn't know what would happen next, but I knew deep down, she wanted Dad to stay. But the other half of her mind rested on building a new bathroom and bringing water into the house. So, whether he wanted to go or not, Dad would have to return to England for another while.

After that, an air of calm fell on the house. Mam was more at ease with herself. I began to think that all this talk about her weak heart had played so much on her mind, that it was affecting her sanity big time. She was more her jovial self again. She joked and played with the boys and sat at the table helping Packy with his homework. Tom and Joe declared that they were too big to need any help. She rose in the morning when Dad was going to work, and she helped prepare breakfast, especially making a pot of porridge on the range. A sod of turf was soaked in a bowl of paraffin oil outside overnight, and together with some small sticks or cipíns the boys had stashed in the shed, the fire lit quickly. One of our new luxuries, which came with electricity was an electric kettle. This was put on about five minutes before breakfast and was ready just in time to make tea. The boys grumbled about having to eat porridge, but Mam had a knack of getting it nice and smooth, and it wasn't sticking to the pot like glue. When poured out on the plate with a few spoonfuls of sugar, and lashings of milk, they ate it with relish, savouring its soft fresh sweetness. This was followed by tea with brown bread and jam, and they were ready to meet the day. When breakfast was over and the house quiet, she sat back into her corner and read some women's magazines which Ellen Walsh had left for her on her last visit.

I found time then to go to the village and post the letter, as well as getting a few much-needed messages. I had to collect the children's allowance too, on that day. Mam used it to buy messages, and to put some by for clothes and shoes for us all. It was usually kept in a biscuit tin in her room, and she dipped into it when required. There was also the Delph teapot on the dresser. Dad kept that replenished with cash for household use and for bills. He topped it up always, before returning to England. Mam's only fear would be someone breaking into the house and stealing it. But that had never happened, and I had never heard of anyone in the area ever being robbed.

Mam had to sign the tickets in the children's allowance book, and it was known at the post office that I was authorised to collect it.

I set out on the bike as usual. I was glad to get away from the house for a while. It was a brisk autumn day. September was closing in, and the countryside was showing its final flush of the year, foretelling the world that soon it would be time to shut down for the winter.

I met Fr Doyle on the street and his usual chant was, 'How's Mam?'

'She's fine thank you, Father.'

'I'll call up to see her one of the days? Is that alright?'

'That's fine, father.'

'Will she know me?'

'Yeah, she will…'

He doffed his hat and kept going.

I stood on the street looking after him. That was a strange thing to say, I thought. But it became clear then, at the post office when I noticed eyes focused on *me*, and then again, I was asked how Mam was.

With the usual answer of 'fine thank you,' it was met with the following statement, 'That's her signature on the allowance book, isn't it?'

'Yes, it is!' I answered rather crossly.

'That's grand! It is wrong to falsify signatures you know.'

'Mam did it!' I exclaimed.

'That's fine, love. I was just wondering was she capable of doing it herself, now that she's not well.'

'Mam's fine!' I shouted, taking the money and the allowance books back. I stuffed them rather quickly into the shopping bag and stormed out of the shop. I stuck the stamp rather angrily on the letter and threw it into the post box. I could have done it inside, but I was angry at what I was hearing. Rumours and gossip spread fast, and heaven only knows what people were saying.

A day or two later, Packy wanted to know who Mad Mary was.

'What do you mean?' I asked.

'I heard some of the boys talking about a woman called Mad Mary at school today, and when I asked them who it was, they laughed and ran away.'

'I don't know for the life of me, who she is,' I said. 'She is not from this parish.' People could be so cruel. I was upset all evening, and when Dad was out doing the evening chores with the boys, I told him I wanted to talk to him privately.

He sent the boys off down the field to round up Tossie to bring him into the stable for the night. I began to cry when they were gone.

'What's wrong Sarah?' he asked.

'Dad, people are all talking about Mam.'

'What did you hear?'

'They are calling her Mad Mary.'

'Pat told me today about it, he wanted to draw out and hit one of those gets who teased him in the village back in August, but he felt it better to say nothing.'

'Why are they doing it Dad?'

'Talk is cheap, love. That's why.'

'What are you going to do?' I asked.

'Absolutely nothing. Walk down that street and hold your head high. Show the world that your Mam is a great person, which she is. If you say anything or do anything, you're adding fat to the fire and they'll have a field day over it.'

'Dad, Maggie at the post office wanted to know was Mam able to write her name. She hoped that the signature was hers.'

'Damn well she knows it was hers. Isn't she looking at it for years?'

'Why do you not get annoyed and cross with people over the things they do and say?'

'I'm too long in the world to let people get the better of me. I just get on with life and let them all go to hell. My father had an expression. He used to say, let them all go to hell, and keep on Pateen and Joe.'

'What did he mean by that?'

'I haven't the foggiest notion, but it worked. It was a way he had of telling everyone where to go in a crisis.' I was amused at this. Dad was never short of a solution. When there was a crisis, he dealt with it. I only hoped that some of his wisdom rubbed off on me. We didn't tell Mam what we knew. It was best to leave her in the dark. It could set her off once again, and now she was in much better form.

Chapter 9

Departure

By the middle of October, whatever casual work Dad was getting, began to dry up as the harvesting had been complete, hay, oats, barley, potatoes and turnips, the mainstay of most of the local farms were all gathered and stored for the winter. The dry stock had been sold off, and farm life was taking a break for the darker months. Little extra work was required on the land, as there was only foddering and milking of cows during this period.

Dad grew restless. He did not want to be at home, and out of work. He was reluctant to return to England, and he avoided broaching the subject with Mam. I knew deep down that he wanted to go, but his heart was telling him to stay. He wondered what the outcome would be if something did happen to Mam. His attitude was, that we'd all get by anyway. He'd find work somewhere, but nothing was coming his way.

One morning, Johnny the Post delivered a letter with an English postmark. It was from Mike, one of his workmates across the water. The tone of the letter was, that there were several jobs coming on-stream, and if he wasn't there in Cricklewood soon, he wouldn't stand a chance. He couldn't say very much now, but he left a phone number to contact him after six o'clock any evening. So, with darkness falling fast now, he set off on the bike to the village to ring from the phone box outside the post office. He put the flash lamp on the bike to guide him home. This meant that he was going for a pint to the pub. Pat was probably joining him. This was often an occurrence in the past, before he departed for England. He'd spend the night before he went, at the pub with Pat, giving him instructions to carry out certain jobs, such as cows calving, or checking that the animals were in good health, and to carry out tasks that were beyond Mam's or his children's reach.

Mam sat and waited at home. She spent the night wondering should he go. At one point, she was saying he should stay. At another point, she was saying he should go, they needed the money. I sat at the table reading the boy's comics to keep myself occupied. He returned at about nine thirty, and I was party to their conversation which would lead to Dad's final decision.

'One part of me says stay, John,' said Mam, 'but then the other half says, go. We need the money. Everyone is getting in running water, and flush toilets and a bath. We should have these things, and so should our children. You want to make the farm bigger. I think you should go.'

'What about *you* Mary? You haven't been well.'

'I'll be alright. I'll tell you what you should do. If that Mike fellow you know would let you use his phone after six o'clock, Sarah could go to the village, and ring you, leaving a message. You see if anything goes wrong, that is if I get sick, you will know very quickly, and you could come home to us in a day or so. When you get there, I could get her to ring you, and get your new address. If you want to send home money, we can get it into the savings in the bank. You see if there is a will there is a way. You'd need to get here quickly, just in case that doctor would take the boys away from us. That's my only fear.'

'I want you to tell me that you are feeling better. I want you to tell me you're not afraid, the way it affected your mind like. I will leave enough money for to keep you all going. It will be up there on the shelf on the dresser in the old teapot. It's about eight weeks to Christmas, and I can come home for a week then, and see how things are.'

I said nothing then, but I was a little concerned with the way Mam was talking. She was hiding from him her true feelings. It was part of her state of mind. What looked fine on the outside was a different kettle of fish on the inside. I wanted to get him on his own and tell him. Mam spent a lot of time talking that night. I left them and went to bed. No one knew her as much as I did. Dad had been away so much, he hadn't seen this develop with her. When he discovered how she was covering up her illness, she brought down this veil again, drawing attention away from the fact that things were not as good as they looked. Dad decided, he was going to go back until Christmas.

Next day, Ellen Walsh drove him to town to book his plane ticket. He was taking an evening flight from Dublin to London three days later. In the meantime, my task was to iron shirts for him, and pack new underwear, as well as a good suit for Sunday wear. Whatever work clothes he needed, he'd take care of himself, when he got there. He was going to stay at Mike's house until Christmas, so it was going to be easier to contact him, if anything happened.

I found it difficult to get him on his own to talk to him, as Mam was always within earshot. But I remained quiet and said nothing. Maybe it was best to leave things be. But I'd have to say something before he left.

He was getting the morning bus to Dublin, which would give him plenty of time to get from the bus station to the airport. I went with him to the end of the road; the bus would stop for him if he put out his hand.

Mam was still in bed when he was leaving and her last message to him was, 'God go with you, John!' The boys walked with us to the end of the road as well, where they said goodbye to him and continued to school. Packy clung to him, and he picked him up in his arms to give him a big hug. I could see a glassiness in his eyes, as he was lonely heading off again. At last, I had a few minutes with him before he left.

'She is not good Dad, you know that.'

'I know that, but she wants me to go.'

'Please keep in contact.'

'When I get there, I will write straight away, and let you know what times to ring me and what days as well.'

'If you are not there, will I be able to leave a message.'

'Aye! Do that, if you can't get me, I'll ring Walsh's.'

'Maybe someday we will have a phone of our own Dad.'

'Please God, we will. There will come a time when everyone will have one.'

'If she needs the doctor will I get him?'

'I'm depending on you, love. You are in charge. If you think you need to get a doctor for her then do so. I'll pick up the pieces later.'

'What if she needs to go to hospital?'

'Only as a last resort. If that happens, don't let anything happen to the boys. It will take me about a day or two to get home, but home I'll come. I promise you that.'

I hugged him then as I could hear the rumble of the bus coming around the bend. Dad raised his hand, and it slowed down, pulling in halfway on the grass margin. The door opened, and he rubbed my cheek as he left. There was a whiff of Bendigo tobacco on his hand, and it stayed there close to me, even after he had left. I watched the bus as it wended its way around the corner, and headed for the village, before driving on to the main road towards the town, and eventually reaching Dublin.

To make a long story short, things did not go according to plan.

Dad wrote a letter, which arrived a few days later, and we had an address and phone number to ring if there was any urgency. Things settled in quietly, and Mam seemed fine most days. She had gone back to her usual routine, rising in the afternoon and sitting by the fire. She gave the boys directions, when they came from school, and I was happy that things were back to normal. Fr Doyle called to see her, and she was in bed. She called him down to the room, and he sat at the side of the bed talking to her. She was glad of the company and he gave her a blessing before he left. It wasn't until the middle of November things changed.

Dad stopped writing, and no money was sent home. To keep in contact with him, I decided to go to the village, and ring Mike after six o'clock. I had only three minutes on the phone, and when I pressed the button to connect me, when Mike answered, my message had to be brief unless I rang back again. Dad wasn't there.

'Where is he?' I asked.

'I don't know,' said Mike, 'he left here last week, and said he would contact me. He found a new job and he'd ring me with details as soon as he got there. That didn't happen, and I haven't heard from him.'

'Will you try and find him, we need to keep in contact with him. Mam's health is not great, and we need to be able to find him.'

'I'll do my best he said. Ring me tomorrow evening.'

I put the phone down having thanked him for his help and signed off. When Mam heard what had happened, it set her back in panic mode again. It was the same old story.

'Why did I let him? I shouldn't have let this happen. What will take place if anything should happen to me?' She kept on ranting on about it and I had to get cross with her to stop worrying, everything was alright.

I rang again the next evening and there was no sign of Dad. After ringing for nearly a week, I gave up altogether and wondered what I should do, to try and find him.

Then Mam had a fall. She fell coming from the room to the kitchen, and I was on my own at the time. I managed to get her to stand up, and she sat on the chair. She was shaken, but I don't think she broke anything. She fell asleep by the fire, and I was afraid she was unconscious. She woke up after about two hours, as the boys had returned from school, and they were cold and hungry.

'Are you alright Mam?' asked Joe, 'you look very pale.'

'I'm fine son,' she whispered.

'Are you sure Mam?' asked Tom.

'Eat up your dinner and get them jobs done, like you good lads.'

When they went out to do the evening chores, she went to bed, and didn't get back up again. I wanted to call the doctor for her later that evening, as I was going to ring Mike, to see if there was any word from Dad. She dismissed the idea completely and wouldn't hear tell of it. She was a little bit shaken, and she'd be alright after a few days.

When I rang Mike, I told him what had happened, but there was no sign of Dad. He suggested calling the police and I told him not to. They might call the guards here, and they'd be on our doorstep. I didn't want to let them know that there were problems at our house.

When I got home, she was asleep, and Tom had taken down the jigsaw that Dad had brought him from England in August. The house was quiet and as a result, she was fast asleep. I told the boys to keep quiet for the rest of the evening, and this they did. Joe was curious as to what was wrong, I was doing a bad job at keeping it from them. When I told him, he too wanted to go for a doctor, but I pointed out to him that it was out of the question. It was up to me to make decisions now. It was the first time I felt that the whole world depended on me. My main concern was my brothers. If anyone knew that Mam was in no position to care for them, they'd be gone like the Larkins. It was up to me to do whatever was necessary, to keep them at home. There was no point in contacting Meg. She was over in England in theatre for the winter. We were not her responsibility, and it would be unfair to ask her. There was no point in going to neighbours for help, they'd send for the guards and an ambulance, and have her brought to hospital. If I could get Dad home, at least we could get a doctor.

Chapter 10

The Sally Army

I had been thinking for several days about ways of trying to contact Dad. Thoughts ran through my head, and I kept thinking of the night I spent in Dublin with Meg and going to the pictures to see *'Whistle down the Wind.'* In that story, the little children were lost and alone, searching for love from their father, whose life was too busy working the farm, depending on their aunt who came to live with them after their mother's death. She provided for their basic needs, but there was no love in their lives. It was, of course, the words of the Sally Army lady who said, *'If you believe in Jesus, he'll take care of you.'* What if I went to them, and asked them for help? Meg said they had a very good track record of helping people find lost relatives. I could give them the information they needed about Dad, and they'd pass it on to their colleagues in England. Meg had shown me where they worked in the city and I knew I could find them myself, as it was not far from the new bus station.

I decided to take the early morning bus to the city and come back on the afternoon one travelling to Galway. I gathered the boys together the night before and explained to them what my plan was. Packy, of course, wanted to go with me, but I said it was too expensive as we needed every penny we could get. I promised to bring them back some sweets as a treat.

Mam was sitting up in the bed, when I told her what I proposed to do.

'You are probably barking up the wrong tree, pet,' she said. 'What gives you the idea that the Salvation Army might be able to help you?'

'Meg said that they often find lost or missing people. They are very good at it.'

'Your Dad isn't lost or missing, he just hasn't written to us, and we cannot do anything till he sends us a contact address.'

'Meg said that they found a friend of hers, whom she had lost contact with.'

'That Meg, she never stops filling your head with silly ideas. She's been my best friend always. If she were my sister, I would probably have a row with her over filling your head with nonsense.'

'Mam, I want to give it a try,' I said.

'Go ahead, pet, but don't expect miracles.'

'You see if we tell the guards, they might start sending people around here, poking their noses in and if they took you to the hospital, they might take the boys away.'

I put my arms around her neck and hugged her. She was very frail, and her breathing was laboured. She hadn't recovered after the fall, and I needed to act fast. Dr Sullivan would have to see her. That was a decision I'd have to make myself, and soon. I'd wait till I came back from Dublin, and then I'd contact the doctor. In fact, he too, might be able to find him for me.

I was up at six o'clock that morning and left instructions with Joe to feed the dog, to put on a good fire in the range, and to give Mam her breakfast before he went to school. Mam said she would stay in bed till about midday, and then sit by the fire, until the boys came home. I warned her not to start doing any house work as the boys would prepare the dinner later.

It was cold and frosty, and the ice was hard on the potholes, which dotted the laneway to the main road. I had to walk the mile to the village, as I was afraid the driver might not see me hailing the bus at our corner in the dark. I was glad when it arrived, into the village and I climbed onboard.

'How are you, alana?' asked the driver.

'I'm fine, thank you,' I said, 'Where will the bus stop in Dublin?'

'Busáras,' he said, 'that's the last stop.'

'Thanks!' I said, and sat down, mid-way down the bus.

There was a red rosy hue to the east, as dawn was approaching. My gaze was fixed on the quiet fields, and passing hedgerows, stopping in villages and picking up passengers as it went along. When we reached Maynooth, the traffic volume began to increase, as the city outer limits approached. But it was still a long way to go. I wondered who each person was, as they travelled on their respective journeys. Were any of them like me, searching for their father? It was like a story from a comic book or a novel. But this was real. My Dad was real, and time was running out for us to try and find him. I kept putting it at the back of my mind. I knew deep down, that Mam was dying, and I didn't want to face the reality of it. Dad was not aware that this was happening. As far as he was concerned, his thinking over in England now, was that everything in the garden was rosy, and as he had done before, he might not write at all, but just turn up for Christmas as normal. Whatever time she had left, I wanted to hold on to it, and I wanted Dad to be there to care for us all, and to stay with us. Whenever he returned, there was no way I was going to let him go away again.

The city was a very busy place. It was alien to my world. It was my second time to visit the place, but it was the first time on my own. With the early rising sun, I was amazed at the reflection of colours from the old buildings, varying from black to bright red, depending on age, and also the colour of the brick. The traffic moved slowly along the quays, and I could soon sense the smells of the city, the Liffey at low tide, as well as diesel and smoke fumes from engines and chimneys.

The city centre fast approached, and it wasn't long till the bus ground to a halt at the forecourt of the bright new bus station. It looked so new, compared to the older buildings of the city, and its beautiful marble-tiled floor and waiting seats. You could even buy newspapers and sweets or go upstairs and buy a pot of tea or a sandwich. This was a luxury I had never seen in my life, and it was marvellous. All one needed was plenty of money, and time to go to these places. Now I know why rich people frequented cities a lot, as the luxuries we missed out on in life living in the country, could all be found here.

I strolled around the bus station, and when I had seen enough, I asked a man at the newspaper booth how to get to the Salvation Army building, and he directed me to a building up the street.

'Are you lost or anything?' he asked.

'No sir! I'm not, but I might as well be.'

'Well, if you need any help, they'll look after you.'

'I know that, but I am only looking for information about someone who is lost.'

'Did you not go to the guards then?'

'No, it's complicated,' I answered, 'I must go, and thank you for your help.'

The man shrugged his shoulders and continued selling his papers and sweets. It wasn't long till I found the place, a bright building, old but quite attractive. It had a welcoming feel to it, and I walked slowly up the steps and entered.

The lady I met took down my details and told me to come back at twelve noon to see Mr Thomas; he'd be my guide and help. She smiled as she spoke, and I was expecting her to say that Jesus would take care of me, but she did not. Her accent was cultured, and it was also Irish. She looked to me to be a very well-educated lady, just like Miss Frost, the Church of Ireland lady who came to our house selling red poppies every winter.

To kill time, I followed the movement of people to O'Connell Street, and the first place I made for was the pillar. I stood under this tall giant structure and looked up. It was difficult to see Admiral Nelson so high up on his podium. To me, it looked as if it was going to topple over, but it was only the racing white clouds across a blue winter sky that created this effect.

I went to the GPO, as we learned so much about the 1916 Rising at school. I remember reading about the leaders who were executed, and the role this building played in the uprising. There was no sign of fighting or Revolution as I entered through the doors. It was such a busy place with people queueing at counters, buying stamps and postal orders, and carrying on with their lives as usual. O'Connell Street was a very long street and after finding the Statue of O'Connell and the bullet hole in the breast of one of the bronze angels, I took the long walk to the other end, and gazed in amazement at the monument of Parnell with the inscription: *No man has a right to fix a boundary to the march of a nation.* It was at this point I realised that these leaders, commemorated on this street, were real people who had lived, and helped carve out our country, O'Connell and Parnell to name but a few. What would they say today, about a young girl who was trying to keep her family together? Would they help me if I asked? Maybe I wouldn't even feature in their busy schedules. I'd just be a name, a number or another lost cause.

I left the monument behind me and began making my way towards Talbot Street. I bought three bags of boiled sweets in a small sweet shop, and I followed the signs to the Pro-Cathedral, to light a few penny candles. I knelt in the quiet of the building, with its candle lights and sounds of gentle prayer. It was silent; a world away from the busy city outside, and the scent of candle wax, polish, and incense were pleasing and relaxing. I lit a candle for each member of my family and knelt in quiet prayer for them all. I called on our guardian angels to mind us and protect us. I prayed for Mam to recover and to return Dad to his family safely. I prayed, to keep us together, and never to separate us, this was the one thing in life above all other I wanted, and I knew that whatever happened I would stop at nothing to protect us all. If Dad were to be found, or to contact us, things would be fine. I blessed myself and walked out into the busy city streets. All my hopes rested on a man I did not know, a man called Mr Thomas.

I thought he was a stern fearful man at first but, when he sat behind his desk opposite me; his face lit up and smiled. He was middle-aged and slightly pot-bellied. He wore thick brown rimmed glasses, and he looked out over them at me when he spoke. His head was bald, but he had many strands of long hair combed from the left side to the right, along the top of his head. This gave the impression that he still had a mop of healthy black hair, and I suppose in his vanity, he wanted to look younger than he did.

He took down all my details, and when he had finished writing, he wanted to know why it was so urgent that I needed to contact my father.

He was a stranger to me, yet I trusted him. I knew he wouldn't go prying into our lives or meddling in our affairs. His task was to attempt to fulfil what I asked him to do, and to leave it at that.

I poured my whole heart out to him regarding the situation at home, how Mam was ill, and refused to go to any doctor, while Dad was away. I told him that I thought Mam was dying, and I was afraid to get the doctor. If the authorities saw that we had no steady income, and that I was at home looking after my mother, the boys might be taken away, and put into care. He could see my distress through my tearfulness, and that I did not know where to turn. Then he spoke to me by asking the question, 'My child, how did you know to come and seek help from us?'

'It was Meg, a very good friend of my mothers. She brought me to the pictures in Dublin last summer. We went to see the film *Whistle Down the Wind* and I saw the children in the film listening to the Salvation Army lady talking at the beginning. When we were out shopping she pointed this building out to me and told me about the work you do. The Salvation Army once helped find a friend of hers, whom she had lost contact with.'

'Well, we do help find lost people, and we have been successful, but we can't always guarantee success.'

'Will you try and find Dad for me?' I asked.

'I will put out a call today. Where exactly would your father be working?'

'He works mainly on building sites. He has worked on roads also.'

'Any idea what city he works in?'

'He has worked in London, Manchester, Liverpool and Birmingham.'

'Any idea where he might be now?'

'It's six weeks since he went. He has not sent any address yet as to where he is staying, but money came in the post every two weeks. We put it by safely and only use what we need for food.'

'Hopefully, if that continues you won't starve.'

'I hope you are right, sir,' I answered.

'You are a very strong and brave young lady, do you know that?'

'I'm not. I'm stubborn and headstrong. I love my family very much. I have three younger brothers and they cannot look after themselves. Until they can, I know I am responsible for them, if anything happens Mam. No one is going to take them away from me.'

'Trust in Jesus,' he said. 'Things will be fine. Can you ring me around midday every Tuesday, and I will give you an update? If we can find your father, you will have him home for Christmas.'

'I can ring from the coin box in the village. No one will know my business from there.'

'That's fine. Meanwhile take it easy and safe journey home.'

He shook hands with me, and I left the place feeling relieved that someone knew my story, and my plight to try and find my father. In so doing, I felt I needed to treat myself. I decided to find Grafton Street and look in the shop windows there. Soon I was lost in the city and its magic, the shops, and smells of coffee and tobacco. If I was rich, I'd buy all the clothes I needed, and the shoes were only heavenly. Someday, I hoped I'd be a rich lady and stay in the Gresham hotel. I'd shop in Switzer's or Clery's, go to the movies and the theatre. I could only dream of such days and in my dreaming, time began to move faster unknown to me. The bus was leaving at three thirty, so I gave myself plenty of time to get back to the bus station. At ten past three, I was walking around trying to find the Galway bus when a conductor stopped me.

'Can I help you miss?'

'I'm looking for the Galway bus.'

'I'm sorry, but that left ten minutes ago. The time for that route changed last week. It leaves at three o'clock now, and not three thirty.'

'Oh my God! What am I going to do?' I exclaimed.

'Not to worry,' he said as he smiled, 'if you are not in a hurry, there's another one at six o'clock.'

I was a bit relieved, but the boys might be worried if I didn't come on the afternoon bus. I decided to go no further. I had nearly three hours to wait. I went upstairs to the café and ordered a cup of tea and a buttered fruit scone. When I finished, I went downstairs and sat in the waiting area with my eyes glued on the bus forecourt. I was not going to let that bus get away without me a second time. It was going to be a long vigil, but I didn't mind once I got home safely.

A heavy murky fog had fallen as we approached Lucan village. The outbound city traffic had slowed down to a crawl. I knew that the bus would be more than an hour late getting into the village. I knew that the boys would have all the work done and the place made ready for tomorrow. I hoped that Mam got up during the day and rested by the fire. I had promised I'd be home as quickly as I could, but of course, having missed the three o'clock bus it was getting late. I was anxious to get home. I hoped and prayed that Mr Thomas would be able to find Dad and get him home to us as soon as possible.

There were about twenty people on the bus, and the driver took the journey in his stride. The slow movement of traffic allowed him to open the biscuit tin beside him, and he began selecting some sandwiches to eat as he drove along. At times, the traffic ground to a halt, and he'd take the sandwich in both hands and wolf it down as quickly as possible.

I peered out the window into the darkness, and I might as well have been in Timbuktu as I had no idea where we were. Whenever we reached a village or a bus stop, he'd call out the name of the place.

'We're in Longwood! Two-minute stop here.'

Later, at the next stop, 'Clonard! Two minutes.'

When we reached Kinnegad the fog began to clear, and the bus began to move faster, and the traffic dwindled as we headed towards Galway. Through the lifting fog, I could see the sky brightening to the east and I knew the moon was rising and a frosty night ahead.

The ritual of stopping at other villages followed, and I began to breathe a sigh of relief when familiar houses and landmarks emerged from the darkness or reflected in the lights of the bus.

It was less than five minutes from Avenstown to the end of our laneway. I stood holding on to an overhead bar, as I directed the bus driver to let me off. As the corner loomed out of the darkness, I could see a figure standing at the side of the road, waiting. It was Tom, and he was standing with a hump on him from the cold. He hadn't even a jacket on, and I wondered why he wasn't wearing it. Didn't he know it was a very cold night?

The bus ground to a halt and the driver said, 'Goodnight, acushla!' as I stepped down. I waited for it to move off, before crossing the road. Tom came running to me, and he was cold, agitated and angry.

'Where were *you*, till now?' he shouted.

'Why? What's wrong?' I asked.

'When we came from school, Mam was lying at the step of the door. She was there for a long time and she was cold.'

'Where is she now?' I asked.

'She is sitting in the soft chair by the fire. She fell asleep and then she woke up. She won't let us go for Dr Sullivan. Why were you so late? We thought you would be home on the afternoon bus.'

'I missed the bus,' I blurted angrily back at him. 'I tried to get the afternoon one home, but the time changed recently, and no one told me. I missed it by ten minutes, and I had to wait for the six o'clock one. That's why I'm late and it's not my fault.'

'Anyway, Mam is not well, and we don't know what to do.'

'Let's go!' I said as I began running up the laneway to our house. Tom ran ahead of me and when he got to the gate, he waited for me as he tried to catch his breath.

When I opened the door, Packy came to me and hugged me tightly. I reached into my bag and I took out the three bags of boiled sweets I bought for them. With the noise and caterwauling of my three brothers, and Joe scolding me for being late, the noise woke Mam up, and she opened her eyes.

'Sarah,' she said, 'I'm glad you are home.'

'You should not have tried to go outside. You promised me you would take it easy till the boys came home.'

'I'm sorry, pet,' she sighed, 'but I wanted to help get things done.'

'Mam, you know everything is fine with the house now. I am going to get the boys to go to the village and get Dr Sullivan to call.'

'You will not,' she scolded, 'I need no doctor, if he comes, he'll put me in the hospital, and what will become of my children then?'

'Well let me get you to bed, you should be resting on this cold night.'

'You get yourself something to eat first, pet. You must be starving.'

'I'll get you to bed first and then I'll eat something.'

Joe helped me get her to her feet. She placed her thin bony arms around our necks, and she walked slowly with us to the bedroom. While I got her ready for bed, Joe put on the pan, and began heating some slices of cold lean bacon on it which had been left over from the day's dinner. Along with that, he fried some brown bread, and when I came back to the kitchen he had it ready on the table for me.

I sat down. I didn't realise I was so hungry, until I began to eat. Then I began checking that all was in order in the house.

'Homework done, boys?' I asked. The answer I received from all three of them was positive, except that Packy wanted me to check his spelling. I examined them one by one, and they were all perfect.

'I think it's time for bed now,' I said to him. He threw his arms around me and hugged me. 'Thanks for the sweets,' he said. He went off to bed quietly, and Tom followed him. They shut the bedroom door and Joe sat staring at me.

'Did you contact Dad?' he asked.

'No, but a very nice man by the name of Mr Thomas took down all the information. It will take a week or two to find him.'

'That might be too late,' Joe exclaimed.

'Shush!' I beckoned, and we talked in a low whisper.

'Another letter came today,' he said, 'There's fifteen pounds in English money in it. There's no letter again.'

He took it out from behind the wireless and gave it to me. When I looked at the stamp, I knew he was no longer in England.

'He's in Scotland!' I said.

'How do you know that?' asked Joe.

'Look at the stamp with the Queen's head on it. There's a picture of a thistle on it also. That means he must be in Scotland.'

The postmark was smudged and unclear. The first two letters were AB, and the last three were EEN.

'Aberdeen!' shouted Joe, 'what's he doing in Aberdeen?'

'I don't know!' I said, 'Maybe he is only after getting there, and when he has an address we can write to Mr Thomas, and he will find him very quickly.'

'I wish he'd write though or send us a phone number. We could ring from the post office.'

I took the money out of the envelope. Taking the tin down from the top of the dresser, I placed it with the rest of the cash. There was seventy-five pounds altogether there now.

'That will do us for a long while,' I said. 'Tomorrow I will write to Mr Thomas and send him the envelope with the stamp on it. It might be of help to him.'

'Sarah, what are we going to do?' he sighed.

'We will see how she is in the morning,' I answered.

'What if she has to go to the hospital?'

'I will look after you all, don't worry.'

'They might take us away from here.'

'They won't, wait and see. Now off to bed.'

Joe turned and headed for the room. Even though he was only thirteen, he was tall and muscular for his age. But beneath that physical exterior, he was still only a child in need of care. He turned before going into bed and said, 'By the way, thanks for the sweets.'

I sent him off to bed and began tidying up the kitchen before I settled down myself. But little did I know I was going to have a very long night ahead of me, a night that would haunt me forever.

Chapter 11

The Long Night

Before going to bed, I checked on Mam and she seemed to be sleeping. I stoked the fire quietly and left the light on in the kitchen. The door to the boy's room was slightly ajar, and I peeped in at them. They were fast asleep. I closed it gently and I was glad to get into bed. I didn't realise how tired I was. It was a long day from six o'clock in the morning. The city was a rumbling noisy place, and between the hustle and bustle of urban life, the noise and the rattling of a rickety bus, coupled with the smell of burning diesel, I sank into a deep sleep.

The whole scene had changed for me. I eased into a world of dreams. I didn't know I was there, but sleep drew me deeper and ever deeper into a better world. It got brighter and warmer by the minute. The cold of winter had vanished. The darkness of night had gone, and I was running through a field of fresh green grass. It was summer. I knew it was summer, as the sun washed my face with light and warmth. The gentle breeze blew my hair backward. I was laughing as I ran. Someone was chasing me. I looked back. Joe was running after me. Tom and Packy were there too. They were running as well, to avoid Joe. We were playing a game of tag. I knew it was difficult to avoid Joe. Sputnik was running hither and thither, trying to be part of the game too. Our laughter was one of happiness. We were never happier in our lives before. It was the same joy I felt back in August, when Dad returned on the bus from England. The sun shone on the trees and hedges. We were out in the pasture behind the house. Tossie the donkey, and the little red cow were in the corner of the field, quietly grazing. They paid no attention to us, as our games in the field were a regular occurrence. It must have been a day in early June. The sun shone on the trees and hedgerows. They were fresh, and in full leaf. The pink and cream hue reflected the sunlight on the hawthorns, and I could even hear the noise of a tractor in a far-off field.

I stopped playing the game, and I lay down on the fresh green grass. It was full of white and pink clover flowers, and there were daisies dotted all over the place. I lay on the flat of my back, looking up at the clear blue sky.

Was this real? It was a day I never wanted to end. I could hear the shouts and merriment of my brothers. and I laughed quietly to myself as well. I turned over on my stomach and pulled a long thraneen of grass and began chewing it, rolling the end of the long stem in my mouth. Sputnik came over to me and sat down beside me, preening and scratching himself as dogs often do. I peered at ground level through the young growing grass, and it was then I could see her. Mam was standing across the field from us. She was smiling and laughing at her children playing. The boys played on and paid no attention to her. Something inside me told me that they could not see her. She was different. She was much younger, and she had a full face. Her cheeks glowed in the sun, and she had her hair draped down her shoulders. She was wearing the dress Dad brought her from England. It made her look like a young girl, and she was moving slowly towards me. I sat watching that beautiful moment in time and wanted to hold onto it forever. Then I had a sudden urge to run to her and hold her. I wanted to hug her and kiss her round rosy cheeks. I wanted her to run with me through the field, to jump over young growing thistles, to run forever and to hold on to the day.

I jumped up and ran towards her. The more I ran to her, the more she seemed remotely distant. As I moved, my legs got heavier and as I tried to reach for her, she moved further away. If this was a dream I began to hate it, as the joy of such a dream began to fade from my world. As I ran towards her, the smile on her face changed and slowly moved from an eternal one to an expression of sadness and sorrow. As I reached for her, she was snatched further away from me again. I stopped in my tracks to catch my breath, and I could see that my brothers played on with their game, unaware that I was struggling to reach out, and hold our mother. As I tried to grasp for her, I could see tears streaming down her face, and she moved her head from side to side as if to say no.

I could hear her thoughts, and she was saying, 'Sarah darling, this is not real. It is too beautiful to be real. This never happened. It never will. My darling child, I have let you all down. I have failed my children. I have not been a good mother. God is punishing me for doing this to you. I'm sorry!' The word sorry kept repeating through the air, echoing across the pasture from hawthorn to hawthorn hedge.

'That's not true!' I shouted back, 'we all love you!'

Then she smiled through her tears, and she was gone. I called her name repeatedly. As I turned around and round searching for her, the trees and grass, the sunshine and blue skies, the dog and my brothers began to melt away. I started screaming, as no one could hear me. I now knew that scream was inside my head, and no one else could hear it only myself. In that deep inner space, reality was just like a castle made of sand that could topple with the slightest breeze. The wonderful dream was fading fast, and I wanted it to stay.

I kept shouting her name, but my calling was silent inside my head. The fading light, and the sunshine now gave way to darkness, and I kept silently uttering her name. Then I thought I could hear her. I stopped running through the darkness to catch my breath. I stopped breathing for a few seconds to listen. I could hear a faint cry through the darkness. As I listened, it got slightly clearer, and began to reach my hearing.

'Sarah!' I could hear her very faint voice.

I listened again and again, and it was the same.

'Sarah!'

Through the darkness, there was a glow once again. and I soon realised I was no longer in a beautiful field, but warm and comfortable in my own bed. There was a shaft of light through the opening in the door from the light in the kitchen. I looked at the clock on the little mantelpiece. It was one o'clock in the morning. I lay back down on the pillow and it was then, that reality kicked in. I heard the voice of my mother call faintly through the house.

I jumped out of bed into my slippers and went quickly to her. She was attempting to get out of bed, but I knew she hadn't the energy to do so. I tried to calm her down. and made her lie back on her pillow.

'I thought you wouldn't come to me,' she said faintly.

'I'm here Mam, you know I will never leave you.'

'You are a beautiful young girl, Sarah. And I will never see you fall in love and marry a handsome young man. I will never see you in your wedding dress. I have failed you, my darling little girl.'

'Stop that Mam, you will have me in tears in a minute.' I didn't know what to say, but soon I began to realise that what I said to her then happened to be the right thing at the right time. I don't know what inspired me, but how I answered and spoke to her that night were not the words of a young girl on the cusp of womanhood, but someone who was much older, and mature, who had been hardened by the world and its strife. I sat in beside her on the bed, covering myself with her top coat and put my arm around her shoulders.

'I want you to go back to sleep,' I said. It was certain now – Dr Sullivan would have to be called in the morning and maybe Fr Doyle. I knew that Mam was dying. I didn't have any fear inside me. In fact, I gathered and nurtured a great strength to be there for her. She might last a few more days, but that was something I could not gauge.

'I will stay with you tonight, Mam,' I said, 'I just want you to go back to sleep.' 'You are a kind considerate young girl, Sarah. Do you know that?'

'I think I inherit that from my mother,' I chuckled.

She gave a low giggle and patted my hand. She became quieter and then said, 'Sarah why did you turn off the light?' It was a moment before I answered. The light in the room was on. I looked down at her. Her eyes were wide open, whatever had happened she could not see.

'It's better this way,' I answered, 'you will sleep easier. I will stay with you don't worry.'

'You know that the day you were born was the happiest day of my life. I always wanted a little girl of my own, and God sent me you. He made a great choice you know?' I patted her hand gently and said, 'Don't flatter me now Mam, that might change. I haven't grown up yet.'

'Nonsense! You are growing into a beautiful young woman. Then after that, he sent me the three boys, one after the other. I love them to bits too you know. They are still only babies, what will happen to them?'

'Nothing will happen to them, Mam.'

'If your Dad doesn't come home, they will be taken away. I know they will. I hear there are terrible places where they send them. Why did I let him go back? It was my own fault for being so stupid. He would have stayed you know, only I acted so irresponsibly, pretending there was nothing wrong.'

'No one was to know that you would become very ill, Mam. Dad didn't realise it either.'

'Hindsight is a great thing, pet. There are so many ifs and buts in our lives, that we often make the silliest of judgements. What will happen to my boys?'

'Don't worry, Mam, whatever it takes, I'll take care of them. I promise you that. No one will take them away.'

'Something inside me tells me that you will, pet. I know that inside that gentle caring nature, hides another person that no one will ever walk on.'

'You're thinking about the day I challenged those go boys in the village, who tried to throw Pat Reardon around.' She laughed gently to herself and then said, 'It's a terrible dark night. I thought the moon was shining. 'It's very foggy out, that's why you can't see the moon.' She stopped talking for a few minutes and then she whispered, 'You will try and find your Dad, won't you?'

'I will, the Salvation Army man will contact him.'

'As long as he doesn't have you singing in the streets.'

'Stop that now,' I said, 'he was very kind, and he is a good Christian.'

'I know love! By the way, did you put that money away safe that Dad sent?'

'I did. I think he's in Scotland. He's gone to Aberdeen.'

'That's him all over. He's not great for writing, but the money keeps coming. He's a good man Sarah, that's why you need to find him.'

'I'll do my best.'

She held my hand tighter, and she closed her eyes. I leaned my head on hers, cradling her on my shoulder. After a few minutes, she spoke again.

'I cannot get it out of my head, but I worry about those boys, especially little Packy. He'll need a lot of loving and minding. Tom is the one who says little. He bottles things up, and Joe is more like yourself.'

'They're strong, the three of them. They'll be fine.'

'I mean it when I say it. I know you will meet and marry a kind young man. I can see you now. You are both by the sea somewhere and he takes you in his arms and kisses you. Then he asks you to marry him and you say yes.'

The child in me emerged again, at that point and I exclaimed, 'No, I'm not! I'm not going to go kissing handsome young boys.'

'You will, my dear,' she murmured. I knew by her now she was exhausted and needed to rest.

'I love you, Mam,' I said.

'I love you too, my darling little girl.'

I held her hand and she slumbered off. I lay there in the quiet of the room, holding her, and thinking to myself of ways to try and get Dad home. I knew he'd arrive at Christmas, which was more than five weeks away. I could feel her breathing quietly and peacefully, and I nodded off into sleep once again. If my dream became a summer meadow this time, at least I was holding her hand, and she could be part of that dream. But they had faded while I slept. I was aware she was there, and I was happy to be with her. It was like those moments she shared with us when we were sick or woke up in a nightmare. She sat in beside us and stayed with us till we nodded off. Now I was here with her, when she needed me at the loneliest part of her life. She was peaceful now. I wasn't aware of it, but she was gently fading away from me, and I slept, as she passed away that night. It must have been about four o'clock, when I suddenly realised that I was feeling cold. I still held her hand and it was heavy. I opened my eyes slowly and reaching up I touched her. Her head felt cold. I went to hold her hand tighter, but it slipped from my grasp. I looked down at her and her eyes were open.

'Are you awake, Mam?' I asked. She did not answer me. She had a vacant look in her eyes, and she was not blinking. I sat up on the edge of the bed, and she slumped inwards. It was then, I knew she was dead. I stayed calm and said quietly, 'I love you, Mam!'

There was a shimmer in my voice as I said it. I was lonely, and terrified, and I could feel that silent scream, inside me which I experienced in my earlier dream. I put her lying down flat on the bed and joined her cold hands together. I didn't want the boys to see her with her eyes open. So, I passed my hand gently down over her face, and her eyelids dropped into a quiet sleep. I knelt beside her, and I whispered an Act of Contrition into her ear.

'O my God, I am heartily sorry
for having offended Thee
and I detest my sins
above all things from the bottom of my heart,
because they displease you.
O my God,
Who art so deserving of all my love
I firmly purpose
by thy holy grace
never more to offend Thee
and to do all that I can to atone for my sins
Amen.'

I began to shiver, when I thought that she hadn't received the last rites from a priest. I kept praying that she was with God. She looked as if she had a smile on her face. Was this an indication that she was with God? I said more prayers over her and finished with a decade of the rosary. I was numb with grief and didn't know what to do next.

I covered my mother's body with the old eiderdown and left her to her peace. I went outside and sat under the haycock my father, Pat and the boys had made the previous August. Winter was creeping up fast. Halloween had been mild, but the rigours of a late November frost was setting in and the quiet landscape around the big haycock had taken an alien and sombre view, as I sat there alone and lonely, not knowing what to do.

I snuggled into the sheltered side of the haycock where it was being sliced away by the great cutting knife, to feed the cow. It was there that night, that I cried my tears, and mourned the death of my beautiful mother. She was everything to me. I always wanted to model myself on her and live my life according to what she believed. She was fair in her dealings with the world and laughed when there was time to do so. She wiped our tears and cured our scrapes and cuts with Dettol and hot water, topped up with a kiss to kill the pain. Our world had turned upside down that night, and I wept quietly into the tea towel I brought with me, and I knew that the boys could not hear me. No one could share my mourning on that cold moonlit night, except the night foxes prowling the nearby bog, or the cow and the donkey in the pasture close by.

It was there, that Sputnik the dog found me. He squealed and nuzzled his nose in under my arm, and I clung to him. I hugged him closely and my tears streamed down his black and white back. It was great to have him there. In his simple animal world, his instincts told him something was wrong. I knew this night would pass away. Tomorrow, the boys would need me to carry them through. How was I going to do it? I would have to find Dad. He had sent some money alright in the form of postal orders and the fifteen pounds in English money that arrived yesterday. I cashed the postal orders for Mam at the post office, and the money was safe on top of the dresser.

If this money stopped, we couldn't carry on without it. I'd have to find him, and now what about our dead mother? The guards would come to our house and take the boys away just like the Larkin children last summer. No one was going to take my brothers away from me. I drew my winter coat around me and when I gathered my thoughts together, I calmed down. If I told Fr Doyle he'd arrange to have her buried in the new cemetery. That wouldn't still solve anything, the boys would still be taken away. The older boys could come home in a year or two, but I might never see Packy again.

I didn't want that to happen to us. I sat alone in the moonlight, into the night wondering what to do, and I decided to leave it till morning to work things out. Soon my crying was over. My mourning for my beautiful mother stopped. At least to the outside world, it stopped. My strength and endurance, had to be borne with dignity and composure, for the sake of my three brothers. I had to be their mother from now on.

A strange feeling came over me, and I knew that come hell or high water, we were going to get by. I didn't know how, but my wise little brother Packy would have an answer. I sat back in the soft chair by the range and fell asleep. I had a restless sleep, and I hoped the boys wouldn't hear me in the kitchen. I wanted to keep vigil over them for fear they'd wake, and find their dear mother covered over with an eiderdown. I wanted to break the news to them myself to soften the blow, and to ease their grieving too.

At eight o'clock, I went to my room and changed into fresh clean clothes and proceeded to stoke up the dying embers in the old black range. It was Joe who heard me first and came into the kitchen. 'How's Mam?' he asked.

'Would you ever waken your brothers?' I said, 'it is time for school.'

'But how's Mam?' he asked again.

'Do as you are told, would you?' I ordered in a nearly stern but not cross voice. Then he looked closely at me.

'You were crying, weren't you?'

'I told you to call the others. Now do as you are told.'

He called his brothers quickly, and they came into the kitchen half dressed. I blocked their path to my mother's bedroom, and they knew by the expression on my face, something was wrong.

'Sit down!' I said, 'sit down around the table.'

'Why are you doing this?' asked Tom.

'Just sit down first.'

'It's Mam, isn't it?' asked Packy.

'I want to see her,' bellowed Joe. I blocked his path and made him sit down again.

'Does she need the doctor?' asked Packy.

'She doesn't need a doctor,' I said calmly. 'She never will again. Mam died in the middle of the night.'

'Don't say such things Sarah Cregan,' roared Packy with tears of anger in his eyes. 'Don't tell lies like that! You'll have to tell Fr Doyle in confession.'

'Do I tell lies Packy?' I answered softly, 'Do I?'

'I want to see her,' he cried through his tears.

'Not yet!' I said. 'Not for a little while.'

Packy banged his fist on the table and began sobbing. Joe was focused on the sycamore trees outside the window, as their last leaves tumbled to the ground in the front. He showed no tears, but I knew his grief was deep down inside, and he was trying to be the man, not the boy he still was. Packy held my hand and cried into my shoulder, as his tears wet my exposed neck. Tom remained silent, a river of tears running down his face. I handed him the old tea towel, and he wiped them away, but they kept coming.

'That's why you were crying,' said Joe. 'Now can I see Mam? You can't stop me!'

It was at this point that I beckoned them to follow me to the room. I held Packy's hand, as I opened the door. The curtains were drawn. I pulled them back to let the light in.

They gathered round the bed and I lifted the eiderdown gently back, showing her now peaceful face.

'It's like she's asleep,' said Tom, who had spoken for the first time since I told them.

'She's not asleep,' said Joe who was fighting to hold back the tears.

'She looks like she is smiling,' said Packy in his broken tearful voice.

'She's happy now,' I said. 'Happier than she's ever been. She has no more sickness and no more pain.'

'Why didn't you tell us she was dying?' asked Tom.

'What could you do?' I answered. 'Mam told me two days ago she was going to die. That's why I was in Dublin yesterday. I was trying to find Dad. I asked the Salvation Army people to help me. They can find lost people and they'll find him.'

'What happened last night?' asked Tom.

'She called me in the night and told me to take care of you all. And that's what I am going to do.'

103

I pulled the eiderdown over her face and closed the curtains again. I shoved them in front of me into the warmth of the kitchen.

'We will eat our breakfast first. Then you will all go to school as normal!' I ordered.

'We can't go!' exclaimed Tom. 'Our mother is dead!'

'That's just it,' I said. 'We know she is dead. But nobody else knows.'

'You mean pretend she is in bed asleep,' said Packy.

'Yes!'

'And how long will we leave her like that?' asked Tom.

'I don't know!' I answered.

'Till she starts to smell,' Joe remarked with a touch of sarcasm in his voice.

'We'll talk about it this evening,' I said, taking a writing pad from behind the wireless on the window. I placed it in front of Packy.

'I want you to write a note to the master,' I said to him. 'Tell him you will not be at school tomorrow. You know the way you can copy Mam's writing.'

'What do you want me to say?'

Dear Mr Browne, the boys will not be at school tomorrow. I have not been well lately, and I need them at home for a few days. Signed Mary Cregan.'

'How do you spell signed?'

'S.I.G.N.E.D.'

'And you want it the way Mam does it.'

'That's right!'

When he finished writing the note, he handed it to me. I put it in an envelope and gave it to Tom.

'Now you must act as if nothing has happened,' I said. I looked around at the three of them. What was in front of me but three lost boys with red eyes from weeping. I made them splash their faces with cold water to try and hide the fact, and I knew that the frost would do the rest. I was now their mother and I would stop at nothing to keep us all together.

'Remember this,' I warned them, 'if anyone finds out that Mam is dead, we might never see each other again.'

Packy came over to me and put his arms tightly around my neck. I could feel him shiver with sadness, but I held him tight, and he relaxed and composed himself.

'Sarah, I have an idea,' said Packy. 'It might work for a little while.'

'What is it, Packy?' I asked.

'I'll tell you this evening,' he said. 'I have to work it out during the day.'

The three boys left for school and I was left alone in the quiet house, to the sadness of death and an uncertain future.

Chapter 12

Packy's idea

When the boys left for school, I closed the door and shoved the bolt shut. I knew I had a thousand and one things to do. On any normal day, I'd have the boys out at seven, milking the cow, but now she was heavily in calf, and no longer milking. The calf was due before Christmas, and I hoped that Dad would be back by then. I fed the hens first, and I knew then that I had to tend to the body of my dead mother. I washed the Delph and put them back on the dresser. I swept the floor, and I kept thinking that I needed to have the place looking as normal as possible. I heated a pot of water on the range, and with soap and water, I washed Mam's body as best I could. I left her night clothes and cardigan on. I went to my room and got the brush and comb set Dad brought me from England. I brushed her hair gently, and I tied it back with two of the slides that came with the set. She looked like a queen, and I sat beside her, and prayed to God to let her into heaven. There was no priest to give her the last rites, and this was something that would haunt me for many years. Then I knelt beside her, saying another prayer, asking her to help me figure out what to do, to try and hold on to our world, and keep our family together.

I held her hand which was cold, stiff and very heavy. I had no fear, only a deep sadness which I thought would never go away. I amazed myself then, and I do so even still, to think that a girl so young, could do what she did. But I know now that any person faced with an impossible situation, will achieve the impossible to survive in this world.

I stood at the room door and looked back at her. She looked radiant, happy and at peace. I promised myself the night before not to cry again, but I did. I made myself a cup of tea at midday and was just relaxing when there was a knock on the door which startled me. I drew back the bolt and opened it. It was Fr Doyle.

'Come in, Father,' I said.

He sat at the table, and I sat opposite him with my back to the bedroom door.

'How is she today?' he asked.

'Much improved, Father. She is sleeping now. Her breathing is much better also. I'd say she will be up tomorrow.'

'I saw the note young Tom gave Master Browne today. I guessed there must have been some improvement when she wrote like that.'

'I agree, Father,' I said, 'She slept all night, and she had a cup of tea this morning. A good sleep will do her good.'

'I won't disturb her so, she's making up for all the wakeful nights she has had of late.'

'Quite true, Father,' I replied, and I breathed a sigh of relief, smiling at him.

'Would you like a cup of tea?'

'No thank you, I'd better be off. When she wakes up, tell her I'll call tomorrow or the next day.'

'I will, Father.'

'By the way, any word from your Dad?'

'Not for more than three weeks.'

'That's odd,' said the priest.

'Dad wouldn't let us down.'

'Have you an address for him?'

'Not now, but I would like him to know that Mam is sick.'

'Let me know what happens, and I will see what I can do.'

He left, and I closed the door. I stood with my heart pounding, overwhelmed for a few moments with delayed shock. I looked at the clock and began to prepare the dinner. I aimed to have it ready by half past three and I worked quietly into the afternoon. Three o'clock came and went, and so did half past three. At four o'clock. I called the hens and they followed me to the shed. When they were secured for the night, I fed the dog and shut him into the shed as well. Then I threw some hay to the cow, and Tossie the donkey in the pasture. There was still no sign of the boys coming from school.

It was shaping up to be a very frosty night.

At half past five, I could hear them coming through the semi-darkness, talking quietly on the road. I met them at the gate with a great sense of relief, and angry with them for not coming home from school immediately.

'Where have you been until this hour?' I scolded.

'Sarah, I told you this morning I had an idea,' Packy shouted angrily back at me, then he composed himself and continued, 'I told the boys going to school and they said it might work.' Packy was the man of the moment and the others nodded in agreement.

'Well you'd better come in and we'll talk about it over dinner,' I said, 'you have just given me the fright of my life. I thought I had lost the three of you.'

We sat down to dinner, but we didn't feel like eating. We looked from one to the other in silence, and then we'd sample the odd morsel. The potatoes were big and flowery, the cabbage was strong and healthy, and there was still an abundance of eggs from the hens. To try and keep some conversation going, I told them about the priest calling, and how we were safe for the moment. Packy said nothing, but I knew he'd have the answer somehow. Then I asked the question.

'What's this great plan?'

The boys looked from one to the other, wondering who was going to speak first.

'Go ahead and you tell her Packy, it was your idea in the first place,' said Joe.

'I think it's a brilliant idea,' said Tom.

'Go on then Packy, and tell me,' I said and don't keep me waiting.'

He lay down his fork on the plate and gazed at all three of us.

'Remember the day Pat Reardon told us the story about his father, and when during the time of the war, his father slept the night in the big coffin room in the graveyard, between the Major and his wife?'

'Well, what does that have to do with our Mam?' I asked.

'Let's put her in there,' said Packy.

'No way, we are not putting Mam in there with all the dead.'

'Why not,' said Tom, 'Mam is dead anyway, and if we were to bury her in the graveyard, she will still be among all the dead.'

'To get into that place we need the key, and how are we going to get that?'

Packy got up from his chair and opened his school bag. He drew from it the large iron key that Pat Reardon's father had made all those years ago. He placed it on the table in front of me. I sat there gazing at it in awe, and then in shock I exclaimed, 'My God you *are* serious, aren't you?'

'Pat Reardon hasn't the key anymore,' said Joe, 'we all went to Pat's place today after school. We watched and waited till he left the house. There are five o'clock devotions in the church today, and Pat always goes to that.'

'You know he doesn't lock the door to his house,' said Tom, 'Packy stole inside and took it off the mantelpiece, and we kept guard. It was in the big box he keeps things in.'

'You stole it then, what next?' I said, raising my hands above my head in despair.

'No, we borrowed it,' argued Joe, 'we will leave it back tomorrow when we are finished.'

'What if someone goes in there?' I asked.

'No one goes in there anymore,' said Tom, 'Pat is the only one. We can hide her body in one of the coffins. No one will look in there.'

'It's the daftest idea, I've ever heard of,' I said.

'What are we going to do then?' asked Joe.

'I have already told one lie today,' I answered, 'how am I going to cover that one up?'

I got up from the table and poured some tea and they all ate some brown bread with damson jam to finish off with.

'There's only one other problem,' I said.

'What's that?' asked Tom.

'It's Dad. What if he comes home and finds out what we did, what then?'

'If Dad comes home, he'll take good care of us,' replied Packy in a tearful voice, 'he'll fix us up, I know he will.' With these words, I knew that I would have to lead them through this crisis and suffer the consequences later. Then Packy continued,

'Until he does turn up, it's our only way out.' Listening to him, I realised that his wisdom for one so young astounded me.

'Alright so!' I agreed, 'but remember, we are committing mortal sins, so we are.'

Packy was quick with his answer as well.

'It's a mortal sin if we lose one another also,' replied Packy, bursting into tears. I stood up and held him close to me. I beckoned the others to come to me too. We clung to each other, standing on the kitchen floor, and they wept together, holding on to that moment of reassurance. I knew then, as a voice hummed in my head, we would always stay together. No one would ever separate us. Maybe this was our mother speaking through us. She was guiding us in this direction to save us somehow.

The first thing Joe did that evening was to light a storm lantern to go catch the donkey. He wanted to spare the battery in the big torch as we'd need it later in the night. Joe and Tom went out together to do this job, while I sat by the range, holding Packy close to me. We didn't speak or say a word, but frightening thoughts went through my head. What if someone finds out that we hid our mother's body, without her ever having the prayers of a priest? With all the lies we were telling, we'd have to live in mortal sin for some years until we were old enough to mind ourselves. Then we could go to a strange priest somewhere and get confession. I put all these thoughts before the boys when they returned, how would we make a good confession?

'What if the priest asks you your name?' asked Tom.

'Tell him a different one,' said Joe.

'That would be a bad confession and then it's another sin and more lies,' said Packy.

'What will we do then?' Tom asked again. Packy answered again in his quiet little wisdom, 'just wait and see, that's all we can do.'

'I'll tell you what I will do,' I said, 'when I'm in the village getting the shopping on Saturday, I'll go in to Mrs Burke's shop and I'll buy some scapulars for us all to wear, and there is also a little card you can carry with you at all times.'

'Why do we have to do this?' asked Tom.

'Written on the card are the words, *in case of accident, I am a Catholic, please notify a priest*. If this happens, the priest will be called, and he will give you the last rites, and you will go straight to God if you die.'

'I don't want to die,' said Packy.

'We have to be well prepared anyway, because of what's happened.'

We decided to wait until after midnight to take Mam 's body to the graveyard. At that time, the world was silent, as sleep crept into each little home. This, of course, was not the case in the Cregan household. The thoughts of what we were going to do, drove any idea of sleep away. We were possessed with an energy that was not evil. But it was nasty at the same time, an energy which drove us on, with a tagline that kept ringing in our heads, *we must survive this*. Our plan was to yoke Tossie the donkey to the cart, and go across the fields to the hill road, through Johnson's Boreen into Keegan's field which led right to the back of the graveyard. It was a journey of about two miles. If we travelled by road it was only a mile distant, but we didn't want to meet anyone or arouse any suspicion. As well as that young Garda Michael Glynn was often on duty at night on his bike. We sat around the table talking about Mam, and the things she did with us. Maybe she had written to Dad, but none of us posted a letter. There was also the possibility that she got Meg to write to him. But she had gone back to Dublin in September. If only she were here now, she would know what to do. She always had answers to everything.

At about nine o'clock, Packy fell asleep with his arms resting on the table. Joe carried him over to the soft chair by the range and covered him with a coat. At eleven o'clock we made more tea. We still talked about how we were going to live, how we'd share the workload, and our hopes that Dad would send us some money regularly. We'd have to tread carefully with great caution. How long we could keep this up I didn't know? The next big obstacle was the impending casual visit of Fr Doyle.

Then when the clock struck midnight we prepared to go. While Joe and Tom readied the donkey and cart, I woke Packy up. He was in a deep sleep, and he was cross and cranky on being disturbed. I gave him a cup of weak tea with plenty of milk and sugar, and when he was finished, he went to the privy out the back of the house, to relieve himself. When he returned, the cold frosty air had wakened him up. He tidied the table while I searched the chest at the foot of Mam's bed for some sheets. I took out two of them. They were made from flour bags. It took four bags to make one sheet. It was a job Mam did in the winter. She stored all the empty flour bags during the year, and on winter nights, she sewed them together, leaving them on the clothes line to bleach for a week, and they'd last for years.

Joe and I wrapped her body in the two sheets and rolled her up in an old eiderdown. Her illness over the last few months meant that she had lost a lot of weight. She wasn't very heavy. We tied it all together like a parcel with binder twine, and the three oldest of us carried her outside, laying her down gently on the cart. Packy stood looking at us silently, as tears streamed down his face. When we returned to the kitchen, I made them all wrap up well against the cold. I stoked up the range as I knew that we'd be very cold when we returned.

'Do you want to ride on the cart Packy?' asked Joe.

'I don't want to,' he answered, 'I want to stay with Sarah.' He held tightly onto my hand and we moved in procession down the garden to the pasture gate. We closed it behind us as we didn't want the cow getting in at the hay.

'Are you all ready?' asked Joe.

'Go ahead!' I said, and we set out quietly across the fields to the graveyard.

Part Two

The Mausoleum

Chapter 13

Night Journey

We were an awesome sight I must say. We were like refugees fleeing from a plundered city, under cover of darkness. Unlike refugees who were looking for a safe harbour, we had something to hide from the world. We did not want to become victims of a society, that could tell us they knew what was best. *We* knew what was best for us. Whether it was my own intuition or fear of the unknown, we were making a secret midnight journey across a field of creeping fog at the end of November.

It was moon bright, and our path was lit by a silvery frosted landscape. The only tell-tale marks were the tracks left by us on the grass. No one would ever notice, as there were no animals in these pastures, at least not for another few weeks, when the farmers released the cattle to graze on the after grass. The remaining leaves on the trees were now saturated by the dew, caused by the rising fog. We could hear the pitter patter of water droplets falling on the ground. By morning they'd be silent as the frost took hold and icicles clung to the branches.

As we moved quietly through the fields, I could not but feel that someone or something was watching over us. Maybe it was our mother's spirit, guiding us on our journey, or the angel who told Joseph to take his family, and flee to safety in Egypt. Maybe it was our guardian angel protecting us. I prayed each day to my guardian angel, a prayer taught to me by Mam, when I was very small. I held Packy's gloved hand tighter and prayed silently as we moved along.

'Oh Angel of God, My guardian dear, To whom God's love, Commits me here, Ever this day be at my side, To light and guard, To rule and guide, Amen.'

I repeated it several times on the journey, and sometimes changed the words to *'ever this night be at my side.'* It was a waning moon that beamed down on us, losing its grip on the last tentacles of an autumn landscape, calling forth the impending dark days of winter. Halloween had passed, and the lost spirits or souls had returned to rest for another year. There was nothing to fear but fear itself. Again, I remembered the words spoken to me by Pat, 'one should be more fearful of the living. Those who have died can never harm us.'

Sheep bleated in a field far away, and a dog barked on a farm a half mile distant, probably at Johnson's. He was aware that there were intruders disturbing the night, but no one would ever take any notice. Our movement was silent. We didn't speak to each other. The iron-shod wheels of the cart made no noise on the deep pile of grass also. Joe and Tom walked side by side, and I followed behind the cart, holding Packy's hand. He was shaking. I held him close to me. He was still crying silently, but his tears had long dried up. There was nothing but sheer emotion for the loss of his mother, coupled with the terrible crime we thought we were committing. We were destined as well, to live the rest of our lives in mortal sin. I felt his deep sadness, but now I was managing to build a wall around it. I was waiting for that wall to be strong enough, so that I could fight to keep us all together.

That night was the longest journey I ever took in my life, as we made our way across the silent fields. Every step of that journey we took, determined for us more than ever, that there was no going back. When we reached the edge of the field, we stopped at the gate, which opened on the hill road. We held our breaths in the silence of the night for fear someone might hear us.

Joe's plan was to open the field gate, cross the road, open the gate on the opposite side of the road which led to Johnson's boreen. Then lead the donkey and cart across, closing the gates behind us. He opened the iron gate back which squealed as he did and held it firmly with a large rock. He crossed over to open the boreen gate and as he did the lights of a car lit up the night sky. He jumped the boreen gate and hid.

'Shut the gate!' he shouted.

I held Tossie's reins while Tom shut the field gate and we pulled Tossie and the cart to the shelter of the whitethorn ditch. The car was being driven slowly, and just as it came to the gate, it stopped.

'I told you, you greedy so and so not to do that. You are not able for the whiskey. Now look at you, a footless son of a skunk, and all you want to do is puke in my car.'

It was Dinny Curly who was driving, but I could not make out who his passenger was. Dinny Curly's Ford Prefect car was his pride and joy, and he kept it immaculate. He was always in demand as a hackney driver to bring people from the village to the town, or whatever their destination was.

The stranger crouched near the gate to our field and began retching onto the frosty grass. The rising fog cleared a path for the moonlight to shine on him and then he stood up, I could see it was Darcy. But where was his car? Where was Meg?

'Where did you say, you were going?' asked Dinny.

'Lynch's B&B. They are expecting me.'

'Maggie Lynch, won't let you in, with the state of you. You'll have to stay at my place tonight.'

The engine of the car was still running, and the lights shone forward on the straight road.

'Would you ever turn that bloody engine off and let me concentrate on what I'm doing,' he grumbled.

'Aye, concentrate on your puking! I'm in no hurry.'

Dinny turned the engine off, and the night air was deathly silent. Then Dinny spoke again, 'You and you're drinking! You should have been a pioneer like me.'

'Yeah! A fat lot of good that would have done me.'

With that, his stomach retched again and up came a flood of bile, vomit and whiskey on top of what came earlier.

'Are you alright now?' asked Dinny.

'Jaysus, that's a lot better,' said Darcy.

'You just can't hold your drink, can you?' asked Dinny. 'At least I'm stone cold sober. You'll have some head on you in the morning.'

'Well, I don't know what to do. She's gone, and she took the car. She could be anywhere.'

'Did you have a falling out?'

'She wanted me to take my sister Eileen out of the home for good, and I wouldn't. You see she's a bit soft in the head, and she can't talk right. She needs minding all the time, and I can't afford to keep her with us on the road.'

'Well, now you have no one.'

'Meg always liked her. She was very good to her, but for me, she was always a burden.'

'You should sleep on it,' said Dinny, 'and figure something out tomorrow. Wait till you see, she will call back tomorrow.'

'Aye, you are right, but now I need to piss.'

Downward from the hedge to the gate, we saw a fountain of urine burst through the bars of the gate. In the panic of the moment, I forgot myself and giggled.

'Did you hear that?' said Dinny.

'I did. I heard something,' answered Darcy.

'Who's there?' shouted Dinny.

'Be quiet, will you?' said Darcy.

'Come out of that,' roared Dinny.

With that he began, to climb unsteadily across the gate and in the spur of the moment, Joe let out a perilous meow like a cat and flung a stone into the trees back the road.

'Will you get down off that gate, ye big eejit,' laughed Dinny. 'It's only a fecking tomcat somewhere.'

Darcy climbed down off the gate again and Dinny shouted into the night, 'Will you cutch, you long-clawed whore and go home!'

We were bursting to laugh as it brought light into the saddest day of our lives.

'Is there any meat at your house, Dinny?'

'There is,' said Dinny.

'Christ, I'm dying for a rasher,' he said in his rather cultured Dublin accent.

'Well, come on then. After all, you got up there. It's a small wonder you're not on the starvation list.'

They got quickly into the car and Dinny started the engine, turned on the lights, and just as they were moving out on the road, the engine backfired. Tossie threw back his head in fright, and Tom let go of the reins. The sudden noise startled him, and away he went galloping across the field. He had enough for one night and ran in circles around the pasture. He was determined no one would catch him. We called Joe, who was quite fast at running. He took after him in hot pursuit, and every time he tried to grab the reins, Tossie swerved and dodged away from him. Finally, Joe made the conquest, by jumping up onto the cart from behind. Suddenly he screamed, and it rang out across the quiet frosty countryside.

'Are you alright?' I shouted.

'Yeah! I forgot about Mam and I fell on top of her.'

He made his way to the front of the cart, climbing onto the shafts, and sat on the donkey's back. He took the reins and pulled the donkey to a stop. It was like a rescue mission from a western movie, where the sheriff saves the lives of many people from certain death in a runaway stagecoach. Tossie slowed down enough for Tom to catch him and hold him at the head.

'I only hope no one heard us,' said Tom.

'It was a near one, though,' I said.

'Only for the cat call, we were finished,' said Tom.

'Come on,' I said, 'we have no time to lose.'

The iron wheels made a trundling sound on the tarred road for a few seconds but when we crossed onto the boreen they were silent again. The boreen was merely a track, bounded on each side by high hawthorn hedges. About a quarter of a mile down the boreen was Keegan's field. The boreen was in sheer darkness and when our eyes adjusted to it we could see well enough to get by. It led us straight into the moonlit field ahead.

As soon as we entered the field, sheep scattered in all directions, but theirs was a silent movement, disturbing nothing but themselves in the process. The night was enfolding deeper now, near to two o'clock, and my feet were cold. Packy was freezing, and I feared for him. I promised him a hot cup of Bovril when we got home. It wasn't long till the steeple-like features of the churchyard loomed before us. It was a relief to see the place, and we quietly made our way to the north corner, where stood the old ruin. There was a low gap on the wall fenced with sheep wire and timber, which gave us easy access. Joe lit the torch to show us the way into the dimly lit churchyard. It was awesome and eerie to gaze inward, as the tall ghost-like shadows of the tombstones, and Celtic crosses stood guard over the souls that rested in that quiet peace. Packy held my hand tighter, as we climbed over the fence. Tossie was tethered to a wooden post, while we three older ones climbed on the cart. and gently lifted Mam's body across the wall. Rigor mortis had long set in and being stiff and cold, made it easier to carry her. Packy shone the torch to give us light, and we soon disappeared into the darkened moonlit glade.

The church ruin itself was a dark mysterious figure against a moonlit landscape, its windows were gaping eyes or holes peering across the darkness, bandaged and stanchioned with ages of gnarled ivy. It stood there, a reminder of our past, our turbulent history and the curse of Black Cromwell, who sought to destroy what it stood for, and the people who once prayed within its walls. But ever defiant, the people didn't give in. For over a hundred years they attended mass on the hills around and buried their dead here among the stones of their faith. Even still, some graves were marked with stones, taken from the old church ruin. Then in more tolerant times towards the end of the18th century, their resting places were marked with headstones, and high crosses which stood there still, withstanding the test of time. But now this place was destined to be soon forgotten. The new cemetery for Avenstown had opened the year before, across the road from this old churchyard. Its gates were now closed, and locked and only a few people tended family plots here anymore.

As we approached the old mausoleum in the centre of the churchyard, it was not unlike a little church too, with its great big steel door closed on the east gable, facing the rising sun. When the Wilsons died out in the 1930's, it was the death knell of this churchyard also. Flanked close by with a yew tree dating back about two hundred years, the great iron doorway was half hidden by a sprawling spindle tree, now gaunt and bare, except for some of its strange pink red berries. I knew about this tree, or should I say, it was more like a bush, as Dad told us he used to cut strong stems off it, when he was young for his grandmother, who made spindles for her spinning wheel. Even when the Wilsons were alive, it was only trimmed back to allow them to open the door to receive deceased members of their family.

Packy was the guardian of the great key. He found it weighing heavy in his pocket, and when he got to Keegan's boreen, he had placed it in the cart in case he'd lose it. Joe took it and placed it into the lock while Tom and I held back the branches. Packy shone the torch, as Joe tried to open the door. Amazingly, the key turned quite easily. But there were tell-tale signs on the lock showing that it had been maintained and oiled. It was Pat Reardon's work, as he still came here to sit among the coffins, even though he claims that it was a long time since he did it. Maybe he came every now and then, to keep the lock maintained, and in working order, just in case he needed to go there. Inside it was dark and gloomy. Cobwebs hung from the ceiling, and traces of ivy had crept in through crevices in the wall, and in the roof.

There was a dead smell in the place, a smell of air, trapped by time, in a dark limbo outside the world of sunlight, moon, and stars. There were about ten coffins in all. The mausoleum had been built in the middle of the nineteenth century, and contained the mortal remains of the last hundred years of the Wilson family. Earlier ancestors lay buried under great headstones or altar tombs throughout the old churchyard. The ten coffins were stacked on two stone shelves, side by side and on top of each other.

'Where will we put her?' asked Tom.

'We can't leave her lying on the ground,' said Packy, 'that wouldn't be fair to Mam.' He was wiping his eyes again and burying his head into my coat.

'Let me look,' said Joe, as he climbed up on the higher shelf.

He checked each coffin, and amazingly the lid was loose on two of them.

'Hey Tom, get up here and give me a hand,' he said.

Tom climbed up beside him, and together they slipped the lid off.

'Show me the torch,' he said.

Packy handed it to him, and he examined the coffin inside.

'Janey Mac Tom, look at this,' he shouted. Tom looked in and exclaimed, 'Wow!'

'What is it?' I asked.

He reached deep into the coffin and held something up, shining the torch on it. It was a perfectly preserved skull. I screamed, and the two boys erupted in peals of laughter.

'Put that back,' I shouted at them, 'that's not funny.' Packy was clinging to me, and cried out, 'Sarah! I want to go home, I'm really scared.'

'Will you two hurry up,' I said.

'You know Tom, I think we can fit Mam in here,' said Joe, 'we can put the lid back on, and if Pat Reardon comes in here he won't know.'

'Who is in the coffin already?' I asked.

Tom read the inscription on the nameplate while Joe held the torch.

'In memory, of
Amelia Jane Wilson,
Who departed this life
15th. Oct. 1856
She sleeps in peace.'

'She won't mind,' said Tom, 'Mam will keep her company.'

They jumped down again, and Packy held the torch as the three of us raised Mam's corpse onto the second level, and then to place her gently on the bones of Amelia Jane Wilson. It was a quick and quiet process, and before we knew it, they slipped the lid back on the coffin again. Packy waved his hand trying to speak through his tears.

'Goodbye Mam, we will love you forever.'

We didn't speak after that, and we left quietly. We locked the door, and the key turned easily again. We dragged the branches of the spindle tree back into position and that feeling came over me once again, that we were being watched. There was nothing there but our footprints, which would fade away in the next few days, weathered and dissolved by the rain and the frost.

'I think we should say a decade of the rosary,' I said. The boys didn't protest, and when the prayers were over, we stood for a few minutes in silence. Then Packy said, 'I don't feel like crying anymore, Sarah.'

'That's because Mam is resting peacefully, and *you* are at peace as well,' I told him.

'Now we must go home and get on with living,' said Joe.

'There's only one problem,' said Tom, 'how do we show the rest of the world that Mam is still alive when she's dead.'

'Pray hard to your guardian angel to protect us all,' I said, 'we'll deal with that tomorrow.'

We went quietly to the gap in the wall, and we climbed onto the cart. Joe took the reins and guided Tossie back across the quiet fields. No one spoke, but I looked forward to the warmth of the fire, and the quiet safety of our house. Even though it appears we had succeeded, I wasn't happy. I was uneasy. There was a feeling inside me that all was not as it seemed. As we made our way home to bed, I wondered how we would make out over the next few weeks, till Dad returned. It might have worked if things went according to plan. But little did I know that this was only the beginning of a long and perilous year ahead.

Chapter 14

An Angel returns

I woke around midday with a start. Sputnik was barking in the shed. I jumped out of bed and opened the curtains, peering out into the yard. The frost had gone, and the sky was filling up to rain. Thankfully, there was no one there. The dog was hungry and wanted to get out. I dressed quickly and went to the kitchen. I did as I always did each morning, I went straight to Mam's room to check on her. But when I opened the door and saw the empty bed, pangs of loneliness erupted inside me, and I felt physically sick. I ran outside to the back of the house and vomited on the turf mould at the shed door. Later I put the whole event down to the stress and fear we had gone through the night before, and this was a release of all that negative energy which had built up inside me. When it had all passed from me, I let Sputnik out, and went inside to prepare his morning feed.

I closed the bedroom door and began the morning chores. Joe heard my movements, and he dressed, and came into the kitchen.

'Are the others awake?' I asked.

'No! They are sound asleep.'

'Well leave them so. Let them sleep on. I want to go to the village and try to leave the key back in Pat's house without him knowing. On no condition let anyone in. If you see anyone, lock the door.'

'I'll do that,' he said. He sat on the chair by the fire and I knew by the white drawn look on his face, the trauma had hit him too. Having survived on false energy, and driven by forces we could not explain, it was taking its toll on all of us. The kettle on the range was beginning to boil, as its singing noise broke the silence. Joe began to shiver and shake.

'Sarah! What are we going to do?'

'Shush!' I said gently, 'it's alright!' I put my arms around this big gentle giant, who was physically, and awkwardly growing fast, and beyond his years. I held him close to me. I was his mother now, and even though we were separated by only a gap of three years, he needed my comfort too. He sobbed quietly on my shoulders for about five minutes, and then I handed him an old tea towel to dry his eyes.

'Are you alright now?' I asked.

'Yeah! I'm fine.'

The kettle was now boiling, and I made us some tea, weak and milky with plenty of sugar. It was Mam's way of easing the stress of trauma and shock.

I wrote out a list of messages I needed from the shop. Looking around, I saw that there was little bread left, and Joe said he'd bake some while I was away. I told him to keep an eye on the cow as well, as her calving time was about two weeks away, I left him in charge and set out for the village.

To the whole world, it was a normal winter day. People on the road waved or asked how Mam was, and I waved back or answered their queries with 'she's fine thank God!' The lies were pouring from me, and I realised that I must be one of the greatest sinners alive. But Jesus forgave sinners, and I prayed he'd forgive me. 'You believe in Jesus he'll take care of you.' The voice of the lady in the film rang through my ears as I entered the village, and I decided to go to Pat's house first, before going to the shop for the messages.

I parked the bike outside the gate, and I knew he was there, as there was smoke billowing from the chimney. I opened the top half of the door as I knocked. He was in my face straight away, and a little excited, as he was not expecting any visitors.

'S-S-Sarah!' he blurted out at me.

'Hi Pat,' I said softly.

'Come on in, girl. I'm only after getting up. I went to bed late.'

'What had you up so late, Pat? You usually go to bed early?'

'I-I-I was reading,' he said and held his head low as he said it. I knew this was not true and I knew also he was not going to tell me. He considered my eyes and in a shocked state, he exploded again! 'A-A-Are you alright, Sarah? You look very pale and washy today.'

'I'm fine Pat, really. I think I had a bit of a stomach bug yesterday.'

'You haven't got your Uncle Pat to look after you. What you need is a strong cup of cocoa to settle your stomach.' It was the last thing in the world I needed. I only hoped, I didn't get the runs after it, the way I was feeling this morning.

Pat opened the press under the dresser and closed it again saying. 'I forgot about that, sure I am out of cocoa this two days. I'll tell you what, you stay nice and warm by the fire girl, and I'll tip up to the shop to get some.'

'Grand so!' I said. Pat left quickly. I could hear the gate squeal as he went out. This was my opportunity. I reached into the shopping bag and took out the great big key. I wiped it in a towel hanging at the end of the dresser and left it back up on the mantelpiece over the range in the tin box where Pat kept odds and ends such as holy pictures, medals, birth certs and some old photographs. I shoved the tin back gently and sat by the fire waiting.

Pat returned about five minutes later with a box of Fry's cocoa, some bars of chocolate and some biscuits.

The kettle was just boiling, and he busied himself with large blue and white striped mugs, hot water, cocoa, milk and lots of sugar. Before I knew it, I was sipping a hot mug of steaming cocoa, and he sat opposite me drinking *his*, and staring me in the face.

'Are you alright now Sarah?' he asked again.

'You spoil me rotten Pat Reardon, you know that?' I smiled back at him, and he giggled.

'I'm glad you are feeling better. I was worried about you.'

'You are one of the nicest people I know, Pat.'

'D-D-Don't start that again, I will always take care of you, you know that?'

'I still won't marry you though,' I teased.

'W-w-who'd marry you anyway,' he laughed, 'You can be a cheeky little strap sometimes.'

I laughed into the mug of cocoa, and as I did, he handed me some fig rolls on a plate. I took one and tasted it, and it was only when I did, I realised how hungry I *was*. Then I took another, and then another. Before I knew it the rest of the packet of biscuits and bars of chocolate were shoved by Pat into the shopping bag. He looked up at me again and said, 'You know Sarah Cregan, I *do* spoil you rotten.'

When I left him, he told me to let him know, if we needed any help with the cow when her time came. I didn't delay on my journey. I managed to get to the shop just as it opened after lunch at two o'clock. I handed the bag and list across the counter, and when I paid for the shopping, I cycled at speed back home. When I made my way up the potholed laneway to our house I was frightened out of my wits when I saw the tracks of a car in the driveway. Someone had been at the house and had gone again.

I opened the door to find a wall of silence within. Meg was sitting in the soft chair by the fire. The boys were sitting in a circle round the range. I knew by the expression on her face that she knew everything. There was no fooling her. Even though I instructed Joe not to let anyone in, there was no way he could refuse to admit Meg, she was Mam's best friend. I stared in horror at her, wondering what was going to happen next. The boys were red around the eyes, as I knew they had wept when giving their account of events, and what had happened the night before. On impulse, I decided it was time to run. Where or why I was doing it, I didn't know. Maybe it would go away, and I'd wake up from a terrible nightmare. As I ran out the door, I heard her call my name out loud. I ran to the back of the house and stopped at the cock of hay. She was hot on my heels, followed by the boys. I had my head buried in my hands in screams of despair and hopelessness.

'Sarah!' she said gently. She dragged me, and unfolded me from my moments of terror, and I buried my head in her arms crying on her shoulders.

'They'll be taken away,' I screamed, 'what am I going to do?'

'You boys get back inside,' she said, 'and tidy away the shopping Sarah brought home.'

The boys went quietly, and we were left alone on the sheltered side of the hay. There was a hint of warmth in the afternoon, and the rain which had threatened earlier had passed quickly over. We sat down on the dry sill of the hay which was made by the cut of the hay knife.

'What have you done, my dear little girl?'

'I can't find Dad, and I promised Mam that I'd do whatever I could to protect the boys. Now they will come and take them all away.'

'Shush!' she said softly, 'you haven't committed any crime.'

'They'll still take them away!' I said. I had calmed down a little and was able to speak in a less terrified or panicked way. She took some folded tissue hankies from her pocket and began drying my tears.

'My dear little-terrified girl, it's not as bad as all that. I'm here now and we will work something out.' She sounded just like my mother. We provided that joy for Meg when she came to visit, as she never had children of her own. So much so, she spoiled us rotten – much to Mam's annoyance at times.

'Let's go inside. We'll calm down and talk around this.' She led me gently back to the kitchen, and the smell of weak milky tea hit me as we entered the warmth of the place. Joe was filling up large mugs of tea for all, an elixir to calm us down again. We sat there silently drinking the tea and listening to the crackle of logs complimenting the burning turf in the range.

'Your poor Mam,' said Meg. 'Why didn't I come sooner? You wouldn't have had to go through all this.'

'We didn't know what to do,' I said.

'I understand, pet. I really *do*. But what made you think of hiding her body?'

It was then I launched into events of the last few days, from the visit to the Salvation Army, to Mam's last hours, Packy's plan to hide Mam's body in the mausoleum, the encounter with Darcy and the midnight flight to the old churchyard.

'My God!' she exclaimed when it was all over, 'this is the sort of thing you'd read about in a novel or something.' We smiled wryly as she said this.

'And even Darcy appears in it.'

'Please don't tell him!' I pleaded.

'My dear girl, after all these years, married to that man, there's little I tell him. The less he knows the better. I gave him the car back this morning as I made him promise me something. But enough about that for the moment.'

'I'm glad you are here, Meg,' said Packy.

'I'm glad I came,' she answered, 'but I would have come sooner.' He went to her, and he hugged her the same way he hugged Mam, when something troubled him. When he sat down again she said, 'We will have to get your Mam back and have her buried properly.'

'No, you can't!' I pleaded.

'Why? Is there something to hide?'

'I want Dad home first,' I said, 'If Dad were here, things would be alright.'

'If we fetch her back tonight, no one will ever know what happened.'

'That means we'll have to steal the key from Pat Reardon all over again. I have only just sneaked it back today. We'd have to make the same journey to the churchyard and back. I couldn't go through it all again. Dad won't be here, and the people would come and take the boys away, just the way the Larkin children were taken away last summer when their mother died. I won't do it! I want Dad home first. We can't! We can't! We can't!'

I kept banging my hands on the table and shouting at the top of my voice, and the mugs bounced and danced with each slam of my hands.

'Well then, the best thing I can do is go away, and pretend that I didn't come here at all, and let you all deal with it on your own.'

'Please don't go, Meg, you will be able to help us,' pleaded Tom. 'We have done awful things, we could go to hell for it.'

'Who in their right minds would send a nice boy like you to hell?' she laughed, 'it's a cruel God who'd allow such a thing to happen. He wouldn't be *my* God, he wouldn't be a Christian God.'

'If Fr Doyle heard you talk like that,' said Joe, 'he'd have you read off the altar.'

'Well, how often then have the likes of me been read off the altar in villages and towns, when a show or play didn't suit the tastes of a particular Padre. I don't see God inside a building or in any place, he's all around you. He's the wind in the storm or the gentle breeze. He's in the waves of the sea. He's in the snow that slows me down in winter.' Then she put her hand to her chest and said,

'He's in here in your heart, where you can talk to him quietly yourself in prayer. He's not in an old cold building. That's why I don't go to mass.'

'Do you see him?' asked Packy.

'You can see him in all of this. He's responsible for it all. He created it. That's why I tell you, no God in his right mind would send lovely children like you to hell.'

'Even if we did something terribly wrong?' I asked.

'What wrong did you do? Did you murder anyone? Did you steal or rob a bank?'

'We stole the key from Pat,' said Tom.

'Forget about that, let's say you borrowed it. You put it, back didn't you?'

'Well then, have you committed murder?'

'No, we didn't!' we chanted emphatically and in unison.

'Some people might think you did something wrong, but the good Lord might think differently.'

'He sent *you* to be with us,' said Packy.

'He sent you to take care of things, and to mind us, till Dad comes home,' said Joe.

'How are we going to get out of this one?' I asked. My question was quickly put on the back boiler and Meg didn't get to answer, as we heard a car rev as it pulled up at the gate outside. Joe ran to the window and looked out.

'It's Fr Doyle,' he exclaimed with panic in his voice.

'I certainly don't want to meet him!' said Meg.

'Hide in Mam's room,' I said, 'I won't let him in.'

The boys made a mad dash for the bedroom and closed the door. I calmly got a tin basin and began filling it with hot water from the kettle to wash the mugs. Just as soon as I started pouring the water, there was a knock on the door, and with that, the latch lifted… and the dark form of the priest appeared in the doorway.

'All's well here, I hope!' he said.

'Very well thank you, Father,' I answered quite cheerfully, 'Come on in and sit down.'

He sat in the soft chair by the fire and crossed his legs.

'This chair feels lovely and warm, somebody must have been sitting on it.'

'I was!' I answered, 'I just had a cup of tea and now I want to wash up.'

'Is Tom here?' he asked.

'He is, Father. He's up in the room. I think he is washing his hair.'

'Tell him I want to see him when he's ready.'

I knocked on the bedroom door and called, 'Tom! Fr Doyle wants to see you when you are ready. He answered with ok. He had been listening to the conversation in the kitchen.

'How is Mam today?' he asked.

'She's grand! She's just resting now. In fact, she is asleep.'

'She's always sleeping when I call, does she need a doctor?'

'No, she doesn't!'

'Well, she must be still awake if she has only drunk a mug of tea. I see five mugs on the table.'

'That was a while ago, Father.' He made to go into the room. With that, Tom emerged from the bedroom drying his hair. His head was wet and later I wondered how he managed to do so. Joe opened the sash window at the bottom and Tom climbed out into the yard. He wet his head with the cold water from the overflowing water barrel and stepped inside again. He was shivering as he dried his hair. I only hoped he didn't get pneumonia out of it.

'You wanted to see me, Father?' said Tom.

'Ah, Tom! The very man!' He stalled at the room door and turned back to talk to him. 'I'm putting together the roster of mass servers for the Christmas season. Is there any chance you will serve at midnight mass for me? It's hard to get young fellows to do that one for me.'

'Of course, I will,' said Tom. 'Dad will be home and we'll cycle there together.'

'Good man yourself, well that's that done! Well now, what about the lady I came to see.'

He pushed past me into the room, and I waited in fear for all to be revealed. There wasn't a sound from the room. I waited for a minute or two, and there was nothing only silence. I decided to follow him in. The curtains had been drawn across and the room was in semi-darkness. Fr Doyle was sitting in the chair at the bed. Meg was lying wrapped up in a blanket and quilt. She was lying on her side facing the wall.

'I told you she was sleeping, Father,' I whispered quietly. I was trembling with fear and anxiety. What would happen next?

'Is it possible to wake her up? I would like to talk to her.'

'No Father, please let her sleep.' He didn't pay any attention to my pleas but began shaking Meg's shoulder gently.

'Are you awake, Mrs Cregan? I would like to talk to you.' Meg made no stir but emitted a gentle snore as he reached in across her.

'Please Father, leave her be,' I said.

'Mrs Cregan, are you sure you are alright?' Meg stirred in the bed.

'Mrs Cregan...' What happened next was so sudden it took me a minute or so to comprehend Meg's actions. She swung her arm around and sleepily saying, 'What's that?' Her arm travelled with such deliberate force that she slammed her elbow into the priest's face, sending him sprawling back on the floor against the window. I screamed as it happened. Meg sat up in the bed with the blanket draped over her head with nothing but her face peering out.

'Oh, my God!' she shouted, 'Are you alright, Father?' The priest got up feebly from the floor. He was holding his nose and blood was oozing between his fingers.

'Let me help you, Father,' said Meg.

Instantly I replied, 'It's ok, Mam. You just relax and go back to sleep. I'll look after Fr Doyle.'

'What made me do that, Father?' said Meg, 'I think I woke in a fright.' As she said this she winked at me and then she twisted her eyes inwards so that both were squinted in over her nose. I was so frightened then to realise that she was teasing me, and it was only later that night that we laughed about it. She lay back down on the bed and covered herself up.

Fr Doyle sat at the table while I got some clean tea cloths and hot water.

'Are you sure you'll be alright, Father?' I asked gingerly.

'I will be grand,' said the priest. The bleeding stopped, just as quickly as it had begun. The boys emerged from the room with mouths open wide, wondering what had happened. I made a face at them while I said, 'Fr Doyle had an accident. Mam got a fright as she woke too quickly, and Fr Doyle fell back.'

The boys made their way slowly to Mam's bedroom, and peering in the door, Meg made a silly face at them from the bed. 'We're going out to the shed, Sarah,' said Joe and they dashed out, all three of them. I knew that when they got to the shed, it would end up in a laughing match as they began to comprehend what happened.

'Would you like a cup of tea or a drink of water, Father?' I asked.

'No thanks, Sarah,' he answered. Then he began to chuckle to himself. 'When I was a young lad, I used to be a good boxer, so I have quite a lot of experience in that area. I have been worried for the past while that your Mam was hiding her illness from us all. I thought by her at the autumn dance, that she had failed a lot. Well, today I can relax. Anyone who could throw a punch like that, and floor a once-champion boxer is in good health.'

'I told you so, Father,' I said. 'She's getting better all the time. She'll be up later for her dinner.'

'I can even see it in her face, she doesn't look as haggard and drawn as she did two weeks ago. Please God, she'll be as bright as a button before too long.'

'I heard that, Father,' shouted Meg from the bedroom, 'I think I'm brighter than a button as it is.' I was petrified that he might go back into the room again. If only she'd keep her mouth shut till he was gone.

'It's ok, Mrs Cregan,' he laughed, 'I think I'll survive this time.'

Chapter 15

Meg's Story

When the coast was clear, and the sound of the priest's car was no longer within earshot, Meg emerged from the room, as the boys erupted laughing once again. I sat at the end of the table in a daze, not knowing what to say or do. She sat in the corner, on the soft chair saying nothing. One by one, the boys stopped laughing, as they eventually saw the frosty cold look on her face.

I began to feel tears force their way once more, knowing that it had happened again. We had told lies, and this time it was to the priest. Then Meg spoke in a low voice and stopping after each word, she said slowly, 'What have I done?'

'I'm sorry, Meg,' I stammered, trying to hold back the tears.

Then she said it once again.

'What have I done?'

The boys held their heads down and sat in silence.

'Do you know I have just done something terrible?'

One could feel that the air could be cut with a knife, as the kitchen fell so silent. There was not a sound to be heard, but the ticking of the clock, and the singing of the kettle on the range.

'Joe, get up on your bike and go bring Fr Doyle back. We'll have to tell the truth,' I said, 'Meg will go to jail if we don't.'

Packy jumped up and screamed, 'No!' He stood in the middle of the floor angrily, breathing heavy and eyes filling up with tears.

'No!' he repeated, but this time in a softer voice, 'Meg fooled Fr Doyle. He will tell everyone that Mam is alright.'

'We might not be so lucky the next time, lad,' said Meg.

'Meg, you can't go to jail,' I said.

'I won't go to jail child. I have been in worse situations before. This world has seen me get into more scrapes imaginable.'

'What will we do now though?' asked Packy.

There was always something uncanny about Packy, and his way of thinking. He stood there with a smirk on his face, and I knew there was some plan up his sleeve. Two days ago, he had concocted the idea of hiding Mam's body. Now there was something else. He went over to Meg and took her by the hand.

'Meg, will you be our Mam?'

Meg gave a wry smile and said back to him, 'I could never replace your lovely Mam. That's the one thing I could never do!'

'But you are an actress, you dress up like many people. You even fooled the priest today.'

'What would your poor father say if he saw all this?'

'Don't worry about Dad,' said Packy, 'stay and be our Mammy till he comes home.'

'Packy could be right,' said Tom, 'you don't do any acting in the winter time.'

'It might work children, and again it might not, and there's another reason I couldn't do it.'

'What's that?' I asked.

'It's Darcy's sister Eileen.'

Then she launched into telling us the story of how she and Darcy met back in the nineteen forties. Eileen was her best friend, and they acted together in theatre in Dublin. She kept telling her about her family, and how they travelled Britain and Ireland with their travelling theatre, stopping in towns and villages, erecting a large tent on village greens, and putting on improvised acting shows for people who would never get the chance to see them.

One summer, they decided to leave the stage and Eileen took Meg to follow the travelling show for a season. After a short while, she began to like the idea, and she joined the cast of *Darcy's Drama and Variety Show*. It was J.P. himself, Eileen's brother who was the big attraction to her. He was handsome and debonair, the real cut of Errol Flynn about him. Meg fell for him, hook, line and sinker, and within two years they were married in Clarendon Street church in Dublin.

Eileen was her bridesmaid, and they settled down to wedded bliss, touring with the theatre during the summer months, from early March until the end of October. It was a busy exhausting schedule each year, but this was her life. She loved the buzz of the stage, and the laughter of audiences, and how they interacted with events on stage. A gun goes off in a dramatic scene, and a small child takes to howl in the darkened tent, prompting a mother or father to exit onto the green, to calm down the frantic child. In some places, the mountainy men or bachelor farmers, stood at the back, caps placed on the side of their heads, gobsmacked at the allure of the dancing girls. In some places, of course, the parish priest had to have a preview of the show, to see if it was suitable viewing for his flock. It happened also, that the priest didn't venture to check out the schedule, only to be confronted by concerned parishioners regarding the morality of the shows, and the influence it might have on innocent people. The result was that the priest spoke off the altar about them, and unknown to him it helped to advertise the company even better, as people flocked there, unconcerned about sinfulness or its consequences. The confessional would sort that out the following week.

Two years into their marriage, Meg got pregnant, but she continued acting on stage right through the summer season, covering up her condition, by taking parts that required long flowing gowns or garments in many period dramas. Her happiness and bliss were short-lived of course, when she collapsed onstage in the last month of pregnancy. She brought a still-born baby boy into the world, and unknown to her, it had been dead for some time. The resulting trauma, and burial in a little plot for the holy innocents, near the village they were performing, had a profound effect on her ever since, and the idyllic relationship between herself and Darcy had changed forever. He forged a barrage of blame against her, over the years for the loss of the baby, and subsequently, there were no other children in the relationship.

The catalyst in all this was Eileen. She kept bringing them together and making peace whenever the relationship broke down. For some reason also, Eileen disliked her brother very much. It was not the typical brother-sister relationship. Whenever he refused to co-operate with her, or to sit down and talk with Meg, she'd refer to some dark secret in their past that she never ever spoke about.

She regarded Meg as the best thing that ever happened in his life, and to treat her with such contempt, was unforgivable. He became the puppet in this relationship, and would always bend to her demands, as well as Meg's. It became more of a business, and working relationship, and the company thrived under the energy of this arrangement.

But the strain of it all on Darcy was too much at times, and he went on binges of heavy drinking, and on several occasions ruined the show, by appearing on stage, totally inebriated, and under the weather from alcohol. The resulting confrontations with Meg and Eileen sobered him up, to such an extent that he'd stay dry for several months until the next conflict.

It was one of these confrontations one summer about ten years previously, that Eileen collapsed, and was rushed to the local hospital. It was a stroke she suffered, which was quite severe, and it was touch and go as to whether she might survive or not. But survive she did, and the months of recovery were slow. The paralysis she suffered disappeared slowly, but she had little power in her left arm and her speech was badly affected. She could no longer act on stage. She did little bit or walk on parts, or helped with the management, and preparation of shows. Eileen's compromised condition saw a change in Darcy's attitude towards her. He felt he could treat her as he liked, and often bullied her, or verbally abused her when Meg was not around. Whatever grip she had on him from her past seemed to abate, as Eileen did not pose any threat in revealing what took place between them, when they were younger.

The show went on as usual, and as the years progressed, the days of the travelling theatre were numbered. The opening of cinemas in towns and villages across the country, pushed their world into the background. But there was still a loyal following in some areas, and it was in these villages that they concentrated their business every year. Avenstown was a loyal follower, and *Darcy's Drama and Variety Show* came to town every August. It was one of Meg's favourite stops, as she was reunited each year with the Cregan family during that week. But five years previously, unknown to Meg, Darcy signed Eileen into a nursing home in the south of England, when Meg was away arranging costumes for the next season's shows. He felt that she was a burden on their business, and they couldn't afford to keep her and make a success of their travelling theatre. It was cheaper to keep her in one of those homes, than to bring her with them from place to place. It led to subsequent breakups and rows between them. But he kept coming back, when the going got tough. He could not exist without Meg. Still, he refused to sign Eileen out, and their love-hate relationship continued. It was after one of these rows that Meg walked out, taking their car with her, and he knew she had returned to the Midlands. He was arranging to meet with her the night before, when Mary Cregan was laid to rest in the old churchyard. That was when we saw him drunk, and very much under the weather. Meg met him in the pub in Avenstown that morning, giving him an ultimatum to go over to England, and bring Eileen back to her rightful place in their home, and with the show. He agreed to do this, and he dropped Meg off at Cregan's to visit for a few days, while he took the ferry over to England.

What met Meg on this visit would probably change things forever. Now she was trapped in our lives and performing the drama of her career. She had unconsciously covered up our deep dark secret.

So, sitting around the warm range late that afternoon, Meg tried to make excuses to get away from what she had just done.

'Eileen is my good friend and I cannot abandon her now. We need to get her back to our Dublin home, and to normal living again. It's just not fair, the way she was treated. She was such a lady. You'd stand to look at her. She was like a film star. She loved fashion. If she saw you wearing something, she'd stop at nothing to get it. She'd buy it if she could. If not, she would plead and bargain with you, till you either gave it to her or sold it to her. That's our Eileen. She was always a winner in the fashion stakes. She was so full of fun at parties, as she sang or played party games, even card tricks. She was always the belle of the ball. Her life is a tragedy now and I want her back home.'

'But you can't go, Meg,' pleaded Packy, 'we need you here.'

'I couldn't do that,' said Meg.

'But you could, we could do up Mam's room, and let you both stay there.'

'What about Darcy?' said Meg.

'What about him?' I asked, 'Isn't he well able to look after himself? Hasn't he enough to do, to get the show ready for the next season?'

I knew that things were changing, and we were getting around her to stay. There was a glint in her eye as she took on board our reasons for having her remain here. Dad could even turn up in the next few days, and things could be sorted out very quickly.

'If I do stay, you lot will have to carry on as normal, school and all that.' The boys nodded their heads in unison. 'I'll make one bargain with you, the minute I hear of your father's return, I'm out of here. I had nothing to do with this, you know. I wasn't even here. I have enough on my plate to look after Eileen, and here I am saddled with you lot. The things I have to do in this life.'

Packy got up from his chair and went to her, throwing his arms around her and clinging to her. It was then she began to cry.

'You poor things,' she sobbed. 'Why would I abandon you? Your poor Mam, one of my best friends and I'm only here by accident. What prompted me to come I'll never know, and look what I found?'

She clung to Packy and held him tight. I knew that she felt responsible for us, and that we needed her so badly. I could see the sadness in her eyes too. Packy was the little boy she never got to hug, her lost little boy.

Chapter 16

The drama begins

The boys set off for the village school the next day, spick and span and smiling. They carried with them specially prepared lunches wrapped in sugar paper and sealed with Sellotape which Meg produced from her bag. She carried a big bag with her always, containing the tricks of her trade, from theatrical makeup to fragments of ribbon, material, and string. Whenever she needed anything for some little emergency, she dipped deeply into it, and found something to solve the problem, whether it was a button, a needle, a pin, a bandage, antiseptic cream or plasters, Meg's big bag always contained something which could be used to solve any of life's little emergencies. It looked as if it was made from pieces of carpet stitched together, with two large leather handles to carry it from place to place. It was durable and strong, and made to withstand the trials and tribulations of travelling from town to town over the years.

She made the boys egg sandwiches that morning and flavoured them with salad cream. She parcelled them in sugar paper and sealed them with the Sellotape. She found three dark blue milk of magnesia bottles, washed them out, and scalded them with boiling water. Then she filled them with milk, which I brought from the village the day before, and the boy's eyes lit up when they saw what she had done. The lunches I prepared were usually rough and ready, brown bread and butter, wrapped in pages from the Westmeath Examiner. She ordered them to bring the sugar paper back, as she could re-use it again.

'When we travel from place to place, we waste nothing. We use and re-use as much as we can. Remember men, that necessity is the mother of invention.' She had them standing in mock military formation as she often did. When she tricked or played with us in the past.

'Now you may all kiss Auntie Meg goodbye,' she said, winking at me and a smirk on her face.

Packy didn't hesitate. He kissed her face and held her close as he did so. Tom followed and gave her a gentle peck on the cheek. But Joe stood his ground. He was a man, and he wasn't having any of it. He didn't kiss women. 'That's for married people,' he protested.

'Come here you,' she said. She grabbed him, pulled him to her, and planted a big loud kiss on the side of his face. He rubbed it away repeatedly with his sleeve, and his cheeks turned crimson red. She held him from her and said, 'you know what, you need to get some practice in sunshine. Someday you will fall in love with a beautiful young woman, and you will never stop wanting to kiss her. Meanwhile, a little kiss on the cheek for Auntie Meg in the morning won't do you any harm.' Joe laughed along with her and returned the compliment by giving her a gentle kiss on the side of her face. Then she pretended to hunt them out the door, chasing them with the tea towel. They laughed and shouted with glee, as they ran out the gate, to escape her gentle taunts.

When they had gone, she closed the outside door, and stood with her back to it. I stood silently looking on, with a gentle smile on my face.

'I feel we need a lot more laughter in this house,' she said. She opened out her arms, and I ran and clung to her. She knew I was crying gently on her shoulders and she held me tight.

'Don't you worry, my little pet, we will sort all this out. Whatever it takes, we will work it out. Just let's pretend that this is a show for the whole world, till your Dad gets here. But then I have to play my part in this as well.'

'I don't want you to get into trouble, really,' I said.

'What I need to start off with, is some of your mother's clothes. Then I can start acting the part.'

She shoved the bolt in the door and said, 'Whatever happens in the next few hours, don't let anyone in.'

She put the bag up on the chair, beside the table, and started rummaging through it, taking out containers of makeup and cream, brushes and powder kits. She laid them out on the table in front of her, and when she had it all ready, she said, 'You don't mind if I use some of your Mam's clothes?'

I led her to the room and began going through her wardrobe. We laid Mam's dresses out on the bed, as well as cardigans and blouses.

'I need one of her bibs as well.'

I found a few of them in the drawer and began putting her clothes back in the wardrobe. I showed her one dress, which Mam had covered in tissue paper, and which was hanging in the corner of the wardrobe. It was the dress Dad brought her from England last summer. She had only worn it once. It was Mam's new good dress, and I wanted to mind it and keep it.

'She looked like a queen that night,' said Meg.

I put it back and I left the room. Meg changed into some of Mam's clothes and came to the kitchen wearing a blue bib, dotted with tiny white flowers. There was a cardigan underneath, and she was wearing a navy-blue skirt, the hem of which showed from underneath the bib. She had the same shape and movement of my mother, but she was a little plumper, as Mam had lost a lot of weight in recent months.

'I have one more thing I need Sarah – a photo taken in recent years of your mother.'

I went back to the room and took down the tin biscuit box from the top of the wardrobe, where Mam kept any photos she had from her young days right up to the present time.

There were many snaps taken with little brownie cameras at the seaside, or beside cocks of hay with friends, when she was young. Then there were some taken with my father at football matches or caught walking the streets of the city by roaming photographers trying to earn a living by taking pictures of weary passers-by. Then we came into the picture. She had baby pictures of us all, and pictures taken at first communions. Ond one of my favourites was the one taken at Lilliput Sports with the waves lapping on the lake, billowing as a backdrop. The one Meg chose was the photo taken at my Confirmation three years previously. Mam and Dad were both standing behind me. Mam was smiling, and she looked happy and healthy. She had her hair rolled up behind, just above her neckline and fastened with clips. It was a fashion common in the forties and fifties, but it was on the wane now. This was the way Mam wore her hair, during the day and in recent years the threads of grey began to appear quite fast.

Meg took the photo, and I helped her roll her hair up, and to fasten it with clips. She took out some powder then, and fluffed it into her hair, to introduce the grey tint Mam had in hers. She then sent me off to feed the cow and the donkey, as well as the dog, and she began to apply makeup to her face.

It was a cold morning, and Sputnik was whimpering to be released from his little shed. He jumped around me, and wagged his tail, following me to the haggard. Tossie the donkey and the cow were peering across the fence, waiting for some fodder. I didn't want to give them too much as there was still plenty of grass in the field where they were grazing, and the hay had to last until spring. I only gave them a little each day, as the cow was nearing her time to have her little calf. Now she needed every bit of nourishment she could get. She was very quiet, and she loved me to stroke the front of her head gently. Old Tossie didn't want to be left out either, and I rubbed him too. What I liked about looking after the animals, was that they never complained, and they had the same temperament always. I stayed with them, while they munched away quietly, and it felt like other days when troubles were few, and the world was a stable and happy place.

Then I was rudely awakened from my few moments of quiet time, when someone spoke behind me.

'Sh-sh-she…is near her time Sarah.' It was Pat Reardon. He immediately realised, that he had startled me when I followed with an alarmed response.

'Oh Pat, you frightened the living daylights out of me.'

'I-I-I am so sorry, I d-d-didn't mean to f-f-frighten you.'

'That's alright, Pat,' I said. I ran to him and hugged him to show that there was no harm done. I knew by him that he could do with a wash and a shave. Pat was someone who could do with some loving tender care, as there were times he went for weeks without washing himself. It was Mam who would remind him every so often, especially coming up to the weekend, not to forget to have a good scrub for Sunday mass. This didn't bother him in the least, but he'd take her advice at face value, and on Saturday evening he boiled a big pot of water on the fire, locked the door, put the tin bath on the floor in the middle of the kitchen, and scrubbed himself from head to toe, and followed that with a clean shave with a cut-throat razor. Next morning, he shone in his Sunday suit, and smiled across at us sitting from the men's side of the church.

'She'll have her calf in about a week,' he said.

'I hope you are around Pat when it happens.'

'You-You know what your father said, no matter what time of the day it happens, send Joe for me.'

Pat leaned across the fence looking at the two animals munching contentedly at the hay. He had a straw in his mouth, chewing happily, and his cap sat at the side of his head.

'How's your Mam today?' he asked.

'She's still in bed,' I said.

'Well, she's up now,' he answered.

'What do you mean?' I asked curiously, and a little bit alarmed by his revelation.

'Well I looked in through the window, and I saw her sitting at the table doing her face and her hair.'

I was annoyed when I heard this. Pat always peeped in the window, before he entered the house. It was something that annoyed my mother a little when she got married but accepted it as part of Pat's personality.

'Well, she told me she wasn't getting up till midday.' Again, I was startled when a voice spoke behind us.

'I'm up now girl and ready to meet the day.'

I turned around and gave a muffled scream when I saw Mam standing there. It was like a flash caught in time, an image in slow motion, something one would see later in a television film, or a movie. Meg smiled at us, and it was in that moment, I thought of the drama Meg said we were performing.

'Mam! I told you to stay in bed.'

'I'm up now, Alana, and I want to get on with things.'

'You-You are looking well again Mrs Cregan,' said Pat.

My heart relaxed a little, when I realised Meg had fooled Pat into believing she was my mother.

'Did you not invite the man in for a cup of tea?' asked Meg.

'I didn't want to wake you up.'

'Come on then, I have the kettle on.'

We followed her back into the kitchen, and she did indeed have the kettle on. Tea followed, and Pat sat in the soft chair by the fire. Within a short while, the heat from the fire began to tease some of the hidden odours from Pat's body into the kitchen air. Meg copped it quickly, and true to form just like my mother she told him that it was time to get the soap and water out.

Pat smiled and agreed with her, saying that he'd be shining like a new pin on Sunday morning. When this conversation ended, Pat could tell her that Fr Doyle had a black and blue nose that morning in the village, and he made no bones about telling everyone that he got it from Mrs Cregan. His story was, that she was well on the road to recovery. With this tale moving around the locality, Meg was acting the part out well. It wasn't till the boys arrived home that evening that her disguise was tested. They stood on the floor in amazement looking at her. At first, they weren't sure, Packy thought initially that it was his mother, and it frightened him, wondering whether this was true, or was she a vision. They didn't know whether to call her Meg or Mam.

'Call me Mam,' she said, 'because be it long or be it short you will call me Auntie Meg in front of someone else.'

The boys were very happy with her new look, and there were smiles all round on their faces as they ate their dinner. All except Packy, who was very quiet and listless during the evening. Meg thought that he might be sickening for something, and he didn't want to finish his dinner. He went to his room and lay on the bed for a while. I didn't bother him, but left him so, thinking that the rest would do him good as the pressure of the past few days was taking its toll on him.

When tea was ready around seven in the evening, I called him to the kitchen, and he came to us, wiping his eyes. He sat quietly at the table. After tea, it was homework time, and it was then that Meg noticed he was finding it hard to hold his pencil, when he was doing his sums.

'What's wrong with your hand Packy?' asked Meg.

'Nothing, I'm fine!'

'Let me see,' she demanded. Packy hid his hands under the table. Then Joe spoke. 'I think you had better tell what happened.'

Packy nodded his head and bundled himself into a heap.

'If *you* don't tell, Packy, *I will*,' said Tom.

'What happened at school?' I asked.

Meg dragged him away from the table, holding his hands. He cried out in pain as she did so. She opened them to find that they were red and bruised.

'Oh, my God!' she screamed in horror, 'Who did this to you?'

Packy wouldn't answer.

'It was Mr Browne, the master,' said Joe.

'Why did he do this? What terrible thing could you have done to be punished like this?'

'He punched Joey Greene in the face,' said Tom.

'Why did you do that?' asked Meg.

'He said something terrible,' sobbed Packy, and he cried loudly into Meg's bib. Then he screamed at the top of his voice. 'I just want to die!' I'd say his screams could be heard by the animals in the field.

'Shush! Calm down, pet,' said Meg calmly and gently. She held him close to her again, and gently caressed his head.

'What did this Joey Greene say?' she asked.

'I thought that of all people, Joey Greene wouldn't say something like that,' sobbed Packy again.

'Why who is Joey Greene?'

'He is the sergeant's son,' I said.

'Well sergeant's boy or not, I want to know what he said to you Packy that made you punch him in the face.' She was holding the two cheeks of his face cupped in her hands and looked kindly into his eyes. Packy knew there was no threat in her voice and he spoke softly. 'He said something terrible about you.'

'About me? But sure, how does Joey Greene know me?'

'I mean, he said something terrible about Mam…'

'What did he say then, come on tell me?'

'He called her a name.'

'What name did he call her?'

'Mad Mary,' said Packy.

It was then that Tom intervened. 'You see, Fr Doyle came into the schoolyard, and was talking to Master Browne. Joey Greene is always listening to what the adults were saying. Fr Doyle, of course, was telling the master how he got the black nose, that it was an accident, and he got it from Mary Cregan when he was visiting the day before.'

'I see, and he was teasing you.'

'Yeah! He was teasing me, and I had enough. I was very angry. I lost my Mam, and I will never see her again, and he called her Mad Mary. I jumped on him for calling her that name, and I began punching him.'

'Then the master came out and brought them in,' said Joe. 'Packy hadn't a great punch though, there wasn't a mark on Joey Greene, but Packy was angry and raging. The master gave him three hard slaps on each hand with a big cane and made him stand in the corner to cool off.'

'What about Master Greene, did he get the works also for name-calling?'

'No, he told him to go out to play.'

'So, he got off Scot free, the one who started it all in the first place.' Now I could see the anger rising on Meg's face. She still held Packy close to her and said, 'I think that Master Browne is a right bully, you know that? He's a young fellow is that what you said, isn't he?'

'Yeah, he is young, and he plays hurling also,' said Joe.

'Well, I think Master Browne has a thing or two to learn about fair play, and how to treat young children.'

She said nothing more but asked me to get a basin of hot water with Dettol in it, and a sponge. She sat Packy down at the table and bathed his swollen hands in the water for half an hour. The smile soon returned to his face, and he declared he was hungry. I buttered some brown bread for him with jam, and he drank some weak warm tea, with plenty of sugar in it. He looked up at Meg smiling, and said, 'You do look so much like Mam.'

'Well, I hope I can be half the woman she was, for a little while anyway.'

Chapter 17

Mad Mary Strikes

There was plenty of drama the next day. Meg was up at the crack of dawn, sitting at the mirror, transforming herself into an image of the dear mother I would never see again. She said little or nothing during that process, and I carried on with getting the breakfast ready as well as lunches for the boys. I called them at eight o'clock, and they sat down to their porridge, boiled eggs with brown bread and butter. I told them there were not many eggs left, as the laying was going off the hens for the winter. I had kept a dozen or so in the cool window of my bedroom for this year's Christmas cake. I had watched Mam over the years making it, and last year I made it myself under her supervision. She was very pleased with the result. I iced that cake Christmas week, and covered the sides with a frilled paper ribbon we bought in town. It had a little ornamental Santa on top, and the edges were surrounded with fancy blobs of pink icing topped with little silver coloured balls, like the ball bearings of a bicycle, only smaller. The boys thought it was great, and the proof in the baking was that it didn't last until New Year's Day.

Thoughts of making this year's cake were going through my head, as Meg plotted her confrontation with Mr Browne. I didn't think she'd do it, but she asked the boys to walk to the school with her that morning. They protested at her decision, and Packy was upset again.

'He'll come at me when you are gone,' he cried.

'No one will lay a finger on any of you again,' she said, 'I'm Mad Mary, and he'll regret it forever if he touches any of you, by the time, I'm finished with him.'

'What if they find out who you really *are*?' asked Joe.

'Didn't I fool *you* lot?' she laughed. They all nodded in agreement.

'Then there's no need to worry, I'll fool anyone else as well.'

She drank a quick cup of tea and disappeared into the early winter light with Packy by the hand, and for all the world she walked and spoke like my mother. I feared for what might happen next.

She was back by midday, and she said very little, except that she had sorted that fellow out for good and all. She sat by the fire, waiting, as I knew someone would call because of her visit to the school.

'There'll be someone here in due course,' she said.

'Who?' I asked.

'Wait and see, Alana, he won't be too long.'

But before that, I must relate what happened that morning at the school. Joe told me quietly that evening as we foddered the cow and the donkey and closed in the hens.

Meg arrived at the school gate just as the master was calling everyone into class. She approached him and said, 'I would like to speak to you sir about an incident at the school yesterday.'

'I'm sorry, Madam,' said Mr Browne, 'but you must call to me after school today.'

'I want to speak to you now,' she demanded.

'I'm afraid you'll have to go,' he said, 'classes are about to begin.'

He walked away from her, following all the children into the school. She stood and waited, till he had gone in and the children had settled into their classes. Soon the classroom doors closed and the day's lessons began.

Mr Browne was standing at his desk laying out books and writing copies for the day, when he heard a series of gasps and giggles from the children. He turned to find himself confronted by Meg, who stood silently inside the classroom door, her arms folded and ready for war. Wearing the red headscarf, she looked so like Mam, as she stood her ground.

'Madam, I said I'd see you after school,' he said, raising his voice as he spoke, 'Would you mind leaving right now?'

'I'll leave when I'm ready,' she said quietly under her breath in a low voice.

'If you don't, I will send for the sergeant and have you forcefully removed.'

'Will it be the same force you used yesterday on a gentle innocent little boy, who tried to defend his family honour?'

'Family honour my foot, he deserved every little bit of it, the little viper,' he sniggered.

'How dare you?' she roared. There were gasps from the children.

'Quiet, you lot!' he bellowed. They were silent again, as they retreated into their amazement, with gazes of excitement and horror.

'I suppose the sergeant has to repay you for not laying a finger on his little darling boy, the one who caused it all, the one who was listening into your conversation with Fr Doyle.'

'He lashed out at the young Greene boy. It was uncalled for, so I had to mete out a suitable punishment.'

'Will you look at you,' she laughed, 'a fully-grown man, about twelve or thirteen stone in weight, and you can't handle a little domestic situation with care and dignity. Then you act violently against a little child. Mr Browne, if I had known you were going to treat my children like this, I'd have had second thoughts about sending them to school here. The only problem is, I don't have a choice. It would be too far to send them a full seven miles into the town on their bikes.'

'Can I ask you for a second time to leave, please?'

'I said I'm not finished with you yet,' she answered with such anger, it looked as if she was going to froth from the mouth.

'Jimmy!' he called to one of the boys, 'Will you get Miss Briody to send for the sergeant?' Jimmy stood up.

'Sit down, Jimmy!' bellowed Meg.

He sat back down again, giggling to himself. He turned to Tom and Joe, giving them the thumbs up.

'Now tell me, sir, and tell me no more – what did you use to hit him with? Let me see?'

'Get out of my classroom?' he shouted.

She ignored him completely as her anger spurred her on even more. Standing against the mantelpiece was a thick sally rod, which she picked up.

'So, this is your weapon,' she said. 'Hands up anyone who has been beaten with this.' One by one the frightened but excited children began raising their hands in the air.

'Isn't that just great?' she laughed angrily and tinted with an element of sarcasm. 'So you've scored with them all, just like on the hurling field.' She raised the stick as if to hit him and he screamed.

'Madam, if you hit me with that you will go to jail…'

'And what about these little children? Will you go to jail for hitting them?'

'You're a mad woman, everyone knows that.'

'I'm nearly finished with you *now*, Mr Browne – if you don't want me to really hit you. But I will if I must. I want you to tell all these children, you will never lay a finger on them again.'

'Get lost!' he gasped.

She raised the stick as if to strike. 'Say it!' she shouted.

'I will not hit them!' he shouted.

'Promise!' roared Meg.

'I promise I will not hit them.'

With that, she broke the stick into three or four pieces, and threw them into the fire.

'I bid you good day, Mr Browne,' she said, and walked calmly out of the classroom, closing the door behind her.

The sergeant arrived a little later. I heard the car at the gate, and Sputnik barked. He knocked on the door and I answered it.

'Is Mrs Cregan in?' he asked.

'She is Sergeant, come on in.'

Meg was sitting at the fire, and she was quietly considering the flames, as the fire door of the range was open, and there was a gentle red glow in the kitchen. He sat on the chair opposite her.

'Mrs Cregan, how are you today?'

'I'm fine, Sergeant, but I'm a little upset by the events of the past two days.'

'Well, so is Mr Browne down at the school.'

'I suppose he gave you his account of the story?'

'Yes, indeed and he is pressing charges for assault.'

'Assault!' she exclaimed. 'I never laid a finger on him. In fact, there must be twenty witnesses there, all those little children.'

'It's your word against his – they are just little children.'

'Is there no one to stand up for them? Just because they are little children?'

'Mrs Cregan, what has come over you of late? It's as if you are a different person. The whole village knows of your recent illness, now you are turning violent. Will you need to see a doctor?'

'When I hit the priest, it was a complete accident. But the only regret I have is that I didn't let that coward have it this morning. Then it would be a great reason for him to press charges.'

'Well, he is going to do just that. I will need you to come down to the station and make a statement.'

'Well, I'm not moving from here. I didn't hit him. I frightened the living daylights out of him, and he deserved every bit of it. It's his pride that's hurt, and maybe it might make him wake up and be a better teacher.'

'You are not coming then?'

'No, Sergeant.'

'I'll be back later then. I may have to arrest you.'

'That's alright, Sergeant. I'll be waiting.'

He stood up to go, and as he did so, Meg spoke quietly again. 'Did Mr Browne tell you how your son was involved in the incident yesterday?'

'Sorry, Mrs Cregan? What do you mean?'

'Sit down there, Sergeant. You haven't heard the half of it.'

He took his notebook out and she told him the whole story from beginning to end, and her anger at seeing Packy's injured hands, and as to how his own son had escaped the wrath of Mr Browne, after having caused the incident in the first place. The sergeant knew that Packy and Joey were friends and whatever happened between them, would be sorted out among themselves as only boys knew how.

'Tell me this, Sergeant,' said Meg. 'How would you feel if your own little boy came home bruised and battered like my little man yesterday? You are a parent too.'

'Well, I wouldn't be happy in the least.' That's the only comment he made on the matter, but I knew his thinking had turned in Meg's favour. He stood up to go once more and placing the notebook back in the breast pocket of his coat, he said, 'I'll tell you what, leave this with me. If he continues to persist with pressing charges, I'll be back later. Meanwhile, you get some rest, Mrs Cregan. You walked to the village this morning, and you walked back. I can see by the colour on your face, you're not feeling the best now.'

'I'm blessed with a great daughter, Sergeant. Only for her, where would I be?'

'Good day, Mrs Cregan,' he said and left.

He didn't return that day. The boys arrived from school in great glee, telling their version of the story, but Meg told them to stop and let the matter be. It had been dealt with, and she didn't want to hear it mentioned again. Then Packy announced that Joey had invited him to play at the barrack house on Saturday. The anger and pain in his hands was diminishing, and he took out his drawing kit after tea and worked away until bedtime.

Next day, Fr Doyle arrived, a little apprehensive to come in for fear that Mad Mary might hit him again, but acting just like Mam, Meg sat in the chair, and chatted quietly to him. The swelling was going down on his nose and he was delighted to see that Mam's condition had improved.

'By the way, Mrs Cregan,' he said before he left, 'I had a visit from Mr Browne early this morning. He has decided to move back to his hometown in Galway. He has been offered a post there, and he has tendered his resignation for Monday the seventh of January. It's a bit of a shock, to say the least. I wasn't expecting a man of his calibre to bow to any pressure. Anyway, I have to make a new appointment in the school.'

'A bit of advice, Father,' said Meg. 'Be careful who you choose. A child who lives in fear won't learn.'

'I will take that on board, Mrs Cregan,' he said as he bid us good day.

I was mesmerised at the end of it all to see that Meg had pulled it off. Her disguise worked. She was amazing. But it was years of experience on the stage that did this. Then she was not unlike Mam in ways, same build, hair much the same and the makeup worked miracles.

In January, a new principal was appointed, Donal Ryan, a Tipperary man, with a great love of music. He had coloured pencils in his breast pocket, and he had a tape recorder. There was a new magic in the classroom, and to Packy's delight, coloured pictures and drawings formed part of the learning process. This helped him to hide his own personal tragedies. Meanwhile, at home, I was ever so careful to keep an eye on the red cow, as her time to calve drew near and it came quick enough.

Chapter 18

Birth

It was mid-December and thoughts of the approaching Christmas season were far from my mind. My wish was that I'd fall asleep and wake up sometime in February when it was over and long gone. I cried myself to sleep at night in my loneliness. I felt responsible for the way I had dragged Meg into the mess I had made. There was no way out for me, only jail or that someone would lock me up forever and throw away the key. Mam came to me in my dreams on many of those winter nights, and my fear was gone by morning.

But where was Dad? It was not like him to go off like that and not keep in contact. What would happen to the boys if what I had done was found out? I withdrew into myself and said very little to anyone. Meg knew my distress, and on several mornings when the boys had gone to school, she sat me down and reassured me that everything would be alright.

'What if Dad is dead? What if he has run away and abandoned us just like the Larkin man?'

'Hush! Hush little petal,' she said softly. 'John Cregan would go to the ends of the earth for his children. He'll make contact soon. There is a valid reason as to why we haven't heard from him. Time will tell.'

It was then I reminded her about the Salvation Army people and my request for them to find him for me.

'Aren't you the clever young lady, Sarah Cregan? What made you go and ask them for help?'

'Do you not remember you told me all about them last summer after seeing the film *Whistle Down the Wind*.'

'I do indeed,' she recalled, 'and you went all the way to Dublin to see them.'

'It happened the day before Mam died. They were so nice, and they said they would help. I didn't want to go to the guards or they'd suspect there was something wrong here.'

'Let's keep our fingers crossed,' she said.

'I hope we hear from him soon,' I sighed.

'Don't! Enough!' she exclaimed as she placed her finger on my lips. 'Let's take it one day at a time?' Then to distract me from these thoughts she said, 'Isn't it time you went out to check on that little cow in the field?'

It wasn't long till I was out in the cold frosty air. I found the cow and Tossie the donkey in the corner of the field. She was standing quietly chewing her cud. So, I knew she was quite happy, and she wasn't in any distress. Tossie came over and began nuzzling me to give him some attention. Three large cocks of hay stood in the haggard the results of the summer harvest. One of them looked as if it had a large slice cut out of it already because of the work of the hay knife. They got a little fodder each evening when they were put into the shed for the night. There was more than enough there to carry us through the winter. On close examination, the cow was a little restless, even though she was chewing the cud. Tossie stopped bothering me, when I threw him in a handful of hay on the ground. I watched her carefully through the afternoon as I knew something would happen before the day was out.

She timed it very well. When the boys came from school Joe took a quick check on her, and came running in, saying she was away in the far corner of the field with a hump on her back. He went post haste on his bike to the village to fetch Pat. His help was needed on this occasion.

It was just nightfall when they returned. I had been keeping a watchful eye on her from a distance in the fading light. The first stars were beginning to twinkle, and the evening spoke of an impending frost.

Pat carried a torch with him, and approached the cow cautiously, as in her distress she could be temperamental at this stage of her labour. Then he called us through the darkness.

'The front hooves are out,' he said.

He reached down deep into his coat pocket and took out a coil of thin rope. He patted her on the back and kept saying, 'Easy g-g-girl! Easy g-g-girl!'

The cow seemed to relax at the sound of his voice. This was Pat's gift, something my father could see in him, and yet he had no explanation for it.

He slipped the loop of the rope around the two new soft hooves and said, 'Now c-c-come and p-p-pull with me.'

He knew when it was the right time to pull, as the cow had her birth spasms and he knew when to stop and wait. Suddenly the head appeared.

'Only a little more to go,' said Pat. Quite quickly, the calf slipped wet, shiny and steaming onto the cold grass. It gave a little yell as it fell, and the cow lowed as well in reply, as if to say, *I'm here!* As she turned around to see her little offspring, the afterbirth began to ooze from her body. Her first task was to lick the little calf to encourage it to stand up.

'It's a little red whitehead heifer,' said Pat.

'Just like her mother!' shouted a very excited Joe. The calf made several bungling efforts to stand up and fell back down again, her long awkward legs folding under her as she collapsed. With a little help from Pat, she stood up before too long. Instinct made her go seek her mother's milk. The night was getting colder and it was now black dark. With the light of the torch shining on him, Pat lifted the calf up in his arms. 'T-t-time to g-g-get her out of the frost. Get behind the cow you two, she'll follow me to the shed.'

Pat led the way across the field to the cow-house in the yard. It had been left with hay and straw bedding. The cow followed Pat. She was a little agitated to see her calf being carried away from her. Every fifteen to twenty yards or so, Pat left the calf down gently. She was reassured when she began to smell and lick her little offspring. Then Pat lifted the calf again and bore it away across the field.

When we reached the shed, he left the calf down in the straw, and she stood in her place at the manger, where she settled down to eat some of the fresh hay. When Tossie shoved his nose in the door to see what was going on, he was quickly hushed away, as he was making a nuisance of himself. He was shoved into one of the far mangers and he was closed off from further intrusion by a little wooden gate. While we were there, he stood with his head across the gate looking curiously at what was going on in the other part of the shed.

The calf soon began drinking her mother's milk, and Pat said he'd leave her for a day till she had filled herself up. Then he'd take the calf away, and train it to drink from a bucket. In a few days, the cow would be giving plenty of fresh milk, and there was going to be loads of butter on the table for Christmas.

We left the cow and her calf to share the darkness and to rest for the night, safe and warm from the frost. For those few brief moments, it was life, as we knew it. It was just like the days when Dad came home and going to the shed full of excitement to see the new arrival. As I lay in bed that night, I recalled a time when I'd hear Mam and Dad talk about what plans they had with the money they'd make from an animal when it was sold off as a yearling. There was often talk of keeping the little heifer for calving and milking, to replace a cow who had reached her older years, and no longer strong enough to have more offspring. There were trips to the town to buy new clothes, shoes, or even to bring home the Christmas. These were happy thoughts. But I wished they were part of my reality in the present living, but the truth was, that I'd never have such moments again. It was still a terrible nightmare. Fortunately, I still had the boys by my side, and I intended to keep it that way. Three weeks had passed since Mam died, and I had managed to keep my family together. If Meg hadn't arrived on the scene, I might not have succeeded in doing so. As she said already, I was taking it one day at a time and to just hope and pray for Dad's return. Despite all that sadness, Christmas as we knew it would have to go ahead. There were greater challenges to meet in the coming weeks more frightening than of late, and the wheels were set in motion next day when Meg got a letter from Darcy.

Chapter 19

Fr Doyle's Concerns

Darcy was in England, and he knew he'd have to contact Meg. Meanwhile, she stayed with us, and he could not contact her by phone at their Dublin home.

The postman gave me the letter with a picture of the Queen's head on it. I knew it was from him. It had a postmark from Devon. She sat down, opened it and read it to herself.

'He's bringing Eileen here for Christmas,' she said.

She handed me the letter and I read it. He had good legible handwriting, and a very nice turn of phrase in his diction, a reflection of his command of language, and his onstage acting experience. He was going to bring Eileen by car and leave her here on Christmas Eve.

'I told him in the letter I wrote to him two weeks ago, I was staying here for Christmas. He was none too pleased about that. Anyway, it's been several years since we spent Christmas together.'

'How does he feel about you not staying with him at Christmas?'

'When he knows I'm down here, it will give him an excuse to spend his time drinking with old cronies in or around the city centre.'

From the letter I read Eileen was looking forward to spending Christmas with a family. He had arranged to pick her up the day after St Stephen's Day and take her back to Dublin. Darcy was it seems, as good as his word.

'I may have to go with them, till she settles in,' said Meg.

'What are we going to do?' I asked.

'Don't worry, pet, we'll work something out, maybe your Dad will be home by then.'

She could still see the worry on my face, and the turmoil that kept churning around in my head. As I cleaned the table, I began to shake. She saw my anxiety and I didn't see her approach. She took my hand and said,

'Stop this! We are all in this together.' She was bordering on being angry with me.

'What if Darcy finds out,' I said.

'Leave him to me. If he hasn't sinned, let him cast the first stone. I know how to handle that man.'

To take my mind off things, she suggested I go to the shop in the village and to buy the ingredients for the Christmas cake. I wrapped up well and brought the soft leather shopping bag hanging on the handlebars of the bike. It was a cold damp morning, and there was a mist floating on the breeze, the early frost was melting away, and it looked as if the rain was going to dampen down the day and draw the dark evening in even earlier.

My head was in a spin. and I was nearly knocked down by a Morris Minor car as I cycled on the main road. The village was quiet, and as I passed the school I saw Packy playing with a team of boys as they kicked a torn leather ball on the cement playground. I knew that his mind was at ease for the moment, and he'd soon have a new master.

Father Doyle stopped me on the street, to tell me that he'd call to the house to finalise arrangements for mass servers for Midnight Mass on Christmas Eve. He thought Joe and Tom would be reliable candidates, even though they'd have to cycle the two miles in the dark.

'I can leave them home after mass,' he said.

'I'll tell them, Father. You can talk to them at Sunday mass.'

'I forgot about that, sure isn't Christmas week their rota for serving anyway?'

He turned to head for the church, and forgetting something he said, 'Oh, by the way child, how's Mam today?'

'She's fine, Father, feeling a little better now.'

'Someone said she does have a heart condition…'

'Mam is fine, Father, I just wish that whoever that someone is, would mind their own business.'

'It's just that lately, she doesn't seem to show any sign of a weak heart. It's me that knows it, a fist in the face or a threat of violence to the headmaster, aren't the hallmarks of someone with a heart condition.'

I began to tremble, not knowing what to say. My own heart began to beat very fast, and I felt like lashing out at him, to tell him to mind his own business. In that instant of just a few seconds duration, I knew I'd have to find the words to answer that, and I did.

'Since when did you become a doctor, Father?'

'I beg your pardon!' he said.

'You seem to have gained a great medical knowledge suddenly. Were you talking to Dr Sullivan? If you were, it was none of his business to say anything to you.'

'You are very eloquent for a girl of such tender years. I'm just worried about her mental state that's all. The question I want to be answered is, is she capable of looking after you all in your father's absence?'

I had no idea what the word eloquent meant, I'd have to look it up in Mam's big Chambers English Dictionary at home. My greatest fear was that someone would come and take her away and send her to the mental hospital.

'Mam is fine,' I said. 'In fact, she will be at mass on Sunday.' I didn't know whether I should have said that or not, as I knew that Meg was a law unto herself when it came to religious matters, having experienced the wrath of many a parish priest, who had questioned the morality of their stage productions down through the years. It seemed to defuse the situation, as the priest backed down in his train of thought with the reply, 'Good! Good! That's great. I'll look forward to seeing her then.'

He turned on his heels and headed for the church, his black soutane giving him an air of floating along the pavement. This was broken by the clatter of his hob-nailed boots on the cement.

My mind suddenly changed when I wondered what Meg might say when I got home. She'd be seeing red, and she did.

'What did you go and do that for?' she shouted.

'I'm sorry!' I replied, tears making their usual track down my face.

'I haven't been to mass for years. Now you are trying to convert me again, and I party to a crime.'

'I'm sorry!' I bellowed again, 'I didn't know what to do. He was trying to find out something. I fear he might be suspicious of something, that's all. I don't want to lose my brothers. They'll take me away and lock me up.'

'Over my dead body,' said Meg, 'there'll be a second dead body before that happens. It just means I must dress up again, become your Mam, and let the whole parish see me as I parade before them. Someone's bound to be suspicious.'

'You fooled us,' I said, wiping the tears away, 'you fooled the priest, the sergeant and of all people, Pat Reardon. You are a master at it.'

She chuckled softly to herself, and then began to laugh out loud. She threw her arms around me, and we laughed through the tears.

'Oh Sarah, Sarah, Sarah! How did it ever come to this?'

I looked up at her and said, 'Mam?' Then I stopped and said, 'Meg!' She placed a finger on my lips again, as she had done before and said, 'You got it right the first time.'

'Mam,' I said again, 'what does eloquent mean?'

'Eloquent! It means you speak fluently. You can be very persuasive, you can express yourself very well to indicate something or getting a message across.'

'I must have done it so,' I said, 'he went away.'

'Remember what I said, we take each day as it comes. If we can get over today, tomorrow will look after itself.'

'Eloquent,' I said softly.

'Yes, eloquent. You will survive, pet, and so will your brothers. I can feel it in my bones and you are learning fast as well.'

'I've learned it from the grand master,' I said.

'Now tell me one thing. What did I send you to the shop for? We seem to have been side-tracked again. This Christmas cake won't be made if we don't do it now.'

That evening, when the boys came home from school, the aroma of Christmas cake cooking in the oven met them at the door. Meg, dressed as Mam, sat in the corner darning one of Tom's socks. She looked up at them, and seeing three smiling faces said, 'Now boys, I want to see a lot more of that, a home without a smile is not a home, it's only a house.

'What do you mean?' asked Tom.

'Think about it, lad, think about it.'

Chapter 20

Sunday Mass

On Sunday morning, we walked the two miles to the village. Meg looked radiant. She had the walk of a queen. She wore Mam's black winter coat, and a woollen hat on her head to keep her warm. Joe and Tom had cycled on ahead to don their soutanes, and black slippers, as well as to prepare the altar with Billy the sacristan, for mass.

As I have said already, she walked like a queen, and when we reached the tarred road, she moved to a slower pace to indicate that even though she was feeling a lot better, things were just not one hundred percent.

'If I'm supposed to have a heart condition, I should go and act the part then,' she said.

We moved at a slow but regular pace to the village. It was a cold morning, and the sun was only showing on the horizon. A gentle frost hung in shady places, as any overnight cloud had dispersed. Near the village, people walking to mass passed us out, saying how glad they were to see Mam looking so well. Afraid that people might pick up on hearing a different voice, Meg pretended she had a cold.

'Take some honey and hot lemon with a few cloves, and a deorum of whiskey, love. It will work wonders,' someone said in passing. A bicycle passed, and the cyclist doffed his hat,

'Great to see ya, Mam!'

A car passed, and the horn blew as a greeting.

'Who is that?' asked Meg.

'It's the Walsh's,' said Packy. 'They're kinda posh.'

'They're not posh,' I protested. 'They are nice people.'

'Are posh people not nice?' asked Meg.

'Yes, they are,' said Packy, 'like you, you're posh sometimes.'

'Thank you, very much young man. Am I not posh all of the time?'

'Well yeah, but Sarah is only saying those things because she fancies Seán.'

'Tell me more then?' said Meg.

'Packy!' I shouted.

'Easy now,' said Meg. 'Are we not going to visit the house of God on a Sunday morning.'

'She fancies Seán,' said Packy.

'I do not!'

'Yes, you do. I saw you writing a letter to him.'

'Packy mind your own business.'

'Well, well! You're a dark horse, Sarah Cregan,' laughed Meg.

'Packy, I'll kill you when I get home.'

'Well, have we not had enough of that lately?' asked Meg. Then she realised she should not have said that. 'I think I will re-phrase that… I want peace in the camp when we get home, is that alright?'

But Packy didn't heed what Meg had said and begun taunting me.

'Sarah loves Shawnie! Sarah loves Shawnie!'

I made a swipe at him, and he ran from me laughing. I knew he was teasing me, but deep down I was glad to see him laughing again.

'He won't be at mass, he's away in college.'

'Oh, posh, posh!' shouted Packy from a distance.

'Now behave yourselves you two,' said Meg. 'We are going into the house of God.' I stopped in my tracks when she said this and looked into her face. It was Mam's words she was using. She winked at me, as the three of us entered the church.

Purple dominated the building in preparation for Christmas. The church year had just begun in early December with the approach of Advent. There was a feeling of hope inside me. The church was full, and the dim light of the building was overcome with pools of low winter sunshine, streaming in through the stained-glass images on the windows. There was a constant chorus of coughing, reflecting the onset of winter colds, and the ever-increasing cooler dark days.

Fr Doyle was dead on time for nine o'clock mass, and the choir from the gallery echoed across the building with, '*O come O come Emmanuel And ransom captive Israel…*

The priest began mass with the words, '*In nomine Patris, et Filii, et Spiritus Sancti. Amen.*

'*Introibo ad Altare Dei.*'

The three servers answered with the responses, '*Ad Deum qui laetificat juventutem meam.*'

Mass continued in this vein. The servers spoke with great clarity and diction in response to the priest's words in Latin. I didn't understand very much of what was being said, as did anyone else in the church, except those who had learned Latin at school. I knew the responses myself, as Mam spent many an hour tutoring the boys when they began serving mass at first.

Meg did not kneel like everyone else, but I could see the impish look on her face as if to say, 'I am not well, I should not be exerting myself.' I turned away from her and left her be. I gazed over at Packy. He considered himself a big fellow now, as he was sitting on the men's side of the church. He was still wearing his cap, which he should have removed when he entered the building. I kept looking over at him, trying to draw his attention to me. Fr Doyle had his back to the congregation praying away in Latin. When Packy did eventually turn around, I pointed at my cap and mouthed the words 'Take it off!' He whipped it off quickly and put it in his pocket.

Meg sat right through mass, and I knew she wasn't interested in it at all. I thought to myself that there was a risk that she might never get into heaven. I offered my prayers during the consecration, that her soul at least might be saved. I prayed for my mother too, in the hope that she had gone to her just reward. She was certainly deserving of it, her remains having been left so unceremoniously in the mausoleum in the old cemetery.

When mass was over we moved slowly into the cold morning air, now much brighter in the winter sunshine.

Someone tapped me on the shoulder. It was Pat.

'G-g-great to s-s-see you out, Mam,' he said.

'And you too, Pat,' answered Meg in a hoarse voice.

As he was about to speak again, one of the village boys passing us out by the gate shouted, 'How's P-p-pat?' as loud as he could.

As quick as lightning, Meg turned around, grabbed him by the scruff of the neck and dragged him back. 'Apologise to this man, you little brat.'

'Oh, it's M-m-mad Mary,' he laughed.

Meg drew out to hit him, but a strong arm caught her hand in mid-flight.

'I wouldn't do that if I were you, Mrs Cregan,' It was Sergeant Greene. She drew her hand back, as a rumble of voices ran through the crowd. In an instant, Meg decided to put on a show, as she would in her own theatrical style. She began to feign a weakness as if her heart was beating fast and held on to the iron railings at the church gate.

'Are you alright, Mam?' I exclaimed, adding my voice to the drama. Then Packy followed suit and began to wail and cry. The young lad who had jeered and taunted Pat had disappeared, and Pat held on to Meg.

'I'll take you home Mrs Cregan, in the squad car,' said Sergeant Greene.

'I'm walking home,' said Meg, in her pretend hoarse voice, 'no guard is taking me home in the squad car. I'm not a criminal, Sergeant.'

Then a white hand touched my arm. It was Ellen Walsh.

'It's alright, Mrs Cregan, we'll take you home in the car.' She was quiet spoken as usual and she too was dressed like a lady. There was an air of kindness in her smile, she was non-judgemental, and she was only willing to help. I thought back to the day I wanted to speak privately to Dad some weeks previously, and she took us to the parlour where no one could disturb us. She turned to her husband and said, 'Bring the car up to the gate, Jim.' He went further up the street to find the car and she said, 'You shouldn't be at mass, love, you should be resting.'

'I'm fine thank you,' said Meg. 'You are so kind.'

The crowd was beginning to disperse, and we led Meg to Walsh's car. It was a big Ford Prefect, and Mrs Walsh sat into the back. She invited Packy and me to join her as well. I went to shove him in front of me, but he decided to wait for his brothers, and they'd all go home together. Meg sat into the passenger seat.

Jim Walsh turned the car, as Sergeant Greene stopped the traffic to allow us to face for home. It wasn't long before the dog greeted us at the gate.

'Will I help you in, Mrs Cregan?' asked Jim.

'I'm fine thank you,' said Meg. I linked her in from the gate, and just as they were about to go Ellen Walsh let the window down and said, 'I'm sure ye want holly as usual for Christmas!'

'Yes please,' I answered. She waved her white-gloved hand out the window and they were gone.

'Meg you have put the heart crossways in me!' I exclaimed.

We laughed together, as we opened the door entering the security of the warm kitchen.

Chapter 21

Seán

On Wednesday, the 19th December 1962, the boys came home from school doubly joyous to the fact that the school had closed for Christmas, and that Mister Browne had said farewell to them as well. He brought canned sweets to the class, and they had handfuls of them wrapped up in their own handkerchiefs. I declined an offer of any, as I feared the crumpled pieces of cloth had been used already today.

'He even shook my hand,' said Packy.

'Well let us wish the man well in his new post, and put the past behind us,' said Meg.

'Should we decorate the house for Christmas?' asked Tom.

'Maybe not,' said Packy, 'Mam isn't here.'

'It's not the same,' said Joe.

'We will decorate the house,' said Meg. 'I'm your Mam for the moment and remember life must go on as normal.'

'When will we begin?' asked Joe.

'No time like the present,' said Meg.

I had bought some rolls of crêpe paper in the village the day before, and Meg showed us how to make paper streamers, by crossing and folding two different colours of paper strips one over the other. Each end is sealed with a straight pin. When complete, the streamer can unfold, and they looked like twisted sugar sticks with two different colours. Several of them are joined together and streamed around the walls from picture to picture. There was a great air of excitement about it all. We didn't hear the dog bark, as there was a knock on the door. When I opened it, Seán Walsh stood there smiling, and holding a big bunch of holly, tied with binder twine.

'Mam told me to bring this over,' he said.

'Leave it down Seán and come on in,' answered Meg from the armchair by the fire.

'Is it okay to do so?' he asked.

'Come on in,' I said, rather bossy, 'Mam is fine, she won't mind.'

Meg looked up at him with a squint in her eyes, and the wool cap pulled down to hide as much of her face as possible.

'How are you Seán?'

'I'm fine thank you, Mrs Cregan.'

'Sit down lad by the fire here, its cold outside.' Seán did as he was told and rubbed his hands together several times and placing them close to the top of the range to make them warm again.

'Have you no gloves on a day like this?' asked Meg.

'I'm fine, honestly.'

'When did you come home?' I asked.

'Last night. I'm delighted to be home for Christmas, just one bigger long stretch, and then the Leaving Cert.'

'What would you like to be?' asked Meg.

'I have often thought about studying medicine, but I'm not cut out to be a doctor. I have thought of one or two other careers. But there's one I'm thinking about, but I don't want to say yet, I have a lot of thinking to do over the next number of weeks.'

'Well I'll pray really hard for you, to help you make your mind up,' said Meg. Mam could not have said it better. It was something she said always, she kept remembering people in her prayers with special intentions and requests for curing illnesses, or for things to improve for people who had fallen on hard times. My only fear was that she might take it too far, and that soon the whole thing would explode in our faces. She could easily find herself in prison, accused of aiding and abetting in a crime, and where would that leave the rest of us? Oh, Dad! Where are you and what's wrong, I thought to myself.

Then Seán saw the worried look on my face and said, 'Are you alright Sarah? You look as pale as death.'

'I'm fine really,' I replied.

'Well I cannot stay much longer.' he said, 'I'm sorry to be in such a rush, but I have to deliver more holly to some of the neighbours around.'

'I'll see you to the gate,' I said.

There was a smirk on Joe's face as I followed Seán out the door. It was a racing bike he had. and he sat astride the saddle with both feet on the road. He was at least six-foot-tall, and his red hair shone golden in the amber winter sunshine.

'You are worrying about your Mam,' he said.

'If only it were as simple as that,' I answered.

'Go on tell me.'

'I can't. Maybe someday but not now.'

'It's Christmas you know, and I would like to see you smile.' He stroked my cheek gently as he said, 'Please don't be worrying. Thank you for writing to me. It was great to hear from someone now and then, it can be a very lonely place, especially when you go to bed at night.'

'I'll write a lot when you go back after Christmas.'

'That'll be great. Anyway, meanwhile, please don't be worrying, your Mam will be fine.' He was a very sweet lad, and I was growing to like him more and more. I could feel his words take my pain away, and the smile he wanted did come. He reached into the breast pocket of his coat and took out a tiny parcel wrapped in red crêpe paper. It sat in the palm of his big white hand.

'Maybe this will help,' he said, smiling.

'What is it?' I asked.

'Go on open it!'

I took it gently in my hands, and the paper came away easily. It was a little purple velvet covered box for holding a piece of jewellery. I opened it gently, to reveal a gold cross and chain.

'It's beautiful!' I chirped. 'Thank you so much.'

'Here, let me put it on for you.' I turned around and he towered over me, as he fastened the chain around my neck.

'There's only one problem,' I said.

'What's that?' He asked.

'I don't have anything for you.'

'You're not getting away that easy, Sarah Cregan,' he said.

'What do you mean?'

'Will you come to the St Stephen's night dance in the parish hall with me?'

'Is this a date?' I laughed.

'I guess it is,' he replied.

'I have no dress and…'

He placed his finger on my mouth stopping me mid-sentence.

'It's not a fashion parade. It's a dance, and I'm not taking no for an answer.'

'Well, I think I must go then,' I replied. 'Seán Walsh, you are a big bully.'

'And a nice one, I hope…'

He hadn't finished speaking when I kissed him. As I did so I could hear Tom shouting from the kitchen window.

'She's kissed him!'

My brothers, the little brats had been watching me. I wanted to kill them, they annoyed me so much. But as I turned around to shout at them to go away, Seán pulled me back and kissed me again.

'Well, you are a very nice big bully!' I laughed.

'See you on St Stephens's night then.' He took off up the hill at speed on the bike, and I shouted after him.

'Happy Christmas!'

'You too!' he shouted back at me, waving both hands in the air, cycling without holding the handlebars.

'Show off!' I shouted and ran to the kitchen door.

My three brothers were huddled in a corner of the kitchen, and giggling as I came in, and then they burst out laughing.

'My goodness, that's a nice present you got,' said Meg. 'You're a lucky girl!'

'She kissed him,' sniggered Tom.

'If I can get you lot, I'll give you a good hiding!' I said, pretending to be angry with them.

'Oh Sarah!' said Packy, 'that only means one thing.'

'What's that?' I asked.

'You will really have to marry him now.'

It was then that the two older boys burst out laughing again, and I laughed along with them. It was good to laugh then, and it was great to feel those brief happy moments. Christmas was taking some of the pain away, but before too long, things would turn against us again.

Chapter 22

Mr Thomas

The shortest day of the year arrived. Midwinter dawned with freezing fog, and the cold air went deep into the bones. At the village shop, Pat tapped me on the shoulder carrying a paper bag full of chocolate bars, toffees, lollipops and barley sugar sticks.

'For you all for Christmas,' he said, smiling his gap-toothed smile.

'Oh Pat,' I said, 'thank you so much.' I put my arms around him saying, 'You are coming for Christmas dinner, aren't you?'

'I-I-I will, no problem! Is your M-m-mam alright?'

'She's fine Pat, back to herself again. She really was annoyed last Sunday.'

'It-it was only young Tommy Grogan,' he said. 'I don't mind him too much. He-he means no harm.'

'It's not a nice thing to do. Anyway, I told you before, Pat Reardon, I'm not going to marry you. I have a new boyfriend now.'

'I-I know!'

'How do you know?'

'I saw you from the fields talking to him. He k-k-kissed you too.'

'You're not jealous, Pat?' I asked, teasing him.

'I will never be jealous of you, Sarah,' he said, and I knew what he was going to say next.

'I will always watch over you, Sarah, till the day I die.'

I placed my hand on the sleeve of his coat and I could feel my eyes all tearful. He would be a great father, if he got the chance.

'One o'clock on the dot Christmas day,' I said.

He smiled and continued down the street, leading his bike, being careful not to slip on the ice which had formed on the footpath.

In the late afternoon, Sputnik barked, telling us that we had yet again, another visitor. I could see a man with a trilby hat and heavy topcoat, standing looking across the gate.

'Is that Sarah Cregan?' he asked.

'It is,' I said.

'It's me, Gregory Thomas from the Salvation Army.'

'Oh, Mr Thomas!' I said, 'please come in.'

He followed me into the kitchen, and he took his hat off saying, 'Good afternoon, Mrs Cregan. I hope I find you well.'

'As well as can be expected,' said Meg.

I introduced my brothers to him, and they stood near the bedroom door gazing at the well-dressed stranger.

'I am on my way to Galway,' he said, 'I will be staying with my sister for Christmas.'

'Make the man a cup of tea,' said Meg.

'No, thank you,' he insisted, 'I won't delay. I don't like this freezing fog. There is something in the wind that is not in the weather. We won't have a white Christmas. Maybe we will have a white new year.'

'The winter pond in the field has frozen over,' said Joe. 'We might be able to go sliding.'

'Have you news for me?' I asked.

'I have good news and bad news,' he said. 'We have found your father, but the bad news is he's in hospital.'

'Hospital!' I screamed.

'He has been a very ill man, but he's conscious now and able to talk.'

'What happened to him?' I shouted in a panic.

'Sarah, please don't shout at the gentleman,' exclaimed Meg.

'What happened to him?' I said more quietly to him, ringing my hands in terror. Packy was sobbing bitterly clinging to Meg as she held him close to console him.

'From what I have been told, it is not quite clear what happened. He had an accident. He left his place in London and went to Aberdeen and then to Glasgow. He didn't give the people in London a forwarding address, that's why they lost contact with him. His intention was to send details to them as soon as he got there and found somewhere to stay. He was going to do the same with you, his family, but he didn't get that far.'

'Was it a car accident?' asked Meg.

'No, it was an accident at work. It happened on the first day of his new job. The foreman on the job took him on in a hurry and sent him up onto the high building they were working on. He told him to call to the office at lunch break and fill out any paperwork which needed to be done. It was going to be very busy for a few weeks, and your father wanted to work long hours, to earn more money to return for Christmas. That is where the mistake was. He had no identification on him. He was new to the area, and no one knew where he came from.'

'What happened to Dad?' sobbed Packy.

'He wasn't an hour on the job, four stories up, when the accident happened. I'm not sure what happened, but the story is, he saved another man's life, a young man. He was the son of one of the contractors on the job. The young man slipped while reaching for something, and a plank on the scaffolding snapped. Your father grabbed the young man and hauled him to safety. A piece of the plank fell away as the lad was hauled to safety and your father tripped. He fell four stories onto the site below. Luckily for him, there was some sort of tarpaulin covering timber near the ground and he fell through it. It broke his fall. That's why he is alive today.'

'How badly injured is he?' I asked.

'He has a broken leg, a broken wrist, and head injuries. He was in a coma for nearly four weeks. When he became conscious again, he was confused for a while and didn't know who or where he was. That's why no one heard from him. He had no identification on him. He had left his suitcase in a locker at the station to collect on his way from work. That's why nobody knew who he was, and no one came looking for him.' He looked up and pointing at me said, 'Then you came looking for him. We couldn't verify his identity till he spoke to us. That was yesterday. Now the hospital in Glasgow has contacted the guards. Sergeant Greene in the village knows the whole story now. He wanted to know Mrs Cregan, why you contacted the Salvation Army, sending your daughter to Dublin to do so, and you didn't tell the guards in the village.'

'What did you tell him?' asked Meg.

'I told him it was none of his business. Mr Cregan had been found and the family needed to come to terms with the situation.'

'You're a very kind man,' said Meg, she was now in her dramatic tearful mode, to show that she was so upset about what happened to Dad, 'Thank you most sincerely for your time and your efforts.'

'I'm sorry the news isn't better,' he said apologetically. 'He has a long road ahead to recovery and you must take great care of him.'

'Will Dad get better?' asked Packy with a sob.

'He will get better, and the doctor will be contacting you when he will be coming home to your local hospital. Right now he's not well enough to make the journey.'

'When will that be?' asked Tom.

'It won't be until the new year,' he said.

'That means Dad won't be home for Christmas,' Packy cried in grief, clinging to Meg, and sobbing his heart out.

'Listen, young man,' said Mr Thomas, placing his hand on Packy's shoulder, 'the greatest Christmas gift you will get this year, is that your father is alive. He is going to get better, and he will be back in the heart of his family. Nineteen sixty-three will be a great year. I feel it in my bones.'

Little did he know the dilemma we were in. One of our greatest gifts was gone forever, and we were trying to deal with that. As happened before, I was dreading the thoughts of Christmas, and I would have preferred to bury my head in the sand and not to emerge until March when the days began to get longer again.

'I'm sorry, Mrs Cregan, Sarah, and these three fine young men here. I regret, the news isn't better,' he said again.

'Our greatest gift this Christmas is Dad's alive, and that's all that matters,' I said.

'I must take leave of you now and proceed on my journey. I will keep in touch with you. You can write to me Sarah and tell me how your father is progressing.'

'I will do that,' I replied.

'I hope you all have a happy Christmas and we'll keep you in our hearts during the season. Good day to you all.' He placed his hat on his head and left.

I went with him to the gate and waved him on. When I went back into the house, the boys were all tearful and weeping. Meg was trying to console them. I decided I had enough and scolded them.

'Look here, we've had enough crying, and tears in this house for the past few weeks. Let's stop this now. Mam and Dad wouldn't tolerate it one bit.'

'They're entitled to be sad,' Meg intervened. 'It will do them good and help them to cope with all of this.' I didn't know what she meant, but in later years in my studies, I knew that by letting all this grief out, helped in the healing process during loss or bereavement. My brave face didn't show for very long, and I too joined them. Why were all these terrible things happening to our family? Why did we deserve it? Was it because I was angry with God, with life, with everything? Would something good ever happen to us again? I had forgotten what Mr Thomas had said, Dad was coming back to us, but we'd have to be patient.

When I settled down to sleep that night, I dreamed of a hayfield in July. Dad was tossing forkfuls of hay onto a cock, topping it and getting it ready for taking home. He was chewing a piece of hay straw. He leaned on his pitchfork. The sleeves of his shirt were rolled up. His trousers were supported by some braces across his shoulders, and a leather belt around his waist. He shoved his hat back on his head and wiped the sweat from his brow. He made his usual sigh of 'Aye!' It could mean anything. He could be happy, or he could be sad. He often said it when he was readying his pipe for a smoke. But in the hayfield, he was happy. He smiled at me through a three-day growth of beard on his face. When would I see that smile again? I knew it would happen. Leaving that thought as a happy one, I turned around on my side, gathering the heavy bedclothes about me to keep away the piercing December cold, and I fell fast asleep.

Chapter 23

Merry Christmas Sergeant Greene

There was little time to mull over what had happened, as Sergeant Greene stopped outside the gate in the squad car. Meg was ready to meet him in her pose as Mam and we knew why he was calling to see us. He knocked on the door, and Joe answered it.

'Good morning young man is it alright if I come in?'

'Come on ahead,' said Joe.

He was a tall man and he had to bow his head forward in case he bumped it on the door lintel. He stood on the floor holding a notebook, and pencil and I said,

'Sit down Sergeant, it's a cold day. Would you like a cup of tea?'

'No thank you, how's your Mam?'

'She will be out in a few minutes, she was just lying down.' Meg had just left the kitchen, pretending to be a little under the weather to emerge when she was ready in her usual dramatic pose.

'I see,' he said, as he sat down by the fire. 'Are you all ready for Christmas?' The boys nodded yes to him, being a little shy of his size, as well as his official presence in his uniform.

I broke the ice by saying, 'I know why you're here, Sergeant.'

'You do? I know, but I'll wait till you're Mam comes down.'

He sat there quietly, with his cap on his knee, twiddling his thumbs, and sighing. Then Meg appeared in dramatic pose.

'Sorry for keeping you waiting, Sergeant.' Her voice was still a little hoarse. She walked slowly, and she really looked unwell.

'Let me help you,' he said.

'I'm fine, Sergeant. I'll just sit here across from you by the fire.'

'I believe you know about John already.'

'We do, Mr Thomas called earlier.'

'I'll come back to that later,' he said.

'Go ahead so, Sergeant, say what you have to say.'

'John is in hospital. He's going to be fine, but he's not fit to be moved back home until well into the new year. He can talk a little, and they told me on the phone from the hospital earlier that he keeps asking for you all. He wishes you all a very happy Christmas, and he thinks about you all the time.'

'What really happened to him, Sergeant?' asked Meg.

'He seemed to have heard of better work on a building project in Glasgow. It was an office building and it needed to be finished in a hurry. He fell on his first day before he could even register with the building office. He has head injuries, as well as a broken leg and wrist. He was unconscious for a long time due to head injuries. He was lucky he didn't injure his spinal cord.'

'He'll walk again, won't he, Sergeant?' I said with a sob.

'It will take many months when he comes home. He's a strong man.'

'He's in God's hands,' said Meg.

'You are very composed about the whole thing,' said the sergeant.

'As I said, Sergeant, he's in God's hands.'

'Are you all ok for Christmas and the new year? Have you enough money, food…'

'We are fine,' said Meg, 'We can manage, and I have plenty of help.'

'That's good. That's good.'

Then he opened his notebook. He seemed to have something written in it and he hesitated before he spoke again. 'I just have one or two things to ask,' he said.

'Go on so?' answered Meg.

'Why did you not come to us at the start? Why ask the Salvation Army in Dublin for help?'

There was a silence in the kitchen. You could cut the air with a knife. No one knew what to say. The silence was deafening, but the tension was broken when a stick burning in the range gave a crackle, and sparks flew out on the floor, dying on the dark cement. He looked from one to the other and waited for a response. For once Meg was lost for words, but as usual in our recent predicament, Packy stepped forward and tugged his sleeve.

'It was Sarah,' he said. 'Mam was very sick and there was no one to go to.'

'She was very sick,' I said. 'I went on the bus to Dublin.'

'You should have come to us,' he repeated.

'Then what would you do, Sergeant?' said Meg, raising her voice. I was afraid she might begin her Mad Mary pose, but she was just expressing her feelings on the matter. She pointed her finger at him saying, 'You'd come and take my children away. They're all I've got.'

'There are people out there who can help.'

'Into a home, or an orphanage never to see them again. Who would care for them, and love them as I do?'

'I know you are having problems with your health now, and I know there are times when you might not be able to cope mentally–'

She stopped him in his tracks and stood up, breathing heavily and shaking her finger at him. I was still afraid she was going to overdo things again.

'Sergeant, I know what happened to the Larkins. You told them they were going to have a day away at the seaside. You took them outside the village to two cars waiting to take them away, to separate them. The little girls brought off to a nun's orphanage and the boy to a place for boys in Dublin. I have heard stories about those places. No one in the whole village around here knows where they are.'

'They are being well looked after, Mrs Cregan.'

'Can you truthfully say that, Sergeant?'

'To the best of my knowledge, they are fine.'

'In other words, you don't know then. You have done your duty, and the rest of us can forget about them.'

'I just asked the question about your welfare, as I am concerned that you are not going hungry or want for anything. If things get too much, I do want to help.'

'Well Sergeant, no one will take my children away. It will be over my dead body.' As she stood there she pretended to have a weakness or a turn, and she flopped back down on the chair.

'I only have the children's best interests at heart,' he said.

'That may be so,' whispered Meg through her gasps. I was tending to her and pulling a cushion up behind her.

'You see the care I'm getting. This is the best nurse anyone could ever have. She is so good to her brothers, and she cooks and cleans for them and for me.'

'If it gets too much for you, girl—'

I interrupted him in mid-sentence. 'I can manage fine, Sergeant!'

'What age are you?'

'I will be sixteen in February.'

'You know where I stand now on the matter,' said Meg. 'We can manage till John gets back. Any heavy work needing to be done, Pat Reardon steps in.'

'A young lady like you needs to get out and meet other young people.'

'She's going to the dance on St Stephen's night,' said Tom.

'And she has a boyfriend,' giggled Packy.

'That's enough now,' scolded Meg. My face went scarlet. I was speechless.

'Will you keep in touch, Sergeant?' she asked.

'I will do that. All I can do is wish you all a happy Christmas.'

As he made to go, Meg called him back. 'Sergeant! No one will take my children away.'

He placed his cap on his head and said again, 'Happy Christmas everyone!'

Chapter 24

Eileen

Eileen arrived on Christmas Eve. Darcy brought her in the car. The gate was opened wide, and he drove close to the door. It was as if the queen of England was coming to visit. Meg stood at the door to block him from entering the house. She didn't want him to find that Mam was not there. He might smell a rat and ask too many questions. She was not dressed up as Mam, as she didn't want Eileen to see her in that pose either. She warned us to call her Meg all the time in Eileen's presence. Our story was that Mam was away in the mental hospital for a few weeks, and that she was caring for them till Dad had recovered from his accident.

I felt a shiver go down my spine when Darcy stepped out of the car. He began to speak in his dramatic Shakespearean mode, which made me shake, and frightened me a little. I was thinking back to the night he knocked on my door in Dublin, looking to come into my room. I was afraid of him. I really was. Meg knew that too, having warned me that he lusted after young girls all the time.

He raised his voice as he spoke, 'What's in a name? That which we call a rose, by any other name would smell so sweet?' He took my hand and kissed it. I tried to draw it away, but he held onto it tight.

'Please, Darcy, stop!' I said in a low voice.

Meg was helping Eileen from the car. She needed some assistance walking to keep her balance. and she used a walking stick. Eileen turned to Darcy as he was speaking and began to shout at him in a loud voice, 'Shut up Darcy! She's not yours.'

'It's alright, Eileen. Don't mind him. Sarah can mind herself,' consoled Meg.

He ignored Eileen's shouts and I still tried to free my hand he continued without taking any notice of anyone. 'But soft! What light through yonder window breaks? It is the east and Juliet is the sun.' The words I recognised were from Romeo and Juliet. I then yanked my hand from his grasp and ran to the door.

'Parting is such sweet sorrow,' he said and doffed his hat again.

'Time for you to go, Darcy,' said Meg. 'Why don't you grow out of your fantasy world too? Eileen is home now, and she will need a lot more care.'

'I know when I'm not wanted,' he grumbled.

'Well you have done your duty for now,' said Meg.

'Happy Christmas, brother,' said Eileen with a hint of sarcasm.

'See you the day after St Stephen's Day, Darcy,' said Meg. 'Happy Christmas!' He reversed the car out onto the road. Blue exhaust fumes permeated the cold frosty air, as he drove across the hill to the main road.

We stood like statues as she approached dragging her left leg.

'This is Packy,' said Meg, 'then Joe and Tom.' She shook hands with each one of them, and when she came to me, she took my hand, and whispered in my ear, 'Watch that Darcy, pet. Just watch it. He's dangerous when it comes to beautiful young girls. I could write a book about him.'

Meg sat her down by the fire and left her case in the bedroom.

She was tired from the journey and a hot cup of tea settled her shakes and her nerves.

'Where is Mary Cregan?' she asked.

'You don't know do you, Eileen?' asked Meg.

'Know what?' she demanded in her usual abrupt voice.

'She's in the mental hospital for a few weeks.' She said little else, except that she'll be home sometime in the new year.

'Poor woman, she must be in a bad state.'

'It's her nerves,' said Meg. 'She'll be fine.'

She then told Eileen, that Mam had a nervous breakdown when she heard of Dad's accident, and that she had volunteered to stay there for a while till she was well enough to come home.

Eileen was content with this story. When she had warmed up again, she went for a lie down to rest after her journey. She was quite frail too, and it was obvious that she needed to be cared for as well.

This was the story we were going to stick to until after Christmas, and Meg was going to be Meg during that period, except if there was an emergency, and someone arrived out of the blue. We'd bridge that gap when we came to it. That evening Meg told Eileen, that we were to pretend that Mam was at home, as she didn't want anyone to know she was away in hospital with her nerves. We hoped the sergeant wouldn't decide suddenly to come and take the children away. How long more could we live all these lies? It seemed as if the whole world was closing in on us, and there was going to be nowhere to run. At least I'd try and enjoy Christmas first.

Chapter 25

Christmas 1962

Joe and Tom went to midnight mass, and I waited until they returned, before I went to bed myself. The ham was boiled, and the goose was ready for roasting the next morning. It was a gift from the Walsh family, and the ham was delivered with the Christmas groceries ordered from the shop in the village. I had the order in, from the week before, and I paid for it from the money Dad had left in the teapot. There was still enough there to carry us into the new year, but I was afraid it would begin to run short once we reached the middle of January.

I sneaked outside into the cold frost to have a few moments to myself, while Meg was settling Eileen down for the night. I went to my usual haunt, the cutaway on the large cock of hay. There was a sharp easterly breeze, and a crunching cold frost in the air. The barrels of water were thick with ice, and I knew Joe would have to break it in the morning with a sledgehammer.

I pulled back some of the frost-covered hay, till I found some nice dry stuff, and I gathered bundles of it around me to keep the cold chill away. I was shoulder deep in the sweet smelling dry grass, and it had a hint of summer still in its pleasing odour. Sputnik jumped up beside me and poked his head under my arm.

The starry sky was spectacular. They illuminated the approaching Christmas morning in their millions, as if they were there for the first time to welcome the Christ Child. If it were any other Christmas but this one, I would have been over-awed with excitement for the approaching festivities. I thought of Dad all alone in that hospital in Glasgow, lonely and deserted, unable to reach us. I knew deep down that his thoughts were with us, and that he'd be home before too long. Then I thought of Mam, hidden away in the old deserted mausoleum. I began to pray on this night directing them upwards into the heavens to her. Then I thought to myself, who was going to listen to them, after all I had done? The guilt rolled through my body in a great shiver, and I was hoping it might just be a dream. But I still had my brothers, and it was my duty to keep them with me. The tears flowed freely again, and I sobbed quietly into the cold dark night.

I felt that Sergeant Greene knew that something was not right in our house. In his right mind, he'd wonder why I would enlist the help of the Salvation Army to find Dad, and not to go to the guards. It indicated that we had something to hide, and he was not able to get under what it was all about. If only I could hold the situation as it was, until Dad was better, then he'd know what to do. I felt like staying the night outside in the frost, and maybe they'd find me in the morning, gone to my mother in heaven, just like the little match girl in the Hans Christian Andersen tale.

Then I saw a light moving on the shed, where Tossie the donkey, the cow, and calf were safe for the night. Was it the star coming to rest on the stable of the little infant of Bethlehem? Then a voice called quietly to me. It was Meg, carrying the storm lantern, Dad used for going out into the dark fields at night. She looked up at me, perched on the hay with the dog at my side.

'Will you come in out of that child, or you will get your death of cold? What are you doing out here, and what were you thinking about on such a cold night? You gave me such a fright! I thought you had run off or something.' I jumped down and brushed the hay straws off my coat. Sputnik stayed where he was, finding warmth in the nest made in the hay. She shone the lantern into my face, and she saw the cold tears streaming downwards.

'Come here!' she said. She left the lantern down on the ground and wrapped her arms around me.

'I'm so lonely!' I sobbed. 'I'm so confused, Mam hidden away in that old mausoleum, and Dad alone in that hospital so far away. What will happen to us?'

'As I have said before, let us take it one step at a time,' she said, consoling my loneliness. 'Let's enjoy Christmas, that's what we'll do. On St Stephen's Day, we will do the same. As each day goes by, the nearer it will get to the time your Dad will come home. I'm not a very religious person, but when I was young, my grandmother told me to visit the crib on Christmas morning, and leave a penny for the infant Jesus. Say a little prayer there, if you have any worries, and they will all go away. I cannot remember if it ever worked but I do it anyway.'

'If it were that easy,' I said, 'there would never be anything to worry about.'

'Let's leave it behind and when the boys come home, off to bed with you. What about a hot cup of cocoa, before bed, it will warm you up?'

'I'm fasting Meg, I'm going to the altar in the morning.'

'You are so like your mother!'

I gave a little giggle when she said this.

'And that's not a bad thing either, she was a great person and a great mother.' She hugged me again and led me slowly back into the house.

I went to eight o'clock mass that Christmas. Everyone else lay on in bed. Mam would have made the boys go to mass for the second time. She'd declare it was good for their souls. But being out so late, on such a cold night, I left them in bed. Packy was up early to see what Santa had brought him, and he took his little parcel down to the bed with him.

I put on my coat, hat, and gloves, and fastened a flash lamp on the bike. I could feel the ice break on the potholes as I cycled through the darkness. There was a sharp east wind biting into my face, and the first rays of light lit up the sky towards Dublin. On the main road, cars drove carefully by, and I passed others on the road walking to mass as I approached the village. The few street lights were still lit, and the visible white frost on the walls and railings, gave the world a festive Christmas look. I stood the bike against the high wall, where in the not so distant past, horse traffic lined the street where the animals were tethered to the railings, jutting out from the wall.

Inside, the church was bedecked with candlelight, as well as electric lights. The outside of the crib was lit by a little red star. Inside a gentle light lit up the figures. It was a lantern with an electric light inside, but it looked as if it was a candle or a flame. The light drew visitors to the side of the altar, where the crib rested in the peace of the building. The figures stood like a snapshot in time, with heads bowed in supplication to the little babe lying in the manger. I knelt at the altar rails, offered that little prayer of hope which Meg had spoken about a few hours previously.

That prayer should help relieve our worries and help disperse any sadness on this blessed day. Then I had doubts once more. What was I doing here? I was responsible for this terrible thing I had done, drawing my brothers, and Meg into the whole plot. I was a sinner, and not alone that I was fasting to receive Holy Communion. When I finished my prayers, I blessed myself, and I whispered, 'Forgive me baby Jesus, forgive me.' I placed a little shiny sixpence with its little image of a greyhound, in the little donations pot on the altar rails, blessed myself once more, and went to my seat on the women's side of the church. I prayed hard all during mass and had great fears of hell and damnation. God would send me to hell and set me on fire if I went to communion. When the time came, and Fr Doyle placed the host on my tongue, nothing happened. I walked in peace back to my seat, with my hands joined, and I felt a great sense of relief. I said another prayer of thanksgiving before mass ended, and I left the church feeling happier and lighter in spirit. The sun had risen to a white frosted landscape. I got a tap on the shoulder, and Pat said without impediment, 'Have a happy Christmas.'

'I'll see you later,' I said.

'No Sarah, you have a full house. I'm going to my cousin in the town for a few days. Father Doyle is leaving me there when all the masses are over. He is having his dinner with his sister who lives there also.' I waved him on, and hurried home to celebrate Christmas.

My little prayer must have been answered. When I got home from mass, Meg was up, and the goose was in the oven. Packy was cheerful and laughing, as he played with the little toy cars Santa brought. I was happy to see him smile. Tom and Joe did the outside chores. There was plenty of fresh milk. The calf was roaring from her little corner of the shed telling everyone she was hungry. Tossie and the cow ignored her wailing, as they were too interested in the fresh hay they had been given. They didn't mind that it had been used as a barrier against the cold in the darkness of early Christmas morning. When the boys had finished the milking, they undid the chain holding the cow in the manger. When she was happy with all the hay she had munched, she ambled quietly through the crisp white frost into the field. She was now totally oblivious to the little calf she gave birth to a short while ago. She was more concerned with eating, than getting on with her bovine life. Tossie followed her, and their hooves left dark prints on the frosty ground.

When Eileen was awakened by the noise and talking in the kitchen, she decided to join us. It was a while before she emerged from the room as she was slow in getting dressed, and it was something she did not want any help with. She was determined in being as independent as possible, now that she had left the home where she was cared for. When she sat by the fire, she requested a cup of tea with some brown bread and butter. It was difficult at times to understand what she was saying, as her voice was slow and slurred. She spoke in a nasal tone, and thus her clarity of words was often lost in conversation. But after a day with us, I was beginning to understand her clearly, as it was up to me to listen more closely when she spoke.

'I didn't have home-made brown bread for a long time,' she said. She watched quietly, as the boys read comics and played with the toy cars.

'Christmas is a time for children,' she said. No one answered, but Meg nodded in agreement as she said so. 'Are you going to visit Mary?' she asked Meg.

'We are not allowed,' said Meg a little abruptly, 'not until her mind is a bit better. Now let's get on with it and enjoy the day.'

The house was very busy for the rest of the morning, and the smells of cooking wafted out into the cold air outside. At two o'clock we sat down to eat. I didn't feel like eating, but when I caught Meg's eye, I decided it was better to do so, and I felt a lot better having eaten a good substantial meal. When all was cleared and cleaned up, there was an element of anti-climax, and no one knew what was going to happen next. Then Eileen captured the moment and said,

'Let's play cards!'

'Poker!' shouted Packy.

'Poker?' she laughed, 'Can you play poker?'

'I can't, but I can learn.'

'Stay away from poker, together with drink, it's the ruination of Darcy. He's probably clowning around Dublin now, with that gang he hangs around with.'

'Aye, let's get on with Christmas!' said Meg.

'What will we play then?' asked Tom.

'Beggar my neighbour.'

'I know that one,' said Joe.

So, the game began, and after four or five games, they switched to Old Maid, and it too ran its course and interest wore thin. Then Eileen suggested another one.

'Kitty come tickle me,' she said.

'What?' the boys exclaimed in unison.

'How do you play that?' asked Tom.

'Deal out the cards there and don't let anyone see your hand.' We took our cards and opened them out in a fan with the numbers facing inwards to ourselves.

'Now you follow the rhyme. I'll start! I have an ace, and I place it face up on the table, and as I do so I say, there's an ace as you can see. Follow in turn around the table, the next person says, there's one as good as thee. Next! There's one the best of three, and the last one says, there's kitty come tickle me. The next person in line chooses any number say five, and says,

There's a five as you can see, There's one as good as thee, There's one the best of three, and there's kitty come tickle me. The game continues until we reach the last card. The last kitty come tickle me card placed on the table means only one thing.'

'What's that?' asked Joe.

'You're the winner!'

'That's easy,' said Packy.

'Ah, but there is a snag,' said Eileen.

'What do you mean?' asked Tom.

'The winner has also to be tickled!'

They all laughed in unison at this, and shouted, 'Come on!'

The game followed the rhyme around the table. As the hands of the cards got smaller, the giggles and anticipation were building, and the last card down on the table was Meg. The boys pounced to tickle her, and she ran down into the room.

'Come on out, Meg, and face the music!' shouted Tom.

'I will on one condition. No tickles, next game please.'

'Alright!' But she knew it was a lame promise. When she emerged from the room, they were ready to pounce. She had smeared her lips with lipstick, and shouted at them, as she edged them away, 'Anyone who comes near me will get a big goozer of a kiss on the face.' The boys ran back to their chairs, and the game commenced again. Next time around, I had the last card and they pounced on me. I screamed with laughter to avoid being tickled. I grabbed Packy and gave him a kiss.

'Yuck!' he said, wiping his face. Eventually, the fun ran out of that game too, and they decided on something else.

'I have a story for you,' said Eileen, 'now listen carefully.'

'I don't want a story,' grumbled Joe, 'I'm not a sissy!'

'It is about the four kings in the deck of cards. Put the four kings out on the table. This is a story for geniuses, not sissies,' said Eileen.

Joe went through the deck of cards, and finding each one, placed them facing upwards, side by side on the table in front of him. Silence fell on the kitchen, as we knew we'd have to listen carefully to Eileen's speech. She spoke slowly, and softly. We were getting used to her nasal tones, as she strived to get her message across to us. The only sounds we could hear was the crackle of sticks in the fire, and the singing of the kettle on the edge of the range, as it approached boiling point. But we listened intently to her story.

'Once upon a time, there were four noble kings. Each had a beautiful kingdom, and each one was married to a beautiful queen. Each year the four kingdoms gathered together, hearts, diamonds, clubs, and spades. Each king had

a son called a knave, and each knave had an entertainer called a joker. The number one knight, in each kingdom was the ace, and they ruled over lesser knights ranging from two to ten. Number ten was probably the peasant or vassal.

Each king gathered at the foot of the great mountain, where the four kingdoms met. It was here, they had their games, jousting, running, archery, skittles, blind man's bluff, chase the fox, and there were awards of gold medals, and gilded swords for the winners. At night, they feasted on wild boar, roasted on a spit, with onions, gravy, leeks, and herbs. They drank red wine and a sweet drink called mead, made from honey. There was harp music and singing as well as dancing and theatre plays. The four kings and their company went home each year, refreshed and renewed from the fun and feasting at the foot of the mountain.

But one year, as the king of hearts and his followers returned home, he found his castle blockaded and taken over by the evil black knight from the dark kingdom across the mountains.

'You can flee from this kingdom or face death!' roared the black knight.

The king of hearts and his entourage had to run for their lives, back the roads they had travelled. They didn't stop until they reached the meeting place at the foot of the mountain. From here, he sent his scouts to call his three comrades back.

After three days, the four kings met in a council of war, and they decided to do battle with the black knight, to drive him back to his kingdom across the mountains.

They met a few weeks later on top of a high hill, overlooking Hearts Castle. The battle raged for three days and three nights. The upshot of it all was, that the black knight and his army were driven back across the mountains forever. The four kings and their armies returned home. But the king of hearts was very sad. He turned to his queen and said, 'one of my three friends were injured in battle, and he must live with his injury for the rest of his life.'

Eileen spoke slowly and dragged the story out, holding the boys' attention through it all, and with the words 'for the rest of his life,' she stopped talking, and there was silence at the table.

'Go on, what happened next?' asked Tom.

'That's it,' she said, 'that's the end of the story.'

'That's no story,' said Packy, rather disappointed. 'Did they live happily ever after?'

'Maybe! You tell me now.'

'Oh, I get it now,' said Joe, 'one of them didn't, the injured one.'

'Clever boy!' said Eileen.

'Which one was it?' asked Tom.

'I want you, to tell me that!'

'Well, it's not the king of hearts,' said Joe, 'he was the sad one.' He pushed the card to one side, leaving the other three facing upwards.

'It was that one,' said Packy, pointing to the king of spades.

'Why is it him?' asked Eileen.

'He has two heads!' joked Packy. The boys broke out into peals of laughter again.

'That's not the answer,' said Eileen, and she wasn't giving the game away.

'Well now, let me see,' said Tom. He pointed at the king of diamonds.

'That's him!' he exclaimed.

'That is correct,' said Eileen, 'but what is wrong with him?'

'I don't know!' they answered in unison.

'How is he different to the others?' she asked.

'Why has he his head turned the other way?' asked Joe.

'He has his head turned the other way, because he lost his eye in the battle, and he has his good eye turned to you.'

'Oh right!' said Joe, 'and you told that great long story just to tell us that he had one eye.'

'That has been her life,' said Meg, 'Eileen *was*, and still is a great actress. See how she has captured an audience of young rascals like you for so long.'

'Have you any more tricks?' asked Packy.

Eileen had more stories and tricks. and it wasn't long till the darkening day called the boys to tend to the animals, milk the cow, and settle them down for the night. After tea, we listened to the wireless for a while. The boys packed off to bed after eight o'clock, and when Eileen retired for the night, the house was left to Meg and me.

'I was glad to see you laughing today,' she said.

'Thank you, Meg,' I answered. 'You are an angel, where would we be but for you?'

'If only I knew, that child, if only I knew.'

Chapter 26

'*The Wren! The Wren!*'

Eileen brought new light into our lives that Christmas, and she too, seemed to be enjoying herself. Her disabilities were overshadowed by her humour and her wit. If one had the power to tell the future, we would have savoured those few days even more, as we were not aware of the dreadful things that lay ahead. But our darkened life had now been overtaken with a short respite of sheer joy, and unimaginable fun, brought to us as a gift for Christmas. The boys were drawn to her, constantly asking for more. She had competitions with them, on the morning of St Stephen's Day, making Mobius strips, with the instruction that the two pieces of paper must come apart, and not end up as one full circular strip. There were then gales of laughter, when her predictions came true. She gave out four strips, saying that the girls were the only people who could separate them. She handed me mine first, and then one to each of the three boys. We began cutting the ring of paper in two. Each end was joined with some gum or glue that Meg had in her bag. As it happened, mine came apart, and the boys, each one, in turn, ended up with their two pieces of paper linked to each other like a chain. In later years, I discovered the secret, when joining the two pieces together, give one end a twist before gluing them together and the chain effect happened, otherwise they separated at the end of the cutting process. The boys thought there was some sort of magic to this and wanted to try again. Meg had anticipated that they'd want to do so, and we were each handed out another ring of paper to cut with the scissors, and the result was the same. I got the inevitable wink from Meg as it began, and I knew the outcome was going to be the same. There was more loud laughter, as the game came to an end. Eileen stated that boys could not cut a Mobius strip in two. Joe knew there was some trick in the process, and he couldn't fathom out what it was.

Next, she handed Tom a long piece of string, telling him to take the ends in each hand and to tie a knot, without letting the two ends go.

'I can't do it,' said Tom.

'Give it to me,' she said. 'Now fold both your arms.' When he did this, she placed the two ends of the string in each of his hands.

'Now open out your arms and don't let the string go.'

When he did this, the string tied into a simple knot.

'Cor!' exclaimed Packy, 'it's magic!'

'Magic is what you make of it yourself, lad,' said Eileen. 'Now I'll show you a trick with a deck of cards, and you can try this out with your friends.'

'Go ahead,' said Joe.

'Select twenty-one cards from the pack, it doesn't matter what ones they are. Now, deal them out in three heaps, with the numbers facing upwards. As they are being dealt out, Joe, choose one card and remember it.'

When this was done, she said, 'Now, tell me which heap it is in.' Joe pointed to the pile.

'Place that heap in between the other two and deal them out again. Remember your card, and which heap it is in.' This pile was placed in between the other two again, and the same thing happened for the third time.

'Now turn the cards around, and keep turning them up, until I tell you to stop.'

Joe began dealing out the cards. and when he was about halfway through she said, 'Stop! It's this one, the king of diamonds.'

'It is!' exclaimed Joe.

'When you play this trick and do it right, it is always the eleventh card. You count each card coming out and stop on number eleven.'

'Janey Mac, that's a great trick,' said Tom. 'Can I try it?'

'Go ahead!' she said. So, began a session of trying the trick out. Sometimes it worked, and sometimes it didn't. An incorrect pile was chosen, or it wasn't placed in the middle of the other two piles, and as well as that not counting correctly to eleven, might have been the problem as well. But the trick itself, provided great joy and interest with the boys all morning.

There were more card tricks, and funny stories as well as tales of times on the road with the theatre company. The morning passed happily and quickly, until it was time for dinner, bringing the Christmas to a close by finishing the last of the goose.

Later that afternoon, Sputnik barked and there was the sound of music from outside. The Wren Boys had arrived. I opened the door to see nine or ten young fellows, ranging in age from about twelve to twenty years standing outside. It was difficult to discern their ages, as they were kitted out in the most outlandish costumes, outfits, or call them what you like. Some had their faces covered in black soot, or ashes as well as lipstick and other paints. They wore hats, some of them festooned with pheasant's feathers and streamers. One boy played a bodhran. There was also a fiddle, and an accordion. Meg decided to disappear to the room, as she couldn't take on mother's role, as she was taken by surprise and it would take too long to get ready.

The musicians struck up with the waltz, *When Irish Eyes Are Smiling*. Eileen stood up and supporting herself using the table, the wall and the door, she stood in the doorway, looking out at the spectacle in front of her. A young man took her by the hand and supporting her down the step onto the icy yard, began to waltz gently with her. Seeing how her body laboured to do so, the young man slowed his pace down to match her ability, and everyone else joined in the singing.

When the music stopped, the young man whom I thought looked familiar winked at me, and called on someone to sing, but the leader of the group, Billy, stepped around as if he was king of all he surveyed. From what I remember of him, he was the son of one of Dad's friends. He carried a stick, like a fishing rod with a string at the top. At the end of the string was what looked like a little bird.

'You killed a little wren!' I shouted. 'How could you?'

'Ah no! my fair young woman,' he said. 'It's made from feathers. How could you catch a wren at this time of the year? So, I had to make one.'

'Thank God!' I said. 'That would be so cruel.'

'Anyway, now let's start!' he shouted, 'Where's the lady of the house?'

'She's not here,' said Eileen.

'Well you'll have to do so,' he chanted. Standing erect and proud in front of Eileen, he began his verse,

Danny Dunne

'The Wren! The Wren!
The king of all birds,
On Stephen's day,
Was caught in the furze,
Although he was little,
His family was great,
Rise up good lady,
And give us a trate,
Up with the kittle
And down with the pan,
Give us a penny
To bury the wran.'

Then the young man who spoke first said, 'Now Johnny, give us a song!'

It was the voice I recognised then, through a face of lipstick and charcoal.

'Seán Walsh, you rogue!' I exclaimed. He turned to me and said, 'Careful now young lady, or you might get a kiss.' He made to run after me, but I ran for the security of the house.

'Come on Johnny! A song,' he chanted.

The boy who stepped forward was around twelve years old, and the air was pinched with a great silence, when his beautiful soprano voice pierced, and melted the cold frosty afternoon,

'Far away a sprig of ivy
Clings around yon cabin door,
Far away a robin redbreast,
Sings a grand old song of yore.

Far away a light is burning,
In yon window fair and bright,
Far away, but not forgotten,
Someone thinks of you tonight.

The Spindle Tree

It may be the golden summer,
It may be the winter night,
Springtime, summer, autumn, winter,
Someone thinks of you tonight.

Write a letter unto mother,
Send your love to dear old Dad,
Tell him that you're feeling happy,
Though you may be really sad.

Never tell this world your troubles,
Smiles are better far than tears,
Tell him that you're going home soon,
Though it may not be for years.

It may be the golden summer,
It may be the winter night,
Springtime, summer, autumn, winter,
Someone thinks of you tonight.'

In the final two verses of the song, Eileen joined in. Even though her words sounded with a nasal and broken tone, her voice was sweet, and it was obvious that in her past, she could hold an audience, acting or singing. When he had finished his song, a big cheer lifted through the air, as voices clapped and cheered. Eileen put her arm around the young lad and kissed him on top of the head.

'You have a lovely voice, young man,' she said. 'You should be on the stage someday.'

Through it all, Meg was listening inside in the bedroom, and she took an odd peep through the lace curtain to view some of the show. This was to be her downfall in the next few minutes. She was extremely taken with the young boy singing his song. When Eileen had finished speaking to the young lad, Billy shouted in a good strong voice, 'You tell me Mrs Cregan's not at home. God dare ye say so, I just saw her there at the window. I can't leave without wishing the woman of the house a very Happy New Year.'

203

He made to run past me to get to the bedroom, and I shouted, 'You can't go in there, she's not well!' This didn't stop him, he pushed past me straight for the bedroom door.

'She's Mad Mary, isn't she? I want to see if she's mad or not.'

Again, it all happened in an instant. Meg started to scream, and she was covered up in the blankets, just the same as the day Fr Doyle was punched in the face.

'Come on Mrs!' shouted Billy. 'It's Christmas and a Happy New Year as well.'

'Go away!' roared Meg.

'I said Happy New Year, Mrs Cregan.'

Then Billy didn't know what happened to him. Meg had Eileen's walking stick with her in the bed. Still not showing her face, she drew the stick out and lunged it forward like a sword, hitting the young man in the chest, winding him, and he fell against the wall. When he caught his breath, he exclaimed, 'She really is mad, so she is!' He grabbed his stick with the makeshift wren, and bolted out the door.

Silence had fallen over the whole place. The music had stopped.

'Please go!' I shouted, 'I told you Mam is not well.'

'She's as mad as a hatter,' he kept shouting.

This brought the whole Wren Boy gathering to an abrupt halt, and they went quietly out the gate, taking their bikes and instruments with them. They headed back to the main road to continue with their revelry. As Billy went over the hill I could hear him shout to the others, 'That woman has really lost it, so she has.'

My head was in a spin, with all that was going through my brain, as I watched them go. We were going to have another visit from the sergeant before too long. Probably not today, or tomorrow, but when word got around about what had happened today, he'd be duty bound to investigate Mam's mental state. My poor gentle mother, who died from a weak heart, was now the talk of the parish, Mad Mary, as portrayed by Meg Darcy, in her latest human drama. I didn't like the way it was going, and I was afraid that they would come, and bring her off screaming. This would force her to reveal who she was, and we were all in trouble thus. In the short term, Meg was going to have to do some explaining to Eileen. When she eventually emerged out of the room, she had transformed herself into Mary Cregan again. Her hair, and makeup looked so convincing.

Then Eileen pounced on her with an abrupt and to the point question. 'Meg Darcy, tell me now, for the love of God, what's going on around here?' Eileen stared at her, bewildered and confused, knowing that something wasn't right in this house.

'Let me explain everything,' said Meg.

'Well, you'd better start at the beginning,' Eileen demanded.

This time, Meg had a slightly different tale to tell. She had found us before Christmas, alone and without our parents. Mam was in a mental hospital, and Dad was missing in England. To keep the family together, she decided to take on the mother's role and she had managed to fool everyone, including the sergeant. The people of the parish were now calling her Mad Mary, and she had no idea how long she could keep it up.

'What about the medical people, surely the local doctor knows about this.'

'Nobody knows,' said Packy. I turned to him wondering what he was going to say now.

'Go on then, tell me,' she said.

'Mam ordered a hackney car from the town and went herself. She didn't want to tell anyone. When we came from school, she was gone. She sent Sarah to the village to do some shopping. When she was gone, the hackney came and she went away in it. She left a note, saying that Dad would be back in about two days, and we were to mind ourselves. She is still there in the hospital.'

'I see! Did anyone go to see her?'

'Yeah, Sarah did,' said Packy. Now he was putting me in a spot.

'I went before Christmas. She is alright, she should be home in about a week,' I said. If I could get to Packy, I didn't know whether I'd give him a slap on the behind or give him a hug. His words seemed to save the day again.

'If you're my friend, Eileen, you will say nothing to no one. Mary doesn't even know that John is in hospital in Scotland. It might upset her too much. Don't utter a word to anyone do you hear?'

'What about Darcy?' she asked.

'Especially your brother Darcy. If he finds out, heaven only knows what he might do or say.'

'Well, I'll be gone tomorrow morning sometime. He's taking me to Dublin.'

'I'll have to stay until their father returns,' said Meg. 'I cannot leave them like this.'

'You're not helping them by putting on that mad charade,' said Eileen.

'It has worked so far,' said Meg.

'You have heard of the boy who cried wolf. Do it too often, and you'll be found out, and where would the children be then? Someone will come and take them away, that's what will happen.'

'Don't say that,' said Meg. 'I'll manage. I mean, we'll manage, all five of us.'

I was beginning to agree with what Eileen had said, and I was fearful that Meg had taken the whole thing just too far.

'What about next year's show?'

'What about it? It can look after itself, for the moment Darcy can deal with it. He's done it before. I have put on the show of my life for the past while, and I have the finest actors with me.'

'They'll send you to prison, Meg. They will!'

'If they do, we'll go down fighting.'

Chapter 27

Walking Back to Happiness

I didn't want to go to the dance that night, but Meg made me. The Walsh family were going and they were collecting me at half past eight. Meg was determined I was going to have a night out. I had suffered so much over the past few weeks, it was time I had a break. She decided that with her experience in theatre and makeup, I was going to be a princess.

She brought her large bag to the kitchen and demanded that everyone be quiet while the makeup went on. She spent quite a while selecting powders, creams, and lipstick from the bag. She was intent on what she was doing, and she chose with precision the colours she required. She brought Mam's big mirror from the dressing table in the room and placed it in front of me on the table.

She did my hair first. She decided on a plait to begin with but felt that it was too girlish for a young woman like me. She opened a large silver coloured purse and took out two pink slides. She pinned my hair back each side, and said, 'They will go with your pink cardigan.' Then I had to face her, as the makeup work began. Eileen sat by the range resting her good arm on her walking stick. Packy and Tom sat at the other end of the table doing a jigsaw, while Joe, having had enough of the procedure, went down to his room to read some comics.

By half past seven, I was ready and went to my room to get dressed. I wore the dress Meg bought me last summer in Clery's along with my pink cardigan and black shoes. When I returned to the kitchen, there was an awesome sigh from everyone.

'Over with you on the floor there, and do a twirl for me,' said Eileen. I spun around and stood smiling at them all.

'I could marry you,' said Packy.

'Go on charmer,' I laughed. 'Get out of here!'

'It's great to see you smile, pet,' said Meg.

It was almost half past eight when Walsh's car pulled up at the gate. Seán came to the door, and Tom let him in. Meg had put on Mam's pose sitting close to the fire beside Eileen.

He was dressed in a black suit, with shiny black shoes, a white shirt, and a grey tie. He was wearing a pioneer pin on his jacket, and he stood there on the floor, awkward and shy.

'Have a good night tonight, both of you,' said Meg.

'Dance the night away!' exclaimed Eileen.

'No kissing!' laughed Packy. His brothers broke out in peals of laughter. Seán began to blush and I warned the three of them to have manners.

'Shall we go?' asked Seán.

'I'm ready,' said I.

'Now young man, I'm giving you the task of taking care of my daughter. She is precious to me,' said Meg, with an element of sternness in her tone.

'Don't worry, I'll look after her,' he answered. 'Goodnight everyone.'

He took my arm, and we went out into the cold frosty night. There had been tiny traces of snow on the grass from the showers on Christmas day. It was a pitch-dark night, except for the cascade of stars across the vast expanse of sky. Ellen Walsh pulled back the front passenger seat, and we climbed into the back.

'Had you a nice Christmas?' Jim Walsh asked.

'We had a very quiet Christmas,' I answered. I knew the conversation was heading towards the incident earlier in the day.

'How is your Mam tonight?' Ellen continued.

'She's fine tonight. She is up, sitting at the range.'

'I do hope she will be well again soon,' she said.

'She gets frightened if someone approaches her too quickly. It's her nerves. Very little upsets her. Billy shouldn't have done what he did today, and he called her Mad Mary. That really upset her.' If I were Pinocchio, my nose would start to grow in that instant. I could hear the words 'Liar!

Liar!' reeling through my head. But another part of me was showing an element of delight at the fact I was getting away with it all the time. But Ellen Walsh, as ever, being the good neighbour, she was, said, 'If I can do anything to help, come to me. She might need the doctor and we could take her to see him.'

'You are all so kind,' I said. 'I'll keep that in mind.'

'Just being a good neighbour, Alana. That's all.'

Seán quietly took my cold hand and winked at me. I felt like telling him he was cheeky, but I didn't mind one bit.

The village was buzzing around the dancehall. Cars were being parked along the street as well as in the school playground. There was very scant street lighting at the edge of the village, and a few local men with strong torches had volunteered to supervise the parking.

Jim Walsh paid for everyone, and we were given cloakroom tickets when we handed in our coats. One ticket had its duplicate pinned to our coats, and the others we put away to retrieve them when we were leaving. A second cloakroom ticket was given to us to call us for supper later in the night.

The hall was brand new, only opened two years. Fr Doyle still had a debt to pay off, and he held several big dances during the year, to offset that expense. He selected key dates during the year, especially bank holidays, Christmas, Easter, and St Patrick's Day. He chose the best young attractions such as these new showbands, to draw the people in. It was a fine, clean and pristine place, with frilled red curtains, trimmed at the edges with interlacing rope and tassel motifs, along the top and bottom. There were steps each side of the stage with gold painted banisters. There were copper coloured metal scallop shells, built into the wrought iron railings.

I asked Seán what the significance of the shells were, and he too had asked his mother the same question. The shells were the emblem of the apostle St James. The hall was named after the local parish church of St James. It was only years later, when I walked the Camino route from the Pyrenees to Santiago De Compostella, did I understand the relevance of the scallop shell in the life of the Saint.

It wasn't long till the band was introduced, and the music began. It bellowed across the hall through microphones, and amplifiers, and it was the loudest sound I had ever heard. There were drums, brass instruments, guitars, and the lead singer was a man. They were all dressed in blue suits, and red bow ties. They were very dapper in their attire, and these new showbands would become the leading popular music bands during the sixties. With the opening song, Helen Shapiro's song, *Walking back to Happiness*, the dancing began.

'Funny but it's true,
What loneliness can do,
Since I've been away
I've loved you more and more each day
Walking back to happiness,
Woopah! Oh Yeah, Yeah!'

Seán sat beside me, and when I looked out on the dance floor, his parents were dancing as well.

'Come on,' said Seán, 'let's go!'

'No, not yet,' I protested.

'Are you shy?' he laughed.

'I'm not shy. I'm not just…shy!'

'That's it,' he said, and he dragged me out on the floor before I had time to protest.

'Seán Walsh, everyone is looking!'

'Yeah, they're all jealous, because I have the prettiest girl on this night,' he joked.

Together we began dancing, making our own steps and moves. I didn't know what to do, but it wasn't long till I was moving to the beat of the music, guided along by this strong but gentle young man. I soon lost my shyness, and I couldn't get enough of the dancing. After an hour or so, we rested, and he bought me a bottle of red lemonade at the shop.

Before long, it was announced that supper was being served, and having already been given tickets for tea, we were numbers twenty-four and twenty-five. We were called for the second sitting, as people were called in groups of twenty. When we left the hall, and went to the supper room at the back, I thought I was deaf from all the loud music. I was fine, just a little ringing in my ears. We were directed to sit down at the red formica-topped tables, and there was a feast of sandwiches, Christmas cake, slices of plum pudding and home-made buttered scones, served with large cups of hot tea. The women's volunteer group did all the catering with donations of food from houses all over the parish, and being such a festive time, there was no shortage of turkey and ham sandwiches as well as seasonal confectionary to feed the multitudes at the dance.

We had just sat down when a shadow stood over me and a familiar voice said, 'C-can I join you?'

It was Pat Reardon, all spruced up, and clean in his best Sunday grey suit. His shaved face made him look much younger, but wrinkles were beginning to show as he approached middle age.

'Sit down, Pat,' I said, throwing my arms around him.

'Hello S-S-Seán,' he said softly, as he sat opposite us with his back to the newly painted wall.

'You look so well tonight, Pat,' I said with a hint of excitement, a reflection of how I was feeling at that time.

'You kn-n-now that's all for you, Sarah,' he joked.

'You know Seán, Pat and I have an arrangement.'

What's that?' asked Seán.

'Firstly, I will never marry him, and he is happy about that. Secondly, he has promised to watch over me always.'

'T-t-till the day I die,' said Pat.

'Are you her guardian angel then, Pat?' asked Seán.

'Y-you could s-s-say that,' he answered.

'Good, guardian angels need plenty of sandwiches, cake, and tea, do eat up and don't be shy, Pat,' said Seán.

'Thank you, Seán,' he said. He was now at ease and his stammer had gone. 'You are growing up to be a fine young man, you know.'

'Are you trying to flatter me, Pat?'

'No, I'm not. I'm telling the truth.'

'Seán wants to be a doctor,' I said.

'That's great, we need a lot of younger men like you around to care for us when we get old.'

'I have to get my Leaving Cert first,' said Seán.

'You will! I know you will, I would love to see you become a doctor.'

'Why is that?' asked Seán.

'Maybe. Just maybe, when I am old and not able to care for myself, it would be nice to have a young doctor to watch over me.'

'You'd never know,' said Seán. 'No one knows what tomorrow will bring.'

We went back dancing again, and I could see Pat watching us from the darkness of the stage. It was a night to remember and a beautiful night. But there were other nights and nightmares to come. Little did Seán know that his words, 'No one knows what tomorrow will bring?' would resonate through my mind for years to come.

Part 3

Snow

Chapter 28

The Fender

I couldn't sleep when I got home. My head was so full of the music of the night. Seán never left my side, and we were watched from a distance by his parents. He never mentioned anything about what happened that afternoon. He wanted to enjoy the night with me, and he knew I needed the break. He bought me another red lemonade before we went home. I didn't drink it, as I'd have to go outside to the toilets and it was such a cold night. The last dance was called, and my head swam with delight as we moved to the sound of *In the Mood*, and other Glenn Miller Classics. Then the hall went quiet for the national anthem, which brought the revelry to a close. We then waited and queued to collect our coats.

It was bitterly cold, and the frost was heavy on the cars, the street, and the pavement. It looked as if it had snowed.

'There has to be snow behind all this,' said Jim Walsh as he and Seán scraped the frost off the windscreen. Ellen took me into the back seat of the car, to try and find some respite from the cold. Jim went to the boot of the car and soaked a rag with some anti-freeze and rubbed it on the windows. It seemed to do the job. The wipers soon loosened and starting the engine, he kept them going to keep the windscreen from freezing up again.

'Remember Sarah, if you need us anytime, just let us know,' said Ellen, patting my arm with her fur gloved hand.

'Thank you so much, you are so kind,' I replied.

'Your mother and father work so hard. Please, God, he will be home soon, and will recover from his injuries. The new year is approaching fast, and I pray for you all the time, and all we can wish for is some new hope.'

I wished there and then I could have shared in her enthusiasm. With the car engine running, the windscreen cleared, and Jim drove away very cautiously on the road. It was a virtual winter wonderland, as the lights caught the glaze of the frost, and the ghostly white of the fog. When we reached our gate, Seán left me to the door, while his father turned the car.

'Thanks for a lovely night, Sarah,' he said.

'Thank you!' I exclaimed. 'It was you who brought me.'

'Will we do it again?'

'Yes please!' I answered with excitement. I had barely stopped speaking when he kissed me, taking me by surprise. Then he stopped suddenly saying, 'I'm sorry, I shouldn't have done that.' I said nothing, but pulled his head towards me and kissed him back.

'That's what you get Seán Walsh for kissing me.'

'Will I get it again?' he asked rather shyly.

'Maybe!' I replied rather teasingly. Then the car horn gave a little quick honk.

'I have to go.'

'Let's do it again so!' I called to him.

'Okay! That's a promise,' he replied. He closed the gate, and then he was gone.

The house was quiet, but the kitchen was warm. I moved so as not to wake anybody up. I stoked the range up again and filled it with turf. I boiled the kettle and made a cup of tea. Mam's mirror was still on the table, and the makeup still looked well on my face. I switched off the kitchen light and went to bed. The music still rang in my ears, and I could not sleep. I blamed the tea for keeping me awake, or maybe it was all the sandwiches and cake. Eventually, sleep did come, and I slept soundly.

I was awakened around ten the next morning with the clatter of buckets, and voices talking in the kitchen. I couldn't sleep on with the noise, so I got dressed and joined them.

Meg was dressed in her best clothes and was eating a boiled egg with brown bread.

'Are you going away?' I asked.

'I'm going to Dublin for the day, something has turned up regarding the opening of the travelling show after Easter. I'll be back tomorrow.'

'Can Darcy not deal with all of this?' I asked.

'He's still out revelling and drinking, and he's not up to dealing with such matters. He was here last night and asked if I would do it. It's part of my life, Sarah, I do the organising, and he does the drinking. I feel that this way of life is on its last legs. It just can't go on like this. I'm meeting with a few of the organising people at my own house this evening.'

'I thought Eileen was leaving today as well.'

'Darcy is collecting her in the afternoon. He's taking her to a hotel in town for a night or two, and then taking her home to Dublin. Eileen has decided to go into a nursing home in the new year. It's a better idea than taking her to our house, as we won't be there at times to care for her. There is a hackney car collecting me soon to take me to the train station.'

'Take care of yourself, won't you?' I asked.

'I promise I'll be back tomorrow. I'm taking an empty case, and I'll bring fresh clothes back with me. You never said how you got on at the dance.'

I smirked and blushed, hanging my head shyly. She could read my reaction like a book, and she began to wax lyrically,

> 'See the mountains kiss high heaven
> And the waves clasp one another;'
> No sister flower would be forgiven
> If it disdained its brother;
> And the sunlight ...

'Stop Meg,' I interrupted, 'you're embarrassing me.'

She smiled and said, 'It's *Just Loves Philosophy*, by Shelley.'

'I don't care what it is but stop,' I still blushed and held my head down.

'Don't be embarrassed. It has happened, hasn't it?'

I didn't answer, but I gave a little giggle.

'Oh dear! You've really done it now!'

'What?'

'You will definitely have to marry him.'

'Meg!'

'I'm only teasing you, pet,' she said and put her arms around my shoulders. 'I know by you, you had a lovely time.'

'I had, I was sad when the dance ended.'

'I want you to promise me one thing again, Sarah. Keep well away from Darcy. When you hear him coming bring Eileen out to him and get the boys to bring her things.'

'Everything will be fine,' I said.

'Just don't be on your own with him, that's all.'

With that, the three boys returned with armfuls of turf to fill up the box for the day.

'Lord, its fierce cold,' said Joe.

'I went down to the winter pond,' said Packy. 'I jumped on the ice and it's as hard as a rock.'

'Be careful now,' said Meg.

'It's only a foot deep,' said Tom, 'It dries up in the summer.'

'Are you coming down, Sarah?' asked Packy.

'No, she can't,' said Meg. 'Not until Darcy collects Eileen. She can go where she likes after that. You boys make sure to return to the house when you hear the car and help bring Eileen and her things out to Darcy.'

'We will,' they answered together, and they were gone. They laughed, and they cheered as they disappeared into the white frost.

'Will you make sure Eileen has everything packed? She's putting things together in the room herself. She won't let me do it. At least it's great to see her do things herself again.'

When I had finished breakfast, the hackney called, and blew the car horn at the gate. There was no bark from Sputnik as he had followed the boys to the pond.

As she was leaving, Meg whispered in my ear, 'If anyone asks about your Mam, she's gone visiting. I'll be back tomorrow on the morning train.'

So now, I was in charge, and I busied myself tidying up the kitchen. Eileen had her breakfast finished. There was dust and ashes everywhere, and I had to sweep it all up. I pulled the fender out to sweep some ashes and dirt, from under the range. There was a pot of water on to boil, so that the Delph could be washed, and with the wastewater I'd give the floor a rub around the range to get rid of ash stains from the day before.

I worked away quietly, and thoughts of the night before, went through my head. The words of the song *Walking Back to Happiness* were on my lips, as I whispered the song to myself. I stood up from the fire, and began dancing around the floor, as if I had an imaginary partner there with me. Then I heard Eileen speak. She had come quietly out of the room.

'Well, what do you think?' she asked. I stood there a little shocked, and embarrassed and then I was horrified at what I saw. She was wearing Mam's dress and good Sunday coat. It was the flowery dress Dad bought for her last summer. I remember how well she looked in it, and she had worn it to the harvest dance in September.

'Take them off!' I yelled at her.

'Isn't that dress beautiful?' she said, totally ignoring my angry plea, 'And what about the coat? Your Mam has great dress sense.'

'Take them off now! That's Mam's best dress and coat. Dad bought her that dress last summer.'

'I'll buy them from her. I'll leave a good price for them. I really like them.'

'No! Put them back please!'

'That's such a pity,' she said.

'Please Eileen, Mam will be very annoyed if she sees her favourite coat and dress gone. She's depending on me to take care of everything for her.'

'She has a great taste in clothes,' said Eileen. 'If ever they fall out of favour with her I'll buy them from her. The dress reminds me of my younger days, especially the flower pattern.'

'I don't think Mam will ever grow tired of these clothes. She wears everything till they are worn and threadbare. She will be glad to know you like them, now please put them back. You know Darcy will be here soon. Do you need any help packing things away in your case?'

'I'm fine child, I can manage alright.'

She went back into the room and I continued cleaning around the range and wiping the fender with a damp cloth. It had gathered a lot of ash and dust during the Christmas period. While I was in that cleaning mode, I decided to dust the shelves on the dresser as well, lifting and wiping the plates and dusting the shelves, and replacing them one by one, wiping the good china cups, and hanging them back on their hooks, gently and carefully.

My world was a lovely place that morning, and I shut out the whole environment around me, as I swayed to the songs, and music of the showband, which went through my head from the night before. I wanted to be carried away again to the hall, the dancing, the sandwiches, Seán's smiles and winks, as well as poor old Pat, my guardian angel.

I was oblivious to the world around me. My brothers were gone sliding on the winter pond, and Sputnik was with them. If only he had barked, I would have been drawn back to reality. I didn't hear a car stop and turn at the gate. The world was made more silent by the white frost, and freezing fog which muffled out the sound of the car engine. I didn't hear the footsteps crunching on the cold dead leaves. I didn't hear the door open, as it had opened quietly, and the cold air was overcome by the warm air of the kitchen. I didn't see the dark shadow stand in the doorway. I heard nothing till a man's voice spoke to me.

'My bounty is boundless as the sea, my love as deep, the more I give to thee, the more I have, for both are infinite...

I screamed when I heard the voice, and one of Mam's good china cups smashed to the floor in a million pieces. It was Darcy. He was drunk, and he reeked of whiskey.

'Now my beautiful, Juliet, I'm here to sweep you off your feet.'

I shivered when I heard him say this, and I made to get out past him, and through the door to run to the boys, he blocked my path. I said in a frightened voice, 'Eileen is nearly ready. She is down in the room. I'll go get her.'

'She can wait now, my precious little diamond. You are the sweetest thing I have ever seen.'

'Go away Darcy! You are frightening me!'

Then he grabbed me and began kissing me, and the smell of whiskey was all over him. I struggled and began pounding him in the chest.

'Oh, playing hard to get, now are we? Look at yourself, all lipstick and makeup. I know you are gagging for it. I could see it in your eyes every time I saw you. You haven't Meg to protect you now, making sure you kept the door to your room locked. I couldn't get any nearer to you, so I sent her off to Dublin on a wild goose chase. That's my Meg, so gullible. Come on, come away with me for the day, and I'll show you a good time.'

'Let me go!' I shouted.

He was holding me firmly, and his fingers were digging into my arms to keep me steady.

'You're hurting me!'

He went to pull me towards him again, and I bit deeply into his hand.

'You little bitch! You little slut!' he exclaimed, and then he slapped me across the face.

What happened next, seemed to be suspended in slow motion in my head. Over the years, it was another nightmare, I had to deal with, which kept coming back, even as the passing years left the incident further back in time.

When he hit me, I screamed at the top of my voice and then he went to hit me again. I continued screaming, and when I looked up, I could see the flight of a walking stick coming down on Darcy from behind. It got him on the shoulder, just at the neck. He was dazed by it and I could hear Eileen shouting as loud and agitated as she could, in an angry broken nasal tone.

'Darcy, you dirty bastard, you never learn, do you? You did it to me remember, and you won't do it to this lovely little girl. She is innocent and pure, and you won't ruin her life, the way you ruined mine!'

'Get away you, go to the room! I'll do what I like!' he roared in a fit of drunken madness.

'Over my dead body,' she answered, clenching her teeth in anger.

She went to hit him again with the walking stick, but he grabbed it, as it came crashing down on top of him again. He held the stick with his two hands in a tug-of-war fashion, and he pushed her away with it. But Eileen's disability meant, that having little power in her left arm to defend herself, she fell helplessly backward, and she crashed to the floor. I could hear the cracking of bone as her head hit the fender, which was still some distance from the range.

There was silence again, as if time had stood still and there was blood flowing from her head forming a pool on the floor. She was still wearing Mam's dress and coat. Her eyes were open, and she stared vacantly at the door. I began to scream uncontrollably, and a minute later, the boys dashed in the door. Packy ran to me, shivering and shaking, and the other boys escaped to the bedroom in fright.

'Eileen! Oh my God, Eileen!' roared Darcy.

'You killed her!' I sobbed. 'You killed her.'

'It was an accident. I didn't mean to do it.'

'What are you going to do now, Darcy? What are you going to do?'

Packy clung to me. He had his thumb in his mouth, and his tears were falling on my hands. I knew he was in deep distress. I turned him away, facing the room door, as I didn't want him looking at Eileen's dead body.

'What are you going to do, Darcy?' I screamed at him.

'Stop shouting at me and let me think,' he said. The big fright he got was now sobering him up.

'Heaven's almighty, I killed my sister!' he exclaimed, as he spoke in a breathless whisper. He considered my face, and I could see that he was now beginning to panic.

'I killed my sister, I did! What am I going to do?'

'Will I get Joe to go for the sergeant?' I asked, gulping breaths of air to help alleviate the shock I was in.

'No, do not!' he shouted. 'I'll deal with this.'

'I'll have to tell Meg.'

'Tell her nothing, leave it to me.'

'What are you going to do then?'

'I'll take her away from here, and deal with this myself.'

'She'll have to know...'

'If you open your mouth again, young lady, I'll kill you too!' He was standing, leaning closely into my space, and waving his index finger at me. It was shaking from the shock.

I moved closer into his space. I wasn't afraid of him now.

'Go on then, you brave little coward – that's all you are. You'll have to kill my brothers as well. Where will that get you?'

He pulled his shaking finger away. Turning to the door he said in a quivering voice, 'Stop this now. I'll take her away from here.'

He darted out the door and returned a moment later with a heavy Foxford rug. He lifted the body up and wrapped it around her. He had also grabbed a towel from the window, and placed it around her head, to absorb the blood which was still oozing from it. With all his might, he carried her body out the door. 'Get me her things,' he said as he headed for the car.

With Packy still clinging to me, I went to the room and picked up her bag. It was on the bed, packed and closed. I brought her walking stick as well. We waited at the door for him to return. He had unceremoniously dumped Eileen's body in the boot of the car. He grabbed the case and stick and was ready to dash off. Then he stopped in his tracks and turned to me and said, 'Sorry!'

He turned the car and took off at speed, as I could hear the wheels spinning on the icy road. To prevent himself from crashing the car he had to slow down.

I took Packy by the hand, rushed inside and bolted the door. I called the boys, but they didn't want to come out of the room. I called them again rather crossly, and they peeped sheepishly around the door to see if all was clear.

'What are you going to do, Sarah?' asked Joe. I was sitting in the armchair by the range, and Packy was sitting on my knee. He had stopped crying. He was still sucking his thumb. His eyes were closed, and he had gone to sleep.

'Get some hot water. Put some Dettol in it, and some Vim. We have to wash up the blood.' Tom and Joe didn't protest, but just proceeded as I ordered. The house was very quiet as they mopped up the blood. They cleaned the fender as well as the floor around it. They turned it over, and washed under it, finally placing it back close to the range. They were ever so careful to make sure there was not a drop of blood to be seen. The only tell-tale sign of washing, remaining long after the floor dried, was the smell of Dettol, and that was a normal household smell. I continued to supervise the clean-up by saying,

'Throw that wastewater into the ditch and wash the bucket out thoroughly. Then dump that old cleaning rag into the fire here.'

When everything was done and back to normal, we sat in the kitchen till near dark. I was numb inside. I didn't know what would happen next. I was soon to find out as before too long Sergeant Greene gave us a call, and he wasn't alone.

The boys were getting ready to milk the cow when the dog barked. The squad car was at the gate, and another car parked behind it. My heart began to pound heavily, and I felt that this was it. Darcy did go to the guards. I would have to tell him everything. I clung to Packy and he stirred in my arms. He was sitting upright on my knee but kept very close to me. Joe and Tom sat at the table next to the window.

There was a loud knock on the door, and I told them to come in.

The door opened slowly, and Sergeant Greene stepped into the warm kitchen. I knew by the frowned expression on his face, he sensed that things were not right. He looked around and surveyed the kitchen as he spoke.

'Hope you are all well here?'

Dr Sullivan was with him. He didn't speak, but he left his medical bag down on the table and sat on the chair next to the door.

We didn't answer but sat there terrified and speechless. You could cut the air with a knife.

'How is your Mam today?' he asked.

We didn't answer, but I began to prepare myself to speak. I would have to tell him she was dead.

'I'm here as I believe there was another incident yesterday, and yet again another assault on one of our parishioners. This is getting serious now. I brought Dr Sullivan along to see her.'

'Your mother may need to go to hospital for a while,' said the doctor.

I anticipated that he knew she was asleep, below in the bedroom, and that Darcy had not gone to the station.

'Will you get her for me please?' asked the sergeant.

I sat up in the chair and faced him. He could sense there was something seriously wrong.

'What's wrong, Sarah?'

'She.... she...' I began to stammer and shake.

'Is she asleep?'

'No! She's...she's...' Then Packy jumped up and began shouting at the sergeant in a frenzied and terrified voice.

'She's gone, Sergeant!'

'Gone!' he answered rather puzzled.

'She went away during the night. We don't know where she is!' Packy was now in his dramatic mode. He ran to the sergeant and clung to him crying.

'Shush! Shush! Stop crying now lad and tell me more?'

I caught the moment too, and kept the lie going.

'I went down to wake her at eleven and she was gone, Sergeant. We didn't rise too early as I was out at the dance in the village last night. She was asleep when I got home.'

'What time was that at?' he asked.

'Around half three, the Walsh family left me home in the car.'

'Could she be gone to relatives or something? Did she drive?'

'She can't drive, we have no car,' said Joe.

'That's odd. She just can't vanish into thin air in such a short space of time, someone, somewhere, must have seen her?'

'Mammy's not well,' said Tom.

'I know that, son. That's why I'm here,' said Dr Sullivan.

'Now, you be a good little man, and wipe those tears,' said the sergeant. 'You must be brave. Your Mam is not well, and she wants you to be strong.'

'Yes, Sergeant,' said Packy.

'You must all be brave,' he said.

'Is she dead?' asked Tom.

'She is missing. We will try to find her.'

'What if you cannot find her?' I asked.

'I cannot answer that,' he replied again.

'What about Dad – will someone tell him?' asked Tom.

'We'll look after all that,' he continued.

'Maybe Mam will be back later,' sobbed Packy. 'I miss her very much. I want my Mammy!'

He began bawling again, and unknown to the sergeant, I gave him a little dig in the ribs, telling him to shut up, and give up the dramatics. He knew what I meant, and he ended the charade, by calming down slowly, and clinging to me for support.

'What about all of you?' asked Dr Sullivan. 'Who will care for you till your mother returns?'

'I can take care of them,' I said, 'I am nearly sixteen years old. I have been helping Mam to look after them for the past few months when Dad was working in England.'

'Are you not still a bit young to care for these three young men?' asked the doctor.

'Please doctor, don't take them away, please! I will look after them till Dad comes home.'

'Your father will not be home for several months, and even then, he'll need care also.'

I knew by him that he was edging to take the boys away, and I had to say something to prevent this happening.

'If you take them away, I will never see them again. I made a promise to Mam, that if anything happened to her, I was to take care of them. I don't want something to happen to them, just like the Larkin children. Where are they now? No one knows where they are. I cannot let you do this. If you try to take them, I will run away with them, and no one will find us.' My voice began to rise in a frenzy and began the dramatics Packy expressed a few minutes earlier, as the tears were rolling down my face.

The sergeant stood up and intervened. He turned and faced the doctor. The doctor had stood up from the chair when he confronted me. Now the sergeant was looking down on him, and he spoke in a harsh and slightly threatening voice.

'Dr Sullivan, could you please stop it now, for a few minutes.'

He did as he was asked, sat down and let the sergeant continue. He turned to me and spoke in a quiet gentle voice. I sat on the chair, ringing my hands and sobbing.

'Sarah! Stop crying, please. It's alright, no one will take the boys away. I just want to ask a few questions.'

I calmed down and listened intently.

'What about money, food, clothes – all of that?'

'We have enough money for about a month. I was helping Mam keep an eye on it, and there are savings in the bank. Dad wanted to buy a little more land and farm full-time. That's why he went back to England.'

'I see, I would prefer to see an adult in the house to help care for you all as well, during this time. Is there anyone, a relative maybe, someone who could stay here with you?'

'Aunty Meg is coming tomorrow to stay,' said Tom. 'She's coming on the morning train.'

'She's not really our aunt,' I said. 'We call her Aunty Meg. She stays with us every summer. She's part of the travelling theatre show.'

'Darcy's, is it?'

'That's right.'

'How long will she stay?'

'The shows don't go on the road till after Easter.'

'I will talk to her when she returns here.'

'Shall I proceed with other arrangements? This situation cannot be left like this,' said Dr Sullivan.

'Are you a married man, Dr Sullivan?'

'Why are you getting personal with me, Sergeant?'

'Answer my question, Doctor, are you a married man?'

'I don't think that's any of your business, Sergeant. As a professional person, I object to your questioning, especially in front of juveniles like these. If you want to question me in this vein, why don't you arrest me and do so below at the station.'

'Don't lose the rag with me, Doctor. I'm not getting personal with you. This is a very delicate situation, and these children are in great pain. They are frightened. They need care and protection. They need us the be there for them.'

'They can receive such care in some of the homes and orphanages in this country...'

'Come back to the real-world, Doctor, and answer my question. I'm not prepared to continue arguing with you on this matter. Now give me an answer, are you a married man?'

He hesitated for a moment, psyching himself up to control his pent-up anger. He was not a happy man to be confronted like this, as he was always in a position in his profession to give orders.

'No, I'm not!' he answered rather sternly. 'And it's none of your business.'

'Well for your information, Doctor, I *am* a married man, and blood is thicker than water. I know where this young lady is coming from. She's here protecting her family. Look around you, is it not evident to you that she is caring very well for them?'

'That's not the point, these three boys will need greater supervision and schooling.'

'They are going to school every day. I know quite a lot about their school days, isn't that right, Packy?' Packy smirked and kept his head down. As he said this he winked at Packy, and I could hear him breathe a sigh of relief. I could feel for the first time, that the sergeant was on our side.

'These children are now under my care, Dr Sullivan, and until I see fit, no one will take them away from here. The orphanages in this country are filled to the brim with children who have no homes to go to. They *have* a home, and a caring mother and father. We have a duty to find their lost mother, and to restore their father to them recovered from his injuries.'

'If that's the case so, I have no business here. If anything happens to these children, it rests on your head, Sergeant. I will file a report on the matter.'

'Do what you must do,' answered the sergeant.

'Good evening, Sergeant,' said Dr Sullivan. He tipped his hat and left quickly.

I closed the kitchen door after him and told Tom and Joe to go do the milking and take care of the animals. I made Packy put his coat on and go with them.

'I can see you are in control of the house, Sarah.'

'I'm used to it, Sergeant. I've had a lot of practice.'

'You are not to worry, I will get the ball rolling as soon as I get back to base. I will alert all stations across the country. She can't have gone too far. Someone somewhere surely has seen her.'

Behind the relief, I felt the sergeant was supporting our situation to remain in our own home. I was ashamed of the façade we had created, how we were deceiving this kind man, and now we were about to deceive the whole country. I was afraid that the affair would go completely out of control. All it would take would be a slip of the tongue by Packy, Joe, or Tom, or for that matter, it could be of my own doing. But there was no turning back, and it was a battle we were going to have to fight for our survival.

Not alone that, I was relieved too, that Meg would not have to play the game anymore. Mam was now officially missing, and the whole world would know before too long.

'Is there anyone you would like me to contact?' he asked. I didn't want to show him I was the perfect mother, not needing anyone's help. I was still vulnerable, and in need of guidance,

'Will you tell Mrs Walsh and Pat Reardon? She is a very kind woman, and Pat helps us out a lot here. I think they should know.'

'I will do that, and I will call back as soon as I have any news.'

'Thank you very much, Sergeant,' I said. He put his cap on, tightened up his coat, to keep out the cold, and he left. It was such a cold evening, I sat at the fire waiting for the boys to return. I began to shake with relief when I sat there on my own.

My head was at bursting point, as so much had happened in the last few months, I only wished Dad could be home. I knew things would be much better when that happened.

Joe returned with a half bucket of milk, his two brothers followed shortly after. When the milk was strained into a cold crock with cheesecloth and strainer, they sat around the table.

They knew by me I was drained of energy. I had not slept well the night before, and we had not eaten since breakfast.

'What will happen next?' asked Joe.

'I don't know,' I said.

'Well I'm hungry,' said Tom.

'You know what, Tom,' I said, 'so am I. We will take down the remains of the ham for the tea, and then we'll talk about tomorrow.'

230

Chapter 29

Cars and Trains

We had finished eating when Ellen Walsh arrived. Jim brought her in the car, and she told him to return at ten o'clock to take her home. She began by being the real little mother hen, putting on the kettle to make tea. She had a shopping bag with her, which contained white bread, cheese, jam, cooked ham, biscuits, tea, butter and even bars of chocolate. She was greeting us in the present moment as if the house was devoid of food. We were poor starving children and needed her own motherly gentle touch. I was too tired to argue otherwise and let her continue with her usual kind neighbourliness. To make room for the meal, she was going to prepare, she put it all away in the cupboard under the dresser till it was needed.

'You poor things, you must be starving. I'll make you some sandwiches.'

We had only just finished our tea of ham and bread, an hour earlier, and I told her we had plenty. But the boys thought otherwise, and the kettle went on, as a flurry of work began with the preparation of sandwiches, and the laying of the table. The Delph, used at the evening tea, had just been placed back on the dresser, and down it all came again for another meal.

I felt drained of energy, but the boys had renewed vigour, having placed the earlier tragic events at the back of their minds for the moment, and were ready for a party. I sat by the fire, staring into the dancing glow of the flames, created by the turf and sticks. My mind was numb from all that had happened. After what felt like an age, I got a tap on the shoulder.

'Drink this, love. It will calm the nerves.' Mrs Walsh gave me a mug of sweet milky tea, which I didn't really want.

'Drink it up. You look exhausted, Alana!' I took the mug from her, wrapping my fingers around it as if it were a baby. The kitchen was warm, but the cold was attempting to penetrate our little house, ice flowers were forming on the kitchen window panes. It was nine o'clock, and I decided it was time to lie down. I left the cup on the table and said, 'I think I'll go to bed.'

231

'Do that, Sarah. I'll take care of the boys,' said Ellen.

The room was freezing cold, and the window was covered with icy flowers. I closed the curtains, undressed quickly, and wrapped myself tight with the blankets. I shivered for a little while until the heat of my own body began to heat me up. Sleep came quickly.

Soon, the darkness and cold of that winter had gone away. It was summer again, and I was out in the fields with the boys, gathering mushrooms. We were stringing them onto a long grass flower strand, the flower head was holding the mushrooms on the chain, created by each cup, stashed one on top of the other.

We had been brave and bold again, we stepped slowly on the fresh cow pats barefoot, and then washed our feet in the cold water of a nearby stream. It was a time when Mam and Dad were making hay, and we were drinking tea out of a flask, and eating sandwiches, as the warm summer day attracted flies, to buzz around our heads. The boys left down the mushrooms, and ran to retrieve young frogs, exposed, when the hay was lifted and turned to dry in the sun. It was warm, and the sun beamed down on us.

Suddenly, the scene changed, and dark clouds raced across the sky. There was darkness and heavy rain and I was alone, standing at the door of the mausoleum. Raindrops fell on the leaves of the spindle tree, twisting together at the hinges of the big door. Then it began to open, and a hand emerged with the fingers opened out, trying to reach for someone or something. I began to scream, calling my mother's name, and it seemed to go on forever. When I sat up in the bed, the light went on.

'Mam!' I screamed, 'Mam!'

'Shush! It's alright, Sarah. It's alright.' It was Ellen Walsh. I sobbed bitterly, as she held me close to her, trying to comfort me. The boys stood in the doorway looking in, and she told them quietly to go back to bed.

'Are you alright, Sarah?' asked Joe.

'She's fine, she's just having a nightmare. Now be good lads, do as you're told and go back to bed.'

They left quietly, and I sat there shaking, as she cradled me close.

'It's only a nightmare, Sarah. Just relax.'

When reality returned to me, I had just remembered that Mrs Walsh was to go home at ten o'clock.

'What time is it?' I asked.

'It's just after five.'

'Why didn't you go home?'

'When Jim called, I decided to stay.'

'Are you awake all this time?'

'I slept on the armchair, and I'm keeping the fire on. There's an unmerciful frost outside.'

'You should have gone home. We'd have been fine.'

'And leave you to those awful nightmares. I decided to stay for the night, but I'll have to go home later in the morning.'

'Thank you very much, Mrs Walsh. You are such a kind person.'

'Shush now! It's time you went back to sleep again.'

I lay back on the pillow, and she turned the light out, leaving the door open a little, to allow some of the kitchen light, to flood in to keep the room free from complete darkness. This time, I couldn't sleep. My mind rambled and wandered, and I wondered what was going to happen next. Suddenly I sat bolt upright in the bed. Meg! She knew nothing yet. She was arriving on the eleven o'clock train. Someone would have to meet her and tell her. What was I going to do? She'd have to be told before she reached the house. I couldn't go to warn her, I'd have to stay.

In view of the circumstances, I couldn't be seen to leave the boys all on their own. Joe. It would have to be Joe. He would be well able to cycle to the town. I knew the road would be icy and dangerous, but if he went early enough, he could take his time. I didn't sleep again, but I got up after seven, and Ellen was asleep on the chair. I woke Joe quietly and whispered everything to him. When he rose just before daybreak, I went to the gate to see him off, but the road was too icy for the bike. He felt it would be safer to walk. 'I'll try and thumb a lift,' he said. 'A lot of the men will be going to work in the town. If I'm early, I'll stay in the waiting room till the train comes.'

I gave him two shillings, and I wrapped him up well against the cold.

'You can come back home in the hackney car with Meg,' I said.

I watched him as he paced himself, walking the white frosty grass verge, to prevent himself from falling on the ice sheet which had formed on the road.

I waited till he disappeared over the brow of the hill. He was getting tall, and I knew that he too would be a young man before too long. My only wish was to see him reach that goal, and to be able to look after himself in the world. I now depended on him to find Meg, and to tell her what happened. I had no idea how she was going to react. I only hoped, she wouldn't blame me for Eileen's death.

It was a cold bleak world when Joe set out that morning. I knew he'd be very careful and that he was strong enough to make the journey. The trees were covered in a thick coat of white frost formed from the freezing dew. The fields were a wonderland ever so bright, white and beautiful, a seasonal Christmas card landscape. But it was damn cold. I went quietly back into the warm kitchen and when Ellen stirred in the chair, I told her that Joe had gone to find Pat Reardon to tell him about Mam.

She then told me the sergeant couldn't find him the day before, as he had called late the night before to check that there might have been some hope of Mam's return. I had forgotten of course, that he said he was going to stay with a cousin in town. When I had time to gather my thoughts together, I never heard tell of Pat having any relatives in town. They had all emigrated to America. Pat's father was the only member of his family to remain in Ireland. None of them had ever returned, and when Pat's father passed away some years ago, there had been no contact with any of them since then.

When Joe reached the main road, it was quiet, except for those who were returning to work in the town after Christmas. It was one of these people who stopped his car, when he raised his hand. Mike Farrell was a mechanic on his first day back after the festive season. He worked at one of the garages in the town. He brought his Volkswagen Beetle slowly to a stop, and Joe waited till it stood rigid on the road before approaching it.

'Good man, young Cregan,' he said in a happy jovial voice. 'Are you heading into town?'

'I am, thanks,' said Joe.

'What has you out so early in the morning?'

'My Mam has run away,' said Joe, 'and we don't know where she is.'

'Don't be coddin' me,' he laughed. 'I'm not in the humour for nonsense like this so early in the morning'

'She did,' insisted Joe. 'On St Stephen's night, and we haven't seen her since. Sergeant Greene is trying to find her.'

'You wouldn't be telling me fibs, now would you?'

'I cross my heart and hope to die.'

'My God!' he exclaimed. 'I hadn't heard. That's shocking! Are you trying to find her?'

'No, I want to wait for the Dublin train. There's a very good friend of Mam's on it. She's coming to take care of us.'

'Is your Da still in hospital?'

'Yeah! Over in Scotland. He won't be home for some weeks yet, not till he is better.'

'Well, you're an unfortunate family, to say the least. I didn't hear about your mother at all.'

'Everyone will know today when the sergeant starts searching.'

'My, my! What a cruel world? Have you a way home with your friend, I could leave you home if you are stuck.'

'I think I am alright. She has hired a hackney at the station. It will collect her, and she will bring me as well.'

'Well, tell me this and tell me no more, why do you have to go meet her? Can she not just take the hackney and arrive at your house? It's strange that you have to make this journey so early in the morning.'

'Well, Sarah wanted to go, but she has to mind my younger brothers. She knows that Mam's friend Meg is very upset, so if she sees someone she knows at the train, it will help her a lot.'

'You know something, Joe? You're a great young lad to do this.'

Joe was relieved that Mike had accepted what he had said. He was stuck for words for a moment, but the right words came at the right time.

'I am so sorry for you all,' said Mike with sincerity. 'I really am. If you need any help, you know where I am. If you want a lift to town for shopping, anything, just give me a shout.'

'Thanks very much,' said Joe.

Mike Farrell continued talking and watching the road with great caution, commenting on what had happened in our family in recent weeks. The car waltzed and rocked gently on occasions, but he managed to keep it steady and in control.

Joe filled me in on all the details of Mike Farrell's kindness and what happened later when he met Meg at the train.

Mike was following a line of cars heading in the direction of the town, working their way on the frozen road, and keeping a safe distance from each other. He deposited Joe at the front door of the station. He thanked him again and Mike handed him a two-shilling piece.

'You're too early for that train, gossoon. Go in there and buy yourself a good big mug of cocoa. It will keep you warm. Come up to the garage if you need me.'

Joe saluted him and went quickly into the warmth of the station. He ordered a hot mug of cocoa, and a bar of dairy milk chocolate. He sat near the window to wait for the train. The two-hour wait felt like a lifetime, but as the winter sun cast away the shadows, the world lit up even brighter than it had been earlier, when Joe left home. This cheered him up a little, and he wished he was out with his brothers in the cold fields, but like me, his reality loomed over him like a great shadow, and he was wondering how he would break the news to Meg.

Just after eleven o'clock, the sound of the approaching train brought intending travellers, as well as people waiting for passengers disembarking at the station, move towards the platform. As it lumbered to a halt, it's brakes screeched, as it slowed down. People disembarked swiftly, and there was no delay for them as they left the station quite fast.

Meg was one of the last to exit the train, and when she saw Joe she knew there was something wrong.

'What's the matter, Joe?' she exclaimed.

'We need to talk before we go home. Something terrible has happened.'

'What's happened to Darcy?' she asked.

'It's not what happened to him. It's what he did,' gasped Joe.

'Shush! Not another word. I want to have a word with the hackney man first and get him to wait for a few minutes.'

She rushed out of the station and Bill Hartley was waiting smiling as usual. She was just about to tell him to wait a few minutes when to her horror, she saw Darcy's car parked at the station parcel's office.

'Could you excuse us for just one minute,' she said, and ran over to the car. It was unlocked, the key was in the ignition. She sat in and started the engine. It quickly fired into action.

'I'm not leaving this here,' she said.

She apologised to Bill, and she paid him the fair he would have charged her for the journey. He was glad in a way, as he wouldn't have to venture out on the treacherous frosty country roads.

'Sit into the car,' she ordered Joe.

'Check the boot,' said Joe.

'Why?' she asked abruptly.

'Just do it!' he said rather crossly.

She opened the boot and Joe was expecting to find Eileen's body wrapped in a rug. But it was empty and pristine clean. There were no traces of blood anywhere.

'What's going on?' she asked. By now Joe was in floods of tears. 'Get into the car and don't make a spectacle of yourself here in front of everyone.'

He sat quickly into the passenger seat and she left the engine running. 'Tell me what it is?' she asked.

'It's Eileen.'

'What's wrong with her?'

'She's dead!'

'Stop it, Joe. I'm not in the humour for tricks.'

'She's dead! She is. She was killed after you left on the train.'

'Oh my God! Oh my God!' she cried. She buried her head in her gloved hands and gave muffled sobs, hiding her face from Joe.

'It was Darcy, wasn't it? It was Darcy.'

'He pushed her, and she hit her head off the fender. There was blood everywhere. Darcy was drunk, and he attacked Sarah. She was screaming, and he slapped her across the face. Eileen hit him with the walking stick, and he pushed her.'

'Where is she now? Where is her body? What did he do?'

'I don't know! He dragged her to the car, and he put her in the boot.'

'Oh, God almighty what is happening? Poor Eileen!' She wept into her hands.

'He said things to Sarah, but Sarah wouldn't tell us. He was going to do something to her, but Eileen stopped him.'

'Did he do anything to her?'

'No, he just made her cry, and go all shaky. What was he going to do to her?'

'Never mind, Joe. Where's Sarah now?'

'She's at home.'

'Is she alright?'

'She's fine today.'

'We'd better get going then.'

'That's not all,' interrupted Joe.

'Heavens above! What else could there be?'

'The sergeant called, and we were going to tell him everything. You were gone, and we didn't want you to be involved in hiding Mam's body.'

'Did you tell him?'

'We were going to.'

'What happened?'

'Packy told him Mam had run away.'

'What did he say?'

'He believed us. He had brought Dr Sullivan to see Mam when Packy told him this. Sarah told the sergeant that you were coming to visit, and you'd care for us till Dad was better.'

'Go on, keep going.'

'Dr Sullivan wanted to take us three boys and put us in care. Sarah pleaded with the sergeant not to let him. The sergeant said we could stay if you were with us. He got Mrs Walsh to stay last night, and that's why I'm here. She might be still at the house when you arrived, and you wouldn't know what had happened.'

'I go away and leave you for one night only, and the whole world comes tumbling down around you again. What are we going to do?'

'You can be Meg, now,' said Joe. 'You don't have to pretend anymore.'

'Neither do you,' she said. 'Your Mam is gone, but now they have to find her.'

'Will they find her?'

'If she's hidden away in that coffin in that mausoleum, surrounded by branches of spindle, she's safe and with her maker.'

She reached over, and she pulled Joe close to her, embracing him, weeping along with him, as he tried to compose himself from too many tears. Still for the little boy it was difficult after all that happened to show a brave face, and she knew this. She held him close, and she knew he was frightened. She could sense his fear, and to crown it all he was freezing cold.

'You poor boy!' she exclaimed. 'What else could happen to you?' She then clung to the steering wheel, grieving for Eileen. Deep down she knew that Darcy would not be coming back. This was the end of the road for the travelling theatre, and her duty now, was to see us safe in the bosom of family life.

'One more thing,' she whispered, and then in a loud voice she screamed, 'Where's that bastard, Darcy? What has he done with Eileen? Where is her body? If I hadn't fallen for his sneaky, warped mind, sending me on a wild goose chase to Dublin, this wouldn't have happened. There was no one there to meet me to plan for next season. I can see it now. He wanted me out of the way to get at your lovely sister. That's what he wanted to do. That mean sleazy good-for-nothing bastard. He was stalking her all the time with his Romeo and Juliet quotes, and I paid a deaf ear to it. I couldn't see through it. Maybe I didn't want to.'

'What was he going to do to her anyway?' asked Joe.

'Never mind, Joe. You are too young to know, so don't ask.'

The frost had cleared on the windshield, and they set out for home. She drove ever so cautiously, and by midday, I could hear the car come slowly to a halt outside. I was shocked to see Meg drive Darcy's car in the gate. What did she do? Did she meet with him, and dispose of the body or what?

Joe beckoned to me and told me about finding the car at the station.

Meg was now back in her theatrical acting mode again and spoke with a slight posh English accent. She looked an elegant lady in her black astrakhan fur coat and fur boots. With a fur hat on her head, she was like some important Russian Princess. She began by hugging us all and clinging to me. She drank tea from one of Mam's best china cups and made a lot of small talk until Jim Walsh arrived to bring Ellen home. She had baked bread and told us she'd be back tomorrow. When the Walsh's had left, she gathered us around her, and she wept with us all over again, this time not for Mam, as our grief for her we had left behind when we too had plunged ourselves into survival mode. This time, our grief was for Eileen. Meg's was twofold – it was

Eileen's death, and the end of the road for her and Darcy. Where he was, she did not know. Suddenly her acting mode kicked into play, as the squad car stopped again outside the gate.

The sergeant was glad to see Meg there. When he saw this elegant lady, well-dressed, and speaking with a very cultured accent, he took his cap off and said, 'Pleased to meet you Madam, and who am I speaking to?'

'I am Margaret Darcy, but everyone knows me as Meg.'

'Are you the lady who has come to mind the children?'

'Well officially, I was coming to visit my good friend Mary Cregan, and to stay in the area for the new year, but sadly as you can see, circumstances have dictated otherwise.'

'So, you are willing to stay then?'

'Of course, I will,' she sighed, becoming a little tearful in the process. 'How can I leave these poor children in such dire straits. I'll stay till their father is well, and please God, hopefully, poor Mary will have returned to us safely.'

'Tell me this, and tell me no more? Have I met you before somewhere?'

My heart missed a beat, as I thought again that the sergeant suspected something, and that now our number was up. Had he seen through her makeup and disguise, which Meg had used to impersonate Mam? Was it her voice, or what?

It was one of those frightening moments again, when this big adventure would come to a sudden halt, and in the unfolding drama, all would be revealed. But as ever, Meg was a step ahead of the posse.

'Have you not been to see the travelling theatre show in the village last summer? In fact, we have been coming here for many years. My husband and I own the company.'

'I know, I remember you had a local boy acting in East Lynne, and everyone was raving about his death scene.'

'That was me!' exclaimed Packy.

'It was indeed,' said Meg, 'and you wouldn't believe how good an actor he is.'

'I'd well believe it,' said the sergeant. 'He was involved in a little bit of drama down at the school shortly before Christmas.'

'What was that all about then?' asked Meg.

'Oh, let him tell you himself later,' said the sergeant.

Meg smirked at Packy, who immediately held down his head, and concentrated on the jigsaw puzzle he was making, letting the conversation continue.

The sergeant turned to me, and I knew there wasn't any progress in the investigation.

'I'm sorry, Sarah. I have opened all avenues of investigation, and there is no trace of your mother. We got word to your father too, and he put a thought to us that maybe she is trying to reach him. We have alerted all ports, especially Scottish ones, but to no avail.'

'What about asking Mr Thomas at the Salvation Army?' I asked.

'Why do you want to do that?'

'He found Dad, so he did.'

'We could have done that job, if you had come to us in the first place.'

'I didn't mean it that way,' I answered apologetically.

'What do you mean, Sarah?'

'You are talking about opening all avenues,' interrupted Meg. 'What Sarah means is, it will help more with the investigation.'

'Can you remember what your mother was wearing?' he asked.

I didn't want to tell him she was wearing her nightdress. Mam was wrapped up, and well hidden in the old mausoleum.

'I don't know, Sergeant, she had several coats. Let me look and see.'

I went to the room and pretended to search in the wardrobe. Mam had a few black coats, so I went with that story.

'Her black coat is gone, Sergeant. I don't know what dress she was wearing. Her blue scarf is gone as well.'

He wrote down all the details and told us there would be a Garda message on the wireless soon, if she didn't turn up.

'Sergeant, please tell me something?' I asked.

'What's that, Sarah?'

'Is Mam dead?'

'I don't know. No one knows. At this point in time, she is a missing person, and until such a time as she turns up or that we...'

He stopped in his tracks and didn't want to continue. Meg looked him straight in the eye and said, 'Finish it, Sergeant, or that you find her dead.'

'If you put it like that...' he answered softly.

Packy began to cry, but there were no tears. He buried his head in my shoulder, and I knew it wasn't for real. He gave me a kick under the table, and I pinched his arm. He kept pretending to sob as the sergeant continued, 'I'm sorry to be so blunt.'

'What will happen next?' asked Meg.

'They've started searching around the parish this morning, in sheds, barns, some abandoned cottages, and even the lake. She could possibly have fallen through the ice there. They have searched along the edge of the lake, the river, even the bog. Bog holes are dangerous places.'

'Will they find her?' asked Joe.

'I hope so, son. I hope so.'

'I'll stay here till they find Mary, Sergeant. These children are fine. I won't leave until there is a more stable situation here.'

'What about your plans for next season?'

'Well, for reasons outside my control – namely a wayward husband, my plans are on hold for the foreseeable future.'

'I see.'

He placed his cap back on his head, and his pencil and notebook back in his breast pocket, he rubbed his hands together, and held them over the range.

'It's hard weather outside. I must leave now and go further with this.'

'Thank you for your help, Sergeant,' I said.

'No problem, girl, no problem. I was hoping to wish you all a Happy New Year, but it isn't a very happy one, is it? At least things should look up, as the days get longer. Good day to you all.'

He doffed his hat and left quickly, closed the door after him, and we sat in the silence of the darkened kitchen. A freezing fog had descended outside, and the air got much colder.

'Oh Meg! What is happening?' I pleaded. 'It's starting all over again. Now we are telling lies to the whole world. If they ever find out, they will run us out of the parish, I know they will.'

'Nothing has happened yet, my dear. That's a very kind man there. He's taking this whole thing seriously and doing his duty to the best of his ability. He has your welfare at heart, and as long as we can keep it that way, and make him happy, the greater chance there is he'll keep you all together.'

Meanwhile, the new Meg stormed into action, and began to commandeer everyone into work mode, so that the smooth running of the house continued, and that life carried on as normal. But life in our little house would never be normal again. Our old world was gone. Things were changing fast, and we had to keep ahead of them, as best we could.

That night Meg sat with me in our parent's room, when the boys had gone to bed, and I gave her my account of what happened the day before. She cradled my hand in hers and listened intently to what I had to say. For some reason, I wasn't tearful or emotional. I was still numb from what happened.

'It's my fault,' she said, 'it's all my fault.'

'No, it's not! How could it be?'

'I trusted Darcy to carry out his duty to his sister. I couldn't read between the lines. Every time he looked at you, he was quoting Shakespeare's *Romeo and Juliet.* He was lusting after you, and I couldn't see it. I didn't want to see it. I even warned you to keep your door locked last summer when you stayed, in case he tried to get into your room. Even when I was leaving yesterday, I told you to be wary of him.'

'He did try before, last summer when I stayed with you. I didn't tell you. He was knocking on my door, and he wouldn't go away. I wouldn't let him in. So, he went away eventually. He was drunk that night, and he was drunk yesterday too. Remember he was gone the next morning.'

'You should have told me, pet. If I had known that, I would have copped on what he was doing yesterday, when he called. You should have told me.'

'I didn't want to annoy you, and I didn't know what was going on.'

'Darcy is a womaniser, Sarah. He cannot keep away from them. I should have left him years ago. But ours was just a business partnership, the theatre and a way of living. I loved that too much to get rid of him. He lusted after many women, especially young girls. I could keep tabs on him, as we travelled the country. I never thought he'd do it to you. I'm so sorry, pet. I really am. I hope he hasn't done any permanent damage to you.'

She burst into tears, and this time it was the reverse. I was cradling her in my arms. She was grieving too, for Eileen as well as the man she thought she trusted. Meg was now in a state of mourning. Her outward show was still an act of theatre. Deep down inside, her whole world had collapsed, and I don't think she knew what way that was going to go now. Her focus was on us, and it would remain so for some time to come.

Over the next few days, I could hear her in the dead of night, in our parents' room, sobbing quietly to herself. I would have gone to her, just as she would have come to me, in my nightmares. I felt she needed that time alone to grieve for her best friend, she thought she had betrayed. If she hadn't insisted in inviting Eileen to stay, she would still be alive.

Then there was Darcy, the handsome debonair young man she once loved. He was now gone, and in her heart and soul, she knew he wasn't coming back. She was now alone in the world, caring for a family who was in mourning too, for different reasons. The whole family unit could be destroyed by bureaucracy, and uncaring people. The boys could be sent away to an orphanage, or an industrial school. She couldn't let that happen. It was her duty to fight for us, and if she succeeded, she'd still have to face an uncertain future alone.

Chapter 30

The Snowstorm

The local searches continued over the next few days, through frosty fields, over hills, and into woodlands. Joe wanted to go help with the searching, but Meg wouldn't let him. She felt that he was starting to think that Mam was out there somewhere in the fields, and he was beginning to lose the run of himself.

The sergeant gave us up to date reports, and according to him, things didn't look too good. People started calling to the house, and bringing large quantities of Christmas cake, plum pudding or brown bread, being neighbourly, and wanting to help as best they could. When it began to get a little out of hand, Meg asked Ellen Walsh if she could tell people to stay away. In view of what happened, it was all too much for the children. A notice was posted on the gate with the words *House Private Please* printed on it. She was hoping that such a request wasn't too harsh, as people were really sharing in the family dilemma, and that they wouldn't feel offended with this request. But despite it all, food parcels were left at the gate during the day, as if they were offerings for residents in a leper colony.

I relaxed more that first day, and in fact, I went to bed in the afternoon, and slept until after dark. The boys played games, read comics and made jigsaws as well as following orders from Meg, to ensure the animals had plenty of fodder and water. The cow and donkey were shut into the shed, and the door bolted to keep them in out of the cold. The cow stood looking in across the wall at her now quite lively calf, romping around the stable, tail up in the air, ready waiting for better weather to go outside. The dog was brought into the kitchen, as she felt the turf shed was too cold for him. It was, as if she knew something was going to happen.

The resulting weather conditions that followed, ensured that it was one of the coldest winters of the twentieth century. The snow began to fall slowly, and steadily at first, in the morning of the day before New Year's Eve. By afternoon it was a blizzard. Meg told Joe to leave the animals in the shed, to feed them there, and not to let them out. Extra turf and wood blocks were brought in for the range, and later in the afternoon, the boys wanted to go sliding on the winter pond in the field, but she wouldn't let them outside the door. They grumbled, groaned, and moaned about it, but to keep their minds occupied, I suggested we make pancakes, served with melted butter, sugar and lemon juice.

Even though they had eaten a hearty dinner with plenty of Christmas cake left by the neighbours, it didn't prevent them stuffing their faces once again with copious amounts of pancakes.

With the snow falling heavily outside, darkness came early, and the light in the kitchen went out. I had to take the old glass table lamp from my room, left there by my mother, when the electricity arrived in our area a few years before. There was a bottle of paraffin oil beside it, and she said it would be needed for emergencies like this.

Curtains were drawn in every room, to help keep them warmer. Small fires were lit in the grates, to keep the piercing cold out during this terrible time.

Just as I had finished washing the dishes, Sputnik, who was lying at the range, pricked up his ears, gave a little yelp, and began to bark.

'Someone's coming,' said Tom.

'Who in their right mind is out on an evening like this? It couldn't be the sergeant!' exclaimed Meg.

There was a knock on the door and I answered it. The faded light of the oil lamp shone out into the darkness at a ghost-like figure standing in the snow. Snowflakes were blowing inwards, and the kitchen began to cool down fast.

'Who are you?' I asked.

The person standing there began shaking the snow from his coat.

'It's m-m-me!' said Pat Reardon.

'Get in here, you silly man,' scolded Meg. 'What has you out wandering around this evening?

She dragged him inwards and closed the door. She pulled the coat off him and opening the door again she shook the snow from it onto the doorstep. Pat was shaking. It seemed as if he was frightened or confused, as well as freezing cold. There was a gash on his forehead, which had bled somewhat, and the blood had streamed down his face, staining the collar of his shirt.

'What possessed you to come up here today, Pat?' asked Meg.

'I heard about Mary,' he said. He began shaking even more, and there were tears streaming down his face. He convulsed and shivered. He was unable to speak. I sat beside him and took his hand. It was deathly cold, and I knew the warmth of my hands began to calm him down. Meg went to the room and brought down a bottle of whiskey.

'Meg, I didn't know you liked whiskey,' joked Tom.

'I don't,' she answered rather curtly. 'It's for emergencies, and this is an emergency.'

In a few minutes, Pat was holding a mug full of hot punch.

'Drink it slowly,' said Meg, 'I don't want you to fall down on me.'

Pat began to chuckle into the mug as he drank and the shaking ceased as he began to relax.

'Are you feeling any better?' I asked.

'I am,' he replied.

He sat there quietly sipping the punch. He warmed up slowly, helped too by the heat of the fire. 'You are all so kind,' he said.

'What happened to your head, Pat?' asked Meg.

'I fell.'

'Where did you fall?' I asked.

'On the road, near the village.'

'Did you not ask anyone for help?' enquired Meg.

'N-n-no. I was alright.'

Meg took a closer look at the wound. 'It's a deep gash. You should have gone to the doctor.'

Before long, she was bathing it with cotton wool, dipped in boiling water and Dettol. A lot of the coagulated blood came away, and the wound looked clean. She covered it with a wad of cotton wool with antiseptic cream, kept in place with strips of plaster she unearthed from her large carpet bag.

'Thank you very much again,' he said.

'You should have stayed at home, Pat,' said Meg. 'You could have died out there.'

'I just needed to see if you were alright. I'll go home now,' he answered, as he stood up to get his coat.

In unison, we all shrieked negatives at him, and Meg insisted he stay in the soft chair by the fire, and sleep for the night till the snowstorm had passed. When asked about something to eat, I discovered he hadn't eaten since the day before. It wasn't like Pat to neglect himself. It was then he told us he had been searching for Mary. He sat at the table and feasted on pancakes, Christmas cake, brown bread and butter, washed down with countless mugs of tea.

The range was warm, and the little fires in the bedroom grates kept the intense cold at bay. We were safe in out of the weather, and I felt happier now that Pat was with us. The burden of keeping our secret safe was overshadowed by the new state of things. Pat knew nothing about Eileen or Darcy. Officially, Mam was now listed as missing. Dad would be home soon, and maybe all our troubles would fade away.

Listening to the wind howling outside, we could see the snow banking up against the windows, when we pulled the curtain back. Whether it was the wind or the snow, but one by one we all headed to bed for the night. I was last to go, as I let Sputnik out to relieve himself. He didn't stay long outside as he soon began to scrape at the door to get in. He stood in the kitchen, shaking the snow off himself and then lay down at Pat's feet by the fire.

Just as I turned to go down for the night, Pat called me back. 'Sarah.'

'Yes, Pat.'

'You know what I have always said to you, that everything will be alright? I know it will.'

'You will always look after me?' I asked.

'I will, you know I will,' he replied gently.

'Goodnight, Pat. Sleep tight.'

I left him there quietly slumbering in the dim light of the oil lamp by the fire. I tucked myself into bed. As I watched the last flickering embers of the little fire in the grate, I thought of Mam, Dad and Eileen and all who were dear to me. I thought of Pat watching over me, telling me that everything would be fine. He had so much faith in human nature, and yet he was very much alone. I wondered was there any hope in his words, or was it just blind faith? But deep down, I didn't share in his enthusiasm.

Chapter 31

Happy New Year

When we woke the following morning, the house was darkened by the curtains still closed. I pulled them back in my room, shivering with the cold. Snow had piled up against the window, and there was only a small patch of light shining in.

I ran to the kitchen and called the boys. Pat stirred in the armchair, covered over with an eiderdown Meg had given him during the night. Sputnik stood up, stretched himself, and began sniffing everywhere. I knew he needed to go out, and soon, before he decided to piddle on the floor. The boys were up and dressed rather quickly, cheering at the sight of all the snow. They wanted to go and throw snowballs, but Meg called to them from the room,

'Breakfast, fire lit, the donkey, cow, calf, hens, all chores must be done first.'

I opened the door, to meet a barricade of snow more than waist high.

'Holy mackerel!' exclaimed Packy.

On examination, the snow had banked against the door, and most of the accumulation fell inwards on the floor. It was still at a depth around knee high, but it was much deeper in places, in drifts up to six or seven feet near walls, ditches, and hedges, where it had gathered, having been blown by the wind, during the blizzard.

Meg was soon up and dressed. Looking out into the snowy landscape, she said, 'There'll be no searching today.'

Pat was tying the laces of his boots, and said he'd help the boys with the chores.

There were still flakes of snow falling, and the cloud was dispersing. But it continued all day with intermittent showers, adding more snow to the ground accumulations.

As jobs were done quickly; fire lit, breakfast prepared and eaten, the boys went outside, wading in the deep snow, they rolled in it and cheered.

Then they tried to throw snowballs. They found that it was too powdery. and wouldn't stick. Joe discovered that if you crunched it hard enough, you could make small snowballs. It was impossible as well to roll the snow into a ball. This was no good, so they went out into the fields, and ran through a great white world, knee -deep in places. But they had to be careful as well, as some of the drifts were ten to twelve feet high, especially against banks and ditches.

After half an hour, Packy arrived inside, complaining of the cold in his hands. Then as the heat came back into them again, the pain got even worse for a short while, till the blood flow in his fingers regulated once more. Soon, the other boys came back in. They too had enough of it. Pat busied himself for the day, making paths around the house, leading to the sheds, and the water barrels. The ice was thick on the barrels, but he broke it with a sledgehammer.

He proved invaluable over those two days he stayed. He was fearful of venturing home alone, and he was glad of the hot food, and the warm fire.

That afternoon he told us of the great snowfalls of 1932 and 1947, when houses were cut off for days, and snow piled right over the rooftops. His father's donkey was lost out in the fields, but they found him alive. Seeing a little hole in the snowdrift, the donkey was covered over completely, but his breath left a little hole where he could breathe. They dragged him through the snow and brought him to a farm shed. When they got him inside, the donkey began to bray with relief, and he was glad to be safe inside out of the weather.

'Will we have enough food,' said Tom. 'I hope we don't starve.'

'Don't worry,' said Meg, 'it will probably go away in a few days.'

But Meg was to be proven wrong. The snow would last well into February, and even going to mass on St Patrick's Day, there were heaps of it piled against the railings and bushes at the church.

The electricity was still out, and we could not hear the radio. We had no idea what conditions were like in the rest of the country. We closed the doors and remained inside out of the cold.

'I wonder what 1963 will bring?' I asked Meg later that evening.

'I hope it will be a better one than 1962,' she answered. 'Things can only get better Sarah, wait and see.' Then within Pat's hearing, she continued, 'I only hope your Mam is safe somewhere. You wouldn't put a dog out in weather like that.'

'Things w-w-will be alright,' said Pat. 'I know they will.'

'I hope you are right about that,' said Meg.

'We'll see,' he answered. 'We'll see!'

That evening, the boys went to bed early, tired and excited with the snow, and looked forward to going out again the next day.

Meg, Pat, and I, sat up to ring in the new year, and Meg brought the bottle of whiskey down out of the room again. She took three small glasses off the dresser and filled each one halfway.

'Now young lady,' she said, 'this is an emergency. We don't have a bottle of wine or champagne, to ring in the New Year, but we have the next best thing. In fact, it's the best and you will have a little drop. It won't kill you.'

'What will Mam say?' I exclaimed. Then I forgot myself, and then realised I had said the right thing anyway in front of Pat.

'You're nearly sixteen, girl, it won't kill you.'

We watched the clock and waited for the minute hand to reach midnight. There were no chimes or church bells, but when the minute hand touched twelve, Meg said, 'Happy New Year! Here's to 1963.'

We touched our glasses, and instead of taking a sip I gulped down too much and my throat began to burn.

'Take it slowly girl! That's all you are getting,' laughed Meg.

Pat chuckled to himself as usual. At least the year began with laughter, and deep down I was hoping that the trend would continue.

Chapter 32

Snowball Fight

The snow brought sunshine by day, and with the paths cleared to the field and the sheds, the boys made their way to the winter pond to slide on the ice.

With constant frost, the snow remained dusty, and wouldn't stick properly to make snowballs. They trampled the snow into the ice, and soon they had a very slippery rink. In their leather boots, the studs in the soles and heels turned them into natural ice skates. They ran from the field, and took off sliding across the frozen pond, cheering and laughing as they did so. Meg and Pat came down to watch with me. He had just decided to venture back home. The main road was now cleared, and he could walk through the low drifts down the boreen, to the main road, and make his way slowly back to the village.

'I'll be back tomorrow,' he said, 'and we'll dig a path to the road.'

'It shouldn't last long,' said Meg, 'you might not have to.' He waved at us and left. He seemed much happier today. The place was quiet, and the snow brought respite. I found myself giggling and laughing at the boys, as they slipped and fell. We were free to be ourselves, and we hadn't to look over our shoulders to see who was coming, or to watch what we were saying. There was a slight warmth in the sunshine, but the cold air caught our steaming breaths, as it disappeared into the arctic weather.

Meg dared me to go out on the ice, but I refused. I was wearing wellingtons. Even though I had two pairs of socks on my feet, they were freezing cold.

'Go on out girl! Have some fun. Go on, I dare you!'

'No, I don't want to.'

'I double dare you,' said someone behind me.

I was startled by the voice. I turned quickly to see a smiling Seán Walsh approaching us.

'You frightened the living daylights out of me,' I said.

'Always watch your back!' he said, mimicking John Wayne or some other cowboy hero.

'Did you walk the whole way here?' asked Meg.

'Dad left me down at the end of the boreen. The main road is passable, but you must drive carefully. A few cars went off the road in the snow, but they are digging them out now.'

'I have never seen it so bad,' I said. 'We might as well be at the north pole.'

'It's worse across the water in Britain. According to the wireless, everything has ground to a halt. Schools are closed and so are the airports. There are no sports fixtures either.'

'That means Dad won't be home for a long while,' I sighed.

Meg, who was watching the boys sliding on the ice said, 'Be patient Sarah, his recovery is very slow, and nothing will happen till it starts to clear.'

'You know what you need,' said Seán.

'What?' I answered rather crossly.

'A good roll in the snow.' He hadn't the words out of his mouth when he grabbed me and keeled me over onto the ground, rolling me along like a snowball. The boys came running to join in the fun and began throwing snowballs at Seán. I was screaming and laughing at the same time. The snowballs disintegrated as they landed on Seán, and looked more like sifted flour on his coat and cap. When he saw the boys ganging up on him in the game, he shouted, 'Right, this demands more recruitment. Sarah, up you get. I need help!'

Suddenly I was standing upright again, and the battle commenced once more. It was handfuls of powdery snow we were throwing, and the more Seán and I threw, the more the boys flung at us. Meg moved a safe distance away from the battleground and stood laughing at us. I knew she was glad to see happy faces, after all the events of the past few weeks.

Then Packy decided to change sides. He wanted to be with me, as I always supported him, when the older boys didn't include him in their games.

After about fifteen minutes, with the five of us looking like snowmen, we decided unanimously to go sliding on the winter pond. I was reluctant to do so, as I was nervous of falling.

'Go on!' shouted Meg. 'I've never seen such great colour in your cheeks for a long time.'

Seán led me cautiously onto the ice, and I could feel as if my legs were going to go from under me. The boys began to show off how well they could do it, and Seán decided to show me how easy it was.

He made a short run to begin his slide, and falling on his backside, careered across the ice uncontrollably. I began laughing at him, but just as quickly, my legs went from under me too. Then I began laughing so loud I couldn't get up. So, the afternoon continued in this fashion, falling, sliding, laughing and chasing each other across the ice. Soon Meg returned to the house, and we continued with our revelry. The weak winter sun, coupled with a sharp north-easterly breeze, ensured that temperatures remained very low, and the cold was deep and penetrating. But our energy was such, that the blood flowed fast in our veins, and we didn't feel the cold.

After two hours of fun Seán said, 'God, I forgot to tell you what I came for. Have you much milk to spare? Our cows are all dry now, and we have no milk till the end of January. There's none for sale in the village. Dad said that your cow was giving plenty of milk.'

He had left an enamel can with a lid on it, and we filled it up for him in the kitchen. He then set out walking for home again, treading carefully in case he'd spill any of the milk.

Chapter 33

The Telephone Call

Next day, Sergeant Greene called in the early afternoon. In the process of clearing the snow, he requested the county council to give access to our place priority, as there was an urgent need to keep in contact with us, if there happened to be any new developments in the search for our missing mother.

There was a team of local men, together with council personnel, out clearing the roads for traffic, and they were busy on our boreen with tractors and shovels, so that a car could drive cautiously, and safely to our gate. They even cleared enough away, so that a car could turn around again. There was a layer of grit thrown on the ice at the gate, to prevent wheels spinning on the frosty ground.

The men worked all morning from sunrise till midday, and it kept my three brothers busy too, in their own way, helping. Pat Reardon was among the volunteers, and he stayed with us afterward for dinner. Pat was a bit more cheerful, as he announced that he had lost his bike on the way to our house during the snowfall. He had left it in the ditch, when he fell. It was recovered during the dig, and it was none the worse for wear.

When Sergeant Greene reached us, he came in when he was invited, and the first thing he asked was, 'Any news on your Mam?'

His request was met with a series of blank staring faces, but Packy spoke up in his usual innocent, but very sensible way,

'She's dead, isn't she, Sergeant?'

'As I have said before, I cannot answer that, son.'

Then Packy began clinging to me again in a very melodramatic mode. He was really making a habit out of this.

'The search was called off, due to the inclement weather,' he said, 'but it will resume again, as soon as conditions are favourable to do so.'

'We understand that,' said Meg.

Then the Sergeant turned to me and said, 'Sarah, you wouldn't mind accompanying me to the Garda Station?'

My heart missed a beat. Was this it? Had he unravelled our secret? Was I being arrested?

'What?' I shouted.

'Don't be alarmed. I won't be locking you up! The telephone line was restored to the barracks today, and I have arranged a call to Glasgow for you, at four o'clock, to speak to your Dad.'

'Oh Sergeant! How kind of you?' I began to feel all choked up with emotion.

He said, 'Now, you can't be doing that on the phone, there's no need to be upsetting your Dad.'

'Can I come?' shouted Packy.

'Me too!' shouted Tom and Joe together.

'I was never in the squad car before,' said Tom.

'Maybe you could arrest us and lock us up,' said Packy.

He reached into his pocket and took out his notebook. 'Let me see then… I could write down here in my notebook, arrested for causing a public disturbance.'

'We are not!' exclaimed Tom.

He looked suspiciously at Tom, and taking his pencil away from his lip, he began writing again. 'Aiding and abetting!'

Meg was smiling to herself. Then Joe intervened on behalf of his brother.

He turned and looked at Joe with the white of his eye, and began writing again, talking out loud as he did so. 'Older fellow arrested for starting a riot.'

'No, Sergeant!' pleaded Packy. 'We're sorry. We won't do it again.'

'Okay then! On one condition.'

'What's that?' asked Tom.

'Your father wants to talk to Sarah on the phone, and he has only a few minutes on the line. You stay here with… Sorry, I have forgotten your name again.'

'It's Meg, Sergeant.'

'You stay here with Meg and look after things. I promise you all though, I will give you a drive in the squad car someday when all the snow is gone.'

'Beezer!' exclaimed Tom.

'That's great, Sergeant. Thanks very much,' said Joe.

'Now Sarah, will you come with me?'

I quickly got my coat and hat and left. I sat in the front seat beside him. The car had just enough room to make it down the boreen to the main road. Coming down the hill, the wheat fields that shimmered like a Mexican wave last summer were gone, replaced with a blazing whiteness, with mounds of snow, not unlike a white desert landscape.

We passed Pat on the road, walking his bike home. I waved at him, and he waved back. The main road was like a skating rink with tyre tracks embedded in the snow.

Sergeant Greene drove very slowly and sat with his chest close to the steering wheel, as the windows were inclined to frost up. He didn't speak, but kept focused on the road ahead, and drove slowly towards the village. There was no traffic on the road, as any cars that got stuck in the snow in recent days, had been recovered and taken home.

As we entered the village, our way ahead was clear too, and the snow was piled up each side of the street, close to the footpath, with just enough room for a person to walk on the ice-covered path.

In my lifetime then, I had never experienced such a snowfall. I was beginning to feel tiresome of this natural spectacle, and I was wishing it would soon go away. With such conditions everywhere, there was no way Dad was coming home soon, and I felt that.

As the car pulled up at the station, even though the street was quiet, the few villagers who were out and about, turned their heads to see what was going on. Curtains moved in the windows and Fr Doyle crossed over from the church to meet me.

'Sarah, we are praying every day for your dear mother's return.'

'Thank you, Father,' I answered.

'I'll get up to visit you whenever I can.'

Sergeant Greene took my arm and led me into the barracks. Garda Michael Glynn manned the counter, and I was led to a chair by the big open fire. It was a spartan place, green painted lower walls, with a cream coloured distemper on the upper half. Apart from a few more chairs, there was little else there, except a smoky-looking mantle clock over the fireplace, and posters giving information about gun and dog licences, the eradication of noxious weeds on farms, and the care needed to keep bicycles in check, especially for cycling at night.

'The exchange will ring at four, and then they will put you through,' he said.

In a few minutes, Kathleen Greene came down the stairs from the upper part of the barracks, where the family lived. She had a cup of tea on a tray with Christmas cake, cut in neat little fingers on a plate.

'Sarah love, drink this and it will keep the cold out. I hope you are all fine up there over the hill. Poor Mary, maybe she's with some friends, and she doesn't know what's wrong. Then this weather doesn't help. I've never seen anything like it. If you need anything up there don't hesitate to ask…'

Sergeant Greene intervened, and stopped the conversation which was set to continue non-stop, pouring too much kindness over me.

'Kathleen!' he said.

'Yes, John?'

'I'd love a cup of tea as well. What about you, Mike?'

'Thanks, Serge!' said Garda Glynn.

'I'll get it straight away,' she said, 'the kettle is boiling anyway. This new electric kettle I got at Christmas is a great thing. I don't have to light the fire in the morning to boil it. The kids are having soup. I could bring you a mug of soup if you want it.'

'Tea will be fine.'

'I'll be back in a few minutes,' she said as she tip-toed back up the stairs again.

Just when I was taking my first sip of tea, the phone rang. Garda Glynn answered it.

'Hang on a minute,' he said, 'it's for you Sarge – the exchange.'

He took the phone and told me they were putting him through to Glasgow. After about twenty seconds, he spoke, 'Hello Nurse, this is Sergeant Greene over here in Avenstown in Ireland. I want to speak to John Cregan, a patient of yours. I rang earlier today.'

There was another silence, and after about a minute he spoke again.

'John, Sergeant Greene here. I want to put you onto Sarah.'

I took the phone and placed it to my ear. There was a crackling sound, and I could hear nothing. Then I spoke, 'Hello, Dad?'

'Sarah!' The voice was very faint and distant.

'Dad, are you alright?'

'I will survive, love, but it will be a while before I'm home.'

'I know that. We are fine too, the boys are grand. They can't wait to get you home.'

'Who's looking after you?'

'Meg is with us. She's going to stay, until you or Mam comes home.'

'What happened to her, Sarah?'

'I don't know, Dad. I just don't know!'

'If only I could be with you!'

'Dad, I need you to get better, and to come home to us. I don't want you worrying about us. We are fine.'

'I hope that will be soon. Please God.'

'We are praying for Mam all the time, but the snow is not helping.'

'It's very bad here too, but they are looking after me very well. By the way Sarah, I'm writing you a letter which will explain everything. I've been doing a lot of thinking about the future. I can't explain it now, it will all be in the letter.'

'I'll look forward to that, Dad.'

'Sarah, there's money in the bank. We have a lot of savings, Mam and me. I have asked the sergeant to get you some money, if you need it.'

'The boys need new boots, as the ones they have are worn with the snow.'

'Talk to the sergeant. He's a good and honest man.'

'I know that, Dad. He's been so kind to us.'

'Sarah, the nurse is telling me here that I have enough said. They generally don't allow patients make phone calls. They brought me down in a wheelchair to the office. I need to rest now, as I'm only out of bed for the first time today.'

'Okay, Dad! We all love you, and everyone in the parish is praying for you.'

'Bye, Sarah! Wait for my letter.'

The line went dead, and I put the phone down. I couldn't hold back the tears. It was joy, combined with sorrow, and loneliness, missing him so far away. There was nothing I could do for him, but just wait till he returned to us. Kathleen Greene was sitting on a chair at the open fire, and she came to me, held me close, and began wiping my tears with the tea towel she was holding.

'It's alright, Alana! It's good to cry, and you have every reason in the world to do so. I have made a hot cup of tea for you. You know that a cup of tea can be the greatest medicine in the world, or so my mother used to say. Sit down there now and take your time.'

I turned to the sergeant and said, 'Dad said you will be able to get money for us, if we need it.'

'Well, we don't want you all to starve, Sarah,' he said with a smirk on his face.

'The boys need new boots for going back to school.'

'I will call tomorrow or the next day. I will talk to the bank manager in town, and discuss the matter with him, so that sums of money can be released to you.'

'You are all so kind, really,' I said.

'Now finish up your tea, and try some of the Christmas cake,' said Kathleen, 'My boys can't get enough of it. I must lock it away in the cupboard. Otherwise, it will be all gone too soon, and it just new year. I made four of them, and there's only one and a half left. I don't know what I will do with them all, the greedy lot...'

'When you are ready to go, Sarah, Garda Glynn will take you home in the squad car,' interrupted the sergeant.

She sat and waited with me a while, talking all the time, small talk mainly. She too, was one of those people whose generous heart was reaching out to those who were in great need. Even though her constant chat could be a little tiresome if not boring, she was there at that time to bring comfort, and I was glad she was with me then.

Chapter 34

A Letter from Glasgow

The snow was here to stay it seems. The first week of January was long, cold and weary. Life went on as normal as we could make it. The boys revelled in the snow, and spent their days sliding on the winter pond, as well as trying to build houses and snowmen with little success, as it remained dusty and powdery. It refused to stick easily. It took a lot of hard pressing it together to achieve any result, and this in turn, saw fingers suffering from the cold, and Packy hadn't learned his lesson to stay away from handling it.

Pat called nearly every day, now that he had recovered his bike. He told us stories he heard in the village about a Volkswagen car driven by some local young men out on the lake.

'It was a mad thing to do,' he said, 'a terrible m-m-mad thing, you could fall through the ice and die.' Now it seemed that everyone was out on the lake, as the ice got thicker by the day.

'Can we go out on the lake?' asked Joe.

'Certainly not!' I answered.

'And let that be the end of it,' said Meg, 'the winter pond is the safest place you could be if you want to go sliding.'

Pat helped the boys clean out the cow-house. The donkey and cow were allowed out in the snow, and they were given hay and fresh water from a bucket.

The hens were left shut in, as the snow set them astray, and they found it too deep to walk on. They could have died if they were left outside. They were quite content to stay on their roosts if they got food and water.

The water barrels had nearly frozen completely, and water for drinking was getting scarce. Meg boiled any water needed for drinking and tea making, and Pat lit a fire inside several cement blocks arranged in a square, to make a fire pit. A large drum was placed on the blocks over the fire, and buckets of clean snow were collected and thrown into the drum to melt, for watering the animals. As each bucket was poured, the resulting amount of water was very little, so it took many buckets to achieve enough water for the next day or so.

Then the boys discovered that if they broke lumps of ice from the barrels, there was a lot more water produced from ice, than the buckets of snow.

Our temporary dutiful mother, Meg, took it upon herself each evening to examine the boys' hands, feet, faces, ears, and hair, as they were quite grubby from their adventures outside. A large pot of water made from molten snow and ice was placed on the range, and they took their turns at the washstand in their bedroom. She filled the ewer with warm water, and taking their shirts off one by one, she washed their heads with carbolic soap. They themselves washed the top half of their bodies.

'Now for the rest of you,' she said to Joe.

'No way! I'm not having a woman looking at me,' he protested.

'Don't worry,' she said. 'I've seen it all before. This is your job. But if I get one whiff of a bad smell, I'll put you standing in a barrel outside the door.'

'You wouldn't dare, would you?' he asked.

'I've never been more serious in all my life.'

'Well, how will I manage to do this then, with you all around?'

'Do what you've always done,' she answered.

'What's that?'

'You wash up as far as possible, and you wash down as far as possible, and if you want to give possible a rub, just lock the door.'

Joe laughed out loud, and then locked the door.

'We're getting so modest, aren't we?' said Meg, winking at me. Then her tone grew a little bit more serious.

'We have to be careful too, Sarah. I wouldn't be a bit surprised if that doctor appears now and again to make sure we're taking good care of them.'

'They won't take them away, not now,' I said.

'It's better to err on the side of caution. I haven't heard how those Larkin children are doing, and no one seems to know. We just have to be so vigilant.'

'Sergeant Greene won't let it happen. I know he won't. He's such a kind man.'

'Maybe not, but I'm just being extra careful, pet.'

When the boys were scrubbed, the dirty basins of warm water were thrown into the hedge outside. The resulting melt, caused by the warm water, tore a great scar in the rounded snow sculptures on the ditch, created by the recent blizzard. It was as if it were saying, 'Please don't destroy me. I'm beautiful. I want to stay.' But the exposing of the darkened hedge was a reminder, that this phase in our time and landscape, was only fleeting, and however long it would take, this would all go away. I felt deep down like the snow that fell that winter, it wasn't real. It was the same as our predicament in a way. I was hoping it was just a bad dream, and it would disappear. If I pinched myself, I would wake up in a summer landscape, making hay, and playing in the fields. But this was reality, and I was drawn back to it day and night.

Sergeant Greene brought me to the town two days later to arrange a cash withdrawal from the bank. I signed my name, and he signed on behalf of my father, then twenty-five pounds was brought home, and put into the kitty. Meg drove her car to town after that, moving ever so cautiously. It was a much slower journey than normal. I bought boots for the boys, as well as a large box of groceries. New batches of fresh bread had been delivered for the first time in days. Food was running low in the town, and everyone breathed a sigh of relief when the shop shelves began to stack up again. As a treat, I bought everyone a bag of chips each, and we sat in the car before we came home eating them with relish. I was glad I had purchased the boys' new boots, as the school in the village reopened on the fifteenth of January 1963. By now the roads were clear of snow, but they were very icy in the mornings.

Joe was pleased to realise that he'd be finishing seventh class in July and could leave school forever. Dad would have something more to say, as I knew he wanted him to go to the technical school in the town, for a few more years, and then be apprenticed to a trade.

When the house was quiet that morning of the 15th, there was a knock on the door, and Seán Walsh came in. He was his smiling self as usual, and he had two apple tarts cooked on biscuit tin lids, baked by his mother.

'She told me to give you these,' he said. Then he paused for a moment, as he took his gloves off, and began to warm his hands over the range. I knew he was hesitating a bit before he spoke again.

'Is everything alright, Seán?' I asked.

'I came to say goodbye,' he said.

'Back to school then?' I continued.

'The last round up… Leaving Cert in June.'

'I won't see you anymore then,' I sighed.

'Don't say that! I'll be back at Easter.'

'And after that, you will be off to college.'

'Maybe! Maybe not!'

'I know you will.'

'If I do go, will you still be my friend?' I thought it strange that he used the word friend. The boys kept saying that we were in love and that he's my boyfriend.

'I thought I was more than a friend,' I said slowly, and a bit apprehensively.

'You know what I mean.' He put his arms around me and held me close. He felt cold from being out in the snow, but I could feel his heart beating and his breath moving in and out. I wanted him to stay forever, but deep down I knew he would never be mine. But family ties were the bonds that would keep us apart.

His was a career and a road through education, paved by his parents, into some university first and a career beyond. Something in the back of my mind kept saying that even though this young man, who was so romantic, gentle and kind to me, was bound by duty to achieve academically and do his family proud. Even if it came to be settling down, a young girl from a struggling small farm on the edge of a bog, was no prospect for someone from a successful agricultural background. His wife would be educated as well, and like his mother, be one of those people who were a backbone of the community. Why they were allowing him to be friendly with me I couldn't fathom out. But then the Cregan and Walsh families were always close neighbours, and maybe the devil you knew was better than the devil you didn't know. Something inside was telling me that Seán was holding something back and didn't want to tell me yet. He was at this crossroads in his life, and these last few months of secondary school were important for him to make decisions. I was probably a barrier to his decision-making, and now that he was heading off once more to boarding school, it was a good thing for him to focus on his future.

Whereas my world was etched in family, the protection of my three brothers, and I hoped to rebuild that family unit again, to help Dad through these difficult times. Seán was a beacon in my life through these dreadful days. I wanted to hold on to him if I could. The kitchen was ours, for that short hour that morning, with nothing but the ticking of the clock, and the singing of the kettle on the range, as well as the warm crackle of sticks and turf on the fire. The cold biting January wind was shut away from us, by the outside door. A beam of sunlight penetrated through the lace curtain on the window, and in that alone, there was a glimmer of hope, and a thought of better days to come.

When Meg returned from the village, Seán excused himself, and said it was time to go home and pack for boarding school. I went to the gate with him to say goodbye.

'Will you write to me this term?' he asked.

'I will. I promise.'

'We are allowed our own private letters now. The priests don't open them to check them. We are now in Leaving Cert, and we were told that we were old enough to take responsibility for our lives. We are allowed visit the post office any evening after classes, if we want to purchase sweets or post letters. It's a break just before study begins. If they saw any unusual messages on the back of incoming letters they will open them though.'

'What do you mean?'

'Like S.W.A.L.K.'

'S.W.A.L.K.? What's that?'

'It means sealed with a loving kiss.'

'Dream on, Seán Walsh!' I laughed.

Then catching me out by surprise again, he kissed me fast and quickly, but I put my arms around his neck and held onto him.

'Don't forget to write. I'll write in two weeks.' He was up on his bike in a flash and was gone. I watched and waited till he had cycled over the hill, and I returned to the kitchen out of the cold.

'You're getting good at that kissing, you know,' said Meg softly under her breath.

'Meg!' I exclaimed.

'I have news for you,' she said, changing the subject.

'News?'

'Yes, I met the postman down the road. There's a letter here from your Dad.'

The envelope was addressed to me. It was thick, and I knew it was a few pages long. It had a stamp with the head of the Queen of England on it, as well as a thistle, the national emblem of Scotland.

'You open it,' I said to Meg.

'It's your letter, pet. It's addressed to you. Take it down to your bedroom and read it. It may be private, between you and your Dad.'

'I keep no secrets from you,' I said.

'Take it down to your room. If you want me to read it, well that's your privilege. In the meantime, go away and read it in private.'

I left her to the morning tasks and closed the bedroom door. I sat on the bed, and I put the letter down beside me. Then I picked it up again, and using a hair clip as a letter opener, I emptied the contents out onto the bed. A black and white photograph popped out of the letter. Dad was sitting propped up in bed, looking rather sad and unhappy. Santa Claus was beside him handing him a present. There was a cage over his leg, covered with blankets. His arm was in plaster and held in a sling around his shoulder. His head was bandaged as well. So, I knew it would have taken a while for him to write the letter. It was dated the day Sergeant Greene brought me, to take the phone call at the barracks. It took nearly two weeks to get here. I opened it, which was a few pages long, and began to read Dad's writing, which was a very small script.

Dear Sarah,

I am so sorry all of this has happened. I should not have listened to your mother. I should have stayed at home. I knew deep down she was not well, and you were the one who pointed it all out to me. She was covering it all up and didn't want to make a fuss. On top of that, the offer from the construction company in Glasgow was too good to let go.

You are a very brave girl to take on all this burden, and I'm so glad Meg is there with you now. She doesn't have to do this. But your Mam and she have been best friends for many years. I don't know how we'll ever pay her back for all of this. I don't want to say it, but where could she be? As well as that, this God-awful weather hasn't helped in the least.

I hope the boys are alright. Sergeant Greene has promised me that they will not be taken away to an orphanage or a home for children, not while Meg is with you.

We still don't know what happened to the Larkin children. Mind my boys and care for them, Sarah. I know you are doing a great job. I'm very proud of what you have done, and I only hope that things will get better.

The construction company have offered me a job in their warehouse shop, when I am on my feet again. They want to compensate me for the accident, and not alone that, for saving that young man's life. My climbing up on the scaffolding days are now over, and I must learn to walk again. It will take many months.

I want to do something for you and your brothers. When I get home, and if we find your mother alive and well, I am going to sell the farm, lock, stock and barrel, and take you all back to Glasgow. You can go to night school. The boys can go to secondary school and learn a trade or get certificates.

I have made a bad job of that farm, and I haven't been there, at home for you.

My heart breaks for you all there, and for your Mam, wherever she may be. I was very sad all Christmas day, but that auld git in the red suit tried to cheer me up by giving me a box of chocolates. You know I don't like chocolates. I gave them to a young nurse, and she brought them home to her mother.

They told me today they will transfer me home, whenever I am able to travel. It might be at the end of January or sometime in February. I arranged with the sergeant to get money from the bank to help you out. There's plenty there to keep us going, but we don't want to run out.

My lovely little girl, I owe you my life. I do hope that things will work out for us. I'm here to stay now. It's where I want to work. When I go back, you are all going with me. They have nice houses here with bathrooms, toilets and running water.

Now, I'm getting tired. There's a matron here like a sergeant major, and she's giving me dirty looks. She's a great nurse though and a great person.

I'll pray for you all every day, and please God, I will see you soon.

Goodbye, God bless,

Dad

I read it over a few times more, and I brought it down to Meg. I gave it to her to read, and I returned to my room, and lay down on the bed. My pillow was wet with tears when she came to me a few minutes later. She stroked my head and said, 'He was missing too Sarah, but he will be coming home. You have found him again. His mind is fine, and if he is able to write like that, he is none the worse for his head injuries.'

'I know that,' I said, 'but what about all our lies? What about Mam and Eileen? You have lost Darcy. Mam won't be coming home. Do we tell him that her body is up there lying in that old mausoleum, while the whole country is searching for her? We are the liars. I wanted you to go away, but you stayed. This was all a big drama. Now he's coming home, and if we tell him what has really happened, it will kill him.'

She kept gently stroking my head, and then she said, 'In that case, don't tell him anything. If your Mam can't be found, then what can anyone do?'

'Then he'll never know what really happened. He'll have to live for the rest of his life, not really knowing.'

'What other choices have you then, Sarah? Do we tell him everything and we all come clean? I'll go to jail, you'll go to an industrial school, the boys sent to an orphanage, and your father left devastated and alone.'

'But what about Pat Reardon? He doesn't know, and sometimes he opens up the mausoleum and hides there.'

'Well, is the body well-hidden then?'

'It's inside one of the coffins. We slipped the lid back on again.'

'I don't think Pat goes opening coffins, does he?'

'I don't think so. If Pat found out, he might tell Dad.'

'What do you think then, Sarah? Do we tell all, or leave things as they are?'

'We'll have to tell the boys then.'

'I know your brothers very well at this stage, Sarah. They know what could happen, and they won't give the game away.'

'And what about you, Meg? What about your part in all this?'

'Let's follow the drama so far. I managed to impersonate your mother in a way she had never shown before. She became Mad Mary. She assaulted a priest, threatened a teacher, had a bad turn outside mass and assaulted a young man with a walking stick. If this were real, Sarah, your mother would now be in a mental hospital. As it happened she ran away, as told to the guards by another great actor, Packy Cregan. Then enter stage left, her best friend to save the day, and take care of her children. I have had no hand, act or part in the whole affair. I'm here taking care of you all now.'

I hadn't thought of it like that before. Except for Eileen's death, it had all worked. Darcy was dealing with that situation somewhere. We had no idea where he was. So, we were set to continue in this vein, in the hope that Dad would make a full recovery.

Chapter 35

The New Master

When the boys returned from school that day, they were in such a rush to get out into the snow to slide on the ice. Meg stopped them in their tracks, as there was homework to be done, the animals had to be tended to, and fuel was needed for the fire.

When work was done, we sat around the table and I read the letter out to them. They were quiet and said very little, wondering how Dad was, and knowing that his body was broken and injured. The photo was proof to them that he was alive.

I omitted to read the paragraph where he said he wanted to take us all back to Glasgow with him. I felt that it wasn't time to give them this information, as there was enough going on in their lives now. Meg agreed with me. It was best to leave that be, till Dad was ready to break such news to them.

When I had finished reading, the only comment made was by Packy, who said, 'Dad is alive, that's all that matters now isn't it Meg?'

'That's true love and let us leave it at that. Now, what about school?'

They were all talk about the new master. He had coloured pencils in his breast pocket, and the best student would get a sixpence on Friday each week. Packy was smiling as well, as the master took one of his pencil drawings out of his copy and hung it on the wall. He pointed it out to the rest of the class and told them to beat that for work. The greatest excitement of all, was that he found the sally rods in the drawer, left behind by Mr Browne. He took them and broke them into small pieces and threw them into the fire.

'He turned to us all,' said Joe, 'then he pointed his finger at us saying, that this doesn't mean he was going to be all soft with us. If we stepped out of line, he'd go to the ditch and cut a fresh one. He had a smirk on his face as he said it.'

'And will he?' asked Meg.

'I'd say not, we all want to do our best for him.'

'I want that sixpence,' said Packy.

Meanwhile, Meg packed them off to the chores. Tom was very quiet in himself and wasn't in a hurry to follow.

'Come on Tom, it will be dark soon,' I said.

'I'm coming! I'm coming!' he answered rather crossly.

'What's wrong with you this evening?' I asked.

'I'm fine! I'm just tired.' He put his coat on and followed his brothers to do the evening chores. Even though there was a stretch in the evening now, but with a covering of cloud, darkness still came early, and more snow followed. It lasted for about two hours, and the roads were covered again the next morning.

The boys headed off to school, looking forward to another day with Mr Ryan. I knew by Tom, he was still under the weather, but he wanted to go anyway. Meg brought them in the car.

Her journey each day brought her to the post office. It was at the post office where the Drama Company collected any mail due to them during the summer season. There was always a hope that Darcy might have written to her or left a message there. Each day the result was the same. She had written to colleagues in the theatre troupes, and to other actors she knew in Britain, to try and contact him. The people in the towns and cities had access to telephones. They were few and far between here in the country, except for the Garda station, the priest, the doctor, the post office, as well as one or two of the village shops. There was a public telephone on the street, but she didn't want to use that, as it wasn't very dependable. On several occasions, she returned with a letter, a postcard, or a short note, but the answer was always negative.

She knew with each communication she received, Darcy was not coming back. There were rumours he had gone to England, or even Australia, but there was no trace of him. She had said time and time again, that if he did return, she would quietly send him packing on his merry way again. But Meg was always very forgiving, and she'd always put the past behind her.

Deep down she knew Eileen's death was an accident, but Darcy's attempt at seducing a young girl of tender years was unforgivable.

On the outside, she was happy, caring and ever so kind. On the inside, she was hurting deeply, and occasionally I could still hear her sob with grief in her room at night. I could have gone to her to comfort her, just as she did for me, but this was her time to grieve. She had put her whole life on hold just for us. In the years that followed, I often thought about her, and all she did to keep us together. She was our guardian angel, or angel of mercy sent by Mam to protect us.

Each morning she returned from the village with her hopes dashed when her quest was negative. She sat by the fire with her cup of tea and had her hour of silence before helping me meet the day's chores in preparation for mealtimes and the coming night. Today she had mobilised herself into action and began baking bread.

Around midday, we thought we heard a car. The dog began to bark, and there was a knock at the door. When I opened the door, a tall fair-haired young man stood there with Tom was by his side.

'I'm sorry, Sarah – It is Sarah, I'm speaking to?'

'That's right! I'm Sarah and who are you? Tom, what is wrong?'

'Are you Mr Ryan?' asked Meg.

'It is Madam. My name is Donal Ryan.'

'Come in out of the cold,' I said to him.

He stepped inside and sat down when Meg asked him to.

'This young man in my class is not very well,' he said. 'I thought I'd leave him home. He's feeling miserable all morning. If he's feeling like that, he should be in bed. Isn't that right, Tom?'

'Yes sir,' answered Tom.

'You are so kind to bring him home, Mr Ryan,' I said.

'Call me Donal.'

'A man deserves his status,' said Meg. 'You are the teacher, and you are Mr Ryan in this house.'

'Whatever you like so,' he answered with a wry smile on his face.

'I take it you are not a local man?' asked Meg.

'Tipperary born, just outside Clonmel.'

'Well, we won't hold that against you,' she joked. 'Sure there are lots of Ryan's in Tipperary.'

'There are indeed!' He then stood up to go, holding his bunch of car keys aloft.

'Miss Briody has taken my class into her room, so that I could bring Tom home. He is complaining of a severe pain in his right side.' Meg went to rub Tom's side and he cried out with pain.

'I think we need to get the doctor,' said Meg.

'When I was twelve years old,' said Donal. 'I had my appendix out. I know by the way Tom is feeling that he could have the same thing.'

'I'll get him to bed. Sarah, will you go to the village and get Dr Sullivan.'

'I'll give you a lift back to the village,' said Donal.

He had a Morris Minor car, and I sat in the front. It smelled of pipe tobacco. It wasn't an unpleasant smell. It reminded me of Dad, when he smoked his pipe on the odd occasion. Again, the countryside had changed little, with mounds and hummocks of snow in the fields, and tracks around the ditches made by the cattle who sought shelter there. The falling snow from the night before had been cut into again by the tracks of vehicles on the road.

'I'm sorry to hear about your parents,' said Donal. 'Father Doyle has given me the ins and outs of life in this little rural parish.'

'I'm hoping Dad will be home soon,' I said. 'He's been so long in hospital.'

'Does he like fishing?' he asked.

'He does. He goes out on the lake sometimes in the summer, and he has caught pike and trout. But that only happens when he is home from England.'

'Maybe later if he's feeling up to it, I'll take him out on my boat.'

'I'd say he'd like that alright. You are so kind.'

'Think nothing of it,' he said.

He left me at Dr Sullivan's surgery, and I had to wait for him to finish his morning clinic. When he was ready, he brought me home with him again in the car, and Meg took him to see Tom in the bed.

He was in great pain, and he didn't hesitate in diagnosing that he had an inflamed appendix.

'Hospital immediately,' he said. He swept Tom up in his arms and carried him to the car.

'You go with him,' said Meg. 'I cannot leave here.' She knew that there had to be an adult presence in the house always, these days. The doctor made no comment but asked me to carry his bag for him. I sat in the back seat, and kept Tom wrapped in a rug to keep him warm. He was at times in tears with the pain, but he was doing his utmost to be brave. He was lying across the seat of the car with his head on my lap, and I kept reassuring him he was going to be fine.

'Am I going to die, Sarah?'

'No, Tom, you are not.'

'The pain is so bad, I know I'm going to die.'

'Stop that nonsense,' I said, 'in a short while, you will be out sliding on the ice again.'

Then he began to cry out with the pain once more. I caressed his cheek for him, but it seemed to do no good. The doctor never spoke as he drove the car slowly through the village, and out onto the open road again. The journey to the town was ever so much longer, as the car had to travel slowly on the freshly packed snow.

At the hospital, the doctor parked at the front door, and ran inside for someone to attend to his patient. Two orderlies arrived out with a stretcher, and Tom was lifted gently onto it. The men carried him up the steps of the hospital, as he screamed and cried out with pain.

'Sarah, don't leave me please!'

'Come along, Sarah,' said Dr Sullivan, 'You can stay with him till they are ready.'

Tom was brought to the theatre, and I followed, holding his hand to comfort him.

'Don't let me die, Sarah!'

'Shush! It's alright.'

'Who said you are going to die?' laughed the nurse, who was getting him ready for surgery.

'I'm going to die!'

'Don't be so dramatic! Who said you were going to die?'

'I know I am!'

'Nonsense! What age are you?'

'Twelve!'

'Well I'm a nurse for over twenty years, and any twelve-year-old who was brought into this theatre to be operated on for appendicitis, has never died on my watch.'

'The pain!'

'I know it's painful, but we will have you as right as rain before you know it.'

I knew by her, she was not telling the truth, she was far too young to be nursing for twenty years. If she was nursing for that length of time, she must have started training when she was about five years old. She was very kind, and reassuring, being ever so cheerful, and it helped Tom relax a little more when he saw there was no rush or panic preparing him for theatre.

When he was ready for surgery, the nurse beckoned me to leave, and I went back out into the corridor. Dr Sullivan had left as he had other patients to attend to in his afternoon surgery in the village. I sat on a chair in the long corridor waiting. Nurses, doctors, trolleys passed by up and down, and no one seemed to notice I was even there. There was that hospital smell of ether, and disinfectant and everything was scrubbed squeaky clean. Darkness began to fall, and then nurses began switching on lights. I didn't feel good. I'd say it was a mixture of anxiety, worry, and not having eaten anything since early morning. Then the theatre door opened, and Tom was wheeled out. They were taking him to a ward.

'How is he?' I asked.

'He's sleeping,' said the nurse. 'There's no need for you to stay, and you can come back tomorrow.'

I turned to leave and remembered no more. The hospital smell, together with everything else, was too much for me. I folded in a heap on the floor. I had fainted. I had knocked over the chair I was sitting on, and the crash brought nearby hospital staff to me. I remembered no more till I woke up lying on a doctor's couch in an office nearby, and a nurse attending me. It was the same nurse who had comforted Tom before surgery. I felt weak and dazed, but I sat up. I thought hours had elapsed.

'Where's Tom?' I shouted.

'Your brother is fine,' she said. 'You fainted a few minutes ago. You will be fine. They are going to bring you a cup of tea in a few minutes.'

'He'll want me near him.'

'He won't. He will sleep the night. He'll be sore and groggy tomorrow. But you can come back to see him.'

'I have no way to get home!' I exclaimed.

'Don't you worry about that. I think your problem is solved. You can come in now Mr Ryan.'

With that, Donal Ryan looked in the door and smiled. 'Everything alright now?' he said.

'Mr Ryan arrived just as you decided to faint young lady. A knight in shining armour here to rescue you.'

I blushed when she said this and held down my head. Donal Ryan just smiled and said, 'I thought I'd call round to see how things were, and I find you in distress. I'll take you home, your Aunt Meg told me everything when I called back after school.'

'Aunt Meg!' I said, 'Yes, she is caring for us.'

'I'll bring Sarah home now, nurse…' He hesitated as he spoke wondering if she would give him her name.

'Brannigan,' she answered.

'What's your first name?'

'That would be telling you now, wouldn't it!' she answered with a smirk on her face. She didn't divulge her name to him, as she felt he was being too forward in his quest for information. Yet there was chemistry in the way their eyes met, and I knew by their smiles something was happening.

'Ok! Thank you again, Nurse Brannigan. Take care of that young man. He's one of my first pupils in Avenstown National School.'

We turned to leave, and we walked down the long corridor towards the stairs. She stood watching us, and as we were about to exit for the stairs she called back.

'By the way Mr Ryan, just one thing!'

'What's that?' he asked.

'My name is Marie.'

'See you soon, Marie. I'm Donal.'

I smiled to myself as we left the hospital into the cold frosty evening. Was I witnessing the beginnings of a romance or what? I kept it to myself, but I knew that I'd watch this space, and see how it would develop.

Tom was in hospital for a week. Each day Meg went to see how he was, driving in the car to the town herself. The weather was still holding out, cold and frosty, and there was little sign of a thaw in the snow. Pat Reardon came every day and helped with the chores in the evenings. He stayed and had his evening tea with us before cycling back to the village. As our everyday life went ahead, around us the search was still going on for Mam, and we were updated regularly by the sergeant.

The neighbours began calling again with offers of help, money, and food. Ellen Walsh popped in regularly with her apple tarts and bakes for the family. Meg wasn't very happy with this arrangement, as she felt we were being treated as charity cases, but I pointed out to her that out here in the country, we looked after each other. People gave willingly of their time, and whatever they could share with each other, especially in times of trouble. Tom's spell in hospital brought another flush of gifted food and treats for him when he got home. Fr Doyle came once or twice with the sergeant on a comforting mission, to reassure us that everything would be okay again.

Meg had gone very quiet in herself, and I knew she was still grieving for what happened, and she couldn't share in the tragedy only with us. Her big worry was what would happen if Darcy's friends began questioning his whereabouts. He would eventually be classified as missing. There were still rumours of sightings in England, as well as Scotland, places where he had played out his acting career in his younger days, yet he wasn't assigned to any theatre house or stage production. She kept saying that as soon as she could leave, she would start searching for him. But in the evening times, she threw her grieving aside, and kept the bright side out for the boys.

When she returned from the hospital, Packy or Joe would ask how Tom was.

'There's not a loss on him,' she'd say. 'When I went in today, he was sitting up in the bed, singing *The Yellow Rose of Texas*.'

'He doesn't know that song,' said Packy.

'I'm telling you now, the nurses have him sitting up, and he's singing that song.'

She knew Packy didn't believe her, but it cheered him up to think that Tom was on the mend.

After his week in hospital, it was arranged with Dr Sullivan to take him home. Meg asked Nurse Brannigan to have him ready for discharge when the doctor called. The boys were out of school early that day to be there when Tom arrived back. At lunch hour, Donal Ryan dropped them home in the car.

Tom arrived around three o'clock, so full of his hospital adventure, and showing off his scar and stitches. He was pale and sickly in the face and put sitting in the armchair beside the range. The doctor left instructions regarding visits to his surgery for check-ups, and the removal of stitches. As he left the three brothers talking and chatting among themselves, he beckoned Meg to go outside, he wanted to speak to her privately. I stayed with the boys, and listened to their chattering and laughing, and Packy wondering when he'd have to have his appendix out. I could hear voices being raised outside, and I gathered that it wasn't a pleasant conversation. I couldn't just catch what the conversation was about, but soon the doctor's car left, and Meg came back inside, and a distressed and angry appearance on her face.

'Sarah, will you come with me to my room for a few minutes? I want to talk to you.'

I followed immediately. Joe was wondering what the matter was, but Meg told him to take care of his brothers, everything would be fine. She sat down on the bed and I sat beside her.

'That doctor is unbelievable. You will never guess what he has done?'

'What's the matter?' I asked rather worried.

'He told me he has paperwork ready to have the boys transferred into the care of some brothers in Dublin. He reckons we are not capable of caring for them. According to him, Tom could have died if it weren't for the schoolmaster who read the symptoms.'

'That's not true! It happened so quickly. He's just looking for excuses to do so.'

'He's been trying since the start to have them taken away. Don't say anything to the boys. We don't need to frighten them.'

'I'll go to the village,' I said. 'Sergeant Greene will do something for us.'

'You cannot go in on your own in this weather. I'll go in the car, and you stay with the boys.'

We returned to the kitchen and Tom had fallen asleep. Joe had put a heavy top coat over him to keep him warm. Packy had begun doing his homework.

'Maybe you should start the evening chores early,' said Meg.

'Pat Reardon has arrived, and he is milking the cow.'

'Oh! That's great,' she said. She left and went outside into the fading evening light. The days were getting longer now and for the first time, there was a softness in the breeze. After a few minutes, she returned with the bucket of milk.

'There's going to be a thaw,' she said, 'at least a little one.'

'Where's Pat?' asked Joe.

'He's gone on an important message for me,' I knew she had dispatched him to find the sergeant.

'Now I think this young man should be in his bed,' she said.

'We put two hot water bottles in it for him,' said Joe.

'You are great young men, do you know that?'

Tom was helped to bed, and the room was warm from the heat of the kitchen.

He was happy to be home, and he fell fast asleep straight away. The house remained quiet, and everyone moved with great care to ensure that he slept peacefully. We didn't know whether the sergeant would come or not. But it wasn't long until we heard a car engine on the road. The squad car stopped at the gate. Sergeant Greene arrived, accompanied by Father Doyle.

They sat down in the kitchen and the first thing he said was, 'Is everything alright?'

'No, it's not,' said Meg angrily.

'What's the matter then?' asked Fr Doyle.

'Boys, will you go down to the room?' I said.

They went quietly to the room and closed the door. They knew that what was being discussed was private and not for their ears.

Then the sergeant spoke, 'Is there news about Mary?'

'I wish there was,' I said, 'but that's not the problem.'

'Go on then!'

'It's that Dr Sullivan. He has the papers prepared to have the boys sent to a home in Dublin.'

'Oh, has he now?' said Father Doyle.

'That's an interesting coincidence,' said the sergeant. 'He has just called to me as well for my signature.'

'Did you sign the documents?' asked Meg.

'I signed no documents. I didn't need to.'

'Why?' I asked.

'Your father is coming home.'

Part Four

Convalescence

Chapter 36

John's Return

It was as if the heavens were on our side. The next day, the snow began to clear, and this meant that there'd be increased activity in the search for our missing mother. With the snow slowly melting, and exposing the fields, rivers and drains, the word on the street now was that they were searching for the recovery of a body. Nothing was said to us, but Meg was told. She felt like saying also if there was any chance they could search for her husband. If he had gone away on his own, it was possible, but when last seen, he was carrying a dead body in the boot of the car. Life was still a drama being acted out, and our little house was the stage. None so great at acting were my own brothers, whom I surmised began to believe that they'd find my mother's body. The thought even entered my head, that we should steal the key to the mausoleum again from Pat Reardon's house, and take the body away, and hide it in the woods somewhere until someone found it. But it was a task I might have to contemplate.

We knew that when Dad arrived home, things would become more official, and the guards and detectives would once again assemble at our gate, and questions would be asked regarding my father's return to England, when Mam's health was so bad. But then it was she, who persuaded him to go in the first place, faking full recovery.

All sorts of thoughts went through my head each night, before going to sleep. The late January winds bringing a slow thaw, rushed against the bedroom window, and the curtains moved ghost-like, lifting and falling gently, as the breeze sifted through the sash windows.

Tom was a little uneasy also, as I had to go to him a few times, as he was having nightmares about dying. There was so much dying and death in our lives, it was influencing him, and Meg reckoned it was due to the after-effects of the anaesthetic. It would wear off after a few days.

One light on the horizon was that I had a letter from Seán the day before Dad's return. I was glad he kept his promise. I knew from the tone of the letter that he was trying to tell me, that we should not become too serious about each other. His duty to his family was to go to college and carve out a career for himself. He wanted us to remain friends always, and that we should still go to the Easter Sunday dance in the parish hall. He wanted us to enjoy this last summer together, before he went away. In one sense, I was glad to read the contents of the letter, as I knew that our lives would change forever, whatever the outcome in the next few months. I knew he had a duty to his family, that love and marriage were something waiting down the road many years from now. His wealthy middle-class background also, would steer him away from a simple little girl, from a cottage at the edge of the bog. His parents, even though they were so caring and kind to us, would quietly wean him away from such thoughts.

I wrote to him that night, and told him about my letter from Dad, and what he had told me regarding taking us away to Scotland to live. His dream of having his own farm had faded, and his period in the hospital gave him a lot of time to think about the future. I knew that our brief time together was special, and I would love him always, for even considering me as his girlfriend. In my letter, I wanted him to be part of my life for the summer, as he waited for the results of his Leaving Cert Exams. I warned him to stop worrying about such trivial matters, and to concentrate on his final months, and his exams. I would see him at Easter, and I made him promise to take me to the Easter dance in the parish hall. I wanted him to buy me some Taylor Keith lemonade, and we'd have sandwiches together. I sealed the letter, addressed it, and I had a stamp for a closed letter, and placed it on the corner of the envelope. When I addressed it, I placed it on the dresser in front of one of the plates. When Meg saw it, she smirked to herself as she passed me by.

'Stop, Meg,' I grumbled.

'I ain't saying nothing at all,' she teased.

'You are teasing me,' I said.

'I'm delighted for you. He's a good lad anyway.'

'I won't be marrying him.'

'Well, not yet anyway!'

'No, I won't be marrying him.'

'Did you have a row?' she asked.

'We didn't have a row. I still love him.'

'That's strange, isn't it?'

'No, it's not,' I answered crossly. I didn't like the way the conversation was going. Maybe I was a little angry over Seán's letter, or maybe it was our own predicament. I knew that there would be no future for us, due to circumstances beyond our control.

'Sarah it's alright! Don't get angry with me. I always have your welfare close to my heart. I want to see you happy, and that means finding the right man in your life, to marry and be happy. I know you would make a wonderful mother and wife. You are the best you know. As I said before, you are the daughter I would always have wished for.'

It only dawned on me then, why she had given her whole life to us in recent weeks. She was telling me that she was being my mother. She would never replace her, but she had given her whole life and career to us until this whole sordid affair could be put to sleep.

I turned to her and put my arms around her. I hugged her close and said, 'I know that now. It's just me. I know Seán and I can never make a life together. He knows it too. Being the gentleman that he is, that is what he was trying to say in his letter to me. We are going to be friends always. I know it.'

'Where does this go from here?' asked Meg.

'First of all, we are going to the Easter dance in the parish hall, and we will let the summer take care of itself.'

'You are thinking about what your Dad said in his letter also.'

'I have a duty to him, and to my brothers. I promised Mam, and I don't want to ever let her down.'

'You know, Sarah, that's the second man you have turned down in marriage in the past few months.' She was talking about Pat Reardon. I smiled as she said it.

'Pat and I have a special bond. He is going to protect me for the rest of his life.'

'You have a strange effect on men, you know,' joked Meg.

'Maybe it's a talent I have!' I laughed.

'I'll say no more,' she said, 'I'll say no more!'

The ambulance trundled up the slushy road, and we could hear the engine as it approached our house. The path from the gate to the front door was clear of snow. The gravel was soft underfoot, but it was strong enough to take the weight of the ambulance, as it reversed in the gate to the door. Two men stepped out, one of them whistling a tune, and cheerful.

'Special delivery for the Cregan family, all the way from Glasgow.'

The boys laughed as he said this, and when he opened the door, they cheered, when Dad sat smiling at them with tears in his eyes. They lifted him down in the wheelchair, and the boys clung to him laughing and crying, so excited to see that he was alive.

'I think you boys need to step back and don't choke your father,' said the cheerful man. 'God knows he's been to hell and back.' I felt like saying that he wasn't alone in his journey there and back also, but we took a different road.

Dad was in such a daze, partly due to his excitement about getting home, but confused, as all sorts of thoughts were going through his head too. When they were wheeling him in the door he saw me, and he held out his one uninjured arm to embrace me. He hugged me tight and through his tears I could hear the words, 'I'm so sorry, love! I'm so sorry.'

I remained composed and just said, 'It's alright Dad. We need to get you in out of the cold.'

They wheeled him into the kitchen and helped him into the chair. When he saw Meg, through his tears he whispered, 'I don't know how I will ever repay you for what you have done.'

'Don't you start this whinging now,' she said. 'It's home to get better, you are. I don't want you dying on us, you know.' Then she realised she said the wrong thing.

He placed his hand up to his eyes, covering them with his fingers. 'Mary! Mary! Where are you?'

'I didn't mean to say that,' said Meg.

'You might as well say it, as think it,' he said.

The ambulance men had fixed up their vehicle and stepped in the door. Meg wanted them to have a cup of tea or something stronger. She was going to head for the carpet bag to get a sample of her whiskey stash, but they declined. They reminded me then so much of the kindly old dutiful policeman in the movie Mary Poppins, declined all forms of refreshments, and returned to duty.

'We are on call at the hospital, and there is always an emergency. Thank you for your kindness, good lady. Meanwhile, I want to see you get better and attending the county hurling finals in town next September. That's a promise, John, alright?'

'I will!' he said. 'And thanks for your help.'

The men left, and the house fell silent. Dad was tearful and emotional, and we were trying to keep the bright side out. He was tired and stressed after his journey from Glasgow. Having spent the night at the hospital in the town, and checked over this morning, he was tired and weary, as well as sad, and down in the dumps. We didn't know what to say to each other, and he sat there in the chair staring into space. We tried to act normally, and as the afternoon progressed towards darkness, the chores began, and a welcome hello from Pat Reardon cheered him up a little.

As always, his words to Pat were of appreciation and thankfulness for his neighbourliness, and loyalty to the family. Pat didn't answer but took a baby bottle of Power's whiskey out of his pocket and put it into his good hand.

Dad smiled and placed it on the table beside him. I knew he was not in the humour of drinking it, and all he needed to do was go to bed. His bed was ready where he always slept with Mam. Meg moved her things into my room, and the spare single bed was made ready for her. She made me promise not to complain if she snored and said that if things didn't work out between us she'd take a room in the village.

Pat was our lifeline over the next few weeks and stayed most of the day to help Dad in and out of bed, get dressed, and to help him to the kitchen in the mornings. We couldn't have managed, as Dad was a big man. His leg was still very weak after removing the plaster and he could only use one crutch as his injured arm was slow to recover. When he went down to bed each evening, Pat went home. Again, we told him he was welcome to stay, if he wanted to sleep in the chair, but he felt that we needed that time to ourselves. Dad's recovery would be slow, and he wasn't prepared for the onslaught of Gardaí calling, and reporters from newspapers that would come our way in the search for Mam's body.

But returning to that first night he returned home, Pat had helped him to bed and after toilet matters were settled in the room, Pat brought the bucket and any contents away to be dumped outside. When Pat had gone home, and the house was quiet, Meg took an early night, the boys had gone to bed, and I was cleaning up the kitchen in preparation for the next day, when I heard Dad call my name quietly from the room. I went to him and sat by the side of the bed. He was lying propped up on the pillows, and the only light shining on him, was the light from the kitchen. Having spent so long in hospital, it would take time to adjusting to home life again. But I knew it was better for him to be back home, in his own corner, and it would help his recovery greatly. There were scars still on his forehead and retreating under his hairline. His broken arm was out resting over the covers, as the white sling hugged close to his neck and shoulders. I kissed him on the forehead and he gently stroked my hair and face. I smiled as he did so, and he was smiling back at me for the first time since he came home.

'I'm blessed you know,' he said.

'Why?' I asked.

'I don't think any man could have a daughter as good as you.'

'Stop that Dad, I'm nothing special.' My thoughts raced back to all the deception over the past few weeks, and the things we were keeping hidden even from him. I did not know in what direction things were going to go, and I gave a little shiver at the thoughts.

'You will always be special to me. The little mother. You have lost your childhood so young, with all the burdens on your shoulders. I'm so sorry Sarah that this has happened to you. I'm so sorry for the boys, Joe, Tom and poor little Packy, the little mite.'

'Dad, they are a lot tougher than you think. You don't really know Packy, do you? I could write a book about him.'

'Then Tom ending up in hospital. It's all too much.' He put his fingers up again to hide his eyes.

'Now, stop that,' I snapped a little loudly at him. 'What's done is done, and we have to move on.'

'If only I had stayed at home. She convinced me that all was well. Why did she do it? If she knew she wasn't going to get better, why did she make me go?'

'Mam shared your dream as well, Dad. She wanted you to buy that extra land, improve the farm, and build an extension to the house with running water and a toilet. She wanted that too. That's why she wanted you to go.'

'But look what it did to her. Whatever possessed her? Father Doyle visited me last night. She nearly broke his nose. Then that young lad on St Stephens day, and she drove the teacher out of the school!'

'I cannot explain all that,' I said. I was lying to him, lying through my teeth. I felt cold, and I knew deep down I was screaming. But I had learned to show composure. My hands felt clammy, and I could feel myself coming out in a cold sweat. He reached down and took my hand. He could feel my distress, and my fear. He held tight to the eiderdown and considering my eyes said,

'Don't be scared, Sarah. There's no need to be afraid anymore. I think you know as well as I do, she's not coming back. Whatever happened to her health and mind, we will never know. She's not coming back, I know it.'

I gazed back into his eyes and we said nothing for a few minutes. I kissed him on the forehead again, and he held his fingers and thumb back up to his eyes to hold back the tears. His mind was racing tonight trying to get a hold of himself, and throwing caution to the wind, was trying to sort out all the confusion inside his head. I held tight to his hand and held it close to me. He knew I wanted to say something, but I was holding back. He could sense my apprehension and then he asked a question.

'What are you trying to say, Sarah?'

'She's dead, Dad. I think you know it too.' It was the first sentence with some truth in it I had spoken in weeks. I didn't elaborate anymore. Our secret would remain intact. He needed to get his health back, and to walk again. I couldn't tell him. The thought of removing the body from inside the mausoleum struck me again, and to place it in the woods, so that it could be found. But once again I wiped it from my thoughts.

'I do! I have known from the first day I was told she was missing. I couldn't say it to you on the phone or in the letter. Sarah, it's her body we want to find now. I won't be happy until we do. I don't know where she went, and I don't know if we will ever find her. I have a lot of questions to answer for the sergeant, and the detectives who are looking for her. They are going to take me to the station in a few days. Sergeant Greene said it was routine, just to gather more information, so that it could help with the investigation.'

'I will go with you, Dad. Please let me go.'

'I need you to stay here. I have never needed you more than I do now. We cannot keep poor Meg here forever. She and Darcy will need to get their act together for the coming year. I'm sure they will be looking for Packy again to act on the local stages.'

'Darcy went away after Christmas. Meg doesn't know where he is. They have been fighting and quarrelling for some time. He's gone, maybe to England or somewhere, but she cannot find him.'

'That happened many times before. But give it a few months, and he'll be back. He's a strange character that Darcy. I could never get my head around him. I was never very friendly with him. But I could never understand him, he spoke in riddles all the time, saying lines from famous plays in his conversation. I don't know how she puts up with him. Whenever Meg wants to go, she should go. I don't know how we will ever pay her back for all she has done.'

'I'm so glad to see you home, Dad. I didn't think I would ever find you.'

'What's all this about the Salvation Army searching for me?'

'It's a long story for another day. Mr Thomas was so kind. He will call to see you someday. He has relatives in Galway, and he will drop me a line in the post when he is coming.'

'Well, I never! There wasn't a day went by that I haven't thought about you. Maybe I shouldn't have worried. But you'll need to get out and meet people your own age. You are growing up fast into a beautiful young woman. You cannot stay cooped up here all the time.'

'I do have a friend now.'

'Is she one of your friends from school?'

'No, Dad!'

'From the town then?'

'He lives locally.'

'A boy!'

'Yes, Dad.'

'Well, I'll be...' he started to laugh. It was great to see him do so.

'Who's the lucky fella?'

'We are just good friends. You haven't seen him for a long time. He is away at school. His name is Seán.'

'The young Walsh lad?'

'Yes, that's him. He's away doing his Leaving Cert.'

'Are you serious about him?'

'No! We are just good friends. He brought me to the St Stephens night dance, and he was here many times before he went back to school. He writes to me also. When I got your letter, and you said that you wanted to take us away from here, I knew we could never be closer. We are going to remain friends.'

'I don't know what to say about that. I have gone and ruined everything for you again.'

'No, you haven't Dad, really! We are just good friends.'

He pulled me closer to him again and kissed me on the forehead. He was smiling, and he seemed to be more relaxed. He had said a lot in a short while, and I knew that his healing had just begun. How it would affect him emotionally I didn't know. All he wanted now, was to try and bring closure to our missing mother. He wouldn't be right until that had happened. I didn't know what I was going to do about it. I would have to talk to Joe, when I got him on his own. The body would have to be moved to the woods. He settled back into the bed, and I covered him, folding his injured arm in under the eiderdown.

'I need to sleep now,' he said. 'I have heard so much in a short while, what with the Salvation Army, and strange men coming to see me, and to cap it all a boyfriend.'

'Just a friend – I told you so!'

'My little baby is a young woman.'

He closed his eyes, and I sat with him till he fell asleep. He was exhausted from all the travelling, pulling and dragging from ambulance to hospital and to ambulance again. Circumstances were changing, and I needed to carry things to the next phase. I knew I wouldn't sleep, but soon we'd have to move the body from the mausoleum, whether I liked it or not.

Chapter 37

Let her rest in peace

The weather remained very cold into February, but the snow had cleared from the roads. There were still the mounds and hummocks which had drifted into ditches, and sides of hills as well as against sheds and outhouses. There were sunny days also, but a cold dry arctic wind held its grip well after St Brigid's day. Dad began to manage his affairs at home, by giving directions to the boys regarding little jobs which needed to be done. Pat was his right-hand man, helping him to get on his feet again, with the aid of a crutch, and walking with him to the gate and back. He was longing for spring to come, so that he could begin to organise turf cutting in preparation for winter. The calf which had grown quite strong through the winter was sold to the Walsh family, as we had enough to cope with just the cow and the donkey. He even talked of selling the donkey, but the boys wouldn't hear tell of it. Deep down he was making plans, looking ahead towards the future, whenever that would be.

He took a trip to the Garda station with Sergeant Greene about a week after coming home, and made a statement, answering any questions that might be relevant in recovering Mam's body. Officially, she was still listed as missing. Renewed searches yielded nothing. Her photo appeared in newspapers also, and the search widened to include England and Northern Ireland. He sat, and he watched and waited. He was quiet and said very little. The boys even kept a distance from him at first. Tom sat with him the week he was at home, following his operation, but Dad spoke very little, even to him.

Tom spent his days reading comics and doing jigsaws as well as resting in his own bed. Whatever the problem was, the broken man who had come home in a wheelchair was not their Dad. They kept very quiet in his presence, and Meg noticed this. He asked her at one stage why they were so quiet.

'They don't want to make too much noise,' she said. 'They want you to make a speedy recovery.'

He lay back in the chair and dozed off to sleep. Meg was feeding him with words of encouragement to cheer him up and give him the reassurance to rise above his injuries. But it wasn't to last long, as Packy was the first to break the ice.

One evening after school, the boys were sitting at the table doing their homework when he spoke up.

'Dad I have a question for you.'

'What is it, son?'

'Did it hurt when you fell?'

'I can't remember. I was injured, I hit my head and I was unconscious.'

'Were you afraid when you were falling?'

'I don't know, it happened so fast. One minute I was high up on the scaffolding, and that's all I remember until I woke up in the hospital a few weeks later.'

'When you were asleep that long did you have any dreams?' asked Tom.

'I cannot remember anything. It's as if that part of my life is a blank. Even when I woke up it was many days before I began remembering who I was, and what had happened to me. It was almost Christmas. I couldn't believe it.'

'Did your leg and your arm hurt?' asked Packy.

'They give you medicine to help stop the pain. It doesn't hurt now, but they are still weak, and I will have to do a lot of exercises before I am right again. The doctors said I might be lame, and I'd have to do light work.' He pulled up the leg of his trousers to show the scars of his injuries. They looked with awe and fear at the recovering scars and words like, 'Wow! Janey Mac,' reverberated from the two older boys but Packy just shouted, 'Beezer!'

The ice was broken; the chat continued with life in hospital, the loneliness of being away at Christmas, and then to hear about Mam missing.

'Don't worry, Dad, we'll always help you,' said Joe.

Joe walked over and sitting on the arm rest, put his arm around him, 'We are so glad you're home. We missed really you!' He hadn't the words out of his mouth when Packy was clinging to him and lying close to his chest. Tom sat on the other arm of the chair, and he smiled and giggled with tears in his eyes. Meg and I looked on, and they sat there with him for the next hour with continued questions about his injuries, as well as life in hospital. He was different to the boys; his injured body was not that of the strong and fit father who had left them in early winter. He had returned, helpless, broken and sad. Their apprehension to sit and talk with him also, saddened him as he didn't want to see them distance themselves from him. So, he talked and spoke gently to them, and promised that things would be better. He still didn't tell them of his plans to take us back to Scotland with him, as he wasn't sure how things were going to turn out.

As the evening drew in, Pat arrived in from the field, where he was foddering the only two animals left. Meg beckoned to the boys to go help him with fuel and milking, but when Dad looked down at Packy, he had fallen asleep. Joe went with Pat outside, but Dad beckoned Tom to stay in, and not to overdo things. He drew his good arm around Packy and let him sleep.

'He's alright! Leave him alone. He needs some comfort. You all do.' He looked at me and winked. It sounded a bit more like my old Dad, but still locked away in there inside himself. It was the first sign though that he was beginning to recover again

What we were going to do about Mam's body began to bother me more and more. I knew Dad was resigned to the fact that she was dead. We could not go and tell him that we hid her body in the mausoleum, it would kill him. The only solution I had, was that it would have to be moved out into the open. I could not talk freely about it now, as Dad was with us, and Pat Reardon spent most of his time at our house during the day. The only way was to try and get Meg away from the house to talk to her, to suggest moving the body. I decided to bide my time and wait for the right moment.

One morning when Pat had arrived to get Dad out of bed, and leave him ready for his breakfast, Meg decided to leave the boys to the school in the car, as the wind and rain were quite strong. It was melting the snow fast, and the landscape was wet dark and dreary, typical weather for February. We were longing for more pleasant days, so Dad could get out and get some fresh air. I decided to go with her in the car, with the pretence that we needed some supplies from the shop in the village. The boys left us at the school gate and waved us on. But before Meg started up the engine, I told her to wait for a few minutes.

'I need to talk to you about something,' I said.

'What's troubling you, Alana?'

'It's Dad.'

'He will be fine,' she said. 'He's improving every day.'

'No, it's not that. We had a long talk recently, and he's resigned to the fact that Mam is dead. He won't rest until her body is found. He wants to take us all to Scotland. He won't do it until her body is recovered.'

'What do you plan to do then?'

'I want to move the body from the mausoleum into the woods.'

'That's a big risk to take. Can you not leave things as they are, and let her rest in peace? No one will ever go near that place.'

'Pat might find her.'

'He won't. I don't think he goes opening old coffins now, does he? He hasn't been there in a long time.'

'I want you to help me, Meg. I will get the boys to give me a hand and move her.'

'No, it's too risky. As it stands she's missing. People often go missing and are never found. Can you not leave well alone?'

'He won't be happy if she's not found. We need to do something.'

'Sarah, I have left my life on hold to help you all through this. I have risked being arrested and jailed. Things have at last turned around for you all. Your father is getting better. I plan to stay until around Easter, till he is more in control of his life. Please don't go and start ruining things, when the whole world sees your plight differently.'

I felt angry with her, and as she spoke, I could see her concern, and anger towards me also. She did not approve of such a move, and I knew I was not going to get any support from her. She sat there staring out through the front windscreen, her hands on the steering wheel, holding on as if it were for dear life. She was speaking softly, and staying composed, knowing that I was still contemplating ruining all that had been achieved in the past few weeks. I had backed myself into a corner, and I began to regret having confided in her in the first place. If only I could turn the clock back.

'I'm worried about Dad's mental state,' I said.

'Your Dad is a strong man. He too faced death also. He's been to hell and back. What has happened your mother is annoying him because he was not there to be with her. He is feeling guilty as a result. That will stay with him for a very long time. I know you are correct in saying that things would improve if her body was found. But we can't do that. You were so worried that your brothers would end up in care, and that you might never see them again. They are safe now. There's nothing more you can do.'

'I don't want to lose him again. I have that great fear that he will go into a decline, and it would affect his health mentally.'

'You can't read the future, Sarah. We can only hope and pray that life will improve for him. Let him take one step at a time, literally. He must learn to walk properly, and without any help. He should build his strength up again, so that he can start working and supporting you all. You have got to remember he was in a very dark place for many weeks, not knowing if he was going to live or not.'

In view of all she had said, I agreed with every word of it, but I was still not happy with the result. It was still possible to move the body, so that someday soon, someone would find it. I knew Meg was not going to be of any help, and after all she had done, I didn't expect her to be. She had her own secrets to hide, and she had to deal with that also. I was still up for taking a risk. If we could bury the body by night, we could move it again to the woods if we had to. I decided to see what Joe might have to say about it. He might give me a hand too. As Meg drove home in the car, she had no more to say on the matter. She was not prepared to be part of all this again. She was just there to support us, she had suffered enough on our behalf.

Chapter 38

Sarah the thief

The following Saturday, the day was fine, and the boys decided to look at the winter pond to see how it had survived being iced up for so long. It had reduced in size and by Easter, it would have dried up for the summer. They discovered that it was full of frog spawn, and they knew that if the pond dried up, all the little tadpoles would die. So, I suggested to them to get a bucket, and some jam jars, and to collect all the spawn and place it in the pond near the Derries. The Derries was a marshy fen close to the bog, and each year it teamed with wetland wildlife. It would be a haven for this doomed frogspawn. Tom and Packy busied themselves gathering up the slippery jelly into jars, and then into the bucket. I told them to make sure every piece of jelly was to be accounted for. I tugged Joe's sleeve and beckoned him to come with me out of earshot of his two younger brothers. I told him about my conversation with Meg, and her position on the matter, and how it might help Dad in his recovery.

I decided to tell him then about Dad's plan to take us back to Scotland. Joe was horrified when he heard this.

'What!' he exclaimed.

'Keep quiet, will you? I don't want the others to know.'

'Why are you telling me then? I don't want to go to Scotland...'

'Stop! I don't want to talk about that now, but I'll kill you if you tell the other boys.'

'Why are you telling me all this?'

'Because Dad will not get better unless the body is found!'

'He's doing fine!'

'Yeah, he's getting better on the outside, but not on the inside. If she is recovered, at least he will know that she rests in peace, and that she is with God.'

'Mam is with God, isn't she?' asked Joe.

'Of course, she is, but if she is missing, he doesn't know whether she is alive or dead. If she is alive, he will be wondering if she is well, and wondering why she never comes home. If she is dead, at least he'll know that she died because of her illness.'

Joe hesitated for a moment, reflecting on what I had said. Between being told about Scotland, and me bringing the whole subject of Mam's disappearance back again, he was confused. He turned one of the buckets we had, upside down and sat on it. With that Packy came running to me, followed by Tom.

'Is Joe alright?' he asked.

'He's fine,' I replied.

'Why is he sitting like that on the bucket?'

'Have you gathered up all those tadpoles yet?' I asked changing the subject.

'Yeah, we nearly have them all.'

'I'll tell you what, will you take the last few out and get Tom to go with you. I have something private to talk to Joe about. It's adult stuff.'

'You're not an adult yet......

'Packy will you do what you're told,' I said rather crossly. 'I said we will follow you in a few minutes.'

'All right then,' he said, and went back to the pond to join Tom, grumbling something under his breath.

Joe looked up and stared at me for a moment. I didn't know what he was going to say.

'What do you want me to do?' he asked.

'I want you to help me get the key from Pat's house and move the body at night.'

'I don't want to do all that again, not ever. No way Sarah! I had nightmares for a long time after that night.'

'Well if Dr Sullivan decides that Dad is not able to take care of us, he will take the three of you away from me, and I might never see you again.'

'I don't want to do it Sarah. Please!'

'Well, you are, whether you like it or not. I can't do it on my own. I don't want to put the younger boys through it all again.'

'So, poor old muggins here has to do it.'

'You are older Joe. You are thirteen now, you are not a child anymore.'

'Please don't ask me to do this, Sarah. I don't want to do it really.'

'Well if you don't I'll do it myself, without your help.'

'What's all this about Scotland again?'

'I'm not telling you because you won't help me.'

'Alright then!'

'You mean you will do it?

'What choice do I have, you will keep at me till I agree, and I don't want to go to Scotland.'

'It might not happen, but we will have a better life.'

'Will you tell me more about it?' he asked.

'We'll talk about it tonight after dark when Pat is gone home. We will go out to the shed and make arrangements.'

We planned to move the body two nights later. We needed to go to Pat's place and steal the key when he was at our house helping Dad. It was as simple as that. Joe would yoke the donkey to the cart again, and we would head across the fields to the old cemetery when everyone was asleep. We had to take great care in what we were doing, and it had to be on a Friday night, as Joe would not have to go to school the next day. It was a long day, that Friday, and I decided to meet Joe after school. It was a fine day, and Meg had gone to town shopping. She decided it was time she did something for herself, and she thought there was a need to wear something new coming into the spring. It amazed me how this lady who had made herself so much part of our lives, could come and live with us in our little simple cottage, and having a beautiful home in the city, lying idle all winter. But there was no one else to share it with, and she had not been too anxious to return. But a change was coming over her; there were letters in the post offering her to travel with a theatre company in England, as she had officially disbanded their own travelling troupe. She was known the length and breadth of the British Isles over the years, and she was once again getting itchy feet. She said she'd stay till Easter, but I had a feeling that as soon as March arrived she would leave us. I didn't want to see her go, as she was the one who had protected us, and kept the authorities away from the door during all this time. She gave me a lift to the village in the early afternoon, and I'd wait at the school gate for the boys. Pat hadn't arrived to help Dad, but Meg said that he was arriving a little later, as he had a job to do for the Walsh's, and he'd be down to the house when he was finished. So that was good news, and we'd have an opportunity to take the key. I waited at the gate, sat on the wall dangling my legs watching cars and people go to and fro. There was a warmth in the sun that day, and the ground was dry. Spring had arrived. I could see snowdrops peeping through some dry dead grass at the side of the road. On the dot of three, the school door opened, and the children poured out. There were a few who were lucky enough to be collected by car, but most them were walking, or were riding bikes. Tom and Packy had to walk home.

'What are you doing here?' asked Tom.

'I want Joe to come with me to the village shop for a message. You and Packy can go on home.'

'Why?' he asked.

'Never mind, just go on home.'

'Is it that adult thing you were talking about the other day?' asked Packy.

'Something like that I said. We won't be long. We'll try and hurry, and we'll catch up with you.'

They went quietly without much more protest, and we waited till they were well out of sight before we walked quietly into the village, following other children who were making their way home. Father Doyle saluted us as he made his way out of the grocery shop, carrying the Evening Herald.

Indeed, we were seen, and even young Garda Michael Glynn waved at us from the window of the Station. We didn't want to look suspicious. At the edge of the village, we turned the corner and into the lane where Pat's house was. Luckily there was no sign of him, and I went in the gate. I told Joe to keep watch, and to let me know if by chance Pat came around the corner. I could be pretending to clean the kitchen for him, if he chanced to return. I often went in there and tidied the place for him if he wasn't around.

Pat never locked the door for long periods and, if he did, the key was under a large stone beside the barrel of water. If he was going to be away for the day, he'd make sure it was locked. I checked to see if it was open or not. I turned the handle and the door creaked open.

'He won't be too long,' I said. 'He must be coming back before going to our house.' So, Joe stood guard, while I tried to retrieve the key. The kitchen was dark as usual, and the range was lit. He lit it every day and stocked it well with turf and sticks before closing the dampers to keep the fire lit and to warm the kitchen in the evening. The kettle was singing on the round ring. I moved it over to the edge, so that it wouldn't boil away. The large tin box was directly overhead on the mantelpiece, and it was just within reach. Pat stored everything in it including money, which he kept just in case there was an emergency, and when it accumulated to a large sum, something in the region of twenty pounds or so, he lodged it in the Post Office Savings Bank. I reached up and was lifting it down when a voice spoke behind me.

'S-S-Sarah, what are you doing?' I didn't know where Pat came from. He was standing behind me in his stocking feet. He had been in his own bedroom.

With the fright I got, I dropped the box onto the range. Pat grabbed it and put it back on the shelf.

'W-w-what were you doing, Sarah?'

With that, Joe came in the door.

'W-w-why are you here too, Joe?'

I didn't know what to say. I didn't want to tell him that I was taking the key, then he might be suspicious, so I said the first thing that came into my head.

'I wanted to borrow some money, Pat.'

'S-s-stealing!'

'No, I wasn't stealing – I was just borrowing it. I was going to give it back.'

'It's stealing so that is. M-m-my mother said never to t-t-take money on anyone without asking. T-t-that's stealing, S-S-Sarah.'

I had backed myself into a corner. In Pat's simple world, taking money on someone was unforgivable, and to him, stealing was as bad as murder. There were tears in his eyes as he looked at me.

'I didn't think you would steal, Sarah! You were my Sarah. I want to protect you for the rest of my life. Then you steal.'

I burst into tears, and he stood staring at me, all caught up in the insult of the moment. His world fell apart, and how was I ever going to gain his trust again?

'Will you p-p-please go, Sarah and Joe. P-p-please go from my house.'

I ran out the door, and Joe after me. I didn't want to go back through the village crying. I'd draw too much attention to myself. I crossed a gate into the fields and began running home. Joe ran after me calling me to stop. The safest place to go was the woods, the place where we wanted to hide Mam's body. Eventually, I stopped, and collapsed under a tree, out of breath and trying to get to grips with what was after happening.

Obviously, Pat had come home, and went to change his clothes before going to our house. I should have checked to see if his bike was in the shed at the back of the house.

'What did you say that for?' asked Joe. 'Why didn't you tell him you were going to get the key?'

'Yeah, great Joe,' I said sarcastically through my fading tears, 'and arouse suspicion. Pat would go there and find her body and that would be it. It was worth a chance, wasn't it?'

'No, I don't think so,' he said, 'now he will never forgive us or trust us anymore. Will he tell Dad? I hope he doesn't.'

'We'll have to get home before he gets to Dad. God knows what he will say.'

'He's probably gone there now,' exclaimed Joe.

We started running again through the woods, till we came to the forest gate, climbing across, we ran through the open fields, scattering Walsh's sheep and their new lambs. I only hope I didn't scare them too much, as some of them had not yet had their lambs. When we got to the road to our house, there was no sign of Pat. Packy and Tom were just approaching it from the main road.

'Hey! shouted Tom. 'What's wrong?'

We climbed the fence and joined them on the road. We were totally out of breath.

'What's wrong with you two?' asked Packy.

'Did Pat Reardon come this way?' asked Joe.

'Yeah, he did,' said Tom. 'He passed us on the road riding the bike very fast a few minutes ago.'

'Did he say anything?' I asked.

'We called to him, but he was all confused and shouting, and he wouldn't stop,' said Tom.

'What's wrong with him?' asked Packy.

'It's a long story!' I said, and I began to run again.

The boys followed me, and their pace grew momentum, from a trot to a race up the rise, and over the hill till we got to our house. Pat's bike was outside the gate. We approached slowly, and as we came to the front of the house, the door was wide open. When I looked in, Pat was sitting at the table, and he had a half a glass of whiskey in his hand. He was shaking, and all upset. I went to comfort him but he drew away. I looked at Dad, and I knew by the expression on his face that he wasn't believing what he was hearing.

'Were you stealing money, Sarah?'

'No Dad, I promise you, I was not stealing.'

'You told Pat you were taking money.' I knelt at his feet, crying into his lap as he caressed my head.

'You were there too Joe, why?'

'She wasn't stealing money, Dad. I promise you.'

'Will you all just settle down, and tell me the whole story,' he said. He pulled over a chair, and I sat down. Pat had calmed somewhat, by now, and after finishing off the glass of whiskey he was more composed.

'If you t-t-take money, it's stealing,' he said.

'Now Pat, you know me a long time. You know my children a long time. I can't imagine that Sarah and Joe went to steal money from you. I'm sure there's an explanation for all this, if we just let them talk.'

'Can I say something?' said Joe.

'Go ahead, son,' said Dad.

'Remember last autumn, you and Pat told stories about long ago, and how people hid in the mausoleum during troubled times to hide from the bad soldiers.'

'That's right, Joe, it was the Black and Tans.'

'Remember you told us too, that Pat used to hide there when you were young. People used to annoy him, and he'd take the spare key belonging to his father and go there. You knew where he was, and you brought him back.'

'What has all this got to do with what happened today?' he asked.

'I never saw inside that place. I said to Sarah one day, that we should sneak the key from Pat's house, and go and have a look. Then we'd put it back.'

'Would you not ask Pat to show you?' asked Dad.

'We thought he wouldn't let us into it, that's why.'

'Did you ever think of asking him?'

'We just thought he wouldn't...'

'Go on, ask him now?'

Joe turned to Pat and asked him softly, 'Would you let us have a look inside, Pat?'

I knew that this was going to be the end. Pat would open the mausoleum and find that things had been moved around. This would arouse suspicion, and we were all going to jail.

Pat turned to me and said softly, 'I don't think so.'

'Why?' asked Dad.

'It's a very sad place. I have been in there many times. I feel it is time to let those poor people rest in peace.'

'I'm inclined to agree with you, Pat,' said Dad.

'Y-y-you were not going to steal any money, Sarah?'

'No, Pat! I wasn't! I would never do that. I didn't know what to say when you startled me like that. I didn't know it would upset you. I'm so sorry.'

'It's alright,' he said. 'I'm so glad.'

I went over to him and hugged him tightly. There was a stale smell from him, and I knew he could do with a wash.

'Pat Reardon, get the hot water out tonight!' I said.

'Sarah!' exclaimed Dad.

The boys started laughing, as did Pat, and then my father. It broke the ice again, regarding the stealing incident. Pat helped Dad from the chair, and for the first time, he was walking alone using a walking stick with his good hand. They walked to the door, and out to the gate, moving slowly.

'You know something, Pat,' he said, 'I'm afraid you will be soon without a job.'

'Please God,' said Pat, 'Please God!'

'There's something else too.'

'What's that?'

'I think it's time to get rid of that auld key and stay away from that graveyard. Let the dead rest. There's no need for you to go there anymore.'

'I think so too,' said Pat. 'I'll d-d-dump that key.'

'Yeah, do that. You'll have peace of mind and you won't be disturbing the dead ever again.'

Dad took out his pipe and lit it. It was the first time he did it since he came home. Looking out the door, I could see a blue puff of smoke rise into the soft late February air. Pat left him and went to help the boys with the evening chores. Passing by, he winked at me, and it was some change from a half hour previously. It's as if the whole event didn't happen at all. Dad could feel the breeze on his face, and just being there, was making his blood flow in his veins again. He was pondering on all that happened, and every so often I could hear him sigh.

'Aye!' he'd say, and look away in a different direction. I put my arm around him, and he turned to me. The smell of pipe tobacco smoke was ever-present in the air, and it was a smell synonymous with him. It wasn't a bad smell, but it was that smell that reminded me of him, even if he weren't present, whether in a bar, or a restaurant, that tobacco smell was *his*, and it was good to know he was there.

'I'm sorry Dad,' I said, 'I didn't mean to upset you.'

'Listen, acushla, all I have been through this winter, I wasn't upset one bit. I know you wouldn't steal money. I know Pat too, and he often got upset like that down the years, and it only took a calm word, and some reasoning to make him see sense.'

'That's why he always had a lot of time for you, Dad. You understand him and know how to help him.'

'I suppose. I don't know what's going to happen to him, if we head off across the water.'

'I don't want to think about that,' I said. 'I'm sure Mr and Mrs Walsh will keep an eye on him. He helps them a lot.'

'Lots of changes happening to us all, Sarah, and I still feel you were cheated of your childhood.'

'That's enough, Dad! I have you, and my brothers, and hopefully Mam also.'

'I don't think that will ever happen,' he sighed.

'We can only pray and hope she returns.'

As we spoke, Meg returned, and we opened the gate, so that she could drive the car into the yard. She got out of the car, and she had many parcels wrapped in brown paper tied with string. As always, she looked like a queen, and today she had a smile on her face.

'Well, go on tell me, did anything exciting take place today?' she asked.

'Nothing exciting ever happens around here,' said Dad, 'only if there was an earthquake or a murder, there's nothing to excite us at all.' Dad turned and walked slowly using the stick to the kitchen.

'Well you're making progress that's excitement enough,' said Meg. She winked at me as she said this, and I helped her bring her parcels in. I was excited to see what she had bought, and I couldn't wait to help her open them.

Three days later, Pat arrived late in the afternoon. That was unusual for him. He rode the bike all four miles to the lake. We wondered what he was doing there.

'I took the boat out,' he said, 'and I flung that auld key into the middle of the lake. N-n-no one will ever get it there.'

There was no way now, I could ever get Mam's body from the mausoleum, and into the woods. Dad would have to live with the fact, that Mam was gone. There was never any hope now of recovering her body.

'Let the whole thing rest now,' said Meg. 'She's really gone and it's time to let her go.'

Chapter 39

Meg's departure

Spring came in March, and the days were brighter. There was a renewed hope in our lives. Dad had the plaster taken off his arm, and he was walking still with a stick, but was now more confident in himself. His appetite returned, and there was colour in his cheeks once more. The cow was again in calf, and we looked forward to another arrival later in the year. Her milk began to drain away, and we had to either buy some in the village or have it delivered to the door.

Ellen Walsh heard that there was a shortage of milk in the house, when she saw me buying a bottle in the village shop. Their shortage at Christmas saw her return the compliment, as some of their cows had spring calves, and they were sending milk to the creamery once again. Pat brought a sweet can full every evening on his way home, as he had to help the family with the sheep during the busy lambing season. It was on an evening in mid-March that he arrived with a box on the back of the bike, and he called the boys. Packy beat the older boys in racing to the gate to see what it contained. As they approached, a little day-old bleating lamb stuck its head out.

'Ah look!' said Packy.

'I thought you might look after her for a while.'

'What about her mother?' asked Joe.

'S-s-she had three of them, and s-s-she didn't take to this one. Mr Walsh is wondering will you rear her as a pet.'

'She's lovely!' said Tom lifting her out of the box. He left her down in the yard, and the lamb began following him.

'There's a bottle of milk for her here, her mother's milk. You will have to give it to her tonight.'

Before we knew it, the lamb was in a box of straw by the kitchen fire, and having drunk half of the bottle of milk, shaking its tail in pleasure, it was tired after its first day in the world, and fell asleep by the fire. They christened

315

her Mollie, and before long she even knew her name. As soon as the first rays of daylight appeared, she began bleating looking for attention and a feed. I warmed the rest of the bottle of mother's milk in a kettle of water and fed her. She was a beautiful little thing, with little black spots on her face. I called the boys to rise and finish feeding her. Joe took her up on his knee, and after a few minutes I could hear him exclaim, 'She's after pissing on me!'

I could hear Dad laughing down in the bedroom, and he shouted up at them, 'That's for luck, boys!'

I didn't think I'd hear any laughter in the house again, but it was a far better place than it had been at Christmas.

When the boys came from school, the lamb followed them to the field, and around the yard, looking for attention. She never stopped bleating, and soon when they called her name she ran to them. After about a week, Mollie was moved to a soft straw, and hay nest in the shed. A little corral, was made for her, and after a night or two of bleating non-stop, she settled into her new bed. They let her out for a while each evening when they came from school. Sputnik was not alone when the boys went down the fields, the lamb trotted after them.

On St Patrick's Day, Meg made an announcement after tea. I knew it was going to come soon, but we weren't surprised when it happened.

'I'm afraid, I will be leaving you,' she said. 'I will be returning to Dublin on the twentieth of March.'

There was silence at the table, and no one said anything. Packy got up, and went to her, clinging to her, the way he used to cling to Mam. Then Dad spoke, 'How will I ever repay you for all you have done for my family?'

'I want to correct you there, John Cregan. They are my family too, and they always will be. They have given me a new lease of life, and a new hope over the past number of weeks.'

'You know what I mean,' said Dad. 'I don't know what I'd have done only for you. My children would have been taken away from me, and I might never have got them back. That's a debt I can never repay.'

'Well let's put it this way, it's paid in full. I have had a great time. It's been very sad too, but it's a time I will always remember. Isn't that right, Sarah?' she winked at me, and I knew it said multitudes.

'I don't want you to go Meg!' said Packy.

'I'm afraid I have to,' she said. 'I can't stay forever. But is it alright if I come to see you sometime?'

'You can come every day if you want to,' said Tom.

'Well, it's a long journey to come from Dublin to visit, and then return home again.'

'You could come by train!'

'I could indeed,' she laughed, 'but I've got itchy feet, and I have to return and do the thing I did all my life. I need to earn some money to live. You lot are an expensive crew to look after.'

'I can give you some money if you need any,' said Dad.

'I'm only joking,' she laughed, 'but I must go and do what comes naturally to me.'

'We'll miss you so much,' said Packy.

'I'll miss you too,' she said. I could see a tear at the corner of her eye, and I knew deep down inside, she was in great pain, the pain of loneliness, as she wasn't sure what the future held for her. She knew I could read this on her face, and I said nothing. I wanted that moment to talk to her myself.

It happened the night before she left. She was packing her bags, which included the big carpet bag full of tricks, she dipped into now and again.

I sat on my bed as I watched her, and we said little. She hung her new summer coat, a bright blue, with large black buttons, on a hanger on the wardrobe door.

'That looks lovely on you,' I said.

'It would look nicer on you,' she replied.

'No, it wouldn't, why do you say that?'

'I'm leaving it for you. It does fit, I know!'

'I can't wear it, it's too nice. It cost you a lot of money.'

'Will you stop judging things by cost? If you think about it, money has no value. We must leave it all behind us. So, if someone gives you a gift, take it and run, girl. If it's taken away from you, you might never get it back.'

'I have no choice then!'

'Exactly!'

'I will wear it with pride,' I said.

'If you have a search around that old wardrobe, there might be a few other items there which will be of use to you when I'm gone.'

I hugged her, and held her close. I could feel her body shake with a sigh, resembling a great sob. I wanted to hold on to that moment with her, and hope that it would never go away.

'Meg, I have something to ask you?'

'What is it?'

'I want you to be my mother.'

'I can't ever replace your mother, you know that.'

'No, will you hear me out. I know that can never happen. But from now on, I want you to be my mother. I don't mean that you will have to marry Dad or anything…'

'Don't you dare try any matchmaking with me, girl. If you do, I'll hit you a wallop that will send you into the middle of next week!'

We started to laugh, and then we began to cry, and after a moment or two of silliness, she took my two hands and said, 'If you want me to be your mother, it comes with a cost.'

'What's that?' I asked.

'Will you be my daughter too?'

'Always! Forever and always!'

We sat there in the room sighing, and talking, and packing things away slowly. I had to sit on one case so that she could close it, and lock it. I made her a cup of tea, and we sat on the side of the bed just saying nothing. I knew there were other things she wanted to say, but she had to be careful, as at times the walls of our house had ears. She took a little red memo notebook out of her bag, and handed it to me.

'All the information you need is in here. I have phone numbers, addresses, and dates of my locations for the summer. If I have an engagement on a certain date, I will be at that address, and I will be available at that telephone number.

If you hear anything about Darcy or Eileen, ring me immediately. If it is urgent, and I cannot be contacted, tell whoever is on the line that Mollie rang. I will know it's important, and I will come immediately. I have arranged with Maura at the post office to keep the line open for you. If you cannot get me immediately, wait at the phone. I have the number, and I will ring you back. I will be working in Ireland until July, and the show moves to Liverpool then. If you need me I have a stand-in, in the play. Put that notebook away safely and don't let it be seen.'

I hid it under my mattress. No one ever went into my room. I only allowed the boys in, if they were invited to talk or sometimes to read. We must have been together there for two hours, when Dad called from the kitchen.

'Are you two women finished nattering up there? Will that daughter of mine come down here, and make her poor neglected father a sup of tae? He wants to go to bed.'

'We'll be down in a minute,' said Meg. 'Do you hear him, Sarah? Playing the martyr, he is. He's well on recovery road, when he's able to give out like that.'

I could hear him laughing to himself in the kitchen.

The boys were mute next morning. She promised to leave them to the school one last time. They didn't feel like eating any breakfast, but she was a little bit firm with them, and they did as she asked. Deep down inside, she was all choked up herself, having to go away. But it would be the first time since Mam died that we'd have no mother figure in our lives. We got so used to her being there, that losing her was the last link we had with Mam. I knew she'd be back again, whenever her time allowed. If there was an emergency in our lives, she was only a phone call away. Her heart was breaking for the boys, and she knew they felt the same. I went with her to the school, and the boys sat in the backseat of the car. Before we left the yard, Joe said, 'Meg, can I give you a big hug and a kiss, before we get to the school? I don't want the other boys seeing me do it. They'll be saying it was all yucky and horrible. Can I do it now?'

'I want to as well,' said Tom.

'Me too,' said Packy.

'All these modest little boys,' she laughed. 'In a few years they'll be really worried if the girls aren't kissing them.'

'Will you stop that?' said Joe.

'We're not like Sarah! She's the one who does all the kissing,' said Tom.

I was laughing to myself, as they got out of the car again. Dad was standing at the door with blue smoke billowing from his pipe. He held it firmly between his teeth in a big grin. I knew he was proud of his little boys, the way they were expressing their farewell to Meg. Yet they were the tough little gents, not wanting the world to see their sadness. Meg held each one of them tight, hugging them, and kissing them, and they went quietly into the car wiping their tearful eyes in their sleeves. There was very little said as she drove to the school. She took her time to share their last moments together. She stopped at the shop to buy them some chocolate, and drove on quickly to the school. I pulled the car seat forward to let them out. They stood at the gate, as she turned the car, and then ran into the schoolyard across the stile.

When we got home, Pat had arrived on his way to Walsh's. He knew she was leaving, and he wanted to say goodbye, too. We carried her luggage to the car and helped her pack it in. She went to the room for the last check on her face and makeup, then walked like a queen through the kitchen. It reminded me of the final scene in a play, when she emerged to take a bow. Dad shook her hand, but she grabbed him in a big hug and planted a kiss on his face.

'You're not getting away that lightly, John Cregan.'

'Thank you for everything,' he said.

She did the same to Pat, who just laughed and giggled as she kissed him.

'You need a woman to mind you, Pat Reardon. You know that?'

'I thought I had one, but she will never marry me,' he smiled at me as he said this.

'You need a mature woman, not a little slip of a thing like Sarah.'

Pat laughed again, and she tossed her scarf around her neck to show that she was leaving, and that now was the time to go. When she turned to me, the tears came. She held me close. There was nothing to say, as we had said everything the night before. Then she whispered in my ear, 'If you need me, use the notebook.' It felt as if we were never going to see her again.

Dad put his arm around my shoulder and held me tight as I wiped the tears away. She reversed the car out onto the laneway, and as she tried to move forward the gears stuck and didn't make contact. It took a while to adjust them, and they scraped and scratched until the car zoomed away across the rise, to the main road. She didn't want to delay in leaving, as the longer she delayed, the more difficult it would be to leave. Dad said nothing but just stood there, and gave his usual sigh, 'Aye!' It meant a lot, and I knew that deep down inside he was sad as well.

'There goes one great person,' he said.

'I know, Dad, I know.'

'This means that you have to be the woman of the house now,' he said. I took his hand and together, we went quietly into the kitchen.

Chapter 40

In the doldrums

The postman arrived at noon, and there was a letter from Seán. Dad saw me bring it to the bedroom, and from his chair, he said, 'Is that from Mr Sunshine?'

'Stop, Dad!' I said. He laughed to himself and turned on the wireless to listen to the news. I sat on the bed, and the blue envelope stared up at me with a stamp showing the map of Ireland on it. As before, I was hesitant to open it, for fear that he might be telling me that it was all over between us. Our agreement to be friends made earlier, I hoped still held, and I prayed that there was no change in that matter. I opened it and read.

Dear Sarah,

I hope that we can still go to the Easter Sunday night dance in the hall. I can't wait to get home. I'm studying round the clock, and I have a lot of decisions to make regarding the future. I will tell you about it at Easter. The Leaving Cert begins in early June, and I will be home at the end of June for the summer.

I hope I didn't upset you, in my last letter, but there has been a lot going through my head now, but thankfully things are much better. I hope that no matter what happens, we will always be friends.

I'm so glad to hear that your Dad is recovering well and walking again. I pray every day for the safe return of your mother. She is always on my mind. The school was freezing cold all through January, and many of us got the flu. I was in the infirmary for three days, but when I began to feel a little bit better, they sent me back to class, as I can't afford to waste any time. On Saint Patrick's Day, we were allowed into the town after mass, and we went to a GAA match in the park. So much excitement in boarding school!

I'm counting the days till Easter. I will be home on Spy Wednesday, and I'll see you at the Holy Thursday ceremonies.

Don't forget to write back, looking forward to hearing from you.

Lots of love,

Seán

322

I didn't write back, as I didn't know what to say. I felt from the letter that he was trying to distance himself from me. It didn't feel like the Seán who kissed me at the gate in the early new year, when he was heading back to boarding school. I put the letter back in the envelope and placed it in the drawer with the other letters I had. I was happy inside, but there wasn't certainty there. I went about my morning chores, while Dad had a nap in his chair. I decided I was going to wear the blue coat Meg had given me, and when I thought about it I went back to my bedroom, opened the wardrobe and put it on. I stood looking at myself in the mirror, and I thought it was gorgeous. I realised then that she didn't buy that for herself. In fact, she had bought it for me. It was a coat a young person wore. But then, Meg was the eternal young person. When I was putting it back in the wardrobe, I noticed something else. It was a cardboard box, loosely closed at the top. I lifted it out onto the bed. Written in ink on the top of it was, *this should keep you in plentiful supply.*

I opened it, and inside was her box of makeup, some of it for theatre use, but there were new supplies of talcum powder, lipstick, eyeliners and pencils, and beautiful brushes for applying makeup to your face. I felt like sitting at the mirror and doing my face up, but I feared that Dad would think I was too vain, and that I'd have nothing better to do. I sat there opening each container and holding them close to my nose, to sample the aroma. There were small bottles of perfume in a box, each one marked with the day of the week in French, denoting that there was a different aroma for each day. I thought they were gorgeous, and I sampled the one for today, and I dabbed some at the back of each ear. I put it back in its own little space. I closed the box and placed it back in the wardrobe. I dressed my bed, and I did the same with the bed Meg slept in at the other end of the room. It was going to be lonely without her, but I knew when the boys came home there'd be plenty of noise and talk, but I was wrong.

When they finally arrived home from school, there was very little said. Joe threw his schoolbag in the corner and said he was going to the shed to let Mollie out, and to feed her a bottle of milk with glucose in it. Tom went with him. Packy went to his room and shut the door. After a few minutes, I could hear him sobbing. Dad told me to go to him and see how he was. He was lying with his clothes on under the blankets. He had his thumb in his mouth, and he was crying into the pillow. The pillow slip was wet with his tears. He sat up and I pulled him close to me and put his arms around me.

'It's alright, Packy,' I said. 'Please don't cry!'

'Why?' he asked.

'What do you mean why?'

'Why do all those we love very much either die or go away?'

'Be careful what you say,' I whispered. But as usual, Packy said the right thing.

'Dad went away and nearly died. Mam is gone, we don't know where she is. Then Meg went away. Are you going to leave me, Sarah?'

'No, I'm not, and get that idea out of your head.'

'Are we ever going to be happy ever again?'

'We will just give it time,' Dad stood in the doorway leaning on his stick. He had tears streaming down his face too. He came over to the bed and sat down beside us. He pulled Packy from my grasp and sat him on his knee.

'Come here, son! I'm never going away ever again. If I ever should go, you will be all coming with me.'

'Are you going to tell him?' I asked.

'We might all leave here in a while, it could be a few months or a year. I have to wait and see.'

'Wait and see for what?'

'I have to wait for Mam to return.'

'Dad, Mam will never come back now, not ever.'

'I want to make sure, son.'

'I know, Dad. I know inside me. She is not coming back.'

'Well, I have to be sure.'

'Where are we going?'

'Scotland.'

'Beezer!' he exclaimed through his tears.

'Would you like that?'

'Only if you will be there with us.'

'I'm never leaving your side, ever again.'

'Well, I can't wait to go. This house has been too sad for the past while.'

'I am inclined to agree with you, lad.'

I left them there and went to stoke up the fire for the night. He sat there, and clung to Dad, his sobs dwindling with every breath. I didn't know how long they were going to sit there, but half an hour later, I peeped in. Dad was asleep with his head resting on the headboard, while Packy lay cradled in his uninjured arm, and he too, had gone to sleep. I went to Joe's bed and took the big heavy coat from the bottom of the bed, and I covered them. I then realised that Dad was making up for time he had lost with his children, and now he was preparing to be mother, as well as father. I knew he was going to do a great job of it.

Chapter 41

Joe's Shiner

There was another incident at school the next day. This time it involved Joe. He arrived home with a note from Master Ryan for Dad. He went to his room and shut the door. Dad sat up in his chair and read the note.

Dear Mr Cregan,

Just a note to inform you that Joe was in a fist fight today with another boy. I am a firm believer in the proverb, 'spare the rod and spoil the child.' I didn't inflict any physical punishment on the lads, as it was a spur of the moment issue. They have both apologised to each other and have promised never to have a repeat performance. I told them that if they wished to be boxers or fighters, to join the club in the town. Joe will tell you what happened, as they have promised me to be truthful to their parents. Ask him also about the punishment I have suggested for them. I'd say you will have no problem with it. I'm sorry to have to send this note to you, as you have enough to deal with now.

Yours Sincerely,

Donal Ryan

I have never seen Dad angry with any of his children over the years, and I knew that on this occasion he would deal with the situation quietly, and with dignity. He showed me the note, and winked at me as if to say, I'm going to have some fun with this guy. In a loud voice, he called out, 'Joe!' There was no answer from the bedroom. He called his name again.

'Joe! You're not deaf, are you?' There was a muffled reply of 'No!' from the bedroom.

'Can you come out here now? We need to talk.'

Slowly the doorknob turned, and Joe came quietly from the room.

When he looked up, I saw that he had a black eye. I gave a muffled laugh, and as I did so he shouted at me. 'Stop laughing at me, Sarah.' I turned my head away and tried to restrain myself from any further laughing.

Dad, of course, added a bit of threat to the conversation, to establish that he was boss in his own home. 'Joe, stop that now! I want to talk to you, I don't want to fight with you. But if I must, I will get you across my knee and give you something you will never forget.'

There was silence as Joe wiped his face, as well as the tears he was holding back with the sleeve of his jumper. Then he spoke softly, 'Alright then.'

Dad turned to Packy and Tom and told them to go out and find something to do. I pretended to be busy at the window washing some plates and dishes from the earlier bread baking.

'I have read this note from Master Ryan, and I must say I think the man is an out and out gentleman. He didn't tell me what happened, but I want you to tell me the truth.'

'It was Teddy Farrell I had the fight with.' I knew who it was, it was his Dad who gave Joe the lift to town in the snow to find Meg at the station.

'Go on,' said Dad.

'It was something he said.'

'I'm listening.'

'He wanted to know did they find my mad mother yet,' Joe held his head down and stopped speaking.

'Continue.'

'I got angry.'

'And then what?'

'I hit him!'

Dad sat up in his chair and looked at the note again. Then he looked closer at Joe and said, 'You know what, Joe, if I was in your shoes, I'd hit him too.' Joe looked up at him with his mouth open wide, as he wasn't expecting the conversation to go in this direction. Neither did I, to say the least. But there was more to come. 'I know how you feel, son. I feel the same way. I'm hurting inside also, and I'm angry too. It's very easy to show your anger by lashing out and hitting someone like that. But it won't get you anywhere. If you were older, it could land you in jail.'

'I'm sorry, Dad,' said Joe.

'Don't be saying sorry, lad. It's me who should be sorry, for letting all this happen to you.'

'People say horrible things sometimes and it makes me mad.'

'I know that. If I got a pound for every stupid thing people said to me over the years, I'd be living in a mansion with a staff of servants.'

'It won't happen again, Dad.'

'I know it won't, but Joe there's one thing that's making me laugh – that's a right shiner you have there.'

Joe laughed through his tears, as Dad chuckled to himself. Then came his usual phrase, 'Aye!' The pipe came out of his pocket, and he began to get it ready to light up for a well-earned smoke. He wasn't finished yet, as he required more information from Joe.

'Tell me this, son, and tell me no more. Has the other lad a black eye also?'

'No, but he has a bruise on his face.'

'He'll live,' he said, and lighting the pipe took a few puffs, which when exhaled filled the house with the sweet pipe tobacco smell. He was contemplating his next question. 'Again, tell me this and tell me no more, what punishment has the master suggested for you both?'

'He told us it was a kind of community work,' said Joe.

'Go on?'

'I won't be here on Saturday.'

'Why? What's happening?'

'The master wants us to go to the schoolhouse, as he had a job he wanted to be done. He has bought a second-hand boat, and he wants us to help him paint it.'

'That will do you both good.'

'I'm sorry, Dad. I won't do it again.'

'I know that, son. I know that. It's a lesson hard learned, but in a few years, you will be a man, and I hope you remember all these things. There will be lots more difficult times ahead, but we are the Cregan's, and we should never let things get the better of us.' He sat there smoking his pipe, and an expression of calm and peace on his face. Joe knew that the conversation was over and proceeded to join his brothers outside. As he passed by, Dad put his fists up to him in a gesture of fun and banter. Joe ran, uplifted and proud.

His punishment was soon becoming a part-time job. Donal Ryan asked him to attend every Saturday, as he wanted to have the boat ready to take out on the lake in July, when the school closed for the holidays. Because of this, Joe's school work improved, and with the impending Primary Cert Exam, Joe was more focused on his work, and wanted to leave national school on a high note.

Each Saturday evening, he talked to Dad about flies and baits, and all the varied fishing tackle which fishermen used on the lake. There were long conversations with Donal Ryan in this regard, and Dad felt it was a way of taking his mind off all those things that were pressing on him for the past few months. Joe was beginning to grow up, and he knew it. He was growing out of his clothes, and as money was still coming from Scotland, he could take them all to town before Easter, and get them new clothes. This was work that was always left to Mam, but he asked me to come along, and help, as he wanted them all looking dapper, and well for Easter Sunday Mass. Clothes shopping was done on Spy Wednesday, and he hired a hackney to take us all to town. He was moving quite well, but he used the walking stick, and we moved slowly through the streets. Indeed, we didn't go unnoticed, as there were many people who came to us, to wish us well, and to share their prayers for Mam's return.

Chapter 42

The Decision

On our way from town on Spy Wednesday, Dad got the hackney driver to stop at the village shop, as there were several items required at home in preparation for fasting on Good Friday. One such item was some smoked haddock, for our one main meal of the day, as there was no meat allowed on Friday. As well as that, I had some shopping to do in preparation for Easter Sunday. The shop had changed in recent times. It had become all modern and extended. Goods were out on shelves, as well as behind the counter, and a new word 'supermarket' was being used instead of the word shop. I picked up a basket inside the door and proceeded to browse through the shelves. There was a lot more in the line of new goods, some of which I had never seen or heard of before. There were boxes of cornflakes. We never had cornflakes, they weren't on Mam's shopping list, as she preferred to make porridge for breakfast each day. I decided to buy a box and have it as a treat for the boys on Easter Sunday morning. There were little chocolate Easter Eggs, and I bought some of them as well. Ellen Walsh was in the shop too, and she was talking to Kathleen Greene. I didn't pass much heed on what they were saying at first, until I heard Seán's name mentioned. Then I was all ears.

'That's great news,' said Kathleen, 'I always knew it was in him. He was always a gentle sort of boy and really cut out for his vocation.'

'He told us the last time we went to visit him, and he has an appointment to meet the bishop next week during the Easter Holidays.'

'When will he be heading off to the seminary?'

'September, shortly after the Leaving Cert results.'

'Heaven's above, it's a great thing he is doing. Won't it be lovely to have a priest in the family? I wonder will any of my boys go down that road. They are good lads, you know. They are at early mass each Sunday, and they never complain. I don't know what we will make of them. They might follow their father into the guards. He would be proud of that. A son a priest! Isn't that just great, and not alone that, he's your one and only child. He's giving his life to God. It's a great sacrifice to make.' As usual, Kathleen Greene would go on talking all day if she could, but Ellen Walsh was in a bit of a hurry, and excused herself, as she made her way to the counter.

Seán's recent silence and apprehension to write to me now became clear. He was making decisions and had chosen a path to the priesthood. When I recalled how he kissed me last autumn, and again at Christmas, was he still trying to make up his mind to a life of celibacy? Was I his pawn? Was I someone he was testing his conscience upon? I mustn't have made much of an impression, as he was now going away to study for many years. I felt betrayed inside, and disappointed. I made my way to the payment counter, and placed the basket in front of the girl who was checking everything on the cash register?

'Have you a bag?' she asked.

I put a sackcloth shopping bag on the counter, and she placed each item in it as she checked everything. She was chewing some gum. It was something I had never seen before either. It was for sale in the shop at two for a penny. I decided not to buy any, as I had been extravagant with the cornflakes and the Easter Eggs.

Ellen saw me and came to me. She didn't see me till now, and she knew that I had heard the conversation between herself and Kathleen Greene.

I didn't want to pretend that I hadn't heard what was said, and she gave her usual smile which was part of her personality.

'And how are you Sarah?'

I replied quickly and to the point. 'I know about Seán. I heard what you both were saying.'

'It's his decision. We had no say in the matter.'

'It's alright!' I replied. 'It's his life, and he can be whatever he wants to be.'

'He's still your friend, you know.'

'I didn't say he wasn't,' I was a little narky with her, even though I shouldn't have, as she was always a great neighbour.

'He was going to tell you tomorrow himself, but now you know. And I'm glad you heard it before the whole world knows.'

'Is that supposed to make it easier for me?' I asked rather abrupt again.

'Sarah, I'm sorry you feel as you do about Seán. He made the decision himself. It was as much a shock for us as it was for you too.'

'I knew something was the matter with him from his letters, but he wouldn't tell me.'

'He didn't tell us either, he kept it all to himself. At the end of the day it was his decision to make, and it wasn't up to us to influence him.'

'Well, if this is what he wants to do, let him do it. I don't want to stop him. It's best I keep away from him, let him follow his dreams.'

'Sarah, you have common sense beyond your young years,' she said in a rather patronising sort of way.

'Mrs Walsh, you don't know the half of it. I won't be going to the dance on Sunday night. It wouldn't do for me to be seen influencing a young lad whose pathway was leading him to God.'

'It's not the end of the world. You said yourself, he's still your friend.'

'Wish him well for me, Mrs Walsh, and thank you for all your kindness for the past number of weeks.'

I paid the gum-chewing young cashier, and taking the bag, walked out of the shop leaving Ellen Walsh and her ever-kind smile, with the curious faces of other local people who were shopping as well.

'You were a long time,' said Dad. 'This poor man driving us hasn't got all day.'

'It's a long story,' I said. 'Now let us get home.'

I was in a bad mood all evening, and the boys kept well away from me. Dad sat in the corner, observing all the activity in the kitchen. I was peeling potatoes and banging pots. Again, I felt that everything I ever held dear, was either dead, or going away from me. Now I was losing Seán. The house was quiet, and by dinner time I knew everyone had enough. It was time for me to get out and go to the place I went when things were bad for me. The rick of hay was still sheltered from the prevailing winds, and the wall created by the cutting of the hay knife provided space for me. It was beginning to lose height now, as most of it was consumed by Tossie and the red cow over the winter. By early May it would be all gone, and there'd be no shortage of feed for them as a new crop of spring grass emerged.

I gathered some dry hay around my legs and sat there staring into the pale spring sunshine. There were still traces of melting snow in the nooks and crannies of the hedge, like little ice sheets immersed in a quiet sheltered mountain valley. Spring flowers were nodding at the brighter light, soaking the sunlight to encourage them to run to seed. Primroses and celandines were competing for the light, and yet they acknowledged each other's presence reaching for the life-giving light.

This was still my refuge. I came here when Mam died last winter, and at times when I just wanted to get away from it all, it was that little space to hold on to. Sputnik sat staring me in the face, panting quietly to himself. I gently rubbed his ears, and just sat staring at the young spring flowers, and the melting ice. Soon a great big shadow blocked the sunlight and I knew it was Dad. He said nothing all evening but waited for his moment to come to me.

'Aye,' he sighed, taking the pipe out of his mouth.

'Go away Dad!' I exploded at him.

'Aye! Well now, you know as much as I do. I'm not going to go away.'

Using his walking stick, he lowered himself onto the hay, and then Sputnik began licking his face. He pushed him away, and he lay down at his feet. He took a tin of tobacco from the breast pocket of his coat. It was a tin with a blue lid, *Mick McQuaid*, with the picture of a smiling man on the front of it. It was that sweet smell of the tobacco that appealed to me, not the smoke itself. It pervaded his clothes and his very being, and I was never threatened by it, even though in later years I came to understand the dangers of smoking, but at that time in the spring of 1963, it posed no threat, but was part and parcel of our lives in our little house, and it often made me smile.

'Come on, out with it. What happened in the shop today?' he asked quietly.

'I met Mrs Walsh.'

'Well, what had she to say for herself then?'

'I don't want to say…'

'Has that young man decided to call it a day with you?'

'No, he hasn't! He's still my friend, but he can never be mine.'

'Some other young lady has taken his fancy then,' he said with a smirk on his face, as he lit the pipe full of tobacco, and blew a cloud of smoke out into the cold air, carrying it away, and disappearing in the breeze.

'No, it's not like that. He has decided to become a priest,' I answered.

The first light of the pipe didn't work, and saying nothing, he drew out a match and lit his pipe again.

'Careful with that match, and don't burn the hay down,' I grumbled at him.

He totally ignored what I said, but I knew he would be careful anyway. He shook it, and threw it out onto the yard, and turning to me he said, 'You know something, you're beginning to sound more like your mother every day.'

'I wish it was her that was saying this to you, Dad.'

'So, do I,' he answered, as he put his arm around me. It was comforting to know he was there for me, his sweet tobacco smell, and the protective feeling it gave me, when I recalled sitting on his knee when I was a little girl.

'He's your first love, you know.'

'Why did he decide to give it all up and go away like that? I thought we had something really nice between us.'

Dad took the pipe out of his mouth tapped the ash on a piece of wood. He was extra careful no sparks fell on the dry hay. He placed the pipe in his pocket, and he sat there thinking. I knew he was lost for words, as he had never had to deal with the romantic comings and goings of a young adolescent girl. This was the sort of thing that I would have had Mam's shoulder to cry on. But she wasn't here. That made it more difficult for me. Dad couldn't cope with all this, and I knew his silence was searching his soul to find the right words to comfort me. He gently stroked my hair, and I waited, knowing that he would have to say something sometime. Then he spoke, 'You know, the first girl I fancied was Brigid Flanagan. She was two years younger than me. She had brown wavy hair and blue eyes. We used to go to the house dances. We both had bikes, and we travelled to the four corners of the parish and beyond…'

'It's alright, Dad, I don't want to know.'

'Just let me finish, will you. When she was nineteen, she decided to go to America. It nearly broke my heart then. I was going to follow her out to New York, but then I didn't.'

'Why didn't you go?'

'Something else happened.'

'What was that?

'I met your mother. She was even nicer than Brigid Flanagan. I was determined not to let her go, so the rest is history?'

'Why did you tell me this Dad?'

'What I'm saying is that there are plenty more fish in the sea. You'll find another young man, just you wait.'

'You're just trying to cheer me up, aren't you?'

'You could say that, but I'm also telling some truths. A beautiful young girl like you, why wouldn't you find someone sometime? Sure, you are only sixteen, alana! You have your whole life ahead of you. Please God, in a few months or a year you will be able to go out to work, or whatever life chooses for you. You will meet people of your own age and go places. There would be no need to lock yourself away here for the rest of your life.'

'What about all this you said about taking us to Scotland? Has that changed?'

'No! That still stands,' he sighed, 'you know why we can't go just yet.'

I had reached one of those weak moments again, where I could easily just say, 'Dad, Mam lies in a coffin below in the old mausoleum.' How would I explain all this to him? A shiver came over me, and he knew he could feel my coldness.

'You shouldn't be out here, or you'll get your death of cold.'

'You should be in at the fire,' I said to him, 'and you after being very ill in hospital.'

'There's only one problem though,' he said.

'What's that?'

'I can't get up. I got down here alright, but now how am I going to stand?'

I started to laugh and so did he. I kept laughing as I could see the colour return to his face. Soon it brought a curious audience from the sheds, three boys and Pat arrived on the scene, he was holding a four-grained fork.

'Did you fall, John?' he asked. 'Are y-y-you alright?'

'That's where you can help, Pat. I sat down here and now I can't get up.'

Pat didn't know his own strength, and he lifted Dad into a standing position, holding him till he found his balance. I handed him the walking stick and we went with him back to the kitchen. Before we reached the door, he stopped and asked, 'What about the dance then?'

'I don't think I'll go,' I said.

'I want you to do something for me,' he said.

'What's that, Dad?'

'The shops will be open in the town on Holy Saturday and I want you to do something for me.'

'I will.'

'I want you to go and buy yourself a nice colourful dress for the Easter dance.'

'That will cost too much.'

'There you go again! You are turning out just like your mother.'

'You're going to town – we are all going to go, we will go in somewhere and eat fish and chips, and you can go and buy a nice dress. We need a day out. We have been stuck in the house all year, wondering and worrying. We just need some cheering up, and especially you, after all you've been through.'

'But we were only there today.'

'I lay in that hospital bed during all those lonely days, wishing I was here with my family. Why not another day in town? We're going to go anyway. We might even get ice cream.'

Chapter 43

All's well in love and war

Seán arrived around midday on Holy Thursday. He waited at the gate, and wouldn't come in. I didn't know whether I should go out to meet him or not. The boys started teasing me that Seán was out there, and he probably wanted to kiss me. I told them to shush, as they kept on at it, I began hitting them with the tea towel.

Dad, sitting in his armchair reading the paper had a smirk on his face and said quietly, 'I think that's enough now, lads. Leave your sister alone.'

They stopped their teasing and giggled to themselves, as Dad began to read his paper again. I continued with my chores, and after a minute or so he looked up again and said, 'Are you not going out to see the young fella?'

'I don't know!' I answered gruffly.

'Well, he has made it his business to call to see you, and I think you shouldn't leave him standing there.'

'Oh alright!' I answered crossly and threw the tea towel on the kitchen table.

I closed the kitchen door as I went out, so that no one could hear what I was saying.

Seán smiled as I approached, and I knew by him, that he was reading how I felt inside. He was leaning on the handlebars of his bike, and I stood inside the gate facing him.

'Hi Sarah.'

'Hi,' I answered, omitting the usual smile I had for him. Then there was silence. You could cut the air with a knife, it was so quiet. He held his head down for a moment, and then looked up again. I knew he wanted to say something but was lost for words.

'It's a lovely day, isn't it?'

'Seán is that all you came to talk about, the weather? I know it's a nice day, but only grown-ups talk about the weather when there's nothing else to talk about.'

'I don't know what to say, Sarah,' he replied.

'Sorry would have been nice.'

'I *am* sorry. I just don't know what to say anymore?'

'You should have told me at Christmas what you intended to do, instead of leading me on like that!'

'I didn't know what I was going to do then, Sarah. I thought I was going to go to college and be an engineer or something…'

I interrupted him and spoke in a rather sarcastic tone, 'Then you had this sudden revelation, the Lord spoke in your ear. He wants you to be a priest.'

'It's not like that. There are priests in my family, and I have given it great thought. I feel I could follow in their footsteps.'

'Family tradition then,' I answered, not deviating from my sarcasm.

'Stop Sarah, please! It's not like that.'

'Well, what then? Tell me. I'd like to know.'

'It's been at the back of my mind for a while, even before I met you. I didn't want to make any decisions until I was sure. Then with Leaving Cert approaching, I had to give it some greater thought.'

'I must have been your guinea pig to experiment on. I'm a failure then if I didn't meet your standards.'

'Stop, please! You sound like an adult or a parent or someone in authority.'

'Seán Walsh, you don't know the half of it. I have had to be mother, father, teacher, guardian – everything for the past couple of months – what else can you expect? God has failed me and my family. I'm the young girl with the mad mother. Mad Mary they were calling her, now she's gone missing. Here I am now losing once more. What can you say to that?'

I was lying through my teeth again, maybe being just that little bit selfish, but I have had to be selfish. Here I was working it around the first person who ever loved me.

He held onto the handlebars of the bike rather tightly, not knowing whether to be angry or to walk away. Then a thought struck me. Why should I stand in his way? It was *his* life too, and he could follow his dreams. Dad's words were true, there were more fish in the sea. It was then the tears came. If I had a pound for all the tears I had shed in the past number of months, as Dad would say, I could build a mansion. Before I knew it, he had dropped the bike on the ground and had jumped the gate. He had his arms around me, trying to comfort me. Then I heard a tap on the kitchen window. I could see the curtain pulled back, and the boys staring wide-eyed at me. I made to go inside and chastise them, when I heard Dad call them away telling them to have some manners. I sobbed on his shoulder and he said nothing, just held me there.

After a few minutes, he spoke again with a quiver in his voice. 'I am so sorry.'

I wiped my tears and held him close, and we said nothing for a few minutes.

'I really am sorry,' he said again.

'I have lost so much lately, I'm angry...'

'Please don't be angry.'

'I'm not angry with you, Seán. I'm angry with life. I don't know what my future will be. Someday you will understand. It's not fair of me to treat you like this. You don't want to know me. Someday you might not want to know me. Believe me when I say this.'

'Why are you saying things like that? Are you going to kill someone or rob a bank?'

'Just don't say anything more about it. You are right to follow your dream. It's just I didn't know how to take it, when I overheard your mother talking in the shop the other day. It was a shock to me, and at first, I thought it was all my fault.'

'As I said in the letters, I want you to be my friend.'

'I know that. How could I do such a thing to such a nice lad? You are better off without me.'

'Please stop saying that, you are beginning to sound as if you had some big deep dark secret. It's as if you are trying to hide something.'

'Maybe I am, Seán, and maybe not. But you must do what you must do. I will have to wait and see what the future has in store for me.'

'Are we still friends?' he asked rather shyly.

'Always,' I said.

'Well, then will you escort a friend to the dance on Easter Sunday night?'

'I can't do that, you are going to be a priest.'

'Whether I am or not, I am still Seán Walsh, and I can ask who I like to the dance.'

'I will,' I answered, 'but I will meet you there.'

'Mam and Dad are going. It's a fundraiser for to help pay the debt on the hall. The whole parish will be there. Can't you sit with us? Mam and Dad will make sure that we behave ourselves.'

He jumped back across the gate again, and taking his bike said, 'We'll be here around nine o'clock.'

He was gone in a flash, and when I turned again, the curtain was raised, and my three brothers, being caught again dipped behind it. I ran to the kitchen and chased them to their room. I was going to flail them with the tea towel. They ducked behind the beds and the wardrobe. They were screaming with laughter.

'Sarah, we are so disappointed,' said Joe.

'Why?' I asked, raising the towel in the air.

'You didn't kiss him this time!'

'She can't!' said Tom. 'He's going to be a priest.'

'Yeah, if you kissed him, it would be a mortal sin,' laughed Packy.

'I'll commit another mortal sin if you don't behave yourselves.'

I closed the door and left them in the room. I sat at the end of the table, and all I could hear was Dad's usual sigh, 'Aye!' I knew that he was going to say something. Then he put the paper down slowly, and looking up at me said, 'I suppose all's well in love and war, then?'

'I don't know what you mean!' I answered pretending to be cross.

'Don't try that with me, young lady. Remember one thing, I can read you like a book. I know when things are going well with you, and I also know when you are in a mood. Right now, you are not in a mood.'

'We are going to the dance on Sunday night.'

'I thought so!'

He folded the paper and began to read it again. After a minute or two, he put it down again and continued, 'Just one thing though, is he still on for the priesthood?'

'Yes.'

'I see! Maybe now we will make a nun out of you.'

I went to hit him with the tea towel, but he grabbed me and pulled me down on his knee. He began tickling me, and I screamed with laughter. I got away and sat at the end of the kitchen table. He was laughing as well. He was getting stronger. I was feeling good again and he smiled back at me.

'We really do have to go to town on Saturday to get that dress for you.' But circumstances outside our control, dictated that the planned trip to town on Easter Saturday would not take place.

Chapter 44

Thinking of nice things

Half an hour later, the dog began to bark, and when I looked out the kitchen window I saw that it was the squad car. Sergeant Greene got out and made his way to the front door. When he knocked, Dad ordered me to let the man in.

I opened the door, and as he stepped inside, I knew that he was on official business.

'Sit down, Sergeant,' said Dad. He sat down and didn't speak until Dad addressed him. 'How can we help you, Sergeant?'

'You know why I'm here, I'd say,' he said.

'If it's the news I'm expecting, don't beat around the bush.'

'We found a body.'

'Is it Mary?'

'I don't know. It was taken from the River Boyne near Trim, this morning.'

'Well, as I have asked already, Sergeant – Is it Mary?'

'I don't know John. It's been in the water for quite a while. There are a few people missing now. There's a young woman from Louth missing since before Christmas. It could be her, but we are not sure. We would like you to come along and see if it is Mary. The missing girl's parents are coming later.'

'So, you are not sure?'

'No, but we would like you to come along and see if it is her. Are you strong enough to come with us? We'll bring you in the squad car?'

'I'll come with you, Sergeant,' he said, getting up from his chair.

Still a little unsteady at times, I knew by him now he was nervous and in shock, and he went to his room to get his coat. He brought his walking stick with him, and the sergeant held the door open for him. He turned to us as he went.

'Take it easy, Dad,' I said.

He smiled at me, patted Packy on the head, and went with the sergeant.

When they were gone, I shut the door, and sat down in his chair.

'What are we going to do now, Sarah?' asked Joe.

'Stop and let me think,' I said.

'It can't be Mam!' said Tom.

'I know it's not her, but it could be Eileen!'

'What if it is Eileen?' asked Joe.

'Dad never met her,' I said.

'Should we go and tell Meg?' asked Packy.

'No, not yet. It might not be her.'

'What if it is her?' asked Joe.

'I don't know,' I said, 'but remember one thing, we know nothing. Even if it is Eileen, we don't know her. The only people who saw her were the Wren Boys. It's not Mam, remember that, we know where she is.'

'Sarah, I'm afraid,' said Packy. 'I'm afraid again. I thought it had all gone away, and now I'm afraid it's going to happen all over again.'

I put him sitting beside me and put my arm around him. He curled up beside me, and I knew I would not get any more work done till Dad came home. I sent the boys to their room, and I sat back in the chair with Packy. He was a little shivery and frightened, and I told him everything was going to be alright.

'Sarah, I still have nightmares about that night in the graveyard.'

'Don't say anything, everything will be fine. Think of some nice things. I have bought cornflakes for you as a treat on Easter Sunday morning.'

'I never had cornflakes.'

'They have them in the new shop in the village.'

'I'd like that.'

'You see, think of nice things Packy, and the bad things go away.'

'I'll try,' he said.

'Remember when Dad came back from England last year, and he brought you the pad and we made charcoal.'

'Yeah, I drew a picture of you,' he said.

'I wanted to keep it, and you said it wasn't good enough. Well, I tore it out and left it in the shed beside the tools.'

'Have you still got it?' he asked.

'No, I thought you might have torn it up,' I said.

'I didn't. It was in the shed for a good while, up to near Christmas. Then it went.'

'It probably blew away with the wind. I will have to get you to do another one, and this time you are not going to tear it up.'

'I promise I won't,' he said.

I could feel that he had calmed down and began to relax. Soon he fell asleep and I laid him gently back on the chair and covered him with my cardigan.

Then just out of the blue, Pat arrived.

'Any news yet?' he asked.

'No Pat, no news. Dad is gone with the guards to see if it is Mam or not?'

'It can't be her,' he exclaimed.

'Why do you say that, Pat?' I asked.

'I just know,' he answered, 'it's too far away.'

'Mam might have gone there by bus or car.'

'No! Not at all Sarah, and the w-w-weather was so bad at the time, with snow and all that. W-w-where could she go in the night?'

'I don't know, Pat!' I began to wonder to myself, where this was all going. Pat had thrown away the key to the mausoleum, and there was no way anyone would find Mam's body now. If Eileen's body turned up, who was to know who she was, and it was something Meg was going to have to deal with. Pat was as much in the dark as Dad was, and Meg's earlier performance as Mam or Mad Mary convinced him that she was around until after Christmas. My great fear was Packy, or one of the other two boys, who in a moment of madness would let the cat out of the bag. Then I would have to face the music. There were times when I woke up at night living the nightmare, wishing to turn the clock back to last October, and to convince Dad not to return to work in England. Pat, as usual, was there to reassure me that everything was alright.

'You know that I will protect you for the rest of your life, Sarah.' He had said it all before, and this time he didn't stammer. It was something said from the heart, and I began to wonder what he meant at times. My childhood soul found this flattering, but my approaching womanhood often made me think was it just an infatuation or what. But I trusted Pat with my life always and wondered why he kept saying this to me.

'It's not her Sarah. I know it.'

'I hope you are right, Pat,' I answered.

I asked him to stay till Dad came back, and he went and helped with the evening chores outside. The spring evening was ending, and tea was over, when the sergeant dropped Dad off at the gate. I knew by him that his journey was a needless one. He came in and sat down in his chair. He didn't speak but gave his usual sigh.

'I'm so sorry, Dad,' I sighed.

'It was that young woman from Louth. All I had to do was look at her to see it wasn't your Mam.'

'It's alright, Dad. It's alright,' I said. I didn't know what to say or how this whole affair was going to end.

Chapter 45

Easter 1963

Easter came quietly, and we all went to morning mass. Eyes were on us again, as word got around that Dad had to go to Meath to check whether the body found in the Boyne was that of Mam or not. The whole incident saw a change in Dad. The progress he was making had turned around. He sat in the chair by the fire since Thursday and wouldn't do anything for anyone. The guilt factor returned to me again, and I was blaming myself for making him suffer. I could end it all by coming clean about everything. I was waking up at night myself again, and with broken sleep as a result, I became cranky and temperamental too.

We walked to the village on that fine, but cold morning. I could feel people looking at me going into the church. I made sure my hat sat correctly on my head. I sat on the women's side, while the boys went to the men's.

Joe served mass along with two other boys, and I had to make sure he was spick and span. His hair sat down neatly on his head, kept in place with a dollop of Brylcreem. He took his job seriously and joined the other boys in answering the Latin prayers of the mass.

I didn't see the Walsh family at mass, but they had probably gone to the early one. I was glad in a way, as I didn't want to meet Seán in such a public place.

I was ready for the dance that night, and I'd meet him there.

This morning I took my prayers seriously, and I prayed so much that I was almost in tears pleading with God, to save us from this awful tragedy we were suffering. I prayed so much that my eyes were red, and people could not but notice my distress. I sat up on the seat, and a lady behind me tapped me on the shoulder.

'Are you alright, love?' she asked.

'I'm fine I whispered.'

'We are all praying for you. We are so sorry you haven't heard anything.'

'Thank you very much,' I whispered.

I turned away again, kneeling as the priest continued with the consecration of the mass. I implored all the saints in heaven to come to my aid, as well as all the angels and archangels. This could not continue, and Dad was suffering too. I began to fear we might lose him, if he wasn't able to cope with his loss. I felt that if he had closure, and that Mam's body was recovered, things would start to improve. The proposed move to Glasgow was on hold, and I didn't envisage anything happening in this regard until that happened. Ideas raced through my head. There was no way we could even get to her body, as it was locked away in a coffin in the mausoleum. If Eileen's body turned up somewhere, that would be Meg and Darcy's problem. So, at this mass, I implored and begged the good Lord to help me. I was at my wits end, to know what to do, and I made a decision that be it long or be it short, I would have to tell the sergeant. I'd suffer jail, or even Dad throwing me out of the house, if I knew it would help him have some peace of mind. He was a man innocent of everything, and it was not fair to see him suffer so much. His physical injuries were recovering, but deep down the mental scars went deep. His mental injuries were also being impinged upon, with the loss of the only person he ever loved.

I went to Holy Communion, and my prayers once more were reaching upwards to heaven in pleading for inspiration, and for closure to the whole sordid affair. I made a promise that morning to God, that if we came through this, I would always look after Dad, and ensure he led a normal life. I'd be there for him no matter what. The boys would eventually go their way in life and leave home. I promised to care for him. It was the least I could do because of what happened. I began to feel an inner peace, and I'd do my utmost to make amends for all that had happened.

The prayers after mass were being recited, and I joined in with everyone else and soon, Father Doyle gave the blessing and he exited the altar into the vestry, as the choir sang a final Easter hymn. When I got to the door outside, Joe was standing waiting in his soutane with a request from Father Doyle for me to go around to the vestry.

I followed Joe, and he went to the boys' vestry to put away his soutane, while Billy the sacristan hung it up with the rest of the vestments. He tidied their altar shoes as well leaving them stored neatly under a little table.

'I could see you were somewhat distressed this morning child,' he said. 'I'm sorry they didn't find your Mam the other day.'

'Thank you, Father,' I answered.

'Just remember, God doesn't close one door, but he opens another.'

'He's a long time opening it, Father.'

'Be patient child!'

'It's easier said than done. I'm worried now about Dad, he wouldn't come to mass today.'

'He will be back soon. I'll come to see him one of the days this week.'

'He would like that. He needs to talk to people. He's wanting to drink also, and I don't want that to happen.'

'I don't know what to say to you. Life has dealt you a hard blow, but you're a very strong young woman, and he's lucky to have you.'

'I don't want to lose him. I don't want to lose my brothers either. Would God forgive me if I did terrible things to keep them all together?'

'I don't know what you mean by that. Are you going to commit murder or something?'

'I don't know what I'm saying sometimes. I just don't know what way things are going to go. I fear for my family. They mean so much to me, and it looks as if it is all falling apart. We need Dad now, and since he went to Meath a few days ago, I can get no good of him.'

'All I can do is pray for you, Sarah. That's all I can do.'

'My prayers are never heard. Sometimes I often wonder if there is a God!'

'Don't ever say that, or even think in that way. Remember, Jesus despaired also in the garden of Gethsemane, that his sweat turned to blood…'

'Look what happened to him, they hung him on a cross.'

'He rose from the dead. Don't you know that? He's with his father in heaven.'

'Well, I don't want any of my family to be with our Father in heaven. Mam is probably there now.'

'We don't know that, do we?' He sounded a little agitated, bordering on losing his temper. But he didn't know that what I was saying was the truth. He didn't say anything more, and I left him there, folding his stole neatly, at the little wooden vestry altar. He was taken aback by what I had said. I was sixteen, saying things that someone of more mature years might say to him. He didn't have the coping skills to deal with human problems, as his brief was to pray, and live a life of prayer. Maybe I was a bit unfair to him, but I was on a journey, not knowing where it was going to take me. I hoped I wasn't going to crack up, as I very nearly said something that could jeopardise our secret. Was I going to murder someone? I wasn't going to do that, or I never would. But I did see someone murdered, killed accidentally maybe. If that ever came to light, I was going to have a lot of explaining to do. I left the vestry and joined the boys at the church door. The congregation had dispersed, and we made our way home.

We didn't say very much, but the boys complained about the hunger, and I promised them a good breakfast. When we crossed the hill just before our house, we could see a black car parked at the gate. Inside, my heart leaped with joy, and we all ran together home. Meg had come to visit us for Easter.

The house was soon filled with laughter. She arrived shortly after we went to mass and she made Dad get up out of his bed. There was the smell of sausages and rashers as she had the pan frying on the range. She had found the box of cornflakes, and it stood like a great skyscraper in the middle of the table.

She had hugs and embraces for us all, as she usually did, and the boys went to their rooms to open the little Easter gifts she had brought them. I was glad they were out of the way for the moment. She knew by my red eyes that something had happened.

'Are you alright, pet?' she asked.

'Yeah, I'm grand,' I answered.

I knew by the looks on her face that she wasn't happy with that answer.

'You know, you're the world's worst liar.'

'Don't even go there,' I answered, 'it's the stuff of nightmares.'

'Happy Easter!' she said as she hugged me close to her.

Dad sat quietly at the table and didn't eat very much. He had very little to say.

The boys attacked the box of cornflakes and would have eaten the whole lot only Meg intervened and told them to leave some for the next morning.

There was an air of festivity with the boys, and it was something I was glad to see. But beneath the façade, Dad sat quietly back on his chair after breakfast. He had little or nothing to say, and after looking at the Sunday Press, which Meg had brought, he cast it aside, and taking his stick with him went quietly to his room.

Meg said nothing, but she was taking it all in, and I knew she would return to it later. There was a sense of unease in the air with myself, and with Dad. But thankfully it went over the heads of the boys.

She helped me tidy the kitchen, and she went with the boys to feed the pet lamb. She was getting quite big now, and she was very well fed, with a fine little fleece forming on her body.

While they were gone, I checked on Dad, and he had fallen asleep. I sat to read the paper, and there was a small piece about missing people as a follow-up to the finding of a body in the River Boyne. Mary Cregan was mentioned also as one of the people the guards were trying to trace. She went missing after Christmas, and there were more pleas from the Gardaí for the public to come forward with any information as to her whereabouts. I knew now, that Dad had read it, and this was the reason he went to his room. I threw the paper on the arm of the chair and went to check on him. He was in bed and was facing the wall. I didn't know whether he was asleep or not and I left him be.

When Meg returned, she suggested we go for a drive to the lake. The day had turned out fine and bright, and I welcomed the suggestion. I went back to the bedroom, and I asked Dad if he wanted to come. He wasn't asleep, and he turned his head to me.

'I'll stay and have a rest. I didn't sleep well last night.'

'I read the piece in the paper, Dad.'

'Is there no end to this nightmare?' he said.

'Things will work out fine, I promise you.' I began to hate myself again, for what I had said, and how I was deceiving him all the time. I knew by him, that he would die too, if he continued in this way.

All the way to the lake, the boys talked as if they never had a conversation for months, and Meg's eyes followed me occasionally, as I gazed out the window at the passing trees and hedgerows.

Joe was all talk about the time he was spending with Donal Ryan, painting the boat, and making it ready for fishing on the lake. He was wishing his life away, as he couldn't wait for the summer holidays to come, as he was promised a fishing trip. The other boys were envious of his excitement, and they voiced their jealousy by calling him a lucky git. He was the one who got to do all the good things. Meg broke the sighs and groans by telling them that she'd show them how to skim stones on the water.

'I never did that!' said Packy.

'Well, I'll show you in a few minutes.'

She drove the car to the lake shore. A new road had recently been created to give motor access to the shore, and spaces were provided for parking, as well as green areas for families to have picnics. She parked the car, and the boys ran to the shore. I sat in the car and decided to watch their attempts. Meg picked up any flat stone she could find, and by throwing it with the flat side parallel to the surface, the stone bounced along, deflected by the surface tension of the water. After a few attempts, the boys began to see their efforts bear fruit, as the stone hopped across the surface before it sank into the shallows. Soon, she left them there, and she returned to the car, sitting in beside me.

She gazed at the boys having their fun down at the water's edge, and after a moment or two, she spoke. 'Come on, out with it then?'

I turned to her, and brushing back my hair I said, 'I'm going to have to do something. I'm going to have to try and get at the body, leave it somewhere it could be found.'

'Weren't we down this road before? The answer love is definitely no! The body is in a safe place, and no one will ever go there, at least not in our lifetime.'

'What about Dad, Meg? What am I going to do about him? Another body will be found and he'll be asked to go identify it. He was doing great, until a few days ago, and when it wasn't Mam, he won't talk now. He's not eating. He's lying in bed. He started drinking whiskey, and I don't like that. I hid the bottle out in the shed. He's going to die with loneliness. If we had a body, at least he could start to live again. I don't want him to die. I'm losing the one thing I really love, and that's my family.'

I cried loud and hard into her shoulder, and she kissed me through my hair, trying to comfort me. She was silent for a few moments, and all I could hear was, 'Shush! Calm down now. It's alright!' She was my mother figure trying to diffuse a sad situation, and she was not able to produce answers for me. I didn't know how she was going to answer me, but she did.

'You still have your Dad! I think you are panicking too much.'

'I can't see any future, Meg. I get so mixed up, and I snap at the boys sometimes. I don't mean to do it, but it happens.'

'Remember, you are still grieving for your Mam. You were there with her, and you were there for her in those last days. You were with her when she died…'

'I fell asleep, and I woke up when she was dead. I wasn't even there for that.'

'You were with her, and the loneliness of her parting was made so much easier for her, as you were there to comfort her in those last moments. She was proud to have her own little girl to keep her company. She died happily, knowing that you were going to keep things going, and look at how well you have done it.'

'I have become mean and angry and selfish…'

'And caring and brave and concerned for her family. Stop saying that, Sarah. You are grieving now. That's what's wrong with you. You hadn't time to do so earlier, your world was on edge. You needed time to grieve for your

Mam, and it didn't happen. It's happening now, and you'll feel a lot better afterward.'

It was then it all exploded. I began to scream my head off, and the tears kept coming. I began to slap my hand off the front dashboard of the car. The boys could hear the noise, and they came running.

'What's wrong with Sarah?' shouted Tom.

'She's alright!' said Meg. 'Now, will you boys just go back to the lake for a little while, and I'll call you. Sarah is feeling a little sad.'

The boys did as she asked, and she sat there holding my two hands. The knuckles on my left hand were bleeding, and I was shaking. She just sat there holding me, calming me down, and after a few minutes, I began to breathe easier. She let my hands go, and then said, 'You've made a right mess of that hand. I hope you didn't break 1anything.' She made me open and close it, and when she was happy with it she said, 'I'll do something with that later when we get home.'

'I'm sorry, Meg.'

'Sorry for what? What did you do wrong?'

'I could have damaged your car.'

'You did more damage to yourself.'

'Will all this ever end?'

'It will. Something will happen, wait and see.'

'And Eileen? Where is she? Where is Darcy?'

'I've no idea. I have people calling from England, and elsewhere looking for him. I tell them that we have parted our ways. I have no idea where he is.'

'And what about Eileen's body?'

'Probably buried in some wood somewhere. We will probably never know.'

'I wish this could end. It's Dad I worry about.'

'For a man who was in a coma for a few weeks, and had multiple injuries, he has come a long way. He too is grieving, but he has injuries inside himself that will take a long time to heal. I guarantee you, someday you will look back, and say thank God, we left it behind. Your brothers will be married with families of their own. So will you. Your Dad will be working in a job that will suit him. Things always work out, but they take time.'

'I'm so glad I have asked you to be my mother.'

She smiled at me, and kissed my tearful face, and letting down the car window she called the boys. They climbed in behind her wondering was I alright, and Packy, as usual, was all concerned. I pulled him to me and gave him a hug.

'I think it's time to go to the town and see can we find some ice cream somewhere,' she said. The boys cheered, and then said, 'What will we do after that?'

'I'll have a very busy time,' she said. 'I have to get your sister ready for the dance tonight.'

As she drove the car off, she knew by my face that I didn't want to go.

'You are going, whether you like it or not.'

I didn't argue with her, but a great calm and peace came over me. The panic I was feeling had subsided. The thoughts still went through my head. How was I ever going to resolve this?

Chapter 46

The Sweetheart I once knew

I went to the dance that night. Meg stayed at home with Dad and the boys. She left me to the hall in the car and she knew that the Walsh family would leave me home. On our way home from the lake, we saw Jim Walsh out for an evening stroll, and Meg stopped the car. She told him she'd leave me to the dance later.

I was very apprehensive about going inside the dancehall. It was a very cold night. The sky was clear, and the moon shone brightly down on the village street. I did not want to go in alone. I waited at the gate as people parked cars and made their way inside. There was great conversation and laughter. It was a sign that spring was in the air, and soon summer would be on our doorstep once more. People spoke to me, and I answered their greetings. I was aware what the subject of their conversation was, as our lives were so much in the local and national headlines of late.

Then a familiar voice spoke to me through the darkness across the road. I turned around to see who it was, and I was glad when I recognised the figure emerging out of the darkness into the moonlight. It was Pat who spoke to me. 'What are you doing out in the cold?' he asked.

'Are you here again to try and find a wife, Pat?' I laughed. He was dressed in a clean grey suit, and his black shoes were polished to a squeaky shine. He had a white handkerchief peeping in a triangle out of the breast pocket of his jacket, and his hair was smoothed down with Brylcreem. He smelled of Old Spice aftershave, or something similar from the counter of Woolworths. I felt that he was on a mission, to try and court a lady and ask her to marry him. But the reality of it was, that there was no lady in the parish who would have any interest in our Pat, and he knew that himself. Fr Doyle had given him the job that night selling raffle tickets again. Anytime Pat was given a task like this in the parish, whether it be at a dance, a sports day or to help in the church, he presented himself well-dressed, clean shaven and smelling of roses.

He smiled when I teased him about trying to find a wife, and once more he gave the answer he always gave, 'I have asked her already, but she reckons I'm too old for her. But I'm still on a promise to care for her for the rest of my life.'

He was keeping this promise. His loyalty to my family had meant no bounds in the past few weeks, since Dad returned, being there for us always whenever he was needed.

'I know that,' I said, 'and I will always love you for it.'

'You are going inside?' he asked.

He was the support I needed, to break the barrier of eyes focusing on me. I began to wonder should I be here at all. Would they be saying, 'Shouldn't she be at home caring for her father and brothers, after all that has happened? Will you look at her there now, out gallivanting, and not a care in the world?'

'Maybe I shouldn't be here, Pat. I know people are talking about me.'

'Talk is cheap,' he said, 'let them talk. Who knows b-b-better than I do about cheap talk?'

'I feel guilty coming out like this…'

'You have m-m-more right to be here than anyone, looking so beautiful on this lovely night. Now, come on before you get your death of cold.'

He took me by the hand, just like a father taking his little girl to school for the first time. I went to pay my few shillings in, but he paid for me. I protested as he did so.

'You're not getting away with that for nothing. I want a dance from you later.'

'That's a promise,' I said, as he left me to go find Fr Doyle.

The floor of the hall was shining. It had been given a good wax polishing, and the place smelled of fresh lavender and cleaner. The damp fusty smell had gone, as the place had been scrubbed out, and cleaned for the night. The band was preparing the stage with sound and instruments. There was a man handing out black and white photos of the group *Billy Hayes and the Wanderers*. They were a local band, trying to make it on the dance scene.

They called themselves a showband, and their music was new, upbeat and modern.

I looked forward to hearing their sound, and indeed to dance the night away. I was looking away towards the stage, when a hand drifted in front of my face holding an open bottle of Taylor Keith red lemonade, with a paper straw sticking out of the top. I turned to face Seán smiling at me. He also held a bottle in the other hand.

'A peace offering,' he said.

'Thank you, Seán,' I answered, 'but you don't have to do that.'

'May I sit beside you?' he asked.

'Are you asking me out on a date?'

'Well, can I sit beside you as a friend?'

'Of course you can. I was only joking.'

He sat down, and we sipped the fizzy lemonade.

The hall began to fill up, and it wasn't long until the music began. Straight away Seán and I were out on the floor for the first dance, a foxtrot. I hadn't a clue what to do, but it wasn't long until we got the idea, as we watched the older people move on the floor, including Seán's parents. The music cheered me up no end, and I was glad I was with him. He needed a friend as well, as he needed to get away from all the study, and decision-making that lay in front of him. He was probably fearful of the months ahead, as he prepared for the road that lay before him. Indeed, I was worried in a similar way, wondering what our future held for us. We drifted to the music, from waltz to jive and foxtrot, and as the night progressed, they played more traditional tunes and songs, and *The Siege of Ennis* were called for, as well as a *Paul Jones*. During the Paul Jones as the ladies in the inner circle faced the men in the outer circle, the music played, and each circle moving to their right in time to the music, faced their next dance partner as the music stopped. I was faced with Jim Walsh.

Of all people, I didn't want to meet him, but we danced together. It was a slow waltz, and he talked to me above the din of the music. The conversation was of course about us, Dad, and the search for the body. I had enough of this with people praying for us, and keeping their fingers crossed for a good result to our dilemma. I turned the conversation in a different direction and said,

'I am so glad for Seán, that he has decided to do what he's doing.'

'We hope he's happy,' he answered.

'So, do I.'

'It's amazing too,' he said, 'he's keeping up the family tradition.'

I knew then, that Seán's decision didn't come entirely from himself, but was more than likely nurtured at the home table by his parents. I only hoped that his decision was the right one for him. I hoped he wasn't blindly going along with this to please his parents.

The music stopped, and the ladies made the outer circle this time. As we moved to the right, I found myself facing Fr Doyle when it stopped. This time it was a waltz. He guided me along and said nothing. I knew that he was lost for words after our conversation that morning.

'Had you all had a nice day?' he asked. Trying to make conversation, having a nice day was something rare in our lives, but it was made even more pleasurable, with the presence of Meg in our house.

'We had a pleasant day, Father,' I answered.

'Did you tell your Dad I'd call to see him?'

'I didn't yet, but I will.'

That was the end of that conversation and we drifted to the music. There was a mixture of golden oldies, Jazz and some of the new pop songs. I felt that I could have been at a function in London or New York, it all felt so new. But then this was only my second one in about four months, thinking back to Christmas, when Seán gave me my first dance. I was glad, when that one was over, and the ladies made the inner circle again. Third time around I landed on some freckle-faced young fellow from out of town. He was visiting relatives in the village, and he spoke with a distinct Dublin accent. It was a jive, and we moved together to the beat, making no mistakes. He was a good dancer, and I enjoyed moving to the rhythm and the sound. My heart was upbeat, and when I finished I discovered that Seán had missed out on getting a partner after the first part of the dance, so he sat it out waiting for me to return.

'Are you hungry?' he asked.

'I'm starving,' I answered.

We made our way to the room upstairs, where the ladies committee provided tea sandwiches, cakes, and buns. We were given a place in the corner at a table, with a few other people I knew, and we tucked in. We weren't long there, when the smell of Old Spice hit me, and Pat sat down beside us. Was this a repeat of the St Stephen's night dance? There was a certain sense of déjà-vous to the situation.

'Don't forget my d-d-dance,' he said.

'I won't, Pat. You have been so busy all night.'

'Can I d-d-drink a sup of tae with ye?'

'If you pour it out,' said Seán.

'B-b-but the women will do it when they come around,' said Pat.

'I'm only joking, Pat,' answered Seán.

The lady came to the table with the large catering teapot, with its double handles. She poured the tea out, and they all tucked into the sandwiches and tea. Pat began to eat ravenously, and I realised that he must not have had anything to eat all day.

Tonight, Pat was all important, as he carried the big biscuit tin with him, selling tickets for the raffle.

He had just deposited all the money he had collected with the people in charge of the door, when he joined us for the tea. He stared at Seán, wondering what he would say next, but I knew what was coming.

'You're g-g-going to be a p-p-p...'

I stopped him in his tracks, as his nervousness got the better of him. I held his hands and calmed him for a moment. 'Shush! Pat, take it slowly. What do you want to say?'

'I know what you are trying to say,' said Seán, 'and the answer is yes, I'm going away to become a priest.'

Pat smiled, and the dark gap of his missing tooth in front, made it look that more comical.

'Y-y-you'll be a great one, Seán.'

'Won't you pray for me?' asked Seán.

'I w-w-will and I know that someday y-y-you will help me, when I n-n-need help.'

'What do you mean, Pat?' I asked.

'S-s-some day you will understand. But I'll need this man's blessing and forgiveness.'

'You don't need forgiveness, Pat. What are you talking about?'

'T-t-that's all I'm going to s-s-say for now,' he said, and he began to wolf down another ham sandwich, and continued drinking his tea. He said nothing more but was happy to be with us. When he was finished, he said, 'Listen, M-m-miss, you have to give me a dance now, so c-c-come on.'

'I'd better keep my promise, Seán, or he'll never forgive me.'

'W-w-well if you won't marry me then, you will have to give me this dance.'

'Come on then,' I said. 'For peace sake, I'd better go.'

We left Seán drinking his tea, and we went downstairs into the music and the melee, and we waited till the present dance was over. He pulled me out on the floor, and as the next dance began, I didn't realise he could dance so well. He was great at doing the waltz, and he guided me through the floor, keeping time to the music, and I was caught in the drift of the song.

Oh, to be in Doonaree, with the sweetheart I once knew,
To stroll in the shade of the leafy glade, where the rhododendrons grew,
To sit with my love on the bridge above, the rippling waterfall,
I'll go no more ever more to roam,
It's my dearest wish of all.

It was a dance I would always remember, and as the years passed, whenever I heard that song played at the county association annual dinner, I thought of Pat and his happiness guiding me around the floor. For him, he felt that he could do just as well as anyone else in the parish, and it was important to be part of the revelry that night. When we finished, he threw his arms, around me and said, 'Remember, everything will be fine. You will have nothing to worry about. You will be happy. I know it.'

'Stop Pat, please. When you say things like that it makes me feel a little scared.'

He put his great big finger to my lips and said, 'I would never hurt a hair on your head, alana.'

'I know that Pat, but I would love to get inside that head of yours. Sometimes I don't understand what you mean.'

'I might not get to say it again, but I will always protect you. No matter where you go, no one will ever touch you.'

I then realised that for the past few sentences, he hadn't stammered or stumbled his words, and he spoke with a determined and excited voice. He returned with me to the tea room and had more sandwiches. We left him there, drinking tea and we returned to the floor. We danced some more, and as the night wore on, Seán said that he was going to take me home.

'Are we going to walk?' I asked.

'Transport has been arranged,' he said.

'You can't drive, is your Dad driving us?'

'No, I'm taking you.'

'A hackney car?'

'No, it's a far better mode of transport. Follow me.'

He took me by the hand, and I collected my coat at the cloakroom, handing in my ticket to make things easier for the lady in charge of the coats. We went out into the light of the only street lamp, giving light at the front of the hall. It was then I saw the bike, chained to the lamppost. I stood and stared as he beheld his mode of transport.

'Mademoiselle, your transport has arrived.'

'You are taking me home on that?' I laughed.

'Yes! That's why we left before the crowd. It is all lit up, flash lamp, rear reflector, rear light, and the brakes are good. You can sit on the crossbar, and I will do the cycling.'

'I'm not getting up on that, it's a death trap.'

'Trust me, my princess, trust me. I shall not let anything happen to you, fair maiden?'

'Seán! Are you losing your marbles or something?'

'Come on, let's go before the crowd come out.'

I giggled and laughed, as I sat on the crossbar. He balanced the bike till I was comfortable. The bar was hard and cold, but I didn't mind, and Seán pushed the bike off with one foot, and the steering began to wobble, as he tried to take control of the pedalling. I screamed as the bike moved off, and he began laughing.

'Stop laughing will you, or we'll fall off!

The wobbling stopped, as the bike gathered momentum, and we moved at ease out of the village into the moon brightness of the night. The flash lamp cast a beam of light on the tarred road, showing us the way, and with the occasional wobble going around corners, Seán was in control. Soon, we reached the turnoff up the hill towards our house, and when we moved uphill, Seán began to struggle with the pedalling, and there was more of a wobble with the steering. We decided to walk to the summit of the hill, and he'd cycle the few hundred yards down to our gateway. My backside was sore and I was lame. We moved slowly, and even though the night was cold, it was a happy occasion. It was a night I didn't want to end. At the top of the hill, I sat back on the crossbar again, and this time he freewheeled down the hill, moving fast. Seán took his feet off the pedals, holding them out in front, and I began to panic a little, thinking that he was going to lose control. I began pleading with him in muffled whispers to begin pedalling again, and as we approached our gate, he declared that the brakes weren't working.

'How are we going to stop?' I gasped.

'We'll just have to wait till we run out of hill,' he answered.

'That's into the bog!'

'Oh dear, it will be a bog hole then.'

'Seán!' I screamed.

But just as we approached the gap into the bog, he brought the bike slowly to a halt using the brakes. I was glad when the bike stopped and I stood on the gravel road.

'Liar!' I said, giving him a little thump on the shoulder.

'I made a mistake, I thought the brakes were not working.'

'And I have green hair,' I said sarcastically.

'Janey, I didn't notice,' he joked.

'Why did you bring me here?' I asked.

'I have something to tell you.'

'What?'

'I'm leaving tomorrow.'

'Leaving?'

'I'm not going back to school until next week, but I'm going away on a retreat to Carlow in preparation for the seminary.'

'You mean this is our last night together.'

'I'm afraid so.'

I didn't know what to think. I felt like thumping him for what he was going to do, but it was his life to do with it whatever he wished. He was following a family tradition, and his decision was partly his choice, and his family duty. I knew I was in much the same boat, with the promises I made to God to take care of Dad. I was sad, and yet I was happy. Seán was that little beacon that cast a light for me in a time of dark shadows, and now it was coming to an end. I think he thought that I was going to be angry with him again, but I placed my hands on his and looked at the soft silver-grey of his face in the moonlight. I smiled at him.

'You are one of the bravest people I know,' I said.

'You're not annoyed with me.'

'No, I'm not. I think you're wonderful to make such a decision.'

'I hope I am doing the right thing'

'Are you having doubts then?' I asked.

'Not really, but I often think that I might be a disappointment to someone like you. I hope I am not letting you down.'

'I will always tease you,' I said. 'Maybe when you are an old parish priest somewhere and I'm an old grandmother in a wheelchair, I can boast that I once kissed that old priest.'

'Can I kiss you again?'

'You can't! Not now, not when you're going away to be a…'

His arms were locked around me, and he stopped me in my tracks kissing me again. I didn't protest, and I could feel his loneliness as he held me. And I wanted that moment to last forever. This was a night to remember, as I felt happy as well as lonely and sad. I had no idea how things were going to turn out. This night was Seán's night, and I wanted to send him off happy. We sat on the roadside bank on his coat, and we held each other close. We could hear the noise of cars on the main road, as people returned home from the dance in the village. No one was going to come our way, as our house was the only one on that road.

We sat there in the moonlight, with only the gentle noises of the night. A fox called across the fields, and a barn owl flew across our path. Occasionally, the sound of a barking dog reached our ears, and we sat in the silence.

'Will I see you again?' I asked.

'I don't know. I will probably be going into the seminary after the Leaving Cert. I'll be home on holidays and that.'

'Dad wants to take us to move to Scotland. He's waiting to see if anything happens about Mam, and he's going to sell the house.'

'We might not see each other again then?'

'Never say never,' I said, 'maybe we will.'

He kissed me again, and this time he wept into my hair. I held him close to me and comforted him. He was this gallant young fellow, yet there was a child within, fearful of the future. In fact, we were both in the same boat.

'I will always remember you, Sarah.'

'We can write to each other.'

'Will we though?' he asked.

'Yeah, we will,' I answered, 'for a while anyway.'

He took my hand and we walked quietly through the moonlight, back up the hill to our gate. The only sound was the clicking of the freewheel of the bike, and our breathing in the frosty air. Our breaths condensed, and we moved in silence. We were sharing this last moment together, and I didn't want it to end. When we reached the gate, he faced me and he kissed me again. He smiled at me. I could see the tears in his eyes reflecting in the moonlight.

'I will always love you,' he said.

'Goodbye Seán,' I said in a whisper. He slowly let my hand go. He turned from me and throwing his leg across the saddle of the bike, he cycled quickly up the hill to the tarred road. I stood and watched him, as his form faded into the moonlit darkness, and I turned to meet Sputnik, who stood wagging his tail at the gate.

I went once more to the remains of the cock of hay and sat down with the dog beside me. I hugged him close to me, and he was warm, with his tongue out panting in the darkness. I had no tears, but I had a feeling that was neither sad nor happy. I was content within. I knew that my duty lay still with my family, just as Seán's duty was to his family and to tradition. This was his vocation, and he was ready to embrace it with both arms. He would be a great priest, serving his community, just like Father Doyle, who was also a person who had a great sense of justice, especially for those less fortunate. I left the dog sitting on the hay. I went inside, opening the door quietly, and turning on the light, Dad was sitting on the chair by the fire.

He startled me, as I was not expecting him to be still up and, as well as that, sitting in the darkness.

'That was very unusual transport you had home.'

'What are you doing still up, you should be in bed.'

'You know it's nearly four o'clock in the morning?'

'You knew I was at the dance, and who I was with.'

'No, I just wanted to say something to you.'

'What is wrong Dad?'

'I'm sorry, Sarah. I shouldn't have carried on like that for the last few days.'

'Meg was talking to you.'

'She made me see sense.'

'Is she in bed?'

'She's not long gone.'

'Ok, goodnight Dad.'

'Sarah?'

'What is it, Dad?'

'We will start the ball rolling this week to move to Scotland.'

'Are you sure you're ready for it?'

'Life has to go on, love, even without your mother.'

I went to him and kissed him on the forehead. He touched my cheek and said, 'You're a great girl, do you know that?'

'Goodnight Dad, now go to bed yourself.'

'Goodnight Sarah.'

Part 5

The Lake

Chapter 47

Measles and Nursemaids

Meg left the next day. She could have stayed longer, but she had got a job helping with management of a summer season variety show in Dublin. For the first time in many years, she was working behind the scenes, and a break was as good as a rest. She had a heart to heart talk with Dad, when I was at the dance. She sat with me in the car before she left and told me everything. She advised him not to sit on his laurels anymore, he was a lucky man to be alive and making such a good recovery. He was fortunate that his children weren't taken away and sent to a children's home. If he continued to sit and brood over everything, to wait for Mam to return, then there was a likelihood that before too long, someone would notice the cracks in his life, and the boys could end up being taken away. He told her about his plans to move to Scotland. She sat with him and wrote a letter to the Glasgow offices of Blake Construction. She was going to post it in Dublin for him. She gave her Dublin phone number as a contact for him. That was the reason for the sudden change, when I got home. She had gone to bed, and he sat in the dark, thinking about his next move. He knew as well, it was a turning point for me, as I too had to let Seán go and follow his vocation.

We sat together in the car, and she gave me instructions once more to contact her if I needed her.

'You have those lists of numbers safe,' she said,

'They are under my mattress,' I answered.

'Write to me as often as you can Sarah, won't you? You can't be going to the village all the time, to use the public phone.'

'I will. I'll keep you informed as to what is happening.'

'Everything will be fine, just wait and see.'

I watched the car till it went over the hill. She was still having problems changing the gears, as I could hear them tearing, as she changed from second to third.

She too was our guardian angel, just like Pat. We were still here, despite all that had happened, and I still had my brothers at home. I often thought of the Larkin children, and how they were spirited away. It would be years before I heard what happened to them. But that's another link in the chain of events which have dominated our lives for so long. It was their story, that made me go to such extremes to keep us all together, and here we were, still a family, and Dad doing his duty to us all.

It was time then to take the next step. It was a waiting game, and Dad said that it would probably be the autumn time or maybe the new year before we could move away.

But life had to go on, and the house would still have to be cleaned, meals cooked, and brothers presented fed and ready for school each day.

Dad still needed the walking stick. In fact, he would need it for the rest of his life, if he was walking any distance. He began going out into the fields, spending time outdoors in the air, checking fences, and ensuring that the ditches and headlands were in good repair. The first move made, was to sell the cow and the donkey, as well as the lamb. Pat Reardon took it on himself to arrange for the cow to be sold at the next market in the town. But there was no need to do so, as Jim Walsh called one evening, and bought all four animals. I was glad this happened, as they would be well cared for, and the cow joined the other milking animals at Walsh's farm. The donkey was put out to pasture with old Charlie, another donkey in retirement, after many years drawing turf from the high banks to the road each summer. The lamb was kept for her wool, and future lambs too. Our little brood was sure of a happy life away from us. The five hens we had, were sent to Farrells; brought unceremoniously by night, when it was easy to catch them on their perches after dark. I was sad to see them all go, and the boys decided that if they remained in Ireland, they'd go regularly to visit their little farmyard friends.

Life went on as normal. Turf was cut to supply fuel for the winter fire, just in case our move didn't take place too quickly, and the now abandoned fields were left to produce meadow. There was still some ready money to be made from the hay, and it was a summer job Dad felt he'd be able to do.

After a visit to the auctioneer, it was arranged that the farm go up for auction when word of his new job with Blakes in Glasgow was confirmed.

It became a ritual every morning, waiting for the sound of the postman ringing his bicycle bell at the gate. On fine days, he waited for the sound of the bike, and if it hadn't arrived by midday, there was no post for us on that occasion.

Sergeant Greene called regularly with updates on the search for our missing mother. One day in early June, there was another call to identify the remains of a woman found in Kildare. She too had been missing for many months, but Dad decided to wait, until it was certain that the relatives of the missing Kildare woman made a positive identification of the corpse.

'I'm hopeful of a breakthrough soon, John,' said Sergeant Greene.

'Well life has to go on, Sergeant, and as you know already, I'll be taking my family away with me to Scotland before too long.'

'Please God, we'll know something by then.'

'I hope you're right,' said Dad.

The days grew longer, and the evenings lingered longer into dusk. It meant some time out in the fields playing for the boys, and as darkness approached so did bedtime. It was in the evening time I took to listening to the wireless, and to events at home and abroad. The first great sad event of the summer was news from Rome that Pope John XXIII was in poor health, and that he was slowly dying. A picture of him hung on the wall next one of the bedroom doors, a picture from the newspaper taken in 1958, when he was elected pope. Mam had it put in a frame, as she had great praise for his Holiness. She always talked about a young boy called Angelo Roncali who came from a poor family of sharecroppers in Lombardy, who made it all the way to the Vatican, to the chair of St Peter. She regarded him as a very holy man and spoke about him regularly as well as in her prayers. One very dull heady morning in early June, the boys returned from school, sent home by Donal Ryan on the instruction of Fr Doyle. The pope had died, and the school was to remain closed for the day. It was a gloomy dead sort of day, and there was thunder and lightning in the afternoon. The world had lost a great friend, Dad said, and maybe our prayers to him might bring news to our doorstep too.

There was news as well from Joe, as he returned to work for Donal Ryan at the schoolhouse to put the finishing touches on the boat. He promised to bring him fishing soon, out on the lake. But something else was to happen to halt his progress onto the water.

Sunday the 16th of June was designated as the day Donal Ryan could take Joe out on his first fishing trip. He was talking about it for days, and he nearly had us all in a spin listening to him. Dad bought him a new fishing rod, with reel, line, hooks, and baits, for his birthday, and he could not wait to get going. But disaster struck on Friday the 14th of June. Joe returned from school not feeling well and had a high temperature. To make a long story short, Dr Sullivan was sent for, and Joe was confined to bed with measles. The trip on the lake was called off for the moment. Donal Ryan did go, that Sunday, but he went alone. Things didn't get easier, as there were other cases of measles in the school, and many homes locally had children bed-bound. The curtains were closed over, as Joe lay there not feeling the best, summer days outside, and not being well enough to even go out and play.

'It's not fair,' he said, 'just as I was about to go out and start fishing on the lake.'

'Stop complaining,' I said, 'aren't you lucky you are not in hospital.'

'I don't care.'

'Joe, get some rest, you will be better before you know it.'

He didn't get much sympathy from me. Dad had started going to the bog with Pat Reardon to heap the turf and have it ready for taking home. Tom and Packy joined them after school, and it annoyed Joe too, that he couldn't go with them. He was stuck with me as nursemaid, and that was how it was going to stay.

Then Dad had a letter from Glasgow requesting him to attend a hearing about his accident. It was to take place in August, and he had to reply to the solicitors who requested him to attend. He was glad that something was happening, and he would not be able to put the farm up for sale until after that.

Tom was struck down with measles next, and I ended up as the nursemaid for the two of them, complaining about having to stay in bed.

They were feeling very sorry for themselves, but they were quite ill during those days. It prompted Dr Sullivan to keep a watchful eye on them. He was ever so attentive to them, but I often wondered was he trying to find loopholes in the care I was giving them. Was he contemplating having them taken away from us once more? But this time I was wrong. One evening late, while Dad was down the fields, he called and seeing that they were improving, but also complaining about their condition, he told them that a few more days in bed would crown them.

'No whinging you two, you are doing well. In a few days, you will be racing through the fields.'

He was closing his medical bag when he turned to me and said, 'Have you ever thought of being a nurse Sarah?'

'No doctor, the thought never entered my head.'

'I have been observing how you have coped and cared for your family over the past few months. You were so kind to your brother, when he got his appendix out. You are so patient with your Dad and keeping the house in such commendable order. As well as that, you must cope with these two rascals, listening to their complaints. You would make an excellent nurse.'

I began to blush when he said this, and I didn't realise that Dad was standing in the doorway having returned from the fields. He listened to what the doctor had said and agreed with everything.

'Only for her, Dr Sullivan, I don't know what I'd have done. She's a great one, and I do agree with you. She'd make a great nurse.'

'Well take my advice, when you go to Scotland. Get some education into her and follow that dream. The nursing profession could do with people like Sarah Cregan. If you need any references or assistance in this matter, contact me here in Ireland.'

'Thank you, Doctor,' I said.

My opinion of Dr Sullivan changed that evening. In his own way, he was trying to keep our best interests at heart, even though I could have lost my family in the process. But he didn't see the importance of family unity, as his world was a clinical one. The welfare of the Larkin children was, to separate them and to lose that family bond, sharing and caring for each other. His eyes had been opened in the past few months, and he was acknowledging how I had managed to keep my family as a unit. I would give all he had said, plenty of thought over the next few months, but up and coming events would put all this on the back burner for a while.

Within a few short days, my two patients were on the mend, and Joe had to wait until the middle of July for his fishing trip on the lake with Donal Ryan.

The summer began to roll on, and other events entered our lives. Dad was a great admirer of John F Kennedy, and he was all ears, when it was broadcast on radio that he was paying a four-day visit to Ireland on his return journey from Berlin. It was this visit to Berlin, where he made the speech '*Ich bin ein Berliner*'. It was a happy time, as things had settled down following the Cuban crisis the year before, and at that time the word among ordinary people was that according to St Colmcille's prophesies, there were going to be three dark days. Opinion later had it, that the Cuban crisis were those three dark days, but such events at the time, were overshadowed by our three dark days when Mam died. Now people saw this visit as a sign of hope. This was the return of a native, whose ancestors left for the new world in dark times, a hundred years earlier. The tea party at Dunganstown, County Wexford, when he visited the old family homestead, was a sign of hope for a New Ireland. This flamboyant tanned, and well-groomed man, was a symbol of what life can give to those who make it a success. For those who had left these shores, whether through forced emigration or by choice, life did offer opportunities to those who were prepared to meet that challenge. Thoughts ran through my head, as to how we might grab that opportunity, and how the boys would adapt to the changes which awaited them before too long. Packy came home from school sporting a sixpence, a prize from Donal Ryan for correctly identifying President Kennedy in the paper. He was the one eating a slice of cake at the party in Dunganstown. Those four days saw Dad read the newspapers from cover to cover, as well as listening to all the radio coverage of the event. There were smiles on his face now and again, as he took it all in.

It seemed that the memory of this event would stay with us for the summer, but like the three dark days earlier, events were to escalate in our lives with the coming of the summer holidays.

Chapter 48

The Fishing Trip

At the beginning of the last week of school, Packy came down with measles, and Dr Sullivan once more kept vigil on the one lone patient. I feared that I might come down with it too, but Dad told me, that I had them when I was about two years old. I was glad to hear that, as I would not like to get them. I had no memory of having them, when I was very small, but I was just as glad. Packy was very ill, and his eyes closed, as there was stuff oozing from them, when he woke up. He found it difficult to open them, and I had to gently rub some flannel dipped in warm water, to clean the stickiness from his eyelids. It hurt him, and he cried on occasion. He also wet the bed when he was asleep, and it upset him when he woke up. He was very weak and was unable to go to the outside privy. I made Joe and Tom sleep in my room during Packy's illness, and I sat up with him at night. They complained each day, that there was a constant smell of perfume in my room. I told them that it was a pity about them. It was a nice smell, and to get used to it. Dr Sullivan told me to make sure Packy drank plenty of fluids, so there were bottles of red lemonade, and diluting orange juice on the three-legged table beside his bed. He woke at night a lot, wanting a drink, and I had to change the sheets on his bed. Dad wanted to take over, so that I could get some sleep, but I managed to grab a few hours each afternoon, when the dinner was over.

Meanwhile, during all this, the school closed for the summer, and Joe waited anxiously for the call from Donal Ryan to go fishing with him. But life on the fields was busy, and Pat Reardon was helping Dad make the hay. The sweet smell of new mown hay carried in through the open window of the bedroom. Even though the curtains were closed, the freshness of the air, may have been part and parcel of seeing Packy begin to return to health. When the high temperature went away, he sat up in the bed, and read comics in the diminished light. He was happy to let me go to the kitchen and continue with the housework.

I had to prepare meals for our working men. I was glad to see Joe and Tom get some colour back on their faces again. Their skin was beginning to clear up, and the red measles' marks were fading. It was something they would never get again. But measles was such a horrible and sickening disease.

Because of this, they had great appetites, and as well as that, both boys were growing fast. It was beginning to show, that Tom was going to be taller than Joe, even though there were two years between them. New potatoes with cabbage and parsley sauce with cooked ham, was the order of the day. They ate the potatoes, skins and all, as the new ones were fresh and tasty. I cooked them big and small, and the smaller ones, I left on a plate like a pyramid, and when they returned in the evening, they ate them cold with a shake of salt.

Packy was only picking at his food, but at least he was drinking fluids, and was beginning to complain that he couldn't go out and join the haymaking in the fields. Dad took his time, and he left a lot of the heavy work to Pat. He sat down occasionally and smoked his pipe. On the third day, when the cocks began to rise in the field, he found Dad fast asleep under a new fresh cock of hay, and the dog lying beside him. He beckoned the boys to come away and leave him be. He knew that a rest like that in the sun would help him, and he left him at peace.

Donal Ryan called in the evening to arrange the fishing trip, and it was agreed to go when the hay was made. To help matters along, the young schoolmaster rolled up his shirt sleeves, and began to hoist the hay into the cocks along with Pat. As it happened he was born on a farm in Tipperary, and haymaking was second nature to him. So, I had to set another place for tea, and he joined us. Joe was all excited, and when he heard that Mike Farrell's son had been out fishing the week before, Tom knew there was going to be a spare place on the boat.

'Please, Mr Ryan, may I come along?' he pleaded.

'Don't be cheeky now, Tom,' said Dad.

'I think it's a great idea,' said Donal. 'I didn't think you wanted to come.'

'Oh, but I do,' said Tom. 'I was just afraid to ask.'

'That's settled then, Tom is coming too.'

Then a little faint voice called from the room.

'What about me?' groaned Packy.

'You're too young,' said Dad, 'when you are older.'

'That's not fair,' he sulked.

'Anyway, you are still very sick, you can't go.'

'I'll take you out some day later when you are well. And I'll bring your Dad with you too,' said Donal.

'Thank you, Mr Ryan,' said Packy.

That settled that. A few minutes later, Packy was asleep and the house went quiet as the men went back to the fields again. It was a beautiful day, but I didn't realise that the fishing trip was going to bring unexpected changes to our lives again.

Donal called to the house at ten o'clock the next morning. Joe was up at the crack of dawn, and he woke the whole house in the process. Packy had a restless night, and as dawn approached he fell asleep. I could have done with a longer sleep that morning, but I was awake early and so was Packy. Dad stayed on in bed as the boys began to make sandwiches, and a flask of tea for the day. I made them include Donal Ryan in the picnic, and they packed cups as well as tea, sugar and two milk of magnesia bottles full of milk for the tea. Joe took great care with his fishing rod, and he checked his baits, hooks and spare line. Packy got up out of bed and sat watching the proceedings. I made him a cup of tea and put a slice of brown bread with strawberry jam in front of him. I was more excited when I turned around and saw that he had eaten the bread with his tea. He was on the road to recovery. He was still very weak, and after about half an hour, he fell asleep on the chair. Joe carried him back to his bed and covered him up. He didn't wake up in the moving, and I was glad as I was busy myself, tending to the older boys' preparation. It was going to be a fine day with a gentle breeze. I warned them to behave themselves, and not to jump about in the boat. I didn't want them to fall in. But I knew that Donal Ryan being the schoolmaster, they'd do everything he asked, and they wouldn't dare to misbehave in any way. This was a day, Joe really looked forward to, and it made me happy to see their excitement too.

When the car pulled up outside the gate, they both cheered, gathered all their belongings, and ran out the door. When Donal saw all they had with them, he asked them a question, 'Are we going to camp out on the lake for a few days?'

'No sir,' said Tom, 'we brought along some sandwiches and tea, just in case we get hungry.'

'We have some for you too as well, sir,' said Joe.

'Well that's great lads,' he said, 'we won't go hungry anyway.' He winked at me, and he helped them pack everything into the Morris Minor car. In a few moments, they were gone, and I hoped that they'd have a great day on the lake.

It was their intention to stay fishing till about six o'clock in the evening and make a whole day out of it. But what took place that day would be a turning point in our lives.

Again, like the morning Joe went to the station to meet Meg off the train, Tom and Joe told me the whole story of their day on the lake, and what had happened late in the afternoon.

It was one of those perfect days weather-wise, and they were both so happy to be out on the water. Donal Ryan was a great teacher, and even taking them out on the lake, he was teaching them fishing skills, something they would never forget. There was never a complaint from them since Christmas, going to school, and they were so enthusiastic to learn, also homework wasn't a chore anymore. Little rewards, and a little praise brought the best out in his students.

His young charges today thought they would never be out on the water. But they followed every direction he had given them, and to Tom's delight, he produced a rod and reel for him to use as well. The lake was about four miles long, and two miles wide. There were little inlets stretching into farmland, and there were large areas of reed beds extending out into the water. Donal told them that the pike kept close to the reeds, as they could hide in the dark shallows and like the Nile crocodile, they lay in waiting, and when an unsuspecting little fish or a little wader or duckling went by, they attacked with a vicious menacing strike, that the poor victims didn't know what happened to them. But the good fisherman could turn the tides on this great hunter of the deep, as the baits attracted Mr pike from his lair into the fisherman's hands.

It was hard to believe that only six months beforehand, the lake was covered in ice and snow, and a car travelled around the shore area on the frozen water. Mounds of snow had gathered in places also, especially near the reed beds.

Now, the soft July breeze waved the tall reeds back and forth in a gentle rhythm, as birds emerged from the hidden areas of the shore. Swans too, with their young grey cygnets swam quietly, bobbing up and down on the water. White woolly clouds floated across a blue sky, shading the sun on occasion, casting cool shadows on the three fishermen.

After an hour, Donal landed a ten-pound pike, which he weighed, and released back into the water again.

'Are you not going to keep him for tomorrow's dinner?' asked Joe.

'A good fisherman returns his catch to the water,' said Donal. 'Remember if you take too many fish away, there'll be none left to catch, and there'll be no fishing. He'll get bigger, and some other great fisherman will come out in a year or so, and land him again, this time he will be a few pounds bigger, and there'll be more cheering and excitement in landing him.'

'Where is he gone now?' asked Tom.

'He's gone back into the shallows there, and he'll be waiting for another little duckling or a young small trout to cross his path.'

'What about the young swans?' asked Joe. 'Will he try and get them?'

'They are too big now, maybe when they were just little fledglings, he might try, but not now.'

A little later, Joe landed his first fish. It was a much younger pike, weighing six pounds eight ounces. It was still a difficult creature to land, and when he pulled him close to the boat, Donal reached out and lifted it aboard with a big net. After weighing it, they released it back into the water again, and the fishing continued.

Around two o'clock, they pulled into the shore and they had a bite to eat. The sandwiches began to disappear quickly, and the tea was very welcome with milk and sugar. Lying down on the short shoreline grass and clover, Tom fell asleep, and in a short while so did Joe. There was a small tarpaulin folded up in the corner of the boat, and Donal covered it over them, to keep the strong rays of the sun from burning their faces. He knew by them both they were still a little under the weather after the measles, and their appetites were great, as their young bodies returned to equilibrium again. He left them lying there, as the sleep would do them good, and he stretched out himself in the sun too, savouring the delights of the summer weather, away from the classroom and teaching, a welcome break from the routine days of learning. He sat back against a large boulder and lit his pipe. One of the pleasures of life he wouldn't deny himself, and he knew when the boys woke up, they'd be rearing to go again, out on the water. Just as he drew his first puff from the pipe, his gaze began to fix on something out in the shallows, among the reeds. It bobbed in the water, and he thought it looked like a human hand. He emptied out the contents of his pipe, and he went quietly to the shore to investigate. About ten yards out on the water, in an open space between the reeds, he could see the object floating on the surface. He waded out quietly, not to disturb the boys in their gentle sleep.

When he reached it, he bent down to touch it, and to his horror, it rolled over in the water, and a badly decomposed human body stared up at him. He stumbled back in the water, falling backward in the shallows, and he sat in the water completely soaking himself and his clothes. The noise of the splashing woke the boys up, and when they saw him stumbling to get up out of the water, he shouted at them.

'Don't come too close boys. Stay where you are.'

'Why, what's wrong?' asked Joe.

'Just do as I tell you now, please!'

The boys stood at the shore. They could see something out on the water, but they didn't know what it was.

'Are you alright, sir?' asked Tom.

'I'm fine,' said Donal.

'What happened?' asked Joe. 'Why did you go out in the water?'

'Can I go out and look?' asked Tom.

'No lad, stay where you are. I can't let you see it.'

'What is it, sir? What is it?' asked Joe.

'We'll have to go immediately,' said Donal.

'Why? Can we not go back fishing?' asked Tom.

'No boys, I have to go to the guards.'

'What's out there, sir? Why will you not tell us?' asked Joe.

He hesitated for a moment, wondering should he tell them or not, but then they'd know eventually, and considering their mother was missing, they had a right to know. Maybe it was her body. He got such a fright, he couldn't tell whether the body was male or female. Why keep it from them? They were two strong young lads, but he would not let them go out to see the body.

'There's a dead body in the water,' he said. 'It's too frightening to see. I can't let you go there.'

'Is it a man or is it a woman?' asked Joe.

'I don't know,' said Donal. 'I got such a fright, that's why I fell in the water.'

'Would it be Mam?' asked Tom.

'I don't know. We'll have to get the guards and they'll find out.'

With that, Tom began to cry. He knew it wasn't Mam, yet all of this had come back to haunt him again, and it wasn't going away. Donal tried to reassure him that everything would be alright.

'Come on now and help me gather everything together. We'll hurry back to the shoreline where the car is. We'll make a little heap of stones here, so that I can mark the spot where we landed.'

'Can we not stay here till you get back?' said Joe.

'No way!' said Donal. 'I will take you home. The guards will want your Dad to identify the body.'

They helped Donal make a mound of stones in the clearing, close to the shore. It was like a pyramid about a foot high. Then they quickly gathered everything up, and Donal cranked the outboard motor. The boat moved quickly across the quiet lake, and before long they reached the shore where he had parked the Morris Minor car.

Chapter 49

A Great Big House of Cards

I was cleaning the kitchen window outside with paraffin oil and newspapers, when I heard the hum of a car engine. I was surprised to see Donal Ryan's car pull up at the gate. It was only after three o'clock, and I wasn't expecting them home till around six. I knew something was wrong, as Tom came running to me. His eyes were red from crying and he ran into my arms. Joe stood motionless and still at the gate, as Donal followed them into the yard.

'Is your Dad there?' asked Donal.

'Why, what's wrong?' I gasped.

'I found a body in the lake,' said Donal.

'Oh, my God!' I exclaimed.

With that, Dad stood on the doorstep in his stocking feet. He had been resting in his room after the dinner. His window was open to let some fresh air in, and he could hear us talking. He held the jamb of the door, as he stepped outside with his walking stick.

'Is it her?' he asked. His voice was broken, as he tried to gasp out the words.

'I don't know,' said Donal. 'I have to take the guards back there in a few minutes. The sergeant is calling here to take me there.'

'I'm coming too,' said Dad.

'I think you should let the sergeant decide that,' he said.

I made the boys go inside, and Dad sat down in the kitchen to put on his boots. A few minutes later, the squad car pulled up at the gate, and the sergeant came in. He knew that Dad wanted to come, but he wasn't prepared to let him view the body at this stage, not until it had been brought to the morgue.

'I'm coming with you, Sergeant,' Dad said again.

'I'm sorry John, but not yet. It may not be her.'

'Who else could it be? There's no one else missing around here for the past six months only her. She's my wife and she needs me.'

'She doesn't need you, John, the woman is dead – if it is her. Stay here with your family. It will take several hours to recover the body from the water. I will call for you in the morning.'

'After all these months, and she was out there on that cursed lake. Why didn't you look for her out there? How did you miss her? Surely someone would have found her.'

'I can't answer that, John,' said the sergeant, 'but we have to move fast to recover the body.'

With that, the sergeant left, and Donal followed him. Dad buried his head in his hands. I laid my hand on his shoulders, and he gave his usual sigh, 'Aye!' Packy called from the room, and I went to him. He wanted a drink. He hadn't heard what was going on, and he asked what was wrong. Tom ran into the room to tell him, and I shoved him out just as quick again.

'What's wrong, Sarah?' asked Packy.

'I don't know. We will know tomorrow. Are you not resting today?'

'I'm going to go for a sleep now,' he said.

'Good man.'

I pulled the blanket up over him.

Dad had gone to his room, and he was lying on the bed. I sat down beside him and took his hand. I knew I had to get to the village to let Meg know that a body had been found. I knew it had to be Eileen. Darcy must have dumped it there and fled. Why did he do that? Why didn't he bury her? Now everything was going to come out, and Meg would have to tell all to the guards. I needed to get a message to her. I calmed Dad down, and I told him to have a rest. He'd have to be up early in the morning.

'Dad, I'm going to the village,' I said. 'Meg told me to let her know if there were any developments.'

'Aye, do that girl,' he said, 'but don't tell anyone.' He turned to the wall, and I covered him with a heavy coat. I hoped that he wasn't starting to revert to the way he was before Easter. I couldn't handle it again, if he did. But now I didn't know what was going to happen next. I told Tom and Joe to keep an eye on Packy, as I'd be back in about an hour.

I didn't delay cycling to the village, and it being Saturday, it was quiet. I placed the bike against the wall outside the post office and went straight to the telephone box. I dialled her home number, hoping she'd be there. To my delight, she answered straight away.

'Something has happened,' she said.

'They found a body today on the lake,' I answered. 'It has to be Eileen.'

I was in a panic, having cycled from home, and she knew by the tremor in my voice that I was in a bit of a state.

'Whatever you do, don't say a word,' said Meg, 'Please Sarah, say nothing.'

'What will I do?'

'Is your Dad gone to identify the body?'

'No, not yet. The sergeant said he would call for him in the morning.'

'Where is your father now?' she asked.

'He's asleep I think. I left him lying on the bed.'

'I'm leaving immediately. I will be with you in a few hours. Whatever you do, say nothing. Promise me that.'

'Alright!' I said, and immediately she put down the phone.

Back home, I told the boys that they were moving back in with Packy, as Meg needed the spare bed in my room. I had no idea, how things were going to go, and I could feel cramps at the bottom of my stomach. Dad got up again and went down the fields. I had to change the linen on the spare bed, and when Packy saw that the boys were moving back in, he was in a mood. He wanted me to stay with him for another while. Then I told him that Meg was coming, and he cheered up. He wanted to get up out of bed, and I wouldn't let him. A silence fell on the house. It was so quiet, that I could hear the clock ticking on the dresser. How were we going to explain this? No one knew Eileen. I could see Dad going to the morgue tomorrow, and when he saw that it wasn't Mam, there'd be a whole new investigation. In time, the body would be identified. Meg then faced questioning, and then be dragged into the whole sordid event. We were playing with this great big house of cards, all that we had achieved in keeping Mam's death a secret, was likely going to come tumbling down around us. They had all handled the game very well. The boys were great at playing along, especially Packy, who was a right little actor indeed. I could now see cars coming to take them away, and I'd end up in a women's prison or a mental hospital. 'There goes Mad Mary's daughter, a plotter and a schemer. Maybe she murdered her mother and hid the body. And that actor woman. The husband has disappeared. Did she kill him also? Did she dump the body in the lake? Where did she bury the husband? Was Mad Mary's daughter in on it also? I feel so sorry for the little boys. They will never be the same again. What part did that peeping Tom Pat Reardon play in it all? And this is Catholic Ireland. What is the world coming to at all?'

These thoughts ran through my head, as it all went spinning round like a bad dream. It was going to kill Dad, and there was no doubt about that.

When he saw me sitting at the table, he could see me tremble, and he said, 'It's going to be alright, Sarah. I know it's her. It can be no one else.'

I wish I shared his certainty.

The hours dragged slowly into evening. I felt a weight lift off my shoulders when Meg's car pulled up outside the gate.

Just before going to bed that evening at dusk, she walked with me down the fields where no one could hear us. She was as concerned as I was, and she had no answers to the problem that faced us. I was surprised at how calm she was, about the whole affair. I put it to her, as to why she was so calm about it.

'It might not be Eileen's body. It could be anyone from anywhere. We must keep calm for the moment. There's nothing we can do until tomorrow. If we start panicking now, it would arouse the suspicion of the guards, and they'll start asking questions. If it is Eileen, the ball will lie at Darcy's feet. He is missing. Blame will fall on him just wait and see.'

'I'm afraid, Meg. I'm just terrified of what might happen. I just can't cope. I'm going to crack up. It just goes on and on.' I began to breathe heavily as if I was having a panic attack, and she grabbed me by the two arms and shook me gently.

'Stop it, Sarah!' she bellowed. 'Stop it now. You are not to say anything. We will just wait and see. Stop it now, Sarah!'

I did as she asked and began to breathe slowly again. She gazed into my face till I had calmed down. I held her close to me, and she patted me on the back saying, 'Shush! It's alright. Wait and see, everything will be fine. I know it will.'

'How do you know it will?' I asked.

'I don't know anything, but I feel it in my water, everything will be fine.'

'Do you need to go to the toilet?' I asked.

She started laughing hysterically, as if she were on the fringe of losing her sanity. When she stopped, she said, 'I feel it in my water means I have a feeling inside me, that it will be fine. It has nothing to do with going to the toilet.'

I laughed along with her again, and it was like a tonic, as I began to calm down. Going back to the house she said, 'Say nothing. You know nothing. The less you say, the less you will have to answer for.'

As usual, Meg brought calm and restfulness to the house, and Packy sat up in bed, bright and cheerful, when he saw her. He had been sleeping all evening, catching up on all the restless nights he had with the measles. He had them far worse than Tom and Joe, and I was afraid he might end up in hospital. I knew that in a few days he'd be running around again.

She sat down on the bed beside him, and pointing her finger at him she said, 'Listen here young man, you are not allowed get measles anymore and that is an order.'

Packy looked at her with a stern and fearful face for a moment, and then realised she was only joking. This reverse psychology Meg used on occasion, perhaps it was part of her acting and training. She could catch them by surprise, and when they realised what she was up to, their concentration on their original problem was refocused and the pain went away. Packy began to laugh, and she beamed her usual big smile at him.

'I didn't know you were not well, young man. But I'm glad to see you're getting better.'

'How long are you going to stay?' he asked. Packy wasn't aware of the day's events, and we didn't say anything to him.

'A few days,' said Meg, 'but I will have to go back to work in Dublin.'

'That's great,' said Packy. Then he turned to me and said, 'Sarah, I'm hungry.'

'What would you like?'

'Some brown bread and jam with a cup of tea.'

We brought him down to the kitchen and sat him at the table to have his little midnight feast. He had lost weight in the past two weeks, and it would take a lot of nurturing and feeding to get him back to good health again. When he had finished, he went back to bed. We went to sleep too, as tomorrow would more than likely shape our future destiny.

Dad was up after seven, and when I heard him stir, I dressed quickly, and went to the kitchen. I had tossed and turned all night, drifting from restless sleep to wakefulness. It was a bright night also, and rays of moonlight beamed in the window. Meg was sound asleep, and her breathing was on the verge of a snore. I was sleeping when I'd heard Dad stir. I was glad to be up with him. He said nothing but sighed and breathed deeply on occasion. He drank a cup of hot tea and wouldn't eat anything with it. He wouldn't speak, but listened for every sound, thinking it was the squad car coming to collect him. Finally, it did arrive, and he left with them to go to the morgue at the hospital in the town. When he was gone, we were free to speak, but I called Tom and Joe aside to tell them not to say anything to Packy.

'Are we going to tell what happened?' asked Joe.

'No, say nothing. We know nothing, and the less they know the fewer questions they will ask.'

'What about Dad?' asked Tom.

'Him too,' said Meg. 'We say nothing. Is that clear?'

The boys did not know what to think. I could feel a lump in the pit of my stomach. We did nothing, but just sat there waiting for the hours to tick away. Packy was hungry again, and he had a fried egg and some brown bread.

'Why is everybody so quiet?' he asked. 'No one is talking.'

'We'll have to tell him too,' said Meg. 'We have to be so careful.'

She sat him down beside her on the side of the bed and asked him a question.

'Do you remember after Christmas, when Eileen was killed accidentally?'

'Yeah, Darcy did it,' he said.

'Remember he took her body away in the car.'

'I do!'

'Well, Mr Ryan found a body in the lake yesterday. Your Dad is gone to see if it is your Mam's body.'

'It must be Eileen,' he said. 'That horrible man must have dumped her in the lake.'

'Well when your Dad comes back, and if it is Eileen, don't pretend you know anything. Is that clear?'

'I know that,' he said. 'I will say nothing to no one.'

'Good boy. If your Dad finds out what happened to your Mam, and what happened to Eileen, it will kill him.'

'Meg, I'm not going to lose anyone anymore. I don't want to be taken away like the Larkins.'

He began to sob softly as she brought him back to bed, and we sat silently in the kitchen again. I could hear the ticking of the clock, and I felt like throwing it out the window. As always, the kettle began to sing on the range, and it drowned out the sound of the clock. You could cut the air with a knife – the house was that quiet. It felt as if we were waiting for the judgement in a court case, waiting for the jury to return their verdict. Random thoughts ran through my head again, and I could hear the local villagers gossiping among themselves, and eyes focusing on me, as I walked alone down the street. There was a hum in their voices as I could not discern what they were saying. But I knew what it was.

'She's the mother killer, and she hid the body.'

'How could she do it?'

'Ah, sure there's a touch of madness in that family. The apple doesn't fall far from the tree. What comes out in the mother, comes out in the daughter.'

'And what about that woman who came from England? She must have killed her too.'

'Isn't it lucky she didn't kill the little boys.'

'The poor gossoons, they're scarred for life.'

I began to panic again and I got that stern stare from Meg once more.

'What did I tell you?' she said.

I thought it would take a long time to identify the body. I wasn't expecting them back until evening, but at around twelve noon they returned. Joe and Tom ran to meet them. There were two cars, the squad car and Donal Ryan's. The sergeant held on to Dad, as he walked slowly with the stick. I knew that it was the same all over again. It wasn't Mam, and he was disappointed once more. The sergeant sat him down in the chair opposite him, at the kitchen table.

'Dad, what is it?' I asked.

He looked up at me, and his eyes changed from a vacant gaze to a glassy tearful hue. He wanted to speak, but he couldn't find the words.

'Take your time, John,' said Sergeant Greene. 'It's alright.'

'I'm sorry, Sarah!' he said, and he burst into tears. Disappointment again, I thought. How was this ever going to end? I'd have to do something.

'It's over, love. It's all over. It's her, it's your mother alright. I found her at last.

'Dad it couldn't be,' I said.

'It is her! Her body was all eaten by fish and animals, she had no face, and her hair had fallen out. She fell and hit her head on the ice.'

'Dad, it's not her. I know it's not her.'

'It is her body, Sarah. There was only one way I knew it was her.'

'What do you mean?' He took a handkerchief from his pocket and dried his eyes, and then blew his nose. He put it back again and looked me straight in the eyes.

'She was wearing the lovely flowery dress I brought her from London last summer. It's a summer dress. Why was she wearing it in the middle of winter?'

'Dad, it's not her. Listen, I have something to tell you.' In that moment of madness, I was going to reveal all. I couldn't live the lie for the rest of my life. The whole charade was getting the better of me. It was as if I had been interrogated for days, and now I had broken. I had deceived everyone, my brothers, my father, Meg. The glass had not only cracked, it had broken. I took a deep breath ready to tell what had happened all those months ago, when there was a scream from the bedroom, and Packy came running in his pyjamas into the kitchen.

He grabbed Dad by the wrists, and he began shouting as loud as he could, 'She was wearing it, Dad! Mam was wearing it that day. She loved that dress because you bought it for her. Dad, Mam wore it all day that day, and she was gone the next day.'

Joe and Tom sat each side of the armchair also, as Dad sobbed quietly. No one spoke. Meg stood at the bedroom door, her gaze focused on me.

I said no more. The panic attack I was about to have, abated. Packy clung close to Dad, crying into his jumper. Dad held him close, and all his grief burst forth also.

'She's not coming back Dad ever, sure she's not?' asked Packy through his sobs.

'No son, she's not. I'm so sorry.'

'Dad will you promise me one thing?'

'What's that Packy?'

'Don't ever go away anymore?'

'I promise you that,' said Dad, 'as God is my witness, I will never leave you.' Tom and Joe each leaned over onto his shoulder, and the outpouring of grief left the kitchen in silence. I wiped away the tears from my face, and he looked up at me again and said, 'We will have to bury her in the new cemetery.'

'What?' I exclaimed.

'We will find a nice little plot for her there.'

What would Meg say? We couldn't bury Eileen in our family grave. I didn't know what to think. I stood up and considered her face. It had changed to a smile.

'Yes, Sarah,' she said, 'she can rest at last in the new cemetery. It's all over now.'

It was then I understood it all. Dad believed he had found Mam. Eileen was going to be buried on holy ground. Mam was already resting in a holy place. In fact, the old cemetery dated back to early Christian times. Dad's mind would be at rest. I looked to the outside door, and Pat Reardon stood across the yard. He wouldn't come inside once there was a crowd there. I could see he had tears too. Meg came to me, and she put her arms around my shoulders.

'It's all over now, Sarah. You understand?'

'I do now,' I said.

Sergeant Greene stood up and made to leave.

'John, I will be back later to make arrangements to release the body after the post-mortem. There's no need to pursue this any further. The case is closed. Thank God for that, this poor family has suffered long enough.'

'I can't thank you enough for all you have done, Sergeant,' said Dad, 'and to you for finding her, young man. I will be ever indebted to you both.'

'I think we should leave you in peace now. I know Father Doyle will be over later to make arrangements for the funeral.'

Then the house was left just to ourselves and Meg. I suddenly felt a great weight lift off my shoulders. I ran to the new hay in the meadow and sat under a fresh cock of hay to gather my thoughts together. I sobbed for a while, and Sputnik nestled into me. Two hours later they found me asleep. When they woke me, I returned to the house to find that people were already flocking to the door, to sympathise with us on the death of our mother.

Chapter 50

Departures

The days that followed were all a haze to me. It was nearly forty years ago. Time and distance have in a sense blotted it out of my memory. It took some time to work it all out in my head. We wouldn't have done it only for Meg. But we did, and I still had my family together. Dad would in time, settle back into a routine, and his whole focus was on us, to protect and prepare us for our own lives.

Those balmy July days were so long ago. The house was full every day, until the funeral was over. Four days after the body was found, it was released to us. The coffin was closed, and we were not allowed to see it.

In later years, Dad would never reveal what he saw, but the only way of identifying the body was the dress. There was also a gash on the head. I could still hear the thud, as Eileen's head hit the fender. But deep down inside, I was still not happy with the outcome. Something within myself told me, that all was not as it seems. It was something I carried with me over the years. I had to accept the deceit bestowed upon Dad in the whole affair. But it was either that, or the whole family unit would fall apart.

Then the radio, and the newspapers had coverage of it all, and television did its own part then. I was so glad, when all the fuss and bother associated with the whole affair, began to settle down.

Eileen was buried in a plot in the new cemetery, with a space reserved for Dad, when the end of his life came. It was something I didn't want to worry about. I'd hope that it wouldn't happen for many years. The faces that came to sympathise that day, are all a blank to me. Many of them too, are long gone to their maker. But they shared our grief in those moments. I was really grieving for my mother. It was put on hold for so long since the events of that night last winter.

But I had tears for Eileen too. She had a sad and tragic life, yet she was such a happy person. I still recall the card games, and the fun the boys had with her on Christmas day. The only blot on the horizon was Darcy. What if he came back? I stood in the sunshine that day with Dad, my brothers, and Meg. Packy held my hand, and I could feel his pain in the tremble of his little hand. Mam's name would appear on the headstone, yet she wasn't there. Eileen would have no marking on the grave at all. We were taken away before the grave was closed in and returned home to neighbours who had taken over the house to provide food and drink for the mourners. People spilled out onto the yard, and they sat on stools, as well as the bank by the road, and they savoured tea and sandwiches, as well as confectionaries such as cake, buns, apple and rhubarb tart.

For the moment our grief had abated, but it would be how Dad coped in the next few months I worried about. Meg stayed a week, and I knew she'd have to go. I didn't get to talk to her very much during that period, as there was always someone within earshot. But the day before she left, she brought me to town and we had tea in the hotel. It was the only place we could talk in private.

She ordered tea and scones, with butter and strawberry jam. We sat in a corner away from rambling ears, and we could talk freely. We weren't in a hurry, and we spent the afternoon talking about all that had happened. Meg was relaxed, and for the first time in a long time, I was in a quiet state of calm. Why did things go the way they did, over the past few months? It was as if someone was there at every turn we made, guiding us in the right direction. When I had time to think about it all, certain things just did not fit. This was something that would always go through my head, as the years went on. We got away with it too easy in the end. It was all down to a dress Dad brought from England, the summer before. I could understand why Eileen was going through my mother's wardrobe, and fitting on her clothes. Meg had told us that she loved clothes so much, she'd want to buy items from you if she took a fancy to them. I had sent her back to take the dress off, moments before Darcy began to force himself on me.

Was it coincidence or what? What did he do with her suitcase and walking stick? Did he take it to Dublin? There was no trace of them in the Dublin house – Meg found nothing. Darcy never even called for his clothes. Everything was still in the wardrobe? What happened Mam's black coat?

Dumping the body in the lake was too obvious a thing to do, if he wanted to hide it and get away. Whatever he did on that spur of the moment occurrence, it scared the living daylights out of him. Wherever he was, he was not coming back, and it left Meg wondering what had happened to him.

Dad's mistaken identification of the body, brought no more investigation from the Gardaí. He was at peace, and preparations were taking place to move away. There was one thing which bothered me a lot. How did Meg feel about the whole affair? As if she could read my mind, she answered my question before I asked it.

'I know what you are thinking Sarah, and the answer is, I'm glad things have turned out the way they have.'

'What about Eileen?'

'She saved our bacon, so she did. The way her body turned up like that, leaving it difficult to identify who she was, left it easier for your Dad to focus on the dress. I knew the state you were in, and if you had said anything, we wouldn't be sitting here today. Eileen is buried on hallowed ground. There is no memorial to her. Her memorial is the happy go lucky way she lived her life, even during those last years following her stroke. I have lost a good friend, but I will always have happy memories of her.'

'It was Packy who saved the day then?' I said.

'You don't realise how clever that little man is. I think his sheer determination along with your own, carried you through the past few months. He is going to put all that at the back of his mind and get on with his life. Your Dad is making a right decision to take you all away from here. Life will go on, but people around here, will always refer to you as the family whose mother turned mad, and threw herself in the lake. There will always be a stigma attached to the name Cregan in the parish. Moving away to a new life, will give you the anonymity to get on without prying eyes, and wagging tongues.'

'What are you going to do?' I asked.

'I will manage just fine. I will keep working, and I have a great circle of friends. I'm not sure what will happen with Darcy. If he comes back, I will probably take care of him. But I doubt if that will happen. If he hasn't made contact in six months, he's not coming back.'

'Will you come back to see us?'

'No Sarah, you don't need me anymore. My work is complete here now.'

'What do you mean, Meg?'

'I won't be coming back. I'm making a clean break now.'

'Why? Why are you not coming back?'

'It's not that I don't love you all. That's the problem. I love you too much. It breaks my heart every time I have to leave.'

'No! I'll come with you. You wanted me to become your daughter. I said I would, now you don't want to see us anymore.'

'That's not true, if I could bring you with me I would. But in view of all that has happened, your duty is to your father now, and your brothers. This was your aim, to keep them all together. Whatever part I had in it all, is over now. I must move on. I have a search to do also. I must find that wayward husband of mine. I married him for better or for worse. Believe me, it was for worse most of the time.'

Recalling that day, and our last conversation together, I thought I'd fly into a blinding rage, to think I was losing someone who was so precious in our lives, for the past few months. I knew deep down she was right, she did have to move on. She was a very lonely person, and her happiness coming to our house was always cut short, when she had to leave again. As she said herself, her heart was broken every time she had to go. It was better to make a clean sweep and go.

I had lost so much in the intervening months, Mam, Eileen, Seán and now Meg. I had to count the cost and hold on to the four most precious people in my life. I couldn't be selfish and expect the same from Meg. I knew she would immerse herself into the theatre where she was happiest. It had been her life for so long. Nothing was going to change that now.

'Will you write to me?' I asked.

She hesitated. I knew she was pondering, as to whether it was a good idea or not. Maybe it was, or maybe it wasn't. I waited anxiously for her answer.

'You still have my numbers. You still have my address. That still stands. You will always be the daughter I never had. I would love to hear how you are getting on. Write to me occasionally, especially at Christmas or Easter. They can be very lonely times.'

'Can I write and tell how I am getting on, and as to how the boys are doing?'

'Please do. I might need cheering up now and again.'

'You know something, Meg. You are our guardian angel here on earth. I believe that to be true. You saved our lives. We would never have gotten away with all this, if it weren't for you.'

'I was there when you needed me, and maybe it was my greatest movie moment. You will have to watch the movie made some years ago, called Sunset Boulevard. It starred Gloria Swanson. She was a veteran actress of the silent movie era. After shooting William Holden, at the end of the film, and his body floating in the swimming pool, she was being taken away by the police to jail. She dressed up in her finest clothes, and the film ends as she declares, she's moving in for her final close-up to the camera. That was me. It was probably the finest movie moment I have ever had. It worked! Our audience believed it. The whole episode could be a movie. Here we are now, after the premier, having tea and scones, and wondering where the next movie will be.'

'I see it all now, it was all a drama, a movie and we were the actors. That is what this is all about,' I exclaimed.

'It's all a fantasy world. It entertains, it deceives. A movie set is not what it seems. Neither is a stage set. Look behind it, and you will see the paper, cardboard, and planks of timber. Outside of that, it is a world of make-believe. This was our world for the past few months. We were the actors and all those who came our way, were watching the drama emerge.'

Some years later I saw that 1950 movie on TV, with William Holden and Gloria Swanson, and I could see Meg, in the dramatic acting of the great lady, as she made her exit at the end of the movie. In 1994, I went to London to see the musical, and I was enthralled by it also.

Memories streamed back to me, of that day in the hotel in town, with the tea, and scones. Meg described the whole affair as being a movie or theatre production. But I had a different perspective of the events, as seen through the eyes of the audience. They couldn't envisage what lay behind those cardboard, and wooden sets.

'The only problem is, they couldn't see the sadness, and tragedy behind it all, which we were suffering,' I said.

'And we will continue to suffer from it. We will be on our guard for the rest of our lives.'

'That's why I'm still not happy with the outcome.'

'Why do you say that?'

'Darcy should have buried the body. He didn't do that. In the end, it was found in the shallows of the lake. If he was running away from killing her, he should have covered his tracks. Why did he want her body to be found?'

'Maybe it was because he was so frightened at the time, he didn't know what to do. He probably panicked and dumped her there.'

'Another thing, I still don't understand. How did he get her there? He would have had to drag her across four fields, from behind the old cemetery. He didn't carry a dead body that journey. Donal came to that part of the shore by boat. There were no boats on the lake at that time, it was frozen solid. He hardly risked carrying it across the ice.'

'I never thought of that,' she said. 'However, it got to be there in that spot, I don't know, and I probably never will. The guards said nothing, they probably think it drifted there. The gash on her head was from the fall. They believe that it was your mother whom they recovered, and she had reached the shore through the fields. She hit her head, and lay on the ice till it melted, and her body sank into the lake. It was probably covered with snow for a long time. That's why no one found it.'

'Things just don't add up Meg.'

'Let it be, it's over, and we cannot turn the clock back. You will have to move on and create a new life for yourselves. Times are changing, and for the better, I hope. Your brothers will have better opportunities for education in Scotland. So, will you.'

'I might try nursing eventually,' I said.

'I'd well believe it. It is you, and only you should follow that dream.'

She held my two hands across the table, and I knew she was lonely. She was being hard on herself and having to let go of all she held dear. She wasn't getting younger either, and she would now have to cut the cloth according to the measure. She wanted to leave without too much fuss. She didn't want to tell the boys she wasn't coming back. She felt she had said her goodbyes before Easter, when she left to return to Dublin. She was only visiting, to ensure that we were taking care of ourselves. She wanted them to think that she'd be returning on her regular visits. She felt they had suffered enough heartbreak, over the past few months. What they didn't know they wouldn't miss.

We sat there into the evening, talking and quietly drinking cups of tea. It was our final moment together, as she wanted it to last as long as it could, and I felt the same.

We returned home in the car to an excited house, as the boys were after finding mushrooms, and Dad was helping to peel them, and to fry them on the pan. She sat quietly watching them for an hour, and at around eleven o'clock she retired to bed.

In the morning, there was no fuss. She had breakfast with us, and she prepared to leave. She placed her small case in the boot of the car, and Packy presented her with a charcoal drawing of our house. She looked at it with tears in her eyes, and said she'd cherish it forever.

'Can I come with you to the top of the hill?' I asked.

She nodded her head gently, and I sat beside her. She drove in first gear to the top and stopped the car.

'Goodbye, my dear little girl,' she said. 'I will always love you.'

'I would love you to stay.'

'I would love to stay too, but I must go.'

'Goodbye, Mum!' I said to her.

She smiled a tearful smile, and I got out of the car. I waited while she made her way slowly to the main road. I ran to the wooden gate and crossed into the field. I sprinted to the summit of the hill, and watched the car move slowly onto the main road. She didn't drive very fast, and it snaked its way towards the village.

It was nearly a year to the day, that I stood at this spot with my brothers, and waited for the bus, taking Dad home from England. The grass was swaying in the breeze, just like a Mexican wave, and I couldn't believe that so much happened in my life since that time. Today, I watched, and waited again to see her leave forever. I wondered what the future was going to bring. Deep down I was not happy with the outcome of events. Our lives had been saved, but I felt for some reason that all was still not well. It would return to me on occasion, as the years rolled on, but I never said a word to anyone about it, not even to my brothers. Nearly forty years would elapse before the past would catch up with me again. All that was in the future. I stood on the hill there, when Meg was long gone. I sat in the long grass and tucked my knees up under my chin. I gave a great sigh of relief, and began at last, to think of the future.

Chapter 51

Moving on

The crowds stopped coming to the house, and our world went quiet. It was time to move on.

Dad went to that scheduled meeting in Glasgow in August, and I cared for the boys for the few days he was away. The sky didn't fall, and no one came to take us away. There had been an investigation into Dad's accident, and the upshot of it all was, that we were to be provided with a house in Glasgow, and Dad was offered a job in the supply shop for the building company. His road to recovery went well, but he required a walking stick for the rest of his life. It was something he got used to, and he didn't complain about it. He was happy with his lot, when eventually he left the tragic events of his life behind him.

By the end of August, the farm was up for sale, and there was to be an auction in the middle of October in the hotel in town. We focused on the move, and what we were going to do when we got to Scotland. I decided that we take it easy, and not to rush into things. We had to decide what we were bringing with us, and what we'd have to leave behind.

I cherished my mother's things so much, her little bits of jewellery, and her photographs. They were placed in a large chocolate box and tied with a red ribbon she used to make into a bow on the top of my head. Most of the furniture was to be auctioned off, and by the time we were ready to leave, we moved into a vacant house in the village for two weeks, as everything was gone. The farm fetched a fair price, and Dad was happy with the outcome. It was purchased by a man whose land bordered ours, and it would add to his holding, making his farm bigger, and more productive. He wasn't interested in the house as such, and we didn't know whether he'd sell it off later or what.

Pat Reardon adopted Sputnik and brought him to live with him. It wasn't such a traumatic change for him, as he knew Pat and lapped up his kindness. He was a great companion for him in those days, after we left, knowing that we were not coming back.

Pat knew that it was goodbye forever for us. If we could have brought him with us we would have done so, but Pat's simple lifestyle, would not suit the busy hustle and bustle of Glasgow. He was more suited to his quiet country life helping local farmers out and collecting the ticket money for the priest at the local dances. He called to the house every day, as we prepared to move, and he sat with Dad into the night. I knew he wanted to be near us, and to savour those moments of friendship, something he was going to lose, and wondered what fate awaited him as he grew older. I knew that the Walsh family would keep an eye on him, and give him some guidance, when it came to hygiene, and he would never go hungry. I often thought about him through the years, and whatever little we learned about him, came from the few lines he wrote on a Christmas card, as well as the one he sent every year for St Patrick's Day.

The night before we left, he came to the house in the village, and stayed well into the night with us. He was tearful and lonely, and he drank a few whiskeys with Dad as a parting gesture. I was ever so conscious of allowing Dad drink too much, but it was his last tipple at home here. He accused me of being bossy like my mother, and this was something he'd say to me through the years, whenever we'd have a little argument or something. When it was time for him to go, he asked me to walk home with him. It was only a few hundred yards from where we were staying, to Pat's place. I held his hand like a little child, and we walked slowly through the dim lit street. It was late November, and the weather reminded me of a night a year earlier, when we trudged through the fields to hide my mother's body in the mausoleum in the old cemetery.

'You will write to me,' he said.

'I will, Pat. I will write to you often.'

'I'm going to be lonely you know. I am going to miss you all.'

'I will miss you too, Pat. Please don't start talking like that, or you will have me in tears. I have had so many of them in the past while, I don't want to start all over again.'

'I know,' he answered, 'but I will still be lonely.'

'Well if you are lonely, think of the nice times we had, when you'd make the hay, and help with the turf, and how we used to have fun throwing the hay on top of you, or hid your hat, or took your bike, and went down the hill for a spin.'

'I will do all that,' he said. He spoke calmly, and he didn't stammer.

'I want you to work hard at not getting yourself excited. If people mock or jeer you, just stop and speak slowly. It will take a lot of work, but you will do it.'

'You are a good teacher,' he said, 'and anything you tell me I will always do.'

'People need you here in the village, Pat. They will always need your help. You are important to them. See how Fr Doyle relies on you at the dances, remember you are an important and clever person.'

'I don't want you to be scared anymore?' he said, changing the subject.

'What do you mean, Pat?' I asked.

'Everything is alright now. They found your mother and they buried her.'

'I know that,' I answered, 'and it is all in the past now.'

'So, there is no need to be afraid.'

'I'm not afraid anymore.'

'Good girl. It's all over you know. You can never have your Mam back, but she is safe with God, and buried in the graveyard. It would have been terrible if they had never found her.'

'They found her, thank God.' I said, lying through my teeth again. I was going to have to forget about all of that. I was running away from the truth, and such secrets I would have to take to the grave with me.

'There is no need to worry ever again,' he said softly.

'And I will never marry you, Pat Reardon, you know that.'

'How could I marry you, you were always my little girl. I never had a little girl of my own, but you were always mine.'

'And you spoiled me rotten always.'

'You were the only one to stand up for me. I can never forget that.'

'So, Meg Darcy said I was the daughter she never had; Pat Reardon said the same. I am blessed to have so many parents in my life.'

He began to laugh quietly to himself, as we reached the creaky gate, leading to his cottage. Then he began to weep into an old dirty handkerchief, he took out of his pocket. I pulled it away from him and said, 'Come here, you big cry-baby, and give me a hug.'

I held him close to me and I didn't mind, he was his still usual stale smelling self. It was only mid-week and he wasn't too bad. My heart was tearing also, but I didn't want to make it worse for him. I knew that he would now be on his own, and the friendship he shared with us for so long, was going to be lost. I hoped that life would not be too harsh on him, and that he would give it a go alone. He had no one in the world except relations in America, and they had never returned. If things had been different, if Mam had not died, or any of the events of the past year had not taken place, we'd still be up there in the little farmhouse, and life would sail on uninterrupted, for many more years.

'I-I-I w-w-will miss you all,' he said again, raising his voice and stammering.

'What did I tell you? Speak slowly.'

He calmed down, and spoke in a quieter gentler voice, 'I will miss you all,' he said again, and spoke perfectly.

'Keep practising that,' I said. 'You can do it.'

'I'll have to go now,' he said.

I planted a kiss on the side of his grey stubbly face.

'Goodbye, Sarah. God bless.' He shut the gate, and opening the flaky green door, he closed it quickly behind him. I stood there in the dim light for a few minutes and went back to the house.

Next morning, we left. The hackney car that brought us to the train station arrived at nine o'clock. The driver's chat was all about the assassination of John F Kennedy in Dallas the evening before. We hadn't heard anything, as we had no radio. But the world moved on despite us, and over the years people often asked what you were doing when you learned of Kennedy's death. We were leaving the country and starting a new life. We didn't speak or say very much, but Packy sat close to me in the back of the car. The boys were all wearing brand new clothes and looked well in their new winter coats. Joe had his hair combed sleekly down on his head and kept in place with loads of Brylcreem.

Dad had visited the farm the day before and walked the land for the last time. 'I will never come back while I'm alive,' he said, 'too many memories.'

Part 6

The Return

Chapter 52

'I will care for you for the rest of my life.'

Dad was true to his word, and this is what happened to us all. We settled in Glasgow as planned, and it took a few years to get used to the new lifestyle. It was strange to adjust to the noise and bustle of city life, the street lights, and the accents. But we lived among those, who had gone before us. Our house was a three-bedroomed semi-detached, and we had stairs for the first time in our lives, as well as running water, a sitting room, a bathroom, a kitchen and an electric cooker. The rent was minimal, and this allowed us to put money by, and in time Dad bought the house. This was something he was very proud of, he felt he was a millionaire.

That first Christmas in Glasgow, he bought a television. The pace of change in our lives accelerated so fast into the twentieth century, that memories of that awful year began to fade away. Dad got the bus every morning, and went to work in the builder's suppliers shop, where he soon adjusted to the light work assigned to him. He donned a blue shop coat, and for the first time in his life he wore a collar and tie to work. He stayed quite sober, and after a few months joined a temperance group organised by the young Irish curate in the parish. He soon joined parish groups and committees, in organising dances, card drives, and concerts, raising much-needed funds for the Catholic parishes.

I often thought to myself that this pipe dream of his, to buy more land and develop our little small farm, to make it more productive, was a lost cause and a money pit. His dream of building an extension to our house, was to fulfil Mam's dream for us all. She was never interested in emigrating, and as a result, he was away for so long each year. If things had been different, Mam would have moved with him to Glasgow and spent several years living there. Maybe in time, they would have returned home again, like many other Irish people. But this was not to be. There was no way we could alter time, and return to those early years, and begin again. We had to make a fresh start, when we had lost so much. But doing so, I had managed to keep our family together. I often breathed a sigh of relief at Christmas time, or on birthdays when I saw my fast-growing brothers laughing and enjoying their new-found life.

The years began to roll by, and I saw them make their way. Joe was to first to venture out into the world. He became an apprentice plumber, and in time, made it his livelihood. Tom began working in a nursery during breaks from school, and followed a career in horticulture, eventually setting up a nursery of his own outside the city. Packy followed his dream, as I had anticipated. He stayed at school and went on to Art College. He became an art teacher, and spent many years helping young people develop their artistic talents, and to express themselves through many art media.

I became their mother, and I observed with pride as they made their way in the world. I watched sadly, as they left home, and moved away into independent living. The house was left alone to Dad and me. He went quiet as usual and gave his usual 'Aye!' sigh as he watched them leave the house.

But they were not lost and gone forever, they came back, and stayed for special occasions such as Christmas, Easter and for our birthdays.

I kept my promise to take care of Dad. I stayed at home for those years, and was there for them all, just as Mam would have done. But Dad knew that I needed a life also, and he encouraged me to go to night classes. I did that for a few years and found myself writing to Dr Sullivan for a reference, as I prepared to train as a nurse. Time moved on, and I worked in Glasgow, living at home with Dad. He wanted me also to try and find a young man to share my life, and he often talked about some young suitable men he knew at work. They'd make fine proper husbands for me. This wasn't to be, as I was content with my life, and I loved my career. Dad and I became soulmates and under my care, he thrived. I suppose it was the care I gave him, that prolonged his life, living to a ripe old age. He had proper meals and worldly comforts, as well as enjoying a greater standard of living. He never talked about home much, but some memories would come to the fore, when a card arrived from Pat in Ireland. He hoped he was being cared for, and that he too was enjoying improved standards of living.

I had occasional letters from Meg, but they got fewer as the years rolled on. Darcy never returned into her life, and he was eventually listed as missing.

It reminded me of the disappearance of Lord Lucan, as he seems to have vanished from the face of the earth. After 1992, her letters ceased altogether. The numbers she gave me no longer worked, and not in use anymore. I presumed she must have died.

Joe and Tom were married when they were in their late twenties, setting up home not far from where we lived, and Dad was happy when the grandchildren began to arrive, eventually reaching a maximum of six. Between them, there were four boys and two girls, and it gave me great pleasure to spoil them, and they gave a new lease of life to their grandad too. Packy remained a bachelor and a career man, travelling extensively every summer, and sending many postcards and photos of all the places he had seen. Our fridge became a shrine to the many magnets he brought, depicting native dancers, kangaroos, kiwis, boomerangs and other memorabilia from all those far-flung places. He came to stay at weekends too, and I could still feel that bond he had when he was young, and the fears he had, that he might be taken away.

When there was a big snowfall around 1982 after Christmas, he talked to me about that time, and the story he spun to Sergeant Greene about Mam running away. He still had nightmares regarding those events, how he was delirious with measles, and he kept shouting at Dad, that Mam was wearing the floral dress, the day she disappeared.

'I'm still not happy about what happened,' he said.

'Why do you say that?' I asked.

Then he proceeded to say the same things I had said to Meg, about Eileen's body ending up in the lake. He often thought about how Darcy had managed to drag her body across the fields to that point in the lake. It would have been an impossible task for someone in the drunken condition he was in. The body would have to have been placed in the lake immediately, as the car was found at the station the next day, when Joe went to find Meg.

I told him about my thoughts also, how I had confided in Meg about the situation. My thoughts were the same, and he wondered why I had never said anything about it.

'Maybe he had some help,' said Packy.

413

'Who would help him?' I asked, 'If that happened, whoever was his accomplice would have said something by now. Darcy could find himself being blackmailed or threatened.' I could never get my head around it. Meg told me to forget about it. If we opened any more doors, we could bring the whole rigours of the law down on top of us. We managed to get away with it. The guards were not thinking the same as us. They believed that the body found, was our mother, who in a fit of madness trudging through the fields, froze to death on the cold lake, having hit her head on the ice.'

'They didn't know what we knew, that's why the case was closed.'

'That's why Dad found closure, the body found was the woman he married.'

'What's going to happen when he dies?' asked Packy.

'So be it, we'll take him home, and bury him beside her in that new cemetery.'

'We have to live with the lies and deceit and all that wheeling and dealing,' he said. 'We will be running away from it all for the rest of our lives.'

'That's what we have signed up for in this life, and we must face it, whether we like it or not.'

'That's why I go away each year, to escape from the past. I often think that if this whole house of cards came tumbling down, I might never get to see the world.'

'Let it go, Packy. You will have to. You are letting it haunt your life. Do like Joe and Tom and find a woman to share your world, raise a family.'

'I would not like my children to have to share the past we have had. If it ever came to light, it would taint their lives also. The mad granny throwing herself into the lake, and none of it was true. Sure, look at you Sarah, why haven't you married and raised a family? You are in the same boat as me.'

'On those many lonely nights, when I had no one to talk to I made a promise that if Dad recovered, I'd care for him for the rest of his life. This is what I'm doing and I'm happy to do that.'

'You were some brave lady to do all you did,' he said.

'I had my accomplices,' I sighed, 'and some of the finest actors Meg Darcy turned out in her little drama theatre in our house.'

'I often thought of going back there,' he said, 'but I'm afraid to. It was home to us during those years, but I know, like all places, it has probably changed too.'

'You will go back someday. I know you will.'

Packy was nearly thirty years of age when we had this conversation, and we never talked about it again. I knew that cloud hung over him always, and he'd show a brave face to the world. But he kept a busy lifestyle, teaching his art and design, as well as travelling when the notion took him. He was still my brave little hero, and he was closer to me, than the two older boys. They never mentioned those events in their lives, as they had moved on with their own, and were so pre-occupied with parenthood. They had found true happiness, and maybe that was the greatest gift I could ever have given them.

I spent many happy years caring for Dad, and he embraced old age with great ease, happy with the physical changes that happened to him. He was mobile till his mid-eighties, using a walking stick to get around. His mind was still bright, and he was great for conversing with any visitors who came to our house. I was glad that his happiness was fulfilled, even though he lost Mam the way he did. He was very grateful for us, for his grandchildren, and his family meant so much to him. In his 90th year, his health failed, suffering a stroke, leaving him confined to the bed for some time. I took some time out of my career to care for him, in his last months, and he began to slowly fade from our lives. In July 2005, he passed away peacefully at home, having received the last rites, something Mam was denied, but I knew in my heart and soul, they were together with the Lord. I called my brothers together, just as I had done the night Mam died, and we arranged to bring him home to Ireland for burial. Packy made it clear he was not coming with us, and there was a long argument with his brothers about the matter. Rather than see him storm out of the house, and distance himself from them, I made them accept Packy's wishes, to remain in Glasgow, and not attend the funeral. They were to travel with me instead.

Arrangements were made, and the undertakers carried out all the tasks in preparation for the funeral, which included the insertion of a death notice in the Irish Independent. Those in the know, who remembered the mad Cregan's from way back then, would recall again, the events of 1963. But it wasn't long till the past started to catch up with us. The day before we left to take Dad to his final resting place, I was at home in the house alone, when the phone rang. I answered it, thinking it was one of our Glasgow friends, sympathising with us on the death of our father. But I was in for a shock. A voice I thought I recognised spoke.

'Is that Sarah?' said the caller.

'Yes, it is. Who is this?

'It's Seán.'

'Seán who?'

'Seán Walsh.'

My heart skipped a beat. It was a very long time since I heard that voice before. Was this the Seán Walsh I fell in love with? I was speechless at the end of the phone, not knowing what to say. Why was he ringing me now? As I didn't respond, when he gave his name, he spoke again, 'Hello Sarah! It is Sarah Cregan I'm speaking to, isn't it?'

'It is,' I gasped. Still not knowing what to say, another silence ensued, and he spoke again.

'Are you alright, Sarah? It's only me, Seán!'

'I know,' I replied. 'Just give me a minute to catch my breath. You are the last person in the world I thought would ring me.'

'Well, it's me alright! I'm not the sprightly little fella, who carried you on the bike into the bog many years ago. I'm as grey as a badger. I'm not slim and trim, as I used to be. I had to have a hip replacement last year, and I'm not yet sixty.'

'Well, I'm plump and matronly. In fact, that's what I am. I'm a matron in a hospital here in Glasgow.'

'We will never get those years back again, Sarah. The march of time declares otherwise. We can only look back and dream.'

'Seán why are you ringing me, especially now? You know Dad has died?'

'That's why I'm contacting you. I'm acting as a messenger for someone.'

'Who or what would want to contact me after all these years?' I asked.

'Someone you loved very much once. He said he would care for you for the rest of his life.' I knew straight away who he meant. It had to be Pat Reardon. I thought he had died, considering we hadn't heard from him for a long time.

'Pat!' I exclaimed.

'The very man. He's still alive, but he's in failing health. He's nearly ninety years old.'

'He was in the same class as Dad in school. They were always great friends. Dad always stood up for him when others wouldn't.'

'He asked me to contact you. I didn't know where to start. I couldn't find any trace of you in directories and other documents. So, I did what you did years ago.'

'What was that?' I asked.

'The Salvation Army.'

'How do you know that?' I exclaimed. I had to sit down in the chair. The only people who knew about that were the guards whom they contacted way back then. What did he know? I was terrified, as to what he might say next. A shiver ran down my spine.

'I have my sources,' he joked. I didn't find it very funny. He seemed to be very amused about it all.

'Sarah! I won't beat about the bush. Pat is dying. He wants to see you. I know in my heart and soul that he will not rest, till he sees you.'

'Why does he want to see me?' I asked. Why was it so important that he was prolonging his life to talk to me? What was troubling him I wondered? Pat should have no troubles. I always said to myself that if anyone had a place in heaven, well he deserved one.

'Pat is in the county home for the past twenty-three years. The authorities had to step in and take care of him. He was injured in the great snowfall of 1982. He was suffering from hypothermia. He had no fire in the house, and he set out for our farm to take refuge. He fell in the snow and broke his leg. It was the luck of God, that the postman found him, and raised the alarm. He was in the hospital for a few weeks. Since there was no one to care for him, when he was recovering, he was placed in the county home. He liked it so much, he decided to stay there. I've never seen him as happy since he went in there.'

The tears were streaming down my face as he told me. I never knew what had happened to him. That was why the cards stopped coming, and we lost contact.

Was I so selfish that I didn't make it my business to go visit him? Again, I could not turn time back, yet I wondered what else Seán had to say.

'I'm chaplain here for the past fifteen years,' he said.

'He said years ago, that he would need you to care for him and to forgive him.'

'Well, it was by accident, rather than design. I was assigned as curate to the town parish then, and part of my brief is chaplain to the old people's home. Pat was a very happy man when I arrived, and I spent many hours talking to him. My father spent his last year in the home too, so he saw me more often than he bargained for.'

'I'm glad he is happy there,' I said.

'Well, let's put it this way Sarah, he is happy, and as well as that he's not happy. He's very restless. It's important that you come to see him after the funeral.'

'Why after the funeral, why not before?'

'I cannot say too much on the phone Sarah at this point?'

'Seán, what is going on? I need to know.' I was beginning to raise my voice in frustration at the way he was talking in riddles, beating about the bush. In fact, I was beginning to perspire, wondering what was going to happen next.

'Seán, I'm frightened at what you are saying. I really need to know what's going on.'

'Ok. Well, I will try and explain it to you, but I cannot tell you everything, and I will come to that also.'

'Go on then.'

'About ten years ago, Pat had a visitor, a lady, someone you knew very well. It was Meg Darcy.'

'Meg!' I exclaimed. 'What did she want with Pat?'

'He asked me to send for her. He didn't give me any reason as to why he wanted to see her, but she came to visit him. She spent a few hours talking to him, and when she left, she had been crying, but she seemed to be happy though. She never returned, and I have had no contact with her since.'

'Why did Pat want to see her?'

'I'm coming to that. You see Sarah, I know everything.'

'What do you mean you know everything?'

'I know everything that took place all those years ago when your Mam died.'

'Yeah, and so does everyone else.'

'What about Eileen?' he asked.

I felt I was going to get sick. Did Meg tell him that? Why would she tell Pat everything? Pat didn't know what took place. We kept it a secret from him. We were afraid he'd panic and give everything away.

'Did she tell him about Eileen?' I asked. I was breathing heavy with anxiety at this stage, but Seán began to reassure me that everything would be fine.

'She told him nothing. Pat knew everything. He is a very clever man. He watched over you all, night and day. I would like Pat to tell you everything. It needs to come from him.'

'Why have I to wait till after the funeral?'

'You see it's like this, when Meg left, Pat wanted me to hear his confession. He wanted forgiveness. He wanted to do what he requested me to do all those years ago.'

'Go on.'

'He told me something in confession.'

'What was it?'

'That, I cannot tell you. What Pat told me I cannot tell? I'm bound by the rules of the Sacrament of Penance. I cannot divulge that to you.'

'You really are scaring me now, Seán.'

'Sarah, for the past ten years Pat has had me on a vigil to watch out for when your father passed away. He knew his body would be brought back home to the new cemetery. He has requested me to tell you, not to come, until as he said himself, John Cregan will have to be dead and buried before I talk to her.'

'Why all the mystery, if you say you know everything, why didn't you go to the guards, and have us arrested and brought back to Ireland?'

'It all rests with what Pat has to say. The things he told me in the confessional will be revealed to you. He will tell you himself. It cannot come from me. My duty as a priest is to keep what I heard to myself. What he told me, is between him and God. He kept me on my guard, to read the death notices in the papers every day. I have been doing that for the past ten years. When I read the death notice to him three days ago, he blessed himself and said, "Thank God!". It wasn't that he wished your father dead, but all the waiting was over, and he could be at peace. I've got strict orders not to bring you to visit him until after the funeral.'

'I am really frightened now, Seán,' I said. 'I'm beginning to wonder, should I go to the funeral or not.'

'Sarah, let me assure you, there is nothing to worry about. Please believe me and trust Pat. Remember what he said, he would protect you for the rest of his life.'

The phone call ended there, and Seán told me that he would be assisting at the funeral mass in the village. He'd take me to see Pat the day after the funeral. I put the phone down, and Pat's words rang through my head. 'I will protect you for the rest of my life.'

With these words, I felt a little more at ease. I had managed to run away from it all, for nearly forty years. How could the whole affair come back like that to haunt me? Pat Reardon was really a very dark horse indeed. He knew so much and pretended to know nothing. He was a very clever man. I always knew that. My mother used to say that there was more in Pat's head than the comb would take out. It meant that he was always prepared for everything that came his way. It was probably due to a survival instinct, that probed at his insecurities. His stammer was always a burden to him. All he needed to do, was have some therapy and classes in voice management. But Pat's world pre-dated all the modern cures and assistance available to people. He was always on the watch. He wouldn't enter the house, if there was a crowd of people there. He had a habit of peeping in windows. It wasn't as if he was a peeping Tom. He was checking to see if it was alright for him to enter, and that it was safe for him to do so. Our house was a haven for him, and he was happy when we were all around him. We were the family he never had, and we moved away not thinking of his welfare. He was alone in the world. We were not there for him, when his house was cold, and he nearly lost his life in the snow. It was as if the winter of 1963 had come back to haunt him. I didn't know whether I should tell my brothers or not. Then I changed my mind and told them. They too were frightened. But they'd have to face the music too. Packy was still adamant, he was not coming to the funeral, and finally his brothers respected his wishes.

I didn't sleep that night. I turned and twisted in the bed and recalled other nights I was restless. They were frightening times then, and I didn't want them to return. I didn't know what was going to meet me when I got home. I began to wonder, did anyone else really know what happened during that year. Nineteen sixty-three would be forever etched in our minds, as a turning point in our lives. It was the year we had to grow up.

Chapter 53

The Return

The following afternoon Tom, Joe and I flew from Glasgow to Dublin. No one knew our mission, but we were very much aware that the remains of our beloved father were stowed quietly in the cargo hold. We had managed to protect him from all the pain and trouble we suffered ourselves, and he would never really know what happened. This was probably the most important journey of our lives. We didn't speak during the flight, but we sat, side by side, staring out the little porthole window at the clouds below us, as well as the sea and islands we were passing over, before we reached the shores of our native land again.

In a sense, I was at peace. Dad died a happy man with his family around him. Gone were those awful days so long ago, but Seán's phone call brought a grave air of uncertainty to our lives again. Joe and Tom said little, but they were prepared to meet anything that came our way in the next few days.

The plane landed at Dublin airport, and we arrived in a city of fast cars and motorways, a changed place from the time we left years before. There was a lot on the news, and in the papers about Ireland; the Celtic Tiger and an economy growing fast, with a more affluent society here. It was evident from the roads and the houses, stretching out into the countryside I once knew. This was a changed place, and I wanted to see how our village had changed too.

There was no one to meet us there, and the hearse was waiting for us to collect the coffin from the plane. A car was waiting to take us back home to the little church, where Fr Doyle said mass in Latin. It was all a spin, and the world we once knew came rolling back to us. The motorway took us swiftly from the city, and we moved westward towards an evening sun.

The Centra shop closed at eight thirty in the evening, which accommodated people coming to and fro to football games, mass, and the occasional funeral. It happened that Fr O'Reilly announced at the First Friday Mass, that there would be a funeral arriving that evening for reception into the church, and burial later in the new cemetery, after requiem mass at eleven o'clock on Saturday. At the previous Sunday mass, he had announced, 'Pray for the repose of the soul of John Cregan, late of Ballyhill, who died in Scotland. Funeral arrangements later.'

As we moved slowly through the busy traffic, thoughts ran through my head once again, as to what people might be saying about us, as we returned after all these years. I reckoned there was great speculation and discussion during the week, as to who this man was. The younger generation could not place, or trace even where he might have lived in Ballyhill.

I knew the older people remembered alright, and could add more light to the mystery, when they came into the Centra shop after collecting their pension at the post office.

'It was a long time ago, a tragedy alright. John Cregan had a hard life. He had to go to England to work, leave his family. Well, this was normal for many people at the time.'

'That's right, but poor Mary, she wasn't well, and she had to cope with four children, and keep things going.'

'What was wrong with her anyway?'

'They say she had a bad heart. Her mother died young, of the same complaint. It runs in the family you know. They hadn't the medicines they have now. It was this, that made her go off the wall, and do what she did?'

'What happened to her?'

'She left her children one night and disappeared. He was in a hospital in Scotland at the time, and he couldn't be found for a long time.'

'Did they find him?'

'They found him alright, but they didn't find her for many months?'

'What happened to her?'

'She was found in the reeds across the fields at the lake behind the old cemetery. She went out in the snow, and never came back. It was a terrible sight, a shockin' tragedy. It was a long time before we all got over it. They buried her in the new cemetery.'

'What about the children? What happened to them?'

'He sold the place and took them with him to Scotland. They never returned, and I wonder will they be with the funeral when it comes.'

I was glad the funeral arrived on time that evening. The hearse, followed by a black car, moved silently through the village. Father O'Reilly was waiting at the church door, having received a call on his mobile, from the undertaker, when he was about two miles from the village. A server stood each side of him, a boy and a girl, dressed in their cream coloured cassocks, with red velvet trim on the sleeves and collars, one carrying the cross, and the other the holy water, to bless the coffin.

A few of the older generation who remembered us, came to the reception at the church, again recalling an event which happened forty years previously.

'I think it happened in nineteen sixty-four.'

'No, it wasn't. It was sixty-three, remember that terrible year, when Pope John XXIII died and John Kennedy was gunned down in November. Remember the big snow. They didn't find her body until July. I will never forget that event. Now it is all coming back as they are laying poor John Cregan to rest.'

'Are the children there?'

'They are there alright, just getting out of the car.'

'There were three boys and a girl. The girl was the oldest.'

'Were there three boys? I can only see two?'

'Can you recall her name?'

'It was Sarah, I think. Yes, it was Sarah. She was the oldest. She kept the family together and looked after the younger ones before her mother died.'

'What about the boys, how old were they when she died?'

'Joe was the oldest, he was fourteen. He was a quiet young lad. The second boy was twelve. Tom, they called him. A wild and funny little fella, and the youngest one was Packy. He was eight when she died. He was quiet and moody, kept to himself a lot, spent his time drawing and colouring. He might have made a good artist. I often wondered what happened to him.'

'There they are, getting out of the cars. I wouldn't recognise them now, and I don't suppose any of them would recognise us.'

'Yeah, but there's one of them missing.'

'I think it's that youngest lad.'

'Quiet now, the bell has rung once. Let's follow them in.'

In my confused imagination, I could nearly hear what was being said, or maybe it was me, again letting it go wild as I used to. I walked behind the coffin, as Joe and Tom helped carry it into the church.

Inside there were about a dozen people altogether. I was surprised that there was anyone there at all.

In the church, I gazed around, and recognised a few of the faces of those who had come to sympathise. Like myself, they were children, when I was growing up in Avenstown, but they were the lucky ones who had the privilege to stay. They would also remember the events that led to Mam's death, the events as seen by the world. But no one knew the deep secrets in our hearts that only we kept. It was all over now, and no one would ever know the truth about what happened in 1963.

I was still a little anxious until Dad was laid to rest. I sat and wondered and waited through the ceremony to see if Seán would appear. But then I realised he said he would assist at the funeral. Joe gave me a nudge now and then, wondering if I was alright.

'I don't know. I'm not comfortable. It's just that it has all come back to me again.'

'It's alright, no one will ever find out what really happened.'

'That's what worries me. What if Seán let the story out?'

'He can't, he said himself he's bound by the rules of the confessional.'

'I am just not comfortable about it all.'

'Will you ever stop, Sarah? You are just paranoid. Forget about it. It is all over.'

The final part of the ceremony was the recitation of a decade of the rosary, and Fr O'Reilly's announcement about the requiem mass, and internment in the new cemetery the next day.

Then the people who had followed the funeral into the church, came up one by one, to sympathise with us, and make themselves known to us. Memories began to flood back once again, of names and faces, some of them happy, others not so happy. I was remembering times when people in a little country village like this, could also be very unkind, and in fact cruel.

Mam's illness was a case in point. Our house was the only one on that road leading to the bog. There was no neighbourliness with some of them. It was this gap, and this distance that may have also been our saving grace. Her story would remain a secret, but now I was not sure.

Just as the last of the sympathisers were shaking my hand, a man in a grey raincoat approached, and introduced himself. He shook my hand and spoke gently to me.

'I'm Seán.'

He had wavy grey hair. His face was still young. In fact, he looked younger than I had imagined. He had filled out somewhat over the years, just bordering on obesity, yet keeping up a fit and athletic image.

I stood and threw my arms around him. I embraced him and held him close to me and sobbed bitterly into the raincoat.

'Now, Sarah,' he joked, 'you didn't miss me that much, now did you?'

I could see that the top of his coat was open, and the priestly collar peeped out at me, reminding me that he was a citadel of Christ, and that I should respect that.

'I'm sorry, Fr Seán,' I sobbed, 'but it has been so long.'

'I'm still Seán by the way,' he said.

He sat down beside us, and he shook hands with Tom and Joe.

'Where's Packy?' he asked.

'He's not here, out of choice. He cannot face the past, and all that has happened,' I said. 'And your phone call didn't help either.'

'I told you that everything was alright.'

'Is it Seán?' said Tom. 'After all that has happened, how else could we be?'

'We shouldn't be talking openly here,' he said. 'Let's go somewhere we can talk in comfort, and without interruption. There's a meeting room at the back of the church, we can go there and talk at ease.'

We followed him to the back of the altar, through the door to the vestry, where Tom and Joe had served mass for Fr Doyle. But it was a changed place. The whole back of the building was a series of meeting rooms, and an office, as well as the vestry. Times had changed in the church, and it seemed that Fr O'Reilly had a very vibrant and active parish. We went to a private meeting room, which had only a few tables and some chairs. We sat facing each other, and Seán went away for a few minutes, to attend to some matter. But I didn't realise that he had organised some tea and sandwiches with some members of the parish council, and in a few minutes, people were milling around us with cups of tea and sandwiches as well as other confectionaries. It reminded me of the parish dances, when we were young, and the tea and sandwiches, sitting with Pat, as he counted his ticket money collected for the raffle.

There was so much rushing through my head now. Pat was in the county home for many years, and now he was dying. I was convinced he had died years ago. He had Seán on the alert for many years to check for Dad's death in the paper. He kept on constant vigil for that day. Now he wanted to see me, and whatever he told Seán in the confessional frightened me. Seán knew everything. That alone terrified me. Was there any chance he told anyone else?

'Why does he want to see me?' I asked again, when the tea and sandwiches were cleared away, and the room was left private to the four of us. It seemed like an age before he answered, and the same thoughts ran through my head again.

'You will not marry me, Pat Reardon,' I used to say to him.

'I will never marry you Sarah, but I will protect you forever.'

That's why I was never afraid of him. Pat Reardon was a kind soul, and I knew he deserved better. He was a mature man, when I knew him, as he ambled slowly, and lumbered through the village, mimicked and laughed at by those who knew no better. Their taunts and jeering didn't faze him one bit, as he was able to rise above this, and considered himself better than they were. He moved through life quietly, and with a pride and nobility way above his station.

Pat Reardon was still alive. But I wondered what he knew, and what he would say. Tomorrow would reveal all.

'As I said to you already, Sarah, I cannot say anything till you see him yourself,' said Seán.

'Come on, out with it Seán,' said Joe angrily. 'What the hell are you playing at? We are mature adults, and we deserve to know what this is all about.'

'Let me put it to you this way again,' said Seán. 'I know what happened. He told me everything in minute detail, all the events that happened during that winter, what happened to your mother, what you did with the body. He told me about Eileen, and what happened to her. He told me how Meg faked being your mother…'

'Stop! Stop! Stop!' roared Tom, banging his fist down on the table. 'That's enough. I thought we were finished with all this. Whatever happened died all those years ago, when we left here forever. I don't want to hear tell of it again. Is that clear?'

'Take it easy, Tom,' I said softly. 'We are not making things any easier for anyone, by blowing your top. You are not making it easier for Seán either.'

'Father Seán,' answered Tom, 'he is a priest, or have you forgotten? He's not that long-lost boyfriend, you were infatuated about when you were a little girl. He's a priest and give him that respect.'

'I'm still Seán, whether you like it or not,' he said. 'You are here to bury your father. It's a difficult time for you all. Let's put Pat aside until after the funeral. You are right to be angry, Tom. It's natural for you to grieve.'

'I'm sorry about that, Seán,' he said still breathing heavily. 'It's just I thought this was all done and dusted. Packy was right to stay away. He always seemed to be ahead of the posse. He could see trouble before it met him.'

'Just like the day the body was found, and he had the measles,' said Joe.

'Don't say anymore,' said Seán. 'As I have said already, let's bury your father with the dignity he deserves, and we'll tackle the next problem after that.'

'Mam didn't have much dignity when we hid her body,' I said. There was a shimmer in my voice as I spoke, and the boys knew it was time for us to retire for the night.

'Say no more,' said Seán. 'Get a good night's sleep, it's a long day tomorrow.'

Chapter 54

The Funeral

There were very few at the funeral, and I was glad of that, but those who did venture, remembered John Cregan and his family. There was no more sympathising with us, as it had been done the night before. A soft mist formed above the tree line and began gently dampening the earth around the village. The bearers lifted the coffin into the hearse, and the few wreaths that came, the evening before, were once more placed each side of the coffin.

I sat beside John our driver, who followed behind the hearse. Tom and Joe sat quietly behind, taking in the landscape of their childhood. It was a place of few people, and quiet fields. Our present environment was of streets, traffic, people, and shopping malls, which was part and parcel of our everyday lives, for more than forty years.

I said very little, as we made our way. Then we passed the old derelict schoolhouse.

'Our last days there were happy ones. Donal Ryan was a great teacher,' said Tom.

'I wonder if he is still alive,' asked Joe.

'I know he married that nurse who took care of you in the hospital,' I said. 'He's probably retired from teaching by now, he must be in his early seventies.'

'Only for him, things might not have turned out the way they did,' said Joe.

'I know,' I answered, 'but enough said for the moment.'

The funeral cortège reached the gates of the new cemetery. I stepped out of the car. More memories came flooding back from all those years ago. Joe and Tom stood by my side, holding back the tears.

I spoke softly, 'It's still there!' I was pointing at the old abandoned cemetery gate across the road. It was through the back we entered on that awful night. It was closed now, and completely overgrown, left to nature to embrace the remains of all the souls who had been laid to rest there, for hundreds of years. A circular stone wall protected it from invasion from the cattle in the surrounding fields, and yew trees reached like spires into the sky, creating dark shadows in the evening, as the sun set in the west, reaching across the road to the new cemetery.

'I wonder if the spindle tree still growing in there?' I asked.

'Please don't say that,' said Tom.

'I just wondered,' I answered.

'Let's not talk about it,' said Joe. 'We promised Seán to leave it until later.'

'We'll talk later,' I said. 'The priest is approaching us.'

Fr O'Reilly took my hand and said, 'We'll proceed now, Sarah, if that's alright with you?'

'We'll go ahead so, Father. Better not keep people waiting.'

We were just going to follow the procession to the graveside, when someone came running into the cemetery. He jumped out of a car and ran to join us. My heart skipped a beat when I saw who it was. It was Packy. He was out of breath, when he got to us, and he was wearing a black suit. I don't ever remember seeing him wear a suit before. He looked quite different, dressed up, with his hair combed back and gelled. I embraced him and cried on his shoulder.

'I'm so glad you came,' I said.

'Well, I had second thoughts when you were heading off.'

'Well you are here, and that's all that matters,' said Tom.

'You must have caught an early plane,' said Joe.

'I did. I got into Dublin at nine o'clock.'

'Why the change of heart?' I asked.

'I thought back to those days when we were young, and we pledged to stay together, and to stand up for each other. It wasn't fair of me to run away from it all, like that. Whatever happens, we are the Cregan's and we stick together.'

'We have a lot of talking to do later,' said Joe. 'It's time now to lay our father to rest.'

Dad's coffin was carried shoulder high again, to the grave, at the far end of the cemetery. There were many styles of headstone, from marble, to Celtic crosses, to simple white metal ones. I knew that the simple white metal crosses, painted white belonged to those who died at the psychiatric hospital, or at the county home, people who had no one to care for them, and their final resting place was just marked by this simple cross. Was this how Pat was to be remembered? It didn't seem fair. I couldn't stop thinking about him, last night. My thoughts should have focused on Dad, but I knew in my heart and soul, that he was at peace. He had a good life, despite all the hardship of the earlier years. He mellowed into quiet old age, and spent those days focusing on his grandchildren, and spoiling them in the process.

The prayers over the grave were said quietly, and Fr O'Reilly blessed the coffin with holy water. A little trowel of clay was blessed as well and thrown in on the coffin. After a decade of the rosary, some local men, who had charge of the grave digging, placed a green mock grass canopy over the open grave.

I breathed a sigh of relief to have seen this. Maybe Mam might be at peace now. But then she wasn't here. I wanted to go to the old cemetery to hug that old mausoleum and pass a prayer to her quiet remains.

When I turned around to shake the hands of some of the people who had followed the funeral, I saw Seán at the back of the crowd still wearing his priestly robes, having followed the funeral from the church. He was on his mobile phone. I felt a little uncomfortable, and strange thoughts went through my head again, just like the day Eileen's body was found. Was I going to crack up again? He stopped talking on his phone, and he approached me.

I pretended not to see him but shook hands with some people who followed the funeral. He stood nearby and waited. As the people moved away from the grave, the gravediggers began to fill it in. I blessed myself, and said a quiet and tearful prayer for Dad, and a very special one for Mam. Dad was the last link I had to this place, and a childhood I had to run away from.

Seán took my hand. It was warm and comforting.

'You probably don't want to see me again, but I had to come for Pat's sake. He sent me on a mission.'

'Why were you on the phone, Seán?' I asked. Then I regretted saying this, as it was probably private. 'I'm sorry I shouldn't have asked that question.'

'That's alright. I was ringing the county home. Pat wanted me to let him know when John Cregan was laid to rest, but not alone that, he wanted to know when the grave would be closed in.'

'Seán, this is getting stranger by the moment. I just wish you'd just come out with it.'

'So this is Seán Walsh,' said Packy.

'And you are?'

'I'm Packy, remember?'

Seán went to shake his hand. Packy hesitated for a moment, and then slowly held his hand out to shake Seán's.

'I'm glad you came,' said Seán.

'Well, Father Seán, I wouldn't know you if I met you on the street.'

'It's been a long time,' said Seán.

'It's a pity we didn't meet again, under happier circumstances,' said Packy.

'We still have a job to do, and there's someone patiently waiting to see you all.'

'What is going on?' said Packy, 'All this secrecy is freaking me out, and I'd have run away from it all, only for these three. We are sticking together, come hell or high water.'

'You will understand when you hear Pat's story,' said Seán.

'It's like something out of an Agatha Christie Novel,' joked Tom.

'I'm no Hercule Poirot,' said Seán.

'When can we talk to him?' I asked.

'Can I contact you this evening?'

'Will you not join us at the pub in the village for refreshments? We can talk there. That's where we are all going now.'

'Thank you very much, maybe I will.'

A warm turf fire glowed in the lounge of Cassidy's Pub and I pulled a stool up close to it, to warm myself after the cold east wind of the graveyard. The Cassidy family danced attendance on us, bringing tea and sandwiches and making sure we were ok.

Packy started again, probing Seán to find out what all the mystery was about.

'Seán, I think you will just have to tell us, for once and for all, what this is all about. I know all those things happened so long ago, and we have a right to know.'

'And I'm not going to tell you. As I have said already, I'm not going to say anything yet. Number one, I'm not going to break the vow of the confessional and number two, Pat wants to tell you everything himself.'

'It's alright, Packy,' I said. 'We all had this conversation with Seán last night, and we will just have to wait till tomorrow as planned.'

'If you like, I can let you see him this evening. I told him you might come today. He's very frail, and he has been waiting for so long, it's not fair to leave him waiting too much longer.'

'Are you all up for it?' asked Joe.

'Will it be too much if we all go?' I asked.

'He can't wait to see you. It's been so long.'

When he had finished speaking to us, I walked with him to the car park, and gave him my mobile telephone number to arrange to meet.

'I will ring you in about an hour,' he said, 'and I will let you know what is happening. Don't be alarmed by all this. I need to get a clearer picture as to what happened all those years ago. I need to do it for Pat's sake. I feel we owe it to him. Things will be clearer when you hear what he has to say. You see I know why he wouldn't say anything, until he heard that the grave was closed.

You see Sarah, he's a very troubled man, and as I have told you already, he wants forgiveness from you.'

A shiver ran down my spine, when he said this, and I knew that there was no way out, but to meet him and talk to him.

When I returned to the lounge I could see Packy was nervous again, and I could see the little boy I cradled then, once again. He was shaking and didn't know what to say.

Talking quietly among ourselves Joe said, 'If we go Sarah, heaven knows what might happen. Maybe we should leave it.'

'What does he know anyway? He is an old man now, and probably doting in his old age? Who'd believe him anyway, if he mentioned things that happened back then?' said Tom.

'It's what he knows about those days that worry me. Remember he was always sneaking around, watching from behind corners. He probably knows everything and said nothing. What has he said already?' said Joe.

'We'll be arrested,' said Tom, 'I know we will.'

I was in tears again at these outbursts, and Packy came to me. With his arm around my shoulder, he told them to stop at once.

'We'll do this together,' he said quietly.

Seán rang an hour later and told me he had arranged to meet with Pat at four o'clock in the retirement home. We all joined hands together, and our silence said, that we were ready to meet whatever troubles were coming our way once again.

Chapter 55

Pat's Story

The old home was a gaunt old Victorian building, built originally as the poorhouse, but at one stage, was used as the hospital, until a new building replaced it in the 1930's. Since then it had been used as a retirement home, for people who were unable to look after themselves, providing twenty-four-hour care, and the comforts of home for those at the end of their days. Even though it looked cold and unwelcoming on the outside, inside it was warm and pleasing. There was a happy and cheerful atmosphere, peaceful, calm and easy-going. Those who cared for its residents, were smiling and ready to provide any needs for the visit Pat was long waiting for. A nurse greeted us and directed us towards a private room away from the wards. Seán was waiting at the door.

'Your visitors are here, Father,' she said.

'Thank you, Bernie,' said Seán. 'I'll take over from here.'

'If you need anything just press the button beside Pat's bed,' she said.

She scurried away to carry on with other duties for needful residents, and the four of us waited at the door for Seán to take us in.

'Are you all ok?' he asked.

'Let's do it,' said Packy.

With that, Seán opened the door quietly. The light in the little room was dim, and the curtains were closed. It was sparsely furnished with just a bed, a locker, a wardrobe and a few chairs. It looked as if Pat had been moved from the ward to this room for privacy, as his health was failing him.

He was in the bed, and he was sleeping. His thin, old wizened hands were out over the clothes, and resting on his chest. His head was smaller, from the man I remembered. His thinning hair was snow white, but his skin was pale and clear. He seemed to have a young face, all the weathered features from a long outdoor life were gone, now replaced with a change in complexion, from a life indoors for the past twenty years or more. He was breathing quietly, and we stayed very still, not to alarm him.

I sat close to him near his head, while my brothers arranged themselves on chairs around the bed. Seán sat the other side opposite me, so that he wouldn't be frightened when he woke up. Seán would probably be the only face he'd recognise. He beckoned me to reach over and touch his hand.

I pressed my hand gently down on his. He woke up quietly and looked towards me. He smiled instantly, and I could see a tear at the corner of his eye.

'My little girl!' he said softly. His voice hadn't changed, but it was softer and weaker.

'Hi Pat,' I answered. I reached over and kissed him gently on the forehead.

'I have been waiting a long time to see you.'

'It's been too long,' I answered. 'I'm so sorry. I should have come back to see you many times. You know I was afraid.'

'I know that, my darling little girl.'

'I'm not a little girl anymore, Pat.'

'You will always be my little girl.'

He looked around at the rest of the party. Then he looked at Seán.

'Tell me who these are, Father Seán. I know who they are, but they are such fine men now.'

'Beside me is Packy, then Tom, and Joe is sitting beside Sarah.'

They all greeted him in unison. I could see Packy's eyes welling up with tears, but he composed himself. He too stood up and kissed him gently on the forehead. Joe and Tom followed. They sat down again facing him, not knowing what to say.

'This is the happiest day of my life,' he said, and then corrected himself by saying, 'In one sense it is, but I lost a great and loyal friend John Cregan. You were all so good to him, and you sacrificed so much for him, especially you Sarah.'

'Do you notice anything different about Pat?' asked Seán.

'I do,' said Tom, 'you are not stammering anymore Pat.'

'I'm not afraid anymore. I was always afraid, peeping round corners and all that. You can all remember it, can't you.'

'We remember you as a great friend, Pat,' said Joe. 'We didn't notice anything unusual about you at all.'

'You are just being kind now, Joe, don't joke with me,' he chuckled.

'You wanted to see us urgently,' I said.

'I have a lot to tell you all. But I won't die in peace, unless you forgive me for the things I did.'

'What have we to forgive you for?' asked Packy, 'Of all people, we should be asking you to forgive us for staying away and leaving you on your own.'

'You did the right thing. John Cregan wanted to keep you all together. He had lost so much when dear Mary died.'

'He did that indeed,' I said, 'and we had him for so long as well.'

'I want to tell you all some things you knew nothing about. I need to sit up in the bed more.'

Seán and I helped him sit forward, by propping his back with more pillows, until he was comfortable. Then he turned to Seán.

'Will you get the box, Father?' he said.

Seán went to the wardrobe, and opening the door, he reached down and took out a large tin box. When I saw it, I recognised it straight away. It was the box Pat kept on the mantelpiece in the kitchen in his little cottage in the village. Seán placed it on the bed in front of him. Slowly, he lifted the lid with his tired, gnarled old hands and reached inside. He lifted out a little paper bag, crumpled with age, and creased from being open quite often. He handed it to me.

'Open it!' he said.

I unravelled the rolled-up bag and reached inside. I drew out three items I hadn't seen for a very long time. It was the brush, comb and mirror, Dad brought me from England in the summer of 1962. I thought I had lost them. I could never find them when I moved to Glasgow. I presumed they were thrown out with the rubbish when we were preparing to leave.

'I have a confession to make,' he said. 'I took them from your room when I was helping you all to pack. I wanted to have something to remember you by, when you were gone.'

He reached into the tin again and took out a sheet of paper wrapped in clear plastic. He handed it to me also. When I looked at it, I nearly screamed in shock.

'Oh, my God!' I exclaimed. I handed it to Packy. It was the charcoal drawing Packy did of me. He wanted to throw it away, if I could remember right. But I wouldn't let him, and I left it in the shed. When I went sometime later to get it, it was gone. Now I know what happened. Pat had taken it.

'Is this what you want us to forgive you for?' asked Tom, 'For stealing these meagre items from our home.'

'No, not at all. I want to show you something else. He reached into the box again, and took out something heavy and large, wrapped in a piece of grubby linen cloth. He handed it to Joe. Taking it, Joe opened the cloth. It was the big metal key, belonging to the door of the mausoleum. I remember Joe turning the key to unlock it and lift the large latch upwards to open that door.

'You said you threw it away,' said Tom. 'What's going on, Pat? Why did you lie to us?'

'Take it easy, Tom,' said Seán. 'It will all come to light soon. Just let Pat speak. He has been wanting to do this for a very long time.'

Pat pointed his long bony finger at Tom and said, 'You see, I wanted to put you all off the scent. It was a distraction.'

He turned to me and said, 'Remember when I accused you of stealing money from me?'

'I do, Pat. I remember it well. I didn't steal any money though.'

'I know that, girl. I always knew it, but again you will understand what I was doing when I tell you all that happened.'

'Are you alright now, Pat?' asked Seán. 'If you want to leave it all, for another time? Tomorrow maybe?'

'No, I won't, Father. I have waited so long for this moment, it's not going to wait any longer.' He seemed to have gained a renewed energy, as if he was recovering some of his lost youth. He was on a roll, and nothing was going to stop him. Seán told us not to interrupt him anymore, but just to let him speak, and to explain everything in his own words. It was what he needed to do. So, Pat began to tell his story…

When I told you, Sarah, all those years ago, that I was going to protect you for the rest of my life, I meant every word I said. Your family were, and still are my family. I had no one in the world to care for me, but your parents welcomed me into their home. Your father, John Cregan, was always my best friend, and he fought battles for me. I used to run away and hide in that old mausoleum. Then he would come and get me and bring me back.

My father didn't care much for me, as he was working all the time. When I was ten years old, my mother died, and they put me away in an orphanage. I had a terrible time there, and I was always scared. It was there I lost confidence in myself. I was afraid to speak. I had a stammer, which happened to me when I was fearful or afraid of something that was happening, or about to happen.

When I was fifteen, I came home again. I looked after my father until he died. He drank himself to death, and he left me with nothing only the cottage and the clothes on my back. I worked for local farmers, and I wasn't treated very well. They laughed at my stammer, and they copied me every time I tried to speak. My only safe refuge was Cregan's house, and Walsh's. I was never afraid when I was with you all.

Mr Walsh gave me plenty of part-time work, and John Cregan always called on me when he needed me, especially, when he had to go away to work. I was so fearful of people, I peeped round corners to see if the coast was clear. I looked in windows to see if it was alright to come into the house. I used to hide, if I didn't want someone to see me. They called me all sorts of names like Peepy Hole or Peeping Pat. I felt hurt by it all. I was not able to fight my battles. I used to get angry, and when that happened, I started to shake, and I was not able to defend myself. Then one day something happened.

A little girl I knew, challenged two grown men, both ignorant louts, who were teasing and taunting me. Yes, Sarah, that was you. You took them on, and you were not afraid. I knew you were special. Fr Doyle sent those boys off with their tails between their legs. I went home that night, and when I was praying to the Sacred Heart in the kitchen, I vowed that if anything ever happened to you, I would do my best, to protect you for the rest of my life. And something did happen. You thought I didn't know about it. But I did. I knew your mother was dying. She called me aside one day, and asked me if anything ever happened to her, would I help John take care of you all. She was thinking about the Larkin children, and how they were taken away, and separated from each other. It was something that haunted poor Sergeant Greene for years.

I used to go up to your house every morning, to watch and wait. When I saw you seeing the boys off to school, I knew everything was alright. I called each night and listened at the window as well. Old Sputnik was so used to me, he didn't bark. When I heard you ordering the boys off to bed, and checking on your mother, I went home through the fields. Then I saw that the key was missing from the box. The only people ever to come into my house was you three. I was wondering what was happening.

But that night something was wrong. I saw the donkey and cart yoked at the gate. I saw you carry something heavy, wrapped in a blanket, out into the yard, and deposit it on the cart. You went down the back, and into the field. It was then I knew what you were doing. I got on my bike and headed by road, round to the cemetery. I entered by the main gate opposite the new cemetery, and hiding my bike, walked to the old cemetery. Crossing the wall, I went to the back gate near the hill road and waited. After half an hour, you all arrived. I saw Darcy getting out of the car, drunk as auld boots, and pissing against the gate into the field. I heard how you disguised your presence by pretending there was a cat. Darcy went away in the car, and I cowered behind some of the old headstones, and waited. I couldn't see very much, due to the moonlight, but I could hear everything you said. I knew how sad you were, and you wondered how you were going to try and get away with it.

I heard the door of the mausoleum creak and open. By then I had moved around closer to you. I was protected by the large clump of spindle tree, close to the mausoleum. It had still a lot of leaves on it, and together with the very dim moonlight, I was hidden from view. I waited till you were all finished and gone, before I set out for home. I went over to your place the next morning, and you were all asleep. I knew that the key would have to be left back, so I waited at home until that happened. When you came, I told you that you needed a great cup of cocoa, and I went to the shop to buy some. This would give you time to put the key back in the tin box. When you left later, after having your cocoa, I checked the box, and the key was back where it was.

The bottom line was, I knew everything that happened. I pretended that Meg was still your mother. She didn't know I knew. But I played along. I was in this as deep as you all were. I knew I had to do something, but I didn't know what to do. I came to the house regularly and helped. I knew Sarah you were trying to contact your father, without letting the guards know. You too were afraid that the boys would be taken away.

Christmas came and went, and this is where things happened quickly. I decided to come visit you in the frost shortly after Christmas. I brought my bike with me, but it was difficult to ride due to the icy roads. I was walking up the hill to your place when I heard a car. I quickly slipped into a gap, hiding my bike in the ditch. It was Darcy in the car. His driving was not great, and I knew he was drunk. He drove quite fast and went over the hill. I knew he was going to your place. When I got to the top of the hill, I could hear laughing and cheering, and I knew that some of you were playing on the winter pond down the field. The car was abandoned, and as I approached your place I could hear you scream. I ran down the hill, and peeping across the hedge, I could see Eileen in the kitchen shouting, and pulling at Darcy. He was shouting back at her.

Then there was a crash, and I could hear you scream again. I heard Darcy swear and panic and wanted help to move her. I saw him drag her to the car. You were too frightened, but I knew what was after happening. I knew what he was going to do to you. This horrible ignorant man was going to hurt you, the most precious thing that ever happened to me. I got so angry, I was going to cross the gate, and beat the living daylights out of him. But then I decided not to. He would pay for this if I was going to die in the process. I ran. Up the hill I went, stumbling on the ice. I fell twice, but I found a better footing in the grass verge. Then I hatched a plan. I would get him. He would never ever hurt you or anyone again...

Pat stopped speaking. He was breathing heavily. He lay back on the pillow with the tears streaming down his face. I held his hand and told him to rest and take it easy.

442

'We'll come back tomorrow, Pat,' I said.

'No! No! Please! I must tell you everything now.'

'Would you like a drink, Pat?' asked Seán.

'Yes, please,' he answered. Seán got him a drink from a jug of water on the locker, and holding the glass to his lips, Pat took a few sips.

I was shocked at what I had heard. I realised that we should have told Pat as well, all those years ago. But maybe Pat didn't want us to know that he knew everything. I was worried about him. He was drawing a lot of energy out of himself to tell us his story. His mind was still as clear as the days forty years ago when all of this took place. What was coming next, I didn't know, and when he was ready, Pat continued his story once again…

I could hear the car turning in haste and the gears creaking, as he tried to manoeuvre it. I knew he was trying to get rid of the body. I saw him dragging it to the car. I kept running till I got to the end of the road. Then I stood in the middle of the road, faced back towards your place. I was going to stop that car. I watched as he slowly changed into second gear and came across the brow of the hill. He began to slow down, as he saw me standing there.

He drew to a halt, and the brakes squeaked as he did so. The wheels skidded on the ice. I didn't know whether the car would stop or not, but it did, about a yard or so from me. I was scared as hell. He got out of the car and shouted at me.

'Get out of the way, fool.'

'No!' I answered as sternly as I could.

'Get out of the way or I'll run you down.'

'I can help you!' I answered quietly.

'Help me! How?'

'I saw it all happen. She fell, it was an accident.'

'Don't waste my time, now get out of the way or else!'

'Or else what?' I asked. I kept my eyes fixed on him. I knew he was in a panic and he was afraid.

'I don't know what else! Just get out of the way.'

'No!' I shouted back at him.

'If you don't get out of the way, I'll run you down.'

'And have another death on your hands. I don't think so.'

'What do you want then?' he asked again. He knew I had him in a corner, and there was nothing he could do.

'I said I could help you.'

'How could you help me?' he said with scorn.

'I could you know!' I spoke as calmly as possible and I discovered I wasn't stammering. I wasn't afraid. I really wasn't. I was angry as hell. I knew what he tried to do to you, and I wasn't going to let him get away with it.

I hadn't known what I wanted to do, then it suddenly came to me. He could hide the body in the mausoleum. I knew there was no way he could see your mother's remains, as you placed her in a coffin along with some of the other Wilsons, who were laid to rest there. It would give him time to think of what he was going to do.

'Go on then,' he said, 'what's this brave plan of yours?'

'There's an old mausoleum in the old graveyard. It is closed now, but I have a key. No one ever goes there. We can put her there till you are ready to bury her.'

'How can I trust you?' he asked.

'You can't, just the way I don't trust you.'

'Well Ha! Ha! Ha!' he said sarcastically, 'Pat the…' He stopped in his tracks again, but I finished his sentence for him.

'Idiot! Isn't that what you want to say? Well, this idiot could get up on his bike now, and go for the guards.'

He began to fold into himself now. He knew he had no choice. But I didn't trust him. I watched his every move. I had seen him on the stage in the village each year. I saw him leering at other young women, and I knew that there was nothing good on his mind ever, the way he treated young women. I could not understand how that lovely woman put up with him for so long…

Pat began to cough, and he sat up straight in the bed. Seán held his back as he breathed in and out. He calmed down after a few minutes, and he sat silently staring ahead.

'Will we leave it till tomorrow, Pat?' Joe asked.

Pat turned in an agitated state and said, as loud as he could, 'Certainly not! I will do this tonight. You don't know how much this means to me. I have waited years for this moment, and I'm not stopping now.'

Seán offered him a drink again, and he accepted. He took a few more sips from the glass and lay back once again on his nest of pillows. He turned and smiled at me.

'I'm sorry to be taking so long,' he said, 'but I'm not as fast as I used to be.'

'Shush! That's alright!' I answered. 'Take all the time in the world.'

'I wish I had more time,' he said. 'It's something I don't have anymore.'

'However long it takes, Pat. We will wait till you are ready.' I placed both my hands in his, and he waited a minute or two before he continued with his story.

Then Darcy asked me to take him to the mausoleum.

'I have to go home first to get the key. It's at my house.'

'Get into the car!' he said. I hesitated as I opened the passenger door. The back seat was down and I could see Eileen's body covered in a blanket or something, her hand hung out from underneath.

'She's dead!' he said rather callously, 'She can't harm you.'

'I'm not afraid of the dead,' I answered just as quickly, 'I'm more afraid of the living. Are you not sad that she has died?'

He started the car, and the gears rasped again, as he moved slowly along the icy road.

'I gave up being sad a long time ago. She was always a burden. Now she's gone. How can I be sad?'

I didn't reply to that, but my heart went out to that lovely lady who was acting as your mother. He probably treated her in a similar manner. He drove towards the village. There was no one around. Being the Christmas season, everyone was indoors. The frost was so cold and heavy, you could see the smoke coming out of all the chimneys, as everyone was huddled up to their fires. At that stage, I wished I was there also. But now I was caught up in all this, and I didn't know where it was going from here.

We stopped on the main street, and I went around the corner to my place. I opened the door and grabbed the key from the box. When I was outside again, he had turned the car, and the engine was running. I got in the passenger side, and slowly we left the village, heading out into the country. I told him to go on to the hill road, and use that entrance, as no one would see us there.

Before long, we reached the gate. I opened it, and he drove on ahead up the lane to the cemetery gate. I closed the road gate and followed him on foot. He had opened the cemetery gate and was ready to move the body. When I got there, I helped him carry Eileen into the cemetery. Darkness was falling, and we would have to act fast. We left deep footprints in the frosty long dead grass, and when we reached the mausoleum, we left the body down so that I could open the door. He ran back to the car again, and I thought I was being left alone with the body, but he returned quickly again with a torch, so we could have a light inside the mausoleum.

We carried her body inside the door, and left it on a stone slab, where coffins were laid before they were stacked in their little alcoves. There was a disturbance on the earthen floor. There were footprints, and signs of activity in recent times. I knew it was from the night you brought your mother there. I didn't tell him but he remarked, 'You haven't been hiding any more bodies here now, Pat, have you?'

He was getting back to his arrogant selfish self again.

'Mind your own business!' I answered.

'I forgot! Sure, isn't this your little hidey hole? You come here to get away from people.' He had been listening to some of the others in the pub when he was in town. He had heard all their tales, as to the things they said and did to me to annoy and tease me.

Something happened there and then, and again it happened so quickly. I thought of you, and I could hear you screaming. Any man who would take a young child's innocence away, was not a man. He was an animal. In fact, animals had more respect for their own kind. He was a monster. I began to breathe heavily, and I let a roar out of me. I lunged out at him. In an instant, I charged at him and punched him in the stomach. He fell on his knees, clutching his stomach. I had winded him. I had had enough of this man. There was an anger inside of me in that moment I couldn't stop. This time I reached down and found a stone about the size of a turnip. It had come away from the walls at some stage and was lying beside the stone slab where Eileen's body rested. I grabbed it and came at him again. I brought it down heavily on his head. He slumped forward on his face.

'You will never ever hurt that little girl or any other girl!' I screamed. As I was roaring these words one by one, I kept bringing the stone down on his skull and I could hear it crack as I did so. It was then I realised what I had done. I had killed a man. I was a murderer. I deserved to go to jail for the rest of my life...

At this stage, we were all in tears. I could see shock written all over my brother's faces. Seán was sitting with his arms around his shoulders, as tears streamed down the old man's face. It was then that it became all clear to me. He had said he wanted forgiveness. He waited all these years to tell Seán his sins, and to be prepared to meet his maker. He wasn't a murderer. That was something I was certain of. He was a man driven to distraction by uncaring people, and he met his match in Darcy, who was a cold selfish human being. Darcy brought the anger out in him. He had done it with such force, Pat became a different person in those few split seconds. He was not prepared to let this man away with his crime as well. He drifted off into a sleep, and Seán called the nurse. He asked if we could be taken somewhere for a cup of tea. We still had unfinished business that night, and it was better to let Pat rest for a little while. Seán came with us to the refectory, and there was tea and some confectionaries left waiting for us. He had instructed the nurse to call us when Pat had woken up again.

'Now I know why he wanted forgiveness,' I said.

'You know then, why I couldn't tell you that. He told it to me in confession.'

'The poor fella,' said Packy, 'how must he have felt all down the years? I mean he had to live with it day and night.'

'We should empathise with him there, hadn't we some terrible memories to put up with and live with too?' said Joe.

'Yeah, but we got away and left it behind,' said Tom.

'The bottom line is, we didn't kill anyone,' I said. 'We were on a survival mission.'

'And you did survive,' said Seán.

'What happens now?' asked Packy.

'It's not over yet,' said Seán, 'he told me a lot more, which you need to hear. We will have to be patient with him. You might be in for a long night.'

I was still shaking from what I heard. Meg never found Darcy. He was dead. Pat killed him. She was searching all her life for him. I knew that when Pat called her to come see him, he must have told her what he had done. He wanted her to forgive him also. Knowing Meg, she would do that. That is why her letters stopped. She was afraid she might end up telling me all this, and she was afraid of the consequences. She knew that I had nearly cracked up a few times, if it weren't for Packy's intervention. My thoughts went to her, as I sipped a cup of tea, and I wondered if she was still alive. I would probably never know, but she was one great lady.

We sat there in the refectory for another two hours. It was nearly ten o'clock when the nurse returned. Pat had wakened up, and he wondered had we left.

He wanted to see us again. He wasn't happy about us leaving. She told him we were having a cup of tea, and he calmed down. When we returned to his room, he was sitting up in bed waiting. He was keeping vigil for this day, and he still had a job to do.

We sat in our original places, and I held his hand, as he surveyed us all again.

'I still can't believe you are all here,' he said.

'We are indeed, in the flesh,' said Packy. 'We are so glad to be with you.'

'You see why I needed forgiveness,' he said, looking me straight in the face. 'I will need your forgiveness too.'

'You don't need forgiveness, now shush!' I said. I kissed his old wizened hand, and he rubbed his other hand gently down my face.

'Oh, but I do!' he said. 'I'm not finished yet. I have asked God for forgiveness. I'm ready to meet him. But you need to know a lot more. I haven't much time left. I know it.'

'Well if you are ready, Pat, we'll let you get on with your story,' said Tom.

He sat forward on the bed again, and his tale continued.

I killed a man. It has haunted me all my life, but I must tell you also what happened after that. I left the mausoleum that night, locked it, and drove the car home. I parked it at the back of the house, and I boiled some water. I washed the inside of the car with soap and water and made sure there were no bloodstains anywhere. I went inside and lit a fire. It was so cold, I thought I'd get my death that night. I boiled a large pot of water on the range, and I washed in the tin bath at the fire. I wanted to get the smell of death off me. There was also a smell of whiskey from him. He was drunk, and I knew it. I changed into some old clothes a man from the St Vincent De Paul gave me, and I burned the ones I was wearing. I sat at the range all night with its front door open, the light off, and stared into the flames. I took Eileen's suitcase and walking stick and burned everything in the fire. It lasted all night. At around six o'clock in the morning, I decided to get rid of the car. I didn't know what to do with it. I couldn't go back to your place. So, I left it at the station. People would think that Darcy had abandoned it and left by train.

I walked back home through boreens and fields in case anyone saw me. Dawn was approaching, and I wanted to hide as best I could. I went to bed. I slept all day. I had nightmares about what had happened, and when I woke up I began to hatch some plan. All sorts of things went through my head. I'd have to get rid of both bodies. What would happen if those little meddling Cregan's stole my key again, and decided to go to the mausoleum to visit their mother? Certainly, I'd have to get rid of the two bodies lying inside the door. I decided to do something the next day, but my plans changed. Word got out that your Mam ran away. Then the snow came and it was impossible to go anywhere.

When eventually I got to your place, I was on a mission to find my bike, which lay hidden in the snow. I did find it but in the process I fell and had to leave it in the ditch. When I got to your place, Meg opened that great big carpet bag of hers and bandaged my head for me. Things had changed. Meg was no longer your mother. Soon, the whole village was looking for her. All our tracks made on that fateful day were covered up in the snow. The old cemetery was searched several times, and no one thought of looking in the mausoleum. But then why should they, it had been closed for years. I helped in the search also. When they finished combing the countryside, they decided to wait until the snow had gone, and a renewed search might yield something. But it didn't.

In the meantime, I prepared to get your mother's body back to her family. On one of my visits back to the mausoleum, I discovered that Eileen had been wearing your mother's dress. A thought struck me. If I took down your mother's body from the coffin where you had left it, I could change their clothes. I decided to give it a try. On another cold frosty night, I went there with a torch to act upon what I was thinking about. It was a difficult task, as both bodies were stiff from rigor mortis. Things had happened to your mother's body even in the cold winter, and I won't go into it.

After a struggle, I got the dress off Eileen's body, and dressed her in your mother's black coat. I put the dress on your mother's body. She was still wearing her wedding ring. I took it off and put it in my pocket. That night I went home and had another hot bath to get rid of the smell. It was coming towards the middle of January, and I went back through the fields one night with a wheelbarrow and brought your mother's body across the fields to the lake. I knew that spot in the reeds where no one would find it.

The ice was thick, and with a covering of deep snow, it was difficult to walk out across it. It was at this point I knew, that if she were found, however long it took, there was nothing to prove it was not your mother. You knew it had to be Eileen. You did not know what had taken place. In my heart and soul, your father, if he was able, would identify your mother. All of you could not say anything, or you would be found out. To make matters worse, and to convince you all that it was Eileen's body, I did something terrible, something that has haunted me for so long.

He began to cry, and I stood up and held him close to me. He was inconsolable. I wanted him to take another break, but he insisted he had to tell us something. What could have been so terrible at this stage? My mind was in a whirl, the whole thing was like something out of a detective novel. He was such a clever and crafty man. He covered his tracks everywhere he went, and the whole world thought differently. We were so focused as children in maintaining our story, and making it as credible as possible, who'd have thought otherwise? Dad did identify the right body. But again, I wondered why he wanted forgiveness?

'What did you do that was so terrible, Pat?'

'Eileen fell and hit her head in your kitchen. There was a gash on the back of her head.' He stopped speaking and looked up at me before he continued. 'If I had left your mother as she was. If she was found with no wound to her head, you'd put two and two together, and realise that the body was not that of Eileen…' He stopped again and began to shake. It was as if his old self was coming back, the nervous Pat who could not speak. He kept looking at me straight in the face.

'I am so sorry, Sarah.'

'Go on, Pat. Tell me what happened.'

'I reached down on the ground before I took your mother's body onto the ice. I rummaged through the snow till I found a large stone. It was stuck to the ground, but after a few kicks, it came loose. I turned your mother's body over and gave a good strong blow to the back of her head. I wanted to make it look as if she had fallen on the ice and hit her head. That's what I did. I had to do that to that wonderful kind lady, my best friend's wife, the mother of the nicest children I have ever known. I had to do this terrible thing to them.'

He sobbed into my shoulder and I calmed him down by just telling him it was alright. After a few minutes, he stopped sobbing, and he stared into my face.

'Will you forgive me for what I did?'

'You poor man,' I said. 'What is there to forgive? My mother was dead. It was her fading body. You did nothing wrong. You saved us all. We didn't know that. You don't need forgiveness. You need ours for not coming back to you, you wonderful, wonderful man. We will never ever be able to repay you. Do you know what you have done?'

'What?' he answered.

'You have given us back our childhood. You have done that.'

'I'm not finished yet,' he continued. He was smiling through his tears now, and I could feel a great burden lifting from his heart as he continued. He took another few sips of water and sat forward on the bed. I could see expressions between horror and relief on my brothers faces also. This was putting a different light on the matter. We spent all those years protecting Dad from the truth. So here, after his funeral, we find a different truth, one that we should have known about, yet he had done so much to make things right for us.

I took your mother's body out onto the ice. It was not as thick among the reeds, and I could hear it crunch underfoot. I knew it was only a few feet deep at that spot and if it broke, I would not drown. I placed it among the reeds, and I covered it with snow. It would not be visible from the shore. There was snow again that night and all tracks I had made were covered over.

I went back the next day to check for myself, and it could not be seen. I could hear people laughing, a little under a mile away across the lake. I peeped through the reeds, and lo and behold there were two cars driving on the ice. One of them was a Volkswagen. They were sliding on home-made toboggans, and one of them had some sort of a contraption on wheels. It had sails on it, and it was hard to control. It kept flipping over. I thought how lucky they were to be so happy. I was cold and hungry, and I was never more frightened in all my life. I returned home and sat by the fire all night. My thoughts were still on your poor mother's body out there on the ice. I wondered would God ever forgive me. Would you all ever forgive me for doing this? I knew one thing though, when the ice melted, it would slip under the water and be found eventually. But I didn't realise it would take six months. Well, you know the rest of that story.

But I still had two bodies to dispose of. When the ground became softer in February, I went one day to the cemetery, and dug one grave. It was easy to do so; the earth was soft from many diggings over the centuries, and I unearthed many bones in the process. I went down good and deep. I dug the grass scraw away in squares and placed it all to one side, and the clay on the other side on a few pieces of mineral felt. The cemetery had been checked again before this, with the melting snow, and no body was found. I dug the grave near the wall next one of the fields, and not far from the mausoleum. From the hill road, any disturbance would not be visible. I dragged Darcy's body out and rolled it into the grave. It fell with a thud. I carried out Eileen's body, wrapped in the blanket she was carried in. I climbed down into the grave and placed her gently on top of her brother.

I closed in the grave hastily, making sure there wasn't a morsel of the clay lying on the grass anywhere. I carefully placed the grass scraws back on top and firmed them in gently. I knew that by late spring, any trace of a disturbance would disappear when the grass grew back. It was a risk I had to take. It was a risk that paid off. By the end of May, the grass was getting long again, and the wildflowers were growing everywhere. Darcy and his sister were gone forever. He was now listed as missing. No mention was made of Eileen at the start. She had left the nursing home into his care, but Meg eventually made it known to the guards that she was missing also. It's an unsolved mystery. I hope it will always remain that way.

But not alone that, there was a very big storm in January. I think it was in 1974. The great big yew tree beside the mausoleum fell. It destroyed the old building. The coffins belonging to the people who were resting there, were re-buried in the new cemetery. The stone was taken away and used in building walls somewhere. The tree was cut up and sold. All the soil and rubble left after the clearance was spread out on the ground, and it would be difficult to find where the Darcy's are buried. They are gone and long forgotten.

He stopped speaking and he smiled. He gave a great sigh as he finished, 'Now you know everything.'

'You waited all these years till Dad had died to tell us?' said Packy.

'I didn't want to say anything until his grave was closed in.'

'So, Mam and Dad are together in the cemetery,' I said. I didn't know whether to laugh or cry. I looked at the boys and said again, 'They really are together!'

'You're some man, Pat Reardon,' said Tom.

'Who'd have ever thought this went on?' said Joe.

'There was a right lot of shenanigans happening on all sides during those years,' laughed Packy. 'It's like a murder mystery.'

'It is a murder mystery,' said Tom.

'Will you stop that!' I said.

'You're a happy man tonight, Pat,' said Seán. He lay back again on his pillows, and he was holding Seán's hand and mine. He was smiling at us all, and we just sat there sharing the moment.

'That's why you made such a fuss about the key, way back then,' said Packy.

'I'm so sorry for accusing you of stealing my money, Sarah. I knew you would never do it, but your Dad played into my plot. He told me to get rid of it. I did that, but I hid it in the rafters of the shed at the back of the house.'

'Pat, you seem to be spending your whole life apologising for something. I'm telling you to stop that now,' I said. 'Remember the way I used to boss you around.'

'You haven't changed, Sarah,' he giggled, 'and you wouldn't marry me.'

'I never married, Pat,' I answered. 'I lost one very good man, and that was enough for me.'

'Don't be making me feel guilty now,' laughed Seán.

'I'm getting tired,' he said, 'but I have more to tell you.'

'Let's not delay then,' said Joe.

I waited and watched each day. Searches continued, and I wondered why they never went near that part of the lake. I went there many times, and I couldn't see the body. When your father went a few times to identify some drownings in different parts of the country, I knew what the answer would be.

Then came the day when Master Ryan took you both fishing. I didn't realise that it would happen so quickly. I knew that your father would identify it as your mother. This he did. Then I could hear you Sarah, getting ready to tell him that it wasn't your mother, but Eileen Darcy. I was outside the door. People had gathered when they heard the news. I was afraid to go in to you. I was waiting for Sergeant

Greene to arrest me. I was ready to step in and say that I had hidden the body. I was going to concoct a story, where your mother came to my house and died. But I knew it wouldn't work. I was beginning to panic when Packy screamed. The poor little mite had been very sick with measles, but he didn't want Sarah to say anything, and he began screaming that your mother was wearing the flowery dress the night she disappeared. The only question asked about this was by your father, why was she wearing a summer dress in the middle of winter? At this stage, the sergeant had enough, your father was very distressed, and Packy clung to him. I could see you, Sarah, looking over at Meg, and she gave you the nod that it was your mother's body. She was prepared to make that ultimate sacrifice also. In an instant, it was all over, and the sergeant told everyone to go home, and let the family grieve for their mother.

'Do you remember what I said to you the day of the funeral?' he asked.

'I do. I have never forgotten it,' I said. 'You said we had nothing to worry about. Everything was fine. You were going to protect me for the rest of your life.'

He looked me straight in the eye. I could see them tearful and smiling. I knew what he had meant now. He kept saying it repeatedly. He would care for me for the rest of his life. He did just that.

'You are a wonderful man, Pat Reardon,' I said, sobbing through my tears. 'I don't know how I will ever repay you.'

'Get me the box again, Father,' he said to Seán. He reached over into the wardrobe and placed the tin box in front of him. Its rusting hinges creaked again, as he reached inside. He took out a piece of brown twig. He placed it in my hand.

'What is it?' I asked.

'You left it in the shed with the drawing. It's the piece of the spindle tree I brought one evening to your house when your father was home. It had little pink berries, and they were just ripening. My mother used to put it in a vase when there were no flowers in the autumn. When I came back home when I was fifteen, I used to gather it and do the same with it. Your mother liked it as well.'

I held it close to me, and I saw him reach into the box again. This time, he took out a little tiny box which was used to hold a piece of jewellery. He handed it to me and asked me to open it. I left the piece of dried twig on the bed and opened the box. When I saw what was inside, I placed my hand over my mouth to prevent myself from screaming in shock. Inside was my mother's wedding ring.

'I've been minding it for you all this time,' he said.

I was speechless. I looked at my brothers. I passed it round to them and they too were lost for words. Packy passed it back to me again, and I placed it on my finger.

'You don't know how much this means to me, Pat,' I said, kissing him again and again on the forehead.

'I think Pat has had enough for tonight,' said Seán.

'What's going to happen then?' asked Packy.

'What do you mean?' asked Seán.

'The ball is at your foot,' he said, 'you know everything now.'

'I have known everything for the past ten years. When Pat asked me to hear his confession, I was bound to the bond of the confessional. He asked me to find Meg.'

'How did you find her?' asked Joe.

'It was easy. I phoned her.'

Pat reached into the box again. He took out a notebook. He gave it to me, and I opened it. In his handwriting, he had written all the addresses and numbers Meg had given me before she left. I knew that numbers would have changed or were extended with area codes. Seán just needed to go to inquiries to check them.

'Where did you get these numbers?' I asked.

'I went snooping around one day when your father brought you all shopping to town. I knew she must have given you some contact addresses and numbers. I got in the window into your room and found the notebook she had given you. It was under the mattress. I sat down in the kitchen and wrote them all down in my own notebook.'

This time I started to laugh. Seán and Joe joined me, and the old man chuckled to himself in the bed. What else did he not know about us? He had followed every move we made and watched over us.

'Pat Reardon, I'm not going to forgive you for this.' He looked at me rather seriously.

'You know why?' I asked. 'You are past forgiveness, you old rascal, you!' I put my arms around him, and I could see a change in him. He was content now, and a great burden had been lifted from his shoulders.

'Shortly after Meg left,' said Seán, 'I tried to ring her just to see if she was alright. All her numbers were no longer in use. There was no reply from her address also. She just broke away all communication.'

'Same here,' I said, 'there were no more cards at Easter or Christmas. I thought she might have died.'

'She had her job done,' said Seán. 'It was time for her to call it a day.'

'You still haven't answered my question,' said Packy.

'I really don't understand.'

'You are the priest. Is it not your duty to inform the guards, now that it is all out in the open?'

'Many years ago,' said Seán, 'your mother's body was recovered from the lake. A lady was killed accidentally, and a man died because of a sudden moment of anger. Darcy and his sister are buried on holy ground. To the world, they are both missing and have never been found. Pat Reardon has been serving a prison sentence all his life. He has had enough. He is at peace now and should be left alone. I'm not doing anything. I'm just so glad, you all now know the truth, and you have suffered enough too. It's time to get on with your lives.'

'Well, I'm tired now,' said Pat. 'I want to rest.'

We left him with a promise to come back. In a few minutes, he had drifted off to sleep, leaving us to our thoughts and our memories.

Chapter 56

Requiescat in Pace

I carried with me the items Pat had placed in my hands, and floods of memories came back again. Some of them I had forgotten. But most of all, I had an important part of my mother's life. It was the ring my father placed on her finger, the day they were married. It was something I would treasure forever. I was ever so grateful to Seán for what he had done. Not alone that, he was there for Pat, when he had no one. He had listened to Pat, who had kept a very lonely secret for too long. We had much to talk about. I went back to the hotel in town, and Packy shared my room, as it had twin beds. Joe and Tom had rooms of their own.

I couldn't sleep during the night. I kept waking up, and thoughts were coming back to me again, about that winter and the snow. I had managed to keep my family together, and now after all these years we were still close, united stronger than ever, and sharing the loss of our dear father. I didn't know what we were going to do about Pat. We were going to return to see him again tomorrow, but I needed to talk to my brothers about him. He was our responsibility now, and it was up to us to do something for him.

Next morning at breakfast, Joe and Tom said they couldn't stay, as they had to return to families and work. Packy was on summer vacation and he decided to join me. We knew that Pat had only a short time to go, and we wanted to be there for him. In the afternoon we returned to the home and Pat was asleep. He had wakened for breakfast, just drank a little water, and began to slumber again. Seán had called while we were there. In recent times, he went there every afternoon just to check on Pat, and arrangements were made to call us in to visit him.

Today, he slept all afternoon. He was drifting in and out of sleep, and Seán maintained that he was slowly leaving us behind. Tom and Joe sat with him for a short while, but they had to get an evening flight to Glasgow. They knew that this was the last time they would ever see him again.

'Tell him, Sarah, that we will love and remember him forever.'

'Don't worry,' I said, 'he knows that now. We were his family really.'

'Tell him we'll help him someday again to milk the cow,' said Joe. With that, he broke down in the front foyer of the home. He was finding it hard to let this great old friend go.

'You will always have happy memories of him,' I said. 'Pat was special.'

Packy and I sat with him that night when my other brothers had left. The place was so quiet, just the sound of another resident calling non-stop for a nurse, just like a little child crying for his mother in the middle of the night. All we could hear was his breathing, which as the night went on, became more laboured. We sat through with him, and a nurse checked every so often. She also brought us a cup of tea, and some pillows if we wanted to drift off to sleep in the green leather armchairs. It reminded me of the night Mam died. I was with her, but I missed her passing, as I fell asleep with my arms around her. But I was there for her at her last moment of life. I didn't want this to happen again. Packy drifted off to sleep, and I left him so. If I had to stay awake, I was determined to do so.

At seven o'clock two nurses came to turn him in the bed, and he woke up. He rallied round and brightened up looking for something to drink.

'You are still here,' he said softly.

'I'm still here, and I'm not going anywhere. Packy is here too. Joe and Tom had to go, and they were sorry to leave. They have to return to their families.'

'And that's where they should be.'

I sat with him until after eight o'clock, and the nurse said nothing was going to happen that day. She told us to go home and rest. She had our phone numbers if any changes occurred in the meantime. She knew we would return for another long night, and it was better we got refreshed, had something to eat, and to get some sleep.

We returned to the hotel and slept most of the day. There was no call from the home, but Seán joined us for a bite to eat in the late afternoon. He had some questions to ask about Pat when his passing came. He didn't want to seem to be jumping the gun, in respect of a funeral, but he was concerned that Pat had no living relatives in Ireland. He didn't want to see him buried with no memorial to him.

'I'm taking care of it,' I said. 'Pat deserves to be remembered, especially by us. No one will ever know what he did, but he is entitled to the dignity and respect due to him. People didn't treat him well at times, but he bore his suffering with great patience and bravery. I don't want to see a simple wooden or iron cross on his grave. There will be a proper headstone for him.'

'I need to say no more then,' said Seán.

'I still haven't got my head around all this,' I said.

'It's a pity you didn't tell me about it when we were young. I could have helped you then.'

'What could you have done Seán? It was our battle, and it wasn't fair to drag you into it. We were fighting a war of survival. I didn't want to lose my family. We worked together then. I didn't want our childhood to be taken away, just like the Larkin children. They were taken away and separated. I never ever heard what happened to them.'

'I can tell you something you don't know. They found each other again. Mary and Ann are living abroad. They are both married, one in England and the other in Australia. Dan eventually found his way home. He went to England, married, and brought his family back here. You won't believe what I'm going to tell you. He bought a house which had been idle for many years. It needed a lot of work, but he turned it into a home for his family. You probably know it, it's up the boreen there on the way to the bog. A certain Cregan family lived there years ago.'

'Oh my God!' I exclaimed. 'We certainly have been away for too long. There have been so many questions answered for me in the past few days. Wait till I tell the others.'

'When this is all over, will you keep in contact, Sarah?'

'I'm not going to have an affair with a priest.'

'We can be friends, you know. You can always say you kissed a priest!'

'You were a young cheeky strap of a fellow then, I was sad to lose you.

I knew I couldn't hold on to you, as I didn't want to drag you into all this.'

'And I had another agenda. I thought then that I was doing all this for my parents and family tradition. But deep down I knew I had a vocation.'

'I might still kiss a priest before I go back to Scotland…'

'I might hold you to that,' he laughed.

'I'm only joking! Why don't you come over to visit Packy and me? We can show you the sights of Bonnie Scotland.'

'I might just take you up on that as well!'

We sat again with Pat that evening. He was a little agitated early in the night, and he woke up calling my name.

'I'm here, Pat, right beside you.'

'I can't see you, Sarah.'

I took his hand and he reached over and folded his other one on mine.

'Packy is here too,' I said.

'I'm sitting on your other side,' said Packy. He reached over and touched the old man's head. Pat smiled and became calmer. A nurse sat with us, as she could see great changes in him during the day. She asked him if he wanted a drink of water. He took a few sips, as his mouth was dry.

'Sure you won't go away, Sarah?' he asked.

'Packy and I will stay with you tonight.'

'You know that I was the happiest man in the world, when I watched you all playing as little children. I knew I would never be blessed with a family. But you were my family.'

'I know that, Pat. I know that now. We loved you very much too.'

'You wanted to marry me when you were five, and I used to tease you about it.'

'Then when I got older, I told you I would never marry you.'

'And I promised to take care of you for the rest of my life.'

'And you definitely did that, Pat. I will never forget that.'

He squeezed my hand and he closed his eyes. A great hush settled into the room, and he sank deeper into a quiet sleep. The nurse decided to fetch Seán. He was at a meeting locally, but he had asked her to call him, and he'd come immediately. He arrived quietly, and he prayed over him, administering the last rites. I thought again of my dear mother, who didn't have this privilege on her deathbed. But I knew she was with God and buried in the cemetery beside Dad now. Packy sat beside me, and Seán stayed as well.

The night drifted on quietly, and I could hear every breath he made getting slower and slower. It was a long night, but I didn't mind. I was glad to be there. It was a beautiful moment to watch him go quietly – shortly before six o'clock he passed away peacefully. His life of suffering was over, but he died a happy man, ready to meet his maker, and reconciled with us for those awful events we shared many years ago. When the nurse lifted the sheet over his head to let his body rest in peace. Seán gave a tearful sigh, uttering in Latin, '*Requiescat in Pace*, Patrick Reardon.'

Epilogue

Pat was buried three days later in the new cemetery. His grave was located close to my mother and father, near the west wall. It was a new area, and the beginning of a new row of graves. In time, he would not be alone. I was surprised to see so many people from the parish, attend the removal in the evening, and the funeral the next day. There were no chief mourners, but Packy, Seán and I were there, to greet those who filed past the coffin.

Fr O'Reilly spoke about Pat, and his time in the community. He said nothing about his treatment by others when he was younger, but focused on his work, helping the parish out, and how he made sure every penny was accounted for, when he sold tickets at the parish raffles, as well as the church collections each Sunday. He spoke about his caring nature for those who were down on their luck, and how he was always available no matter the weather, to help with sowing, turf cutting, and harvesting. He gave an account as well, of the years spent in the home, the rug making and other crafts he mastered, to keep himself occupied, and to maintain an active mind. He spoke of his patience, as his health failed him, and how he was prepared to leave this world without any fear or fuss.

The people who filed past the coffin were strangers to me, but one man made himself known, apologising for not being present at my father's funeral. He had snow white hair, and looked quite fit and well for his age, probably around seventy years old or so.

'You don't know me,' he said.

'I'm sorry. I haven't a clue,' I answered.

'Donal Ryan, the auld master.'

I took his hand and was reluctant to let it go.

'It's been so long,' I said.

'Too long. But I'm here now, for your Dad and for Pat.'

'By the way,' said Packy. 'I've still got that sixpence.'

'You're joking me!'

'I'm not. I kept it. I took it out every so often, and it gave me the encouragement to follow my dreams.'

'Did they come true?' he asked.

'I teach art in a grammar school in Glasgow.'

'I'm so glad to hear that.'

'Are you still teaching?' I asked.

'I retired five years ago. I'm babysitting now. My wife and I take care of our two grandchildren. Our son and his wife both work. They have a mortgage, and we take care of the kids. Just loving it, we are.'

I could see that others wanted to talk to us, and we had to let him go. He joined us after the funeral for a few drinks, and a chat about those days in the distant past.

I heard also that Sergeant Greene had passed away a few years before. He was buried in the cemetery too. We said a prayer at his grave while we were there. Our time was running out, and we'd have to return to Glasgow. There were so many people I met at the funeral, that I began to recall names and faces. Again, many of them had missed Dad's funeral, and they were glad as well to have made the journey. There was a feeling that the years were rolling back. I could feel myself being drawn there. Now that the past was safe for us, I was feeling more at home again.

I arranged with the headstone maker to place a new one, over my father and mother, as well as on Pat's grave. He was going to be remembered. I made sure of that. He was another father to us and was there when Dad was not around. We had two guardian angels looking after us during those terrible days. Meg came into our lives and made sure we were safe and secure. Pat watched over us, unknown to us, as we tried to deal with our pain and loss. Speaking in riddles, he told us what he had done. He knew that our lives were safe, when we left. He kept his promise to me, and I was his little girl, the little daughter he never had.

The day before we left, Packy and I, walked and wandered the roads and fields of our childhood. We made a journey to the old cemetery, now overgrown and unkempt. The gates were padlocked, and they were rusting away. They hadn't been opened for years. We crossed the fields to the lake, to the spot where Mam's body was found. It was still quiet and peaceful. The lake reeds were waving gently in the breeze, and the water was lapping on the shingle and stones. Little flurries of foam, lined the shore in places, and two swans were leading their four young grey cygnets out on the water, floating like sailboats, quietly and peacefully, leaving a gentle wavy trail behind them. We sat on the rocks for an hour or more, and we recalled a time, when there was ice and snow, and the cold watery grave our mother found when the thaw came. It was a different world now, and the events of 1963 were long forgotten. It was time for us to let them go too.

While I was there, I had something to do, that Pat had failed to do when we were young. I reached into my shoulder bag and fumbled for something I brought with me.

'What are you doing?' asked Packy.

'You'll see.'

I took out the large piece of cloth with the old key of the mausoleum wrapped in it. Even though it looked clean, preserved with the grease and oil, Pat had rubbed on it over the years, it was beginning to rust, and shone a brighter red in the sunlight.

'I have to finish this for Pat,' I said.

'If you let me, I can throw it further. Remember I was always trying to be better than my brothers at throwing stones in the water.'

I gave it to him, and he stood facing the lake. He reached as far back as he could, and he hoisted the old key skywards. It tumbled through the air, as if it were moving in slow motion, and it landed in the deep, about twenty yards out. It gave a gentle splash as it hit the surface, and it sent gentle ripples outward in tiny waves in a full circle till they were broken by the shoreline. I was expecting a hand reaching out of the water to grab it, just like Excalibur in the old Arthurian legends, but the ramblings of my imagination didn't come to life magically, and the key sank to its resting place at the bottom of the lake.

We stood there staring into the water, focusing on the quiet scene and the far shore.

'Remember Pat told us he threw it in the lake,' said Packy.

'He was making sure, we would never go to the mausoleum again,' I said, 'or else his whole plan was in jeopardy.'

'I hope he's at peace now,' said Packy.

'He is. Please God, he is,' I answered.

We left the lake behind, strolling back to the old cemetery, and followed on, across the fields which marked our journey on that cold frosty November night. The landscape and territory of our childhood had changed little with the passing years.

Finally, we arrived in the field at the top of the hill close to our old home. I could see it in the distance now, altered and changed, a beautiful bungalow, a happy home for a man, who had his childhood taken away from him too. It had a happy countenance about it, with a well-manicured hedge, a lawn, and some flowers. There was a swing in the garden, where once we had large cocks of hay. I was happy to see this. Life goes on, and memories fade.

We sat at the top of the hill, and the field of corn which stretched down to the road, waved in the breeze, keeping time and rhythm to the rise and fall of the pulses of air. The clouds raced across the sky, blotting out the sun, and leaving the shining land mottled in different shades of green. I was back again, barefoot and running down the hill with Packy by the hand. That was the happiest summer of our lives, and one of the last ones we shared in this place.

The landscape was still the same, the trees, the hedgerows, the gates, and headlands. The birds flew high in the sky. It was as if time had stood still. I often imagined myself out here, when my thoughts rambled back to those times, and I wanted to smell the grass, the earth, and the leaves. Even the cowpats in the fields had that earthy country smell which drew me back. This was a moment I wanted to last. Then a thought came to me. There was no need to run away anymore. We were no longer fugitives to the past. We could share this space, this place, and this time again, whenever we wanted. It left me a little choked up, as I thought about it. We had our memories to share. Those who had gone, my mother and father, Pat and Meg, wherever she was, whether she was alive, or gone to her just reward, I'd never know. They shared this landscape with us, and it would go on, unchanged even into our own ageing years. We had to leave soon, but with a different feeling about it all. I turned to Packy, and taking his hand just as I did when he was a little boy, I squeezed it gently.

'You know something,' I said.

'What's that?'

'There's something we can do now whenever we want to.'

'Yeah?'

'We can come home again.'

The End